"Gena Showalter's stories hum with fast pacing and characters that leap off the page. Pick up one of Gena's books! You won't be disappointed!"
—*USA TODAY* bestselling author Julie Kenner

Playing with Fire
"Another sizzling page-turner from one of the premier authors of paranormal romance. Gena Showalter delivers an utterly spellbinding story!"
—*New York Times* bestselling author Kresley Cole

"Charming and hilarious...I was hooked from page one."
—*New York Times* bestselling author MaryJanice Davidson

"The versatile Showalter takes the nail-biting elements of her exciting paranormals...and blends them with the wit and humor of her contemporary romances...to make a delicious offering spiced with the best ingredients of both."
—*Booklist*, starred review

"Sizzles with sexual tension!"
—*New York Times* bestselling author Sharon Sala

"Wow...Gena Showalter always takes us on a fantastic ride."
—*USA TODAY* bestselling author Merline Lovelace

Animal Instincts
"Bold and witty, sexy and provocative, Gena Showalter's star is rising fast!"
—*New York Times* bestselling author Carly Phillips

"Showalter writes with a sparkling humor that keeps the story light without losing poignancy."
—*Booklist*

"Filled with expert storytelling, page-melting sex and touches of humor, this is a fantastic book!"
—*Myshelf.com*

Jewel of Atlantis
"Showalter has created a ripe mythological world populated with fascinating creatures and dark lore.... For extraordinary escapism, read this book."
—*Romantic Times BOOKreviews*

"Shines like the purest gem... Rich in imagery and evocative detail, this book is a sterling example of what makes romance novels so worthwhile."
—*A Romance Review*, 5 stars

Heart of the Dragon
"Lots of danger and sexy passion give lucky readers a spicy taste of adventure and romance."
—*Romantic Times BOOKreviews*

"Filled with steamy sex, adventure, and a sprinkle of humor...a fantastic book!"
—*Myshelf.com*

The Pleasure Slave
"Gena Showalter is gaining the reputation of a master wizard who enchants her readers."
—*Harriet Klausner*

"This couple is dynamite and Tristan's intense sensuality will have you sweating. [*The Pleasure Slave*] is definitely going on my keeper shelf."
—*The Romance Studio*

The Stone Prince
"Sexy, funny and downright magical! Gena Showalter has a lyrical voice and the deft ability to bring characters to life in a manner that's hilarious and absorbing at the same time."
—*Katie MacAlister, New York Times* bestselling author of *The Last of the Red-Hot Vampires*

"A most rewarding read...*The Stone Prince* is definitely a keeper!"
—*Romance Reviews Today*

GENA SHOWALTER

The VAMPIRE'S BRIDE

HQN™

Recycling programs
for this product may
not exist in your area.

ISBN-13: 978-0-373-77359-6
ISBN-10:   0-373-77359-5

THE VAMPIRE'S BRIDE

Copyright © 2009 by Gena Showalter

Printed in U.S.A.

Dear Reader,

Since the first title in my Atlantis series, *Heart of the Dragon,* was published in 2005, I've been asked how I thought to combine the lost city of Atlantis with the creatures of lore. The answer is simple: what if. What if the gods hid their greatest mistakes inside Atlantis and that's why it's buried under the sea?

That single question branched into a thousand others, each more intriguing than the last. What if a dragon shape-shifter is forced to guard the portal that leads to his home, tasked with killing anyone who enters—even the woman of his dreams *(Heart of the Dragon)*? What if a modern man is sent inside the forbidden city to steal its greatest treasure...who just happens to be a beautiful female he can't resist *(Jewel of Atlantis)*? What if the king of the nymphs can seduce everyone he encounters—except the woman he loves *(The Nymph King)*?

Now, in my brand-new tale of Atlantis, *The Vampire's Bride,* I have the chance to answer the question readers have been asking for years: what if the villain in all those earlier stories, the vampire king who has tortured and hated and warred, got a story of his own?

I hope you'll join me on these journeys through Atlantis, where the creatures of myth and legend walk, peril lurks around every corner and forbidden passions ignite.

Wishing you all the best,

Gena Showalter

Other sexy, steamy reads from

GENA SHOWALTER

and HQN Books

Lords of the Underworld
The Darkest Night
The Darkest Kiss
The Darkest Pleasure

Atlantis
Heart of the Dragon
Jewel of Atlantis
The Nymph King
The Vampire's Bride

Tales of an *Extra*ordinary Girl
Playing with Fire

Other must-reads
The Stone Prince
The Pleasure Slave
Animal Instincts
Catch a Mate

**More stunning tales from Gena Showalter
are coming your way in 2009!**

To Jill Monroe (the author, not the hard-hitting journalist of Author Talk) for loving vampires as much as I do.

To Sheila Fields, Donnell Epperson and Betty Sanders for saying, "What about a paranormal *Survivor*?"

To Pennye Edwards for always taking care of me.

To Kresley Cole, Melissa Francis, Marley Gibson, Kristen Painter, Louisa Edwards, Maria Geraci, Pamela Harty, Elaine Spencer, Deidre Knight, Roxanne St. Claire and (again) Jill Monroe for making me laugh— and spit up blueberries.

Lastly, to Jill Monroe (the hard-hitting journalist of Author Talk, not the author) for asking the questions readers really want to know.

Acknowledgments
To the two ladies who help and guide me every step
of the way: Tracy Farrell and Margo Lipschultz.
I couldn't do it without you!

PROLOGUE

LAYEL, KING OF THE VAMPIRES, hated son of Atlantis, fought so fervently against his chains that the metal cut past skin and muscle, nearly slicing into bone. He did not care, continued to struggle. What use were his hands without his beloved to caress?

Susan. Inside his mind, the name was a prayer, a scream of desolation and a wail of sorrow, all twisted into an agonizing spiral of shame. How could he have allowed this to happen?

"Release him," someone said. Layel would have looked at the speaker, but he could not pull his gaze from his woman. Or rather, what was left of her. "Let him see up close what he has wrought upon himself."

Footsteps pounded. There was a tug on one wrist, then the other, and the chains gave way.

Weak, nearly drained of blood, Layel tried to step away from the iron fence that propped him up, but his knees gave out and he collapsed. With the impact, hot breath abandoned him and reality settled deep. *I'm too late. They kept me chained long enough to ensure she could not be turned. I cannot save her.* He gagged. Gods, oh, gods.

Susan lay a few feet away, her once vibrant, beautiful body now stripped, violated and burned. Around him, the dragons responsible laughed, their voices floating in and out of his consciousness.

"…deserved this and more."

"…and look at him now."

"…pathetic. He never should have been crowned king."

Layel had left Susan in his palace, safe, happily drowsy and snuggled in bed, while he and a contingent of warriors doused a fire in the surrounding forest. He hadn't known the fire had been started purposely until it was too late.

Oh, gods, oh, gods, oh, gods. A choked cry escaped him, blood spraying from his mouth. What seemed an eternity ago but could only be hours, he'd returned to an ambush, Susan's screams echoing in his ears. The anguish he'd heard as she'd shouted for his aid, the pain he'd seen contorting her features as she'd pleaded with the dragons for the life of their unborn child…both would haunt him into eternity.

Susan.

By the time he'd fought his way to her, she'd already gone silent, her expression frozen in misery. The silence had been ten thousand times worse than the screams and writhing physical agony.

Dead. She was dead. Layel had failed her in every possible way. And in his grief, the very dragons who killed her had managed to capture him. They'd torn him from Susan's lifeless body and chained him to the gate in front of the palace. Then, oh, gods, then they had dragged her body in front of him, taunting him with her death.

His gagging became heaving, and he emptied the contents of his stomach. A meal Susan had prepared for him, eyes glimmering with amusement. And later, for dessert, she'd flicked her lovely dark hair aside and offered her vein, knowing just where the biting would lead.

Arm shaking uncontrollably, he reached for her. The tips of his fingers brushed the hollow of her neck. No pulse. Dirt mixed with blood, caking her charred, still-hot skin in clumps. "Susan," he tried to whisper, but his voice no longer worked. His throat was raw from screaming, pleading and desperate bargaining. But nothing had helped. The dragons hadn't disappeared and Susan hadn't returned to life.

Though he was still surrounded by the enemy, he was unable to take his eyes off his mate. He knew, soul deep, that this was the last time he would ever see her. *My love. My sweet love.*

Stay in bed, she had beseeched only a few hours ago. *Make love to me.*

I cannot, love, but I will return quickly. That, I promise you.

She'd pouted a bit, pink lips dipping prettily. *I can't bear to be without you.*

Nor I you. Sleep, and when I return, I'll make you forget I was ever gone. How is that?

Promise?

Promise. He had kissed her softly and strolled from their chamber. Content, satisfied. Happy. Assured of a future together.

"Now you can suffer as we have suffered," one of the dragons spat, tearing him from his cherished memories.

In the background, Layel could hear demonic laughter. His gaze lifted, and he saw several red, glowing eyes peeking from nearby bushes. An audience of demons, he realized. How long had they been there, watching? Could they have helped Susan? Probably. That laughter… They'd seen—and enjoyed—everything.

"Your people drained our loved ones, blood-drinker, and so we burned yours."

Ignoring them, Layel gathered his remaining strength and crawled as close to Susan's body as he could get, leaving a trail of crimson behind him, hot tears pouring down his face. The dragons didn't try to stop him. His shaking intensified as he awkwardly gathered her in his arms. There was no smile of greeting, no whispered endearment.

Her once pretty face was swollen, bruised and smeared with soot. Her silky dark hair was gone, singed to the scalp. He had loved to wrap those strands around his palms, loved to hear her purr for his kiss.

Closing his eyes against the horror of what had been done to her, he hugged her close, so close, before gently laying her back down. He could not bear to sever all contact, however, and smoothed a fingertip over the seam of her lips. They were still hot, burning him as smoke rose from her parted teeth.

Susan. Eyes stinging, he crouched all the way down and placed his temple upon her rounded stomach. There was no movement inside of it. Not anymore. *I love you. Oh, gods, I love you. I am sorry I left you. So sorry. Come back to me. Please. I am nothing without you.* To the crystal dome above, he prayed, *If you will not bring her back to me, let us bargain. Take me instead. Return her to life and take me. She is everything that is good. She is light. I am darkness and death.*

No response.

"Enough sniveling. Now you will listen. We are going to allow you to live, *king.*" The words were sneered by the dragon leader, a towering hulk of muscle and rage. "And with every breath you take, you will remember this day and the consequences of allowing your people free rein."

Layel barely heard him. *Susan, sweet Susan.* None had been as gentle, tender, loving or kind. Her greatest crime was—had been, he corrected with an inward roar—loving him.

She had been his everything. Yet his precious human had been slaughtered. For his lack of leadership, the dragon had said. She had been tortured because Layel had wanted nothing to do with the vampire throne and had refused to place restrictions upon the army under his command as his father had.

"I've awaited this moment for many months," another of the hated beasts said, spraying him with a stream of fire.

The flames settled in Layel's cheek, crackling, singeing deep. He gave no reaction, didn't even open his eyes. Truly, he felt nothing except the razor-sharp edge of his grief. If the gods would not heed his cries, he wanted to remain in this spot forever, wanted to die with his woman and child. His family.

"Look at him. Look at the mighty Layel, reduced to *this*."

All of the dragons laughed.

"I can see why you liked her, vampire. That tight little sheath took me all the way to the hilt."

"I liked pumping into her mouth, feeling her throat close around me."

"I think *she* liked what we did to her. You heard the way she whimpered…"

Finally Layel's eyelids cracked open, tendrils of hatred and rage blooming, growing, consuming him. Overshadowing his grief, becoming all that he knew. He glanced at the surrounding forest. The demons were still there, still giggling like children. Most of the nearby trees were charred, offering little refuge. Next he glanced at the expanse of dragon warriors. There were eight of them, their stances cocky, assured. Their golden eyes blazed with triumph. Except…

Whatever they saw on his face caused them to lose their smiles. A few even backed away from him.

Perhaps they had forgotten that vampires could fly. Perhaps they thought a broken, bloody man could do no damage. They were wrong.

"SUSAN!" Layel leapt up and attacked, his war cry an echo of all the pain inside him.

The agonized screams that next cut through the forest far eclipsed any that had ever come before them.

CHAPTER ONE

Two hundred years later

JUST A LITTLE CLOSER, *fire-bastards. Just a little bit closer.*

Hidden by lush, dewy foliage, Layel watched as the dragon army marched through the detestably named Forest of Dragons. Where they were going, he didn't know. *Why* they were going, he didn't know, either. He only knew that he was going to relieve them of their burden. A young—human?—female was bound and gagged inside a portable prison. That prison was balanced by two wooden beams slung over several of the warriors' shoulders, swaying with their movements.

Obviously, she was their enemy.

He didn't know the girl, but a dragon's enemy was his dearest friend. And he didn't like his friends being bound.

The dragons continued to march forward, slowly, steadily. He motioned for his own army to hold…remain composed. They obeyed without hesitation. Since that dark day two hundred years ago, he had happily led his men with an iron fist—straight into a never-ending war. His will was not questioned. Ever. Not without severe consequences.

"…not going to end well," Brand, second-in-command of the dragon soldiers, was saying. Golden light seeped from the crystal dome that surrounded all of Atlantis, forming a halo around his pale, braided hair and disgustingly handsome features.

Brand was strong, brave, loyal to his king, kind to his people. A pity he was a dragon. Had he been born even a demon, Layel thought perhaps he would have liked him. As it was, he wanted Brand alive long enough to take a mate. A mate Layel would then steal. Brand would suffer, for a little while at least, and then Layel would gut him.

Brand had not been one of the warriors present all those years ago—none of the warriors here had been present, for Layel had slaughtered them all. Remembering their deaths, he smiled. Not all of them had faded quickly. Some he had lingered over, enjoying their pain, taking his time with every slice and bite.

Still, killing those responsible hadn't been enough. Not for the horrendous crimes that had been committed against Susan. Hadn't he been blamed for the actions of others? It was only fair to use that same logic against the dragons.

Only when Layel had obliterated the entire race would Susan be avenged. And only then would Layel deserve to join her in the hereafter. *Soon, my love. Soon.*

"If her sisters see her like this, there will be a war," a dragon called Renard said.

Renard was a dark-haired tyrant who, Layel knew, had studied how best to kill every race in Atlantis. The demons, the nymphs, the centaurs, the gorgons and all the other creatures the gods had deemed mistakes in their quest to create humans. Of them all, Renard hated vampires most and was always eager for a fight.

Eager himself, Layel ran his tongue over his elongated teeth.

"What else could we do?" an irritated voice proclaimed.

Tagart. Untamed, almost feral, with black hair and an even blacker heart. He was loyal to no one and was even jealous of his own king. "One more word out of that girl's mouth and I would have cut out her tongue. We *had* to gag her."

All of the soldiers nodded. Each was taller and more muscled than the last, and each had a long, menacing sword strapped to his bare back, nestled between the slits that hid his wings. Layel collected those swords and hung them on his walls as trophies. He used their bones as furniture.

"Whatever our reasons for binding her, they won't understand. Even though we're taking her back to them. Kind of. If we can find their camp." Brand again. "She's their beloved, their future queen."

Sisters…beloved…queen.

Amazons, Layel realized.

His lips curled in another slow grin. Fierce creatures, the Amazons. Devoted to each other, bloodthirsty, though they mostly kept to themselves unless provoked. Oh, yes. And vicious. Legend claimed that anyone who threatened an Amazon would soon find his deepest fear bearing down on him. A shadow, a determined phantom that would devour him whole.

Yes, the stories of their conquests were endless, though Layel himself had never fought one, never tasted one. He had no interest in doing so, either. Always before, they had been a nonentity to him, unworthy of his time or consideration, for he existed simply to torment the dragons. Nothing more.

But now his mind whirled with ways he might be able to use them. Perhaps he should not liberate this captive, after all. Perhaps *he* should find the Amazon camp, lie and tell them the dragons meant the girl harm, perhaps meant to kill her in front of them. The dragons would have their asses handed to them by little girls. Now wouldn't that just be—

A loud, piercing war cry sounded.

What seemed like hundreds of warrior women but could only have been a handful suddenly burst from the trees. They were scantily dressed, breasts covered by thin strips of leather, waist and thighs covered by some type of frayed skirt. The vast expanse of skin visible was painted in blue, the color marking royalty.

"Big mistake, dragons," a woman shouted.

"Your *last* mistake," another called.

What a bright day this was turning out to be. Layel would not have to search for the Amazons, after all.

Blades were anchored to their muscular arms and legs, and death radiated from their fierce expressions. Most were as tall as the dragons, but a few were petite, almost…fragile looking.

In the span of a single heartbeat, a battle was raging between the two races.

Weapons were twirling, men and women grunting and blood splattering. The metallic scent wafted to Layel's nostrils, sweet and tangy. He breathed it in deeply, felt it sweep through his entire body, fuse with sinew and bone and ignite a guttural hunger.

"Now!" Layel shouted to his men.

Together, they rushed forward. How he would have loved to simply materialize in the midst of battle, but he could not. None of them could. Well, not if they hoped to survive. A vampire could materialize anywhere he wanted with only a thought, but there were consequences. Once they reached their destination, they were drained. Exhausted. Unable to move for hours. Escape was the only time the ability proved useful, and he didn't want to escape this.

As he reached the dragon masses, sword swinging, slicing, light from the upper dome warmed his sensitive skin, all the hotter as it blended with the dragons' kiss of fire. He did not allow either to slow him, however. Sweat streaked down his chest and back. His wrist flicked left and right in constant motion, giving his blade a fluidity that cut through dragon flesh as smoothly as if it were cutting through water.

He reveled in every drop of crimson that he spilled, rejoiced with every body that fell. Every pain-entrenched shout brought a new smile to his lips. More than anything, he loved seeing his opponents' golden eyes as their minds registered his blow. They always widened; horror always filled them. The light inside always died right along with them.

Later, when the fighting was done, he would have to stalk through the masses and remove their heads. Dragons, like vampires, healed quickly. He liked to eliminate any possibility of regeneration. But right now, with fire dancing in every direction, he could only cut their decayed hearts in half.

Two dragons rushed him from different angles.

Ducking low, he arced his sword forward with one hand, slashing through one warrior's stomach while withdrawing a dagger from his waist with his other hand, then reaching out, leaning…stretching…and stabbing the second warrior in the groin. There was an unholy scream.

Both warriors collapsed.

Grinning, he leapt back into motion. Someone swept in front of him and managed to nick his side. He hissed, saw that one of his men, Zane, was already chopping his way forward to aid him. Layel didn't go in for the kill himself but kicked the dragon in the stomach, sending him flying in Zane's direction. Seeing this, the battle-hungry vampire spun, sword singing with lethal menace.

Seconds before the dragon's head rolled, he unleashed a blistering stream of flames. As the body dropped, those flames found a target on Layel's cheek. He wiped at the charred, sizzling skin. Felt a warm trail of dragon blood drip down his arm. Grinned again. He still held the dagger and the blade gleamed a vivid crimson.

"You are well, yes?" Zane asked him, breath sawing in and out.

He nodded. *More. Need more.* Needed to inflict more injury, more carnage. His focus landed on a nearby dragon already engaged in a fierce fight with a vampire. Layel stalked forward and swung, gutting the creature without warning. There was a grunt, a jerk. The body toppled. Did Layel mind striking from behind? Never. Fighting fairly would ensure nothing but failure.

Another dragon railed at him. Moving faster than the eye could see, he stabbed the bastard in the belly, pulled out, stabbed in the heart, pulled out again and stabbed in the neck. Only three seconds had passed. Too quick, too easy, he thought.

More.

Brand, ripping an Amazon off his chest and tossing her to the ground, came into view. Yes, Layel thought, tracing his tongue over his sharpened teeth in anticipation. That one. That one would die today. No more waiting. He would not simply incapacitate the bastard; he would kill.

Layel kicked and bit his way through the ranks, gaze locked on the dragon captain. Halfway there, he heard a growl behind him, pivoted to dispatch the threat swiftly and return his attention to Brand. But his sword slashed and clanged against another sword, jarring him. No easy, unprepared kill this time, apparently.

He blinked as an Amazon swirled in front of him, swinging at him a second time. *Clink.* Scowling, he blocked her third thrust. *Clang.*

"I do not wish to hurt you," he gritted out.

"How admirable," she replied drily—before swinging at him again.

He twisted to the side, barely escaping the sharp tip. Had she just mocked him?

Wind gusted past them, lifting her cerulean-colored hair off her face. Suddenly Layel was granted a full view of breathtaking, incomparable beauty. Beauty even the war paint couldn't hide. Beauty that nearly felled him. Definitely rendered him dumb, for he ceased moving. Brand who?

Layel hadn't taken the time to appreciate the beauty of a woman in two hundred years, yet he was helpless to do anything but drink this one in, this fantasy come to life. It was as though she exuded something…magical? Something that forced the eye to her. Something that would not release its hold. But Amazons weren't able to weave spells. Only dragons could.

He continued his scrutiny of her, searching for signs of a dragon relative. Her eyes were so bright a violet they sparkled like freshly polished amethysts. Long black lashes. Slightly rounded cheeks. Flawless, bronzed skin where the paint had washed away. Unlike most of her hulking sisters, she was of the petite variety, barely reaching his shoulders. No, no dragon.

From her fluid grace to her perfect curves, she was sensual and exotic, ready for a bedding rather than a battle.

"You should not be here. I could have killed you, woman." He didn't mind killing females, had done so on many occasions, but it would have been a shame to destroy something so lovely. His jaw clenched as he realized exactly what he was thinking. Damn her. He did not regard women with any kind of desire. Not anymore.

One corner of her lush, red mouth kicked up, causing his stomach to tighten. "Please," she said, voice sultry, like a dream. "You'll need a few centuries' more sword practice before you have the skill to eliminate me, vampire." She swung at him yet again, this time aiming for his neck.

There were no creatures faster than the vampires, and he managed to arch backward with swift precision as the blade soared just over his nose. "And you fancy yourself my tutor? I think not." But he admired her confidence.

"What are you doing here?" she demanded. Another swing.

Another block. "Helping you."

A tinkling laugh escaped her, floating over his skin with the surety of a lover's caress. His stomach tightened again. He scowled, mouth thinning over razor-sharp teeth. How was she affecting him like this?

He had not experienced even a single wisp of need since—*do not think of Susan. You will lose focus.*

Growling, he swung at the Amazon. She blocked the harder blow and frowned. Better. A frown was better than a laugh. And so he did it again. Slashed at her, using all of his might. When their swords next met, both of their bodies vibrated from the impact.

Her delicate nose twitched. In irritation? Amusement? Delight?

Surely not the latter two.

"*This* is how you help me?" she demanded.

"No. That was me, helping myself. Now this is me, helping you." With a swift jerk of his arm, he tossed his dagger. The tip embedded in the neck of the dragon racing toward her from behind. "See the difference?"

She spun, surveyed the fallen, dying warrior. When she faced Layel again, there was no longer any question about what emotion she experienced. Irritation. "Well, we don't need your help and will not grant you any type of boon for offering it."

"Your gratitude is humbling. Fortunately, cutting out the hearts of my enemies is boon enough for me."

The pink tip of her tongue emerged and traced over those lush lips, smearing war paint. All the while she eyed *his* lips. Had his words…excited her? Shock rooted him in place, staying his sword. Such depravity should have disgusted her. And her excitement should have disgusted him.

Should have.

He hissed at her, suddenly as desperate to get away from her as he was to dispatch the dragon army. "Get in my way again, Amazon, and I will take *you* down." Perhaps he would not need to, he thought, before he could turn from her. Already another dragon closed in behind her.

Layel's vehemence seemed to shake her out of her inactivity. She returned his hiss with one of her own. "Try, and you'll die like the dragons." As she spoke, she stabbed behind her, sinking the apex of her sword into the very dragon that had been sneaking up on her. She gave a twist of her wrist, digging her weapon deeper, causing even more pain for the injured man.

Her gaze never left Layel.

The warrior fell to the ground, a final gasp echoing from him.

Layel didn't waste another moment. He moved around and behind the woman and her lethal beauty, knowing he was nothing more than a blur to her. She didn't have time to turn when he kicked out his leg. Contact. Her ankles knocked together. She grunted and toppled to her knees. But she was back on her feet in the next instant, spinning around and glaring at him.

Except there was no anger in that glare. Only vulnerability. Raw vulnerability. It was the kind of look a woman gave a man she was considering taking to her bed—but knew she should resist. A look *he* had resisted from others, without hesitation, for what seemed an eternity. *She's dangerous.*

Layel backed away from her, a spark of panic igniting.

"You knocked me down," she said, breathless.

For years he'd assumed his heart was withered, dead. And yet, hearing the excitement in her voice, the foolish organ sped to life, nearly beating through his ribs. *Keep moving away, damn you.* "Yes," he said, his legs suddenly heavy. "I did."

"But…you knocked me down."

And he would do more if she approached him again. He'd have to. Something about her…

He should not have to remind himself that desire was not something he wanted in his life. He would avenge Susan's death, and then he would join her. Nothing and no one else mattered.

"Play nice with my vampires, little girl, and I might save a few dragons for you. If not, I'll come for you. And when I find you, I will take your head and hang it beside my throne with all the others I have collected in my long life. Doubt me not." With that, he flashed her a dark grin and pushed his way into the thick of battle, through the raging fires, Brand once more in his sights.

CHAPTER TWO

THAT BASTARD! Delilah thought. That bloodsucking fiend. That black-hearted warrior. That…man! He had no conscience, no sense of fairness. And she…liked it. A sigh slipped from her, and she nearly melted to the ground in a boneless heap of feminine delight.

The warrior had dropped her to her knees. No one had ever dropped her before. No one. She was too strong, too fast, too menacing and too eager to exact revenge. And if she could not, her sisters were more than willing to see the task done, which every species in Atlantis knew.

But the vampire had acted against her without reservation or remorse. What was worse—better?—was that he could have done so much more. One moment he'd been in front of her, the next he'd been behind her. He could have sliced her throat as he'd done to so many of the dragons, and there would have been nothing she could've done about it.

Well, she could have *died.* But where was the fun in that?

She should have been wary of such skill. She wasn't; she was excited. Which was foolish! Number eight of the ten Amazon commandments: never fight an opponent face-to-face if you couldn't defeat him. Wait and stab him in the back later. The vampire could have defeated her. Utterly. Would have. Yet she'd practically begged for more.

The thought of his cunning made her pulse leap and her blood heat as if dragon fire had somehow seeped through the war paint, past her skin and straight into her veins. He'd tripped her, and she had wanted to kiss him for it.

Yes, all right, fine. She had spent many nights lying awake, wishing for what she couldn't have and shouldn't want: a man strong enough to risk her sisters' ire and claim her. A man who didn't think of her as too violent to enjoy for more than a few nights. A man who gave as intensely as she did, who would fight for her with the same ferocity she brought to every battle she joined. A man who would topple any barrier to reach her.

A man who would view her as the most important thing in his life. A prize to be won and cherished.

All of those desires embarrassed her, however, and were not something she would—or could—ever mention aloud. Not if she wanted the respect of her tribe. She was a warrior; they all were. Battle came first. Love, never.

Besides, she'd tried love. Or at least, had given herself to a man. He hadn't been forced to accept her. Hadn't been picked during the Ceremony of the Chosen, where Amazons decided which slaves to bed. No, she'd met him on the battlefield. She'd gone to stab him and he'd kissed her. Intrigued, flattered, she'd let him live, had even snuck out of camp later that night to see him. *You're the one for me,* he'd told her. *I knew it the first moment I saw you.* But after the loving had finished, he'd walked away and had never looked back. She'd been nothing more than a passing fancy, an enemy to use, a woman to sate himself on and, later, a bad memory to bury.

Her fault, though. If she hadn't secretly watched other races over the years, melting at the sight of men fighting for their women, doing anything and everything to protect them, the need for a love of her own wouldn't have sprouted. A need that was a clear violation of the third commandment: if you begin to desire more than a bedding from a man, kill him or he'll take you from your sisters, betray you.

A rage-drenched snarl resounded through the forest, claiming her attention. She thrust her sword forward, twisted the hilt, then slammed it backward. Both in front of and behind her, a dragon warrior dropped at her feet.

Another dragon sprinted toward her. Silly men. They were strong soldiers. She knew that, had fought a few of them before, but she was stronger. Despite her delicate appearance.

Delilah raised her dagger, ready to meet this new opponent. One of her sisters stepped in his path, however, and the two became locked in a fierce battle of clanging, sparking metal. All too soon, the weaker, still-in-training Nola fell against the brute's powerful sword thrusts. The man threw his sword aside, ready to use his meaty hands.

The first commandment: always aid a sister in need.

Steps sure and quick, Delilah reached her sister's side— only to realize proudly that she needn't have bothered. The Amazon shot to her feet and met the dragon warrior's fists with a high kick. He grunted, stumbled.

Nola is fine, and you have a mission. Delilah turned, eyeing the macabre scene before her. Blood, grunting, collapsing bodies. All necessary. She had come here for a specific reason: to find and rescue her sister by race, Lily.

Where are you now, sweet Lily? Before attacking the dragons, Delilah had seen her in the cage. Since then, there had been no sign of the girl. *Come on. Show yourself.* Lily had disappeared a week ago, and they'd tracked her to the dragon palace and followed the warriors into this forest. Better to ambush them there. Whether the dragons had taken her or she'd gone willingly was not important. They had bound her hands and mouth. They had imprisoned her.

For the first, they would suffer. For the second, they would die.

Lily was a child, an innocent, and their future queen. Delilah—and all Amazons—doted on the girl. At thirteen, she was charming, precious, amusing. Everything the rest of the Amazons were not.

Bring my baby home, the queen had instructed Delilah, her chin trembling. Seeing the usually staid Kreja near tears had been a torture all its own. *You know what to do with those who harm her even in the slightest way.*

Every warrioress fighting this battle would do anything, everything, to preserve Lily's sweet innocence—if the dragons had not destroyed it already. If they had… Fury clouded Delilah's vision, winking red and black.

Concentrate. Several warriors had already morphed into their animal form, flesh replaced with scales, serrated tails whipping back and forth, wings flapping and claws slashing. They would be harder to kill that way, but she relished the challenge.

From the corner of her eye, she caught a flash of white hair and glowing crystalline eyes framed by long black lashes. Features almost too pretty to be male. Sensual, exotic. Her heart gave a strange leap. The vampire who'd knocked her to the ground. He could have been the god of wickedness and temptation, and she would not have been surprised.

What was his name? The question whispered through her

mind before she could stop it. *He doesn't matter, remember?* Why, then, could she not tear her gaze from him?

He disappeared in the midst of the crowd. Two enemy warriors clomped toward him, their bodies monstrous and scaled, faces elongated and teeth like sabers. Would the vampire be strong enough to fight them both?

As excited as she was by the thought of his success, a part of her was…scared? Her brow furrowed. No. That wasn't possible. Nothing scared her. Not battle, not pain, not death. Yet she couldn't deny the unsteady rhythm of her heart just then. What if the vampire was struck down? There were so many around him, all going for his neck.

Delilah's attention again snagged on Nola, who still fought a few inches away and was not faring as well as Delilah had hoped. Nola was not one of her closest friends, was too solitary to have *any* friends, but the tribe came first. Always.

Shoving the vampire from her mind once and for all, Delilah leapt at the dragon engaging her sister, propelling him to the ground and allowing Nola to finally sink her blade into his chest.

He roared. "Damn it, woman!" He lay there, panting, intermittingly staring at his chest and Nola with fury, but he didn't get up again. "That hurt."

"Good." Ninth commandment: never leave a fight without first injuring your opponent in some way. Delilah whipped around, ready to fell another. But once again, she found herself searching for the vampire. Not forgotten, after all. Surrounded by countless adversaries as he was, he would surely be cut down. Despite the prowess he'd demonstrated, he was only a man. A breathtaking, commanding man, but as fallible as all his brethren.

Panting, Nola followed the line of Delilah's gaze. "Shall we cut out his heart?"

"Don't even scratch him. The vampire is mine," she said, the words tumbling from her before she could stop them. Fifth commandment: what's yours is your sisters'. Nola had just as much right to him as she did.

There was a shocked pause. "The chaste Delilah finally chooses a male? I must meet him." Nola rushed forward and inserted herself into the throng of Amazons, dragons and vampires. The latter two attempted to shoo her away while continuing to fight each other. Their lack of attention cost them, and they began falling like raindrops during a storm, her sword flashing like lightning.

Did Nola plan to win the vampire for herself? At first, Delilah stood unmoving in astonishment. Stoic Nola always kept to herself, had never fought for a male prisoner and only warred when commanded, despite her growing skill. By nature, she was a watcher, not a doer. She would not want the vampire. Would she?

Perhaps I am not the only one fascinated by his strength. Seething with sudden fury, Delilah stalked forward. What she would do when she reached the thick of the fray, she didn't know. If only cleaving Nola's head from her body were an option.

The illicit thought had her gasping. Were she to say something like that aloud, she would be sentenced to death.

Someone pushed her to the ground before she'd gotten halfway to her target. The vampire had done the same and it had excited her. This…didn't. She rolled to her back. There was no time to rage, though, as this newest threat leapt on top of her and pinned her. She looked up and saw that it was the last dragon she'd stabbed. He'd already partially healed—and clearly wanted more. She wiggled her arm free to slice him.

"Oh, no, you don't," he said, fingers clamping around her wrist.

"Oh, yes, I do." She worked one of her legs between them and kicked him in the face. His body twisted to the side, lifting his weight, freeing her. She stood, kicked him once more, aiming for his oozing wound. He jerked, then stilled, eyes closed. Satisfied he wouldn't come for her again, she marched away, catching sight of the vampire and watching him move with lethal grace and fluidity, his weapons extensions of his arms, as if he had been born with them in his hands.

Behind him, a dragon opened its mouth to spew a stream of fire.

"Nola!" she shouted, too far away to shove him out of the way herself. But the Amazon was distracted by the tail being swung at her, and didn't hear her cry for help.

Swiftly, Delilah withdrew one of the daggers criss-crossed at her back and tossed it. The tip wheezed through the air before embedding in the dragon's chest. There was a chilling howl, but thankfully no fire.

The vampire spun, and his gaze collided with hers. A sizzle of awareness swept through her, stronger than the one she'd experienced at their first encounter. He glanced at the dragon falling to his knees, then inclined his head in acknowledgment of Delilah's action. Disappointment joined ranks with the awareness.

What did you expect? That he'd blow you a kiss? "Your gratitude is humbling," she called, echoing his earlier words to her.

Without a word, he pivoted and attacked another of the

fire-breathers, seeming unconcerned as flames danced over his skin, charring and blistering. The more steps she took toward him, the more opponents jumped in her way. And as Delilah fought her way to him—no, to her friend, damn it!—she saw Nola dive low, slide past a dragon that had just stabbed a vampire in the stomach and slice into its scaled ankles. There was another roar as the creature dropped, no longer able to stand.

Delilah reached her then. The white-haired vampire had vanished.

"Where's Lily?" Nola asked her, panic layering her voice. Ribbons of black hair whipped across her delicate face as she searched left, then right. A loner she might be, but she loved Lily as much as the rest of them.

Delilah followed the direction of her gaze—and finally found the cage Lily had occupied. It was empty. No. No, no, no. "Surely one of the others freed her and carried her to safety."

"That was not the plan. She was to be taken, cage and all to keep her safe and snug, out of harm's way. Most likely she picked the lock herself. She knows how, we made sure of that at least."

"True. All right. You sweep the north, and I'll head south. We'll find her."

Nola nodded, and they were off.

Delilah raced through trees, twigs slapping her face and arms. Rocks dug past the soles of her boots. All the while, she kept her eyes to the ground, searching… searching…there! Three sets of footprints came into view. One was delicate and bare, two were large and booted. Male.

All three were headed toward the Amazon camp.

The dragons wouldn't know the way, which meant Lily was being chased.

Enraged, Delilah increased the speed of her steps, her own haggard gasps ringing in her ears. For once, she regretted the fact that Lily had not been instructed in the art of battle like all the other Amazons.

Sweet Lily, the queen's only child. She'd been a tiny infant, born too soon and constantly sick. She should have been killed at birth, or at least later as it became apparent she would never be strong enough for war. But no one had been able to do it. She'd captured their hearts from the first.

And so, sickly as she'd been, the girl had not been taken from her mother. Had not been thrust into combat training at the age of five. She hadn't been beaten for revealing any hint of weakness, like tears and sadness. Hadn't been slashed and hurt, then thrown into the elements to learn how to survive while her body screamed in pain and the world around her supplied nothing but bone-chilling ice or skin-melting heat.

On her own, Lily would die.

Violated, Lily would probably *want* to die.

I'm coming, sweet. I'm coming. Where are you? Where—

A terrified scream pierced the air, an answer to her prayers. Her nightmares.

Lily! Still sprinting, Delilah unsheathed the remaining daggers at her waist. She burst through an emerald thicket—and found Lily being held down, her ankles tied, her arms flailing as she tried to free herself from the men subduing her.

"Let me go!" she shouted.

"You brought war to our doorstep, girl. Now you're going back to our king whether you want to or not."

Tears streamed down her cheeks; she whimpered. "I just want to go home."

With a leap, Delilah was there. She elbowed one man in the temple, spun and kicked the other in the neck. Both crashed to the ground with dazed grunts. She didn't give them time to recover. Arms crossing, she tossed her remaining blades. They embedded in each target's chest. There was a gurgle, there was a howl, then both men slumped over, every beat of their hearts edging them closer to death.

"Lilah," Lily cried, removing the ties at her ankles. She scrambled up and threw herself into Delilah's waiting arms. The girl was shaking, sobbing, those warm tears still trickling down her cheeks.

Delilah remained on guard as she stroked a hand through the girl's silky hair. "I'm here now. Everything will be fine."

"I didn't mean…the blood…my fault…" Lily said between sobs. "I just wanted to be strong like you. Prove myself. Explore. When I stumbled upon the dragons, I decided to ambush them and bring home their claws as proof of my skill. I've been practicing on my own, but they wouldn't fight me back. Just took me to their home and locked me up so I'd stop trying to hurt them and they could figure out what to do with me. I'm sorry. So sorry. I just… I'm not a child."

"I know, sweet. I know." Anything to calm her. Even a lie. Lily was dissatisfied with her life? Before disappearing, Lily had offered nothing but smiles and laughter. She'd been a radiant glimmer of light among otherwise dark, violent warrioresses. She'd been doted on, coddled, and she'd seemed to soak up the attention.

"If someone dies because of me…"

"You know better." Delilah cupped her jaw and lifted

until they were peering at each other. Watery green eyes stared up at her, branched with red, slightly swollen from her tears. "Your sisters will be fine. They are warriors to the core, and the fire-breathers will not defeat them." And what of the vampires?

Her pulse gave another of those strange flutters, the blood instantly heating in her veins.

Lily shuddered. "Promise?" she asked weakly, hopefully.

"Your need for a promise is insulting."

"I'm sorry. I would never insult you on purpose, but I'm also scared for the dragons. They didn't hurt me, were actually kind."

"That doesn't matter." Her voice hardened. "They should have let you go immediately. Instead, they kept you. Locked you up. Your mother has been wracked with worry."

"But—"

"If we are lenient in this matter, other races will think such treatment of you will be tolerated. We will be seen as weaklings, and we will find ourselves under constant attack. Therefore we must fight now to prevent worse conflicts later." The lesson had been beaten into her until it was as natural as breathing.

A sniffle, a nod.

"Now. It's my turn to extract a promise from you." As she spoke, she scanned the forest. So far, there had been no indication they were being watched or followed. That didn't mean they were completely safe, however.

Lily nibbled on her bottom lip but nodded.

Oh, this girl, Delilah thought with a sigh. Tomorrow, she was going to issue a request to the queen asking that Lily be trained for combat. She didn't want the girl fighting, but she did want her better able to protect herself. "Promise me that you will never leave our home without permission again."

"Promise," was the instant reply. No hesitation. "I've never been so frightened, Lilah. Men are not the frail, feeble beings I thought they were."

No, they weren't. The vampire… Delilah tightened her grip and tried to blank her mind. "If you break this promise, baby girl, dragons and vampires aren't the only thing you'll have to fear. Understand?"

Lily shuddered. "Yes."

"Then let's find the others and go home."

WHILE THE BATTLE CONTINUED to rage, Layel searched the clearing for the blue-haired warrioress but saw no sign of her. He was surprisingly disappointed, which was completely unacceptable. First desire, now a craving to see her?

Hopefully she had been slain. *Yes, hopefully,* he thought, though some hidden part of him screamed *no.* Better she die in battle than torment Layel's mind a second more. His thoughts belonged to Susan. Only Susan.

"I should have known you'd be nearby," a voice snapped behind him.

Layel rotated and found himself facing both Brand and Tagart. Finally. Oh, finally. They were still in human form, more vulnerable to attack. He grinned slowly, raising one arm and pointing, blood dripping from his hand. He'd abandoned his blades a while ago, preferring to make the kills more personal with nails and teeth. "You."

"Yes, me. It's time to end this, Layel," Brand said.

"Your friends tasted good," he said, wiping his mouth

and knowing he smeared more crimson across his face. "But I think the two of you will taste better."

A black curtain of rage fell over Tagart's blood-splattered features. The warrior's stomach was sliced open and bleeding, but he didn't seem to notice. "Killing you is going to be a pleasure, vampire."

"A pity you think so, as you'll never be granted the opportunity to see it through."

A muscle ticked below Brand's eye. "You'll suffer for all you've done to our friends and all you plan to do to us, vampire. You know that, do you not?"

"I know nothing of the kind. It's *because* I suffer that I've done all I have to your friends. And, yes, I have loved every moment of this." Layel might have killed the dragons that raped and burned Susan, might have taken some of them to his dungeon and tortured them for weeks before delivering the final blow, but he didn't think he would ever tire of hurting their brothers by race.

Truly, he lived for one purpose: to wipe out their entire lineage.

"You invite war!" Brand snapped.

"Funny, I thought I had invited it two hundred years ago. Did you just now receive your invitation?"

"I did. And here's my acceptance." Tagart stalked several steps forward before Brand grabbed his arm, holding him still. The dark warrior looked ready to shake off his commander's grip and attack.

"Not yet," Brand said. Then he roared loud and long, morphing into his dragon visage. His clothing ripped away, floating to the ground, and green scales overtook his skin. A snout lengthened his face, claws stretched from his fingers and his teeth sharpened to dripping points. Wings sprouted from his back, gossamer and clear, deceptively innocent as they spread toward the trees. Tagart's transformation quickly followed.

"Come and get me, little hatchlings," Layel told them.

A spew of fire, then Brand and Tagart were flying toward him. Layel sprang at them, ready, so ready. "Susan!" he shouted. His war cry. A constant reminder of what had been taken from him, of what he fought for, of what he would die for.

Except he never reached the warriors.

Midway, Layel's entire world blackened and crumbled piece by piece into nothingness. Nothing around him, nothing in front of or behind him. The ground, his only solid anchor, opened up and swallowed him, his body suddenly careening down a long, dark void. Round and round he twirled. Grunting, he flailed for another anchor but discovered only capricious air.

Ignoring the panic sweeping through him, he forced his breathing to slow, his heart to cease its erratic patter. *Transport. Now!* He tried, but a moment passed and nothing happened; he continued to fall, his body a solid mass. Teeth grinding together, he spread his arms and attempted to fly. But the invisible chain tugged him down…down…down…never slowing, refusing to relinquish its hold on him.

Shock and rage joined the panic and sped through him with sickening intensity. He didn't know what was happening, didn't know *how* it was happening. Only that he could not stop it.

His hand slapped into something hard. A man, he realized. A man's chest. The male grappled for him, fingers clawing for purchase. Layel hissed, his arm soon ripped to shreds. Thankfully, he spun out of reach—and slammed into the softness of a woman's body. She gasped, the sound low, frightened. *How many?* he wondered, even as he hit—a horse? There was a whinny.

Someone screamed. Someone else whimpered. All the while they continued to plummet, no landing in sight.

IN THE MIDDLE OF THE FOREST, Delilah shoved Lily behind her back. Danger suddenly lurked nearby. She could sense it, almost smell it as a presence, a power, thickened the air.

"What's wrong?" Lily whispered, her terror palpable.

"Stay behind me." Delilah reclaimed the daggers she'd used to slay the dragons, her grip tight. *Where are you?* She scanned trees, leaves, shadows. There, to the right, something was rattling branches together. Her lids narrowed, eyes focusing, but she couldn't make out a form. Just—

A gasp tore from her lips as that something sprang into view, as clear as the air she breathed but thicker, like water. She had no time to react, no way to attack. Then it was there, right in front of her, consuming her, sucking her into a black hole.

"Lily!" she screamed, daggers ripping from her hands as she thrashed her arms, desperate for some type of security. She found nothing. Only air. The more she tumbled, the more wave after wave of dizziness assaulted her, slamming with enough force to double her over. Shouts, grunts and groans pierced her ears, as discordant as the bells that tolled when an Amazon died.

"Lily!"

"Amazon," a familiar male voice called, rising above the chaos.

"Vampire?" Her heartbeat should not have calmed. The

sweat just beginning to bead over her skin shouldn't have cooled, but it did. She shouldn't have been relieved, but she was. As she grappled for him—a touch, she only needed a touch—her head slammed into what must be a jagged rock and she grunted, thrown from the vampire by the force.

Stars winked over her eyes, the white lights thickening, expanding, becoming all that she saw. Somehow that light was more terrifying than the darkness, a ray of hope dashed in the cruelest way.

"Reach for me," the vampire commanded.

"Can't," she tried to say, but the word congealed in her throat.

In the end, she didn't have to reach for him. She hit another wall and flew forward. Their bodies collided, knocking the air right out of her lungs. Instantly the terrible white faded into welcome darkness. All of Delilah's muscles slackened and her head lolled against something hard. The vampire's fingers latched around her arm, hot and strong and more necessary than breathing. She wrapped herself around him, wanting to cling to him forever.

Take what you want. It's yours. The sixth commandment rang in her head. She knew beyond any doubt its Amazon creator had not meant snuggling against a male and placing her safety in his hands. Still she held on. *Don't let me go,* she thought before slipping into the oblivion.

CHAPTER THREE

LAYEL BLINKED open his eyes, murky light coming into focus, a combination of bright and dark, clarity and haziness. Fighting confusion, he groaned against a sharp ache in his temples. Where was he? What had happened? He'd been on a battlefield, yes?

Yes, he thought, absolutely sure. The scene flashed through his mind: him, rushing toward his enemy, blade raised. Brand and Tagart in dragon form, flying at him, death in their golden eyes. And then he'd been plucked into nothingness.

Now he was…lying down, he realized. Atop sand. Another ache, followed by a thickening fog, broke his stream of understanding apart. He squeezed his eyelids shut. One heartbeat passed, two. As he'd hoped, the fog thinned and his thoughts realigned. Had he been injured fatally before reaching Brand and Tagart and now rested in eternity?

Not yet, he nearly screamed. *I am not ready. I have not avenged Susan.*

Calm. Think. He *had* been injured, he remembered that. Cut in the chest, one arm shredded. If he was alive, those injuries would still be present. Shaking, he slid one hand under his shirt and rubbed up and down his chest and arm to be sure. Scabs greeted him, and his mouth curved into a half smile.

So…what had happened? he wondered again.

In and out he breathed, the scent of salt and coconut filling his nose. Familiar. The crash of turbulent waves resounded in his ears, washing against the shore. Again, familiar.

Once more he opened his eyes. Slowly this time, allowing the light to reach him gradually. At first he saw only white, puffy…*things* floating across a limitless expanse of blue. Not familiar. The half-smile mutated into a deep frown. Usually a crystal dome surrounded Atlantis, arching and jagged. Where was he?

Focus. Gingerly, he sat up.

Spots of gold and rose flickered before his vision. In, out, he continued to breathe. When the spots faded, lush palm trees in different shades of green and white, from the brightest emerald to the palest jade and ivory, came into view. He turned his head—and had to massage his temples to tame another sharp ache. Soft sand stretched into clear azure ocean, the water undulating into foam, misting, blushing under the stroking beams of a bright orange…ball.

A ball that burned his skin far worse than the dome ever had, he noted, frown intensifying.

His eyes watered so badly he had to cast his gaze back to the sand. That did not lessen the burn, but the burn soon became the least of his worries. Bodies were scattered throughout the sand. Unconscious. Dead?

Layel remained in place and studied the male closest to him. Zane, he realized, who was no longer cut and bruised. The warrior's chest was rising and falling, proof he still lived. Thank the gods. Next he saw—he tensed. Several feet away, Brand lay sprawled on his back. Though he had morphed into a dragon during the battle, ripping away his clothing, he was now human and dressed. Beside him sprawled Tagart. Human and dressed, as well.

As though it had never left him, only ebbed to the back of his mind, rage tore through Layel. Rage that their fight had ended so abruptly, rage that the dragons were not dead.

Whatever had happened to bring them to this strange land, Layel suddenly didn't care. The dragons had to die. Should be dead already. Scowling, he jumped to his feet. He swayed against a surge of dizziness, unsteady, but stumbled forward anyway. He reached for his daggers, every ounce of his determination pulsing from the tips of his fingers.

The blades were gone. A growl echoed in his throat, growing louder, fiercer, when a quick body-pat revealed every piece in his arsenal was gone.

He didn't slow. Using his teeth to rip out their jugulars would work just as well. Still, a few weapons would have been nice. Just in case. No matter, though.

Almost upon them…almost…he slammed into an invisible barrier.

Every bone in his body vibrated from the impact, and that cursed dizziness again swept through him. He blinked in confusion, lifted his arms and pressed at the air. What in Hades? There was some sort of…shield?

Yes, yes, he realized. That's exactly what it was. Clear, unseen, and yet solid, preventing him from moving another inch. He banged his fists against it, but it held steady. He clawed at it, but it did not crack. No, it snapped two of his nails from their beds, causing blood to flow down his hands. He rammed his shoulder into it, nearly dislocating the bone, but the shield did not even shake.

Damn this! He would not be denied. Would lose a limb

if necessary. What did physical pain matter when faced with such a delightful outcome? As he threw his body against the barrier over and over again, he glared at his still-sleeping enemies. Never had a time been more ripe for vengeance. Soon…

Next to the dragons were two Amazons, one of whom happened to be his bloodthirsty, blue-haired wench. *Not mine,* he corrected instantly, fervently. But he couldn't deny the sight of her caused his breath to heat and singe his lungs. Couldn't deny his blood quickened.

As he'd fallen through that dark void, he'd heard her raspy voice and had grabbed on to her limp body. She'd been warm and soft, a torment to him. And yet, he'd been oddly protective of her, cradling her against him, marveling at her sea-kissed scent as he recalled the way she'd looked at him on the battlefield, as if he were a miracle and a devil wrapped in the same tempting package.

He didn't recall letting go of her, yet they had clearly been parted. Now, he drank her in when he should have looked away.

She appeared rumpled, as if she'd fallen asleep after a vigorous hour of lovemaking and had only now awakened for more. Her eyes were slightly uptilted, the lids at half-mast and shadowed by long dark lashes. Her nose was small and dainty, her lips still red and lush. And her skin…more was revealed, smooth, amber-rich, each pulse point hammering deliciously. A large bruise covered the left side of her jaw. Her breasts—

Do not think of her like that, you disgusting pile of dragon droppings. Females were off-limits to him.

Layel tore his gaze from the Amazon and renewed his study of the other creatures, only then realizing he'd stopped pounding at the air shield. All were beginning to stir, sitting up and rubbing their faces. He might not be able to reach them—yet—but he could hear them. Moaning soon overshadowed the hum of the waves.

There were two nymphs, a male and a female, pushing to a stand and staring at the beach of creatures in confusion. Around them were one pair each of minotaurs, demons, centaurs, formorians and gorgons, the snakes atop the latter's heads hissing and baring fangs much sharper than Layel's. Two of each race. Why two?

What in Hades is going on? he wondered yet again.

The Amazon scrubbed a hand over her delicate face, barely painted now with the remnants of swirling blue designs. Those designs etched onto her temples didn't smear. Were they tattoos? She was blinking, as though she couldn't quite believe what she was seeing.

You're looking at her again. He growled and returned his attention to the dragons, his rage intensifying. He shoved at the invisible wall. Still there, still unyielding. His fingers were bloodied and tattered now, nearly useless. His shoulder was completely out of its joint.

He needed to think, to plan. More than that, he needed to find shade. What skin was bared now felt as if it were blistered. Probably was. Hating the thought of retreat, hating himself, he edged backward, trying not to draw unwanted attention as he stopped beside Zane and crouched, gripping the vampire's shoulders and shaking.

Zane's eyelids popped open and he hissed, swinging a claw in reflex. Quick as a heartbeat, Layel bowed his back, managing to evade a fatal slice to the throat. "Calm," he commanded quietly.

Seconds passed as the vampire oriented himself. "What happened?" Zane demanded roughly, on his feet a moment later. The consummate warrior, he braced his legs apart as his hands fisted at his sides, prepared to initiate battle. His eyes were dark, flat, and he looked hungry for blood. Like Layel's, his skin was red, beginning to blister.

"I'm not sure." Layel rose and motioned to the others with a tilt of his chin. "One moment we were fighting, the next we were not."

"What is this place?" Zane's gaze circled the surrounding area. "Why do I feel as though I'm on fire?" He patted himself down, snarled. "And where are my weapons?"

Something Susan had said long ago, after they'd made love out in the open, under Atlantis's sparkling dome, suddenly drifted through Layel's mind. His mouth fell open in astonishment. *I wish we could travel to the world of my people. Just for a little while. With all the stories my family used to tell me, I think we would love it.*

He'd held her tighter, afraid she'd somehow slip through his fingers. *Tell me about it.*

She had, in great detail, as if she'd already visited it in her dreams. A seemingly never-ending expanse of blue—sky. Fat, puffy white masses—clouds. A glowing orange ball—the sun.

"I think…I think we are on the surface world." How? Why? "I know we could tolerate the daylight under the dome, but the sun's light must be stronger. Harsher. And the weapons? Vanished."

"Surface?" Zane's mouth fell open in a mirror of Layel's expression.

"We must find shade. Now."

"Our battle—"

"Can wait."

Together they backed up, neither willing to give the

other creatures their backs, shield or not, and moved into the thicket of trees. Instantly Layel's body cooled.

He sighed. "We will remain in the forest until we figure out what's going on." Even if that meant avoiding the dragons. Right now they seemed to have the advantage, the sun caressing them like lovers rather than hated foes.

"We should make new weapons," Zane said.

"Yes." But he didn't move another inch. Could barely form a coherent thought. The blue-haired Amazon had just popped to a stand, her eyes wild. She reached for something at her waist—probably a blade—found nothing, and scowled. Like him, like Zane, she patted herself down. Also like the both of them, she found herself completely unarmed.

Someone had taken all their weapons.

He watched as she spun in a circle, studying, gaping. When she spotted the other Amazon, she rushed forward.

"Nola!" she cried, so loudly Layel had no trouble hearing her from his new sanctuary. She bent down, locks of silky hair tumbling over her shoulders, and shook her sister.

The dark-haired female moaned and rubbed at her forehead, eyelids cracking open. "Delilah?"

Delilah. The name played through his mind. Delilah… Delilah…soft, feminine, exotic. A name that bespoke midnight fantasies and insatiable passion. A name that could send the strongest of men to their knees. When the thought registered, Layel stiffened. *I will never speak that name aloud,* he vowed. Too…dangerous.

"I'm here," the woman in question said. "Right here."

The one called Nola massaged her temples, her lips pulled in a tight, pained frown. "What happened?"

No doubt it was a question everyone on the beach would ask.

"I wish I knew." Delilah looked left and right, searching again, gauging, and then she was staring over at Layel, the shadows nothing to her.

The force of that violet gaze jolted him. Made his muscles jump. For a moment, he was light-headed again and there was a pain in his chest, exactly where his heart resided, as though it were once again healthy and whole. How was she doing this?

Apparently he wasn't the only one suffering a strange response. The Amazon's pulse pounded in her neck—he couldn't see it, but he could sense it, hear it—every erratic beat like a summoning finger. His mouth watered, preparing to feast even though he had gorged himself during battle. When he sank his teeth into that woman he would… His jaw clenched painfully. *What are you doing? You will never taste her.* Since Susan's death, the only blood he allowed himself was the blood of his enemies. And the supply was vast. He was never without, didn't need to take from anyone else.

Who was this Amazon, that she was able to tempt him to forget? She was lovely, yes, but she wasn't Susan. Would never be his sweet, gentle Susan. And he would not defile his love's memory with fanciful thoughts of another.

Delilah pounded toward him. "Who did this to us? How were we brought here? Do you know?"

Layel ignored her. Her raspy voice was as seductive as her body and he'd already made the mistake of softening toward her several times. He would not do so again. Being polite to her would encourage familiarity between them when he craved only distance.

"Vampire."

He turned his face away from her, wondering how she'd breached the invisible wall. *Do not even think of her.* All of the creatures had risen and were now pairing off, growling and hissing at their enemies, though none could seem to get within striking distance. Unlike Delilah, they were met with the same obstruction he had encountered.

"Demons," Zane suddenly spat. He marched forward, his intent to slaughter evident with every step, their agreement to remain in the shade obviously forgotten. When he, too, hit the clear barrier, he paused and shook his head. Banged his fist against it once, twice. Paused again. Screeched an unholy sound of frustration. A second later, he attacked the air with a vengeance, screaming curses and promises of brutality all the while, oblivious to the cruel sun.

Layel didn't even try to rein in the vampire's rage. They had been together only a few months, and in that time he had learned that Zane could not be subdued until exhaustion gripped him. The male had spent centuries as a demon queen's consort—willing or unwilling, Layel didn't know. He only knew the experience had left the warrior wild, uncontrollable, and so volatile Layel only utilized him during battle.

There was no better killer than Zane.

Layel waited until the warrior's actions slowed and his screams quieted. An eternity, surely. He strode to him, away from the Amazon, and placed a warning hand on one of Zane's tense shoulders.

Panting, the vampire whipped to face him, fangs bared to bite. Zane stopped himself in time, and Layel withdrew his hand, his point made.

"For some reason, we cannot hurt them." Yet. "You must remain calm."

"I want those demons on a pike," the warrior snarled.

"And I want the dragons' heads to roll."

Silence enveloped them as they stared at each other in understanding. Their enemies might be different, but their pain was not. Layel only wished he knew what had been done to the warrior.

Finally Zane nodded. But a muscle ticked below his left eye, contradicting the easy acceptance. "What should we do?"

"We shall learn the layout of this land." Maybe they would find the perfect place to ambush the others. If the invisible wall did not stop them again. "Maybe as we do so, we will learn the reason we were brought here."

"Where are my weapons?" Brand suddenly shouted, drawing Layel's attention. The dragon soldier was searching the sand for his blades, grains flying in every direction. "Tell me or I will burn this—"

"Mine are missing, as well," Tagart growled. His side no longer bled. Unfortunately, he'd already healed.

"Look!" someone said, their shock cutting through the commotion.

"Is that… Can it be…?"

Intrigued, Layel twisted. He found himself peering at a large crystal dome several miles away, which stretched above the rolling waves and momentarily blighted the luminous rainbow that glittered at the water's edges.

Atlantis, he realized, dread curling his stomach. How was that possible? It lay far beneath the surface world. But he was looking right at it, standing on land he'd only ever heard stories about. Wasn't he?

Could their hidden world be tiered, with layers he had not known about? Could he still be inside Atlantis, just in another part? If so, there would be a way home. He had only to find it. Perhaps the same way he'd gotten here—the tunnel that had tugged him down, down, down.

How had he stumbled upon the tunnel, though? A god? They were certainly powerful enough to create such a transport, moving more than a dozen creatures from one location to another in seconds, stealing their weapons and erecting a shield to prevent them from killing one another.

Could it be?

The gods were not something he usually considered. They had neglected the Atlanteans for thousands of years, only returning a few months ago. Or so he had heard. He himself had yet to encounter one. What possible reason could they have for whisking two of every race to this island?

Unable to stop himself, he stood helpless as his gaze once more sought the Amazon. She was still watching him, those inviting lips pursed as if she was lost in thought, trying to decide on the best course of action. A tendril of hair caressed her cheek, and he found himself wondering if her skin was as soft as he remembered. Found himself jealous that his fingers were not what caressed her.

Oh, no. No, no, no. There would be none of that, he reminded himself, determined to repeat the mantra as many times as necessary. His eyelids narrowed to tiny slits, and the spark of hatred he'd felt earlier grew. Intensified. Perhaps it was best that his weapons had been taken from him. He might have killed the Amazon right then for daring to claim desires that belonged only to Susan.

"Should we swim out?" one of the gorgons asked the crowd.

A debate arose.

"Come," Layel told Zane. He ignored the sense of loss that assaulted him as he once again pivoted. Swimming, he was confident, would prove pointless. Someone powerful wanted them here, so here they would remain. "We have weapons to make."

Sweat glistened on the other vampire's face as he nodded. "I cannot relax until I have blades in my hands."

They moved deeper into the thicket, the dewy foliage about to wrap around them completely. "We will—" Layel hit another invisible wall and cursed.

Snarling, Zane kicked out his leg. "No one should be able to hold us like this."

"Trapped," someone said behind them. "The forest is blocked."

"What should we do?" another demanded. A female.

Layel twisted, saw the two nymphs had followed him, and scrubbed a hand down his face. Valerian, the nymph king, was his only true friend, the man's followers his allies. These two were more beautiful than most, both boasting pale hair and vivid blue eyes. Features so pure and perfect they far surpassed the radiance of the sun.

"Broderick," he acknowledged with a nod. "Why aren't you trying to swim back to Atlantis?"

"Several reasons. The first is that I'm not convinced it will do us any good—and I'd just as soon stay warm and dry if that's the case. The second is that I trust you more than I trust any of the other creatures here. Where you go, my sister and I will go. Have you any idea what's going on?"

"All I know is that our way is being blocked, which must mean we are not to leave the beach. Perhaps if we return, whoever has done this to us will finally reveal himself." *Bastard.*

"We can hope." Walking back, side by side, Broderick said, "Word is you were battling dragons again."

"Yes."

"Win?"

"Not yet." But he would.

"They are not bad men." Valerian had recently allied himself with the dragons to save his mate. Layel had understood the need for such a union, even if he despised it with all of his being. He would have done no less for Susan. "They are respectful of our women, aid us in our defense of our palace, never strike at us in spite. They—"

"Are not up for discussion." Having reached the edge of the trees, Layel was careful to remain in the shade. He studied the creatures anew. They were divided, whispering in their groups of two.

Or maybe not so divided after all. "There's only one other avenue of escape. Who's with me?" The proclamation came from Brand as he stalked toward the water. The others were quick to follow him.

A moment later, there was a splash, then another and another. Every creature save Layel, Zane and the two nymphs entered, swimming for the dome. Even Delilah. Her head bobbed up and down with the waves.

He gritted his teeth. *You must stop seeking her out.*

"Should we follow them?" Zane asked.

"They'll return," he replied confidently. "There are powers at work. Strange powers, strong powers. As I said, we are clearly wanted here. There will be no escaping."

He watched as arms and legs peeked above the water, some scaled, some lined with horns, some humanlike. Five minutes passed. Ten. Fifteen. Twenty, thirty. No one gained any distance. No matter how hard they fought the ocean, they remained a few feet from the beach.

One by one, they gave up and crawled to shore, exhausted and panting. Delilah was the last to exit, which spoke volumes about her character. Strong, determined, unwilling to admit defeat.

He should not admire her for that.

She was scowling as her gaze latched on to his. She lumbered into a march, her expression darkening the closer she came. All of her war paint had washed away, revealing golden skin tattooed with intricate designs the same luscious shade as her cerulean locks, swirling around her face, upper arms, waist and thighs.

What little clothing she wore clung to her curves.

Soaked tendrils of hair were plastered to her, dripping liquid down her stomach and thighs. His gaze followed several droplets, and his blood heated as if he were baking in the sunlight again. Oh, to lick them up…

Zane tensed and stepped in front of him. "Enemy approaching."

"Let her come." *If* she could. Would the air shield stop her this time?

Curious, Layel kept his hands clenched at his sides. Part of him hoped she would be allowed to reach him. He had tried to ignore the sensual power she wielded, the awareness that sizzled every time he looked at her. He had tried, and he had failed. It was past time the madness ended. Susan deserved better from him. And there was only one way he could think of that would halt his new desires permanently. Death.

As he was not yet ready to die, that left one option. Killing the Amazon. He would not be upset about it, would not miss her. He didn't even know her.

"Do not touch her. Do not even approach her, no matter what she does or says."

The command surprised them both, but he did not rescind it. She belonged to him, her last breath his to deliver.

Eyes narrowed, Zane moved out of the way. He stared Delilah down as she stalked past him, still no hint of the air shield in evidence.

She tossed the man a withering glance before once again focusing all her fury on Layel. "A bodyguard," she said, brows arched. "Afraid of a little girl, vampire? I don't know why, but I expected better of you."

That she was now inches from him, practically in his face, her sea-kissed scent tormenting his nose, electrified him. He'd just decided to kill her. Could he, though? he wondered now as his gaze locked with hers. All that violet…a man could get lost. His hands still rested at his sides, the muscles lax. *Do it. Strike!* Not even a twitch.

"I don't care what you expected. Your opinion has no value to me." Cruel, yes, but necessary. If he couldn't hurt her physically—*what's stopping you? Simply act, move*—he would have to hurt her emotionally. Anything to preserve the distance between them.

Her mouth fell open, pain shimmering in her eyes. Pain she quickly masked.

Has to be this way, he reminded himself, since he clearly wasn't man enough to slay her. "Don't come near me again, woman. Don't look at me, don't even breathe in my direction."

As he spoke, she ran her tongue over her teeth. "As if I'm the only one doing the looking. But I'll tell you what, vampire. I'll stop looking at you, if you'll stop looking at me."

His jaw hardened—and he refused to admit what else hardened at the sight of that pink tongue. "Done." He forced himself into motion, attempting to sidestep her.

She stiffened and jumped back in front of him. "Stay where you are. There are a few more things we need to work out."

True to his word, he kept his eyes averted from her. "No. Now, out of my way, Amazon." A mistake, letting her get close to him. Besides being too hot, his skin was suddenly too tight for his bones and his stomach was knotted.

"You're being very rude," she said. "I've killed men for less."

"Do you want a prize?" he asked drily. Still, he managed to face the beach. Her sea-salt scent continued to tease him, strong, lovely. Hauntingly familiar.

"I'll settle for your testicles in my trophy tent."

That did *not* amuse him. "Perhaps later. At the moment, I need them." He headed for Brand, who sat near the water's edge, knees drawn to his chest. His back was to Layel, his braided blond hair as soaked as Delilah's. Obviously the air shields were down, not just for Delilah but for everyone, creatures now touching one another.

As if sensing him, Brand hopped to his feet and spun. His lips curved into a grin, animosity flaring as if there had been no break between battles. "I expected you sooner."

"I live to disappoint you. Ready to die?"

"Come and get me, bloodsucker."

"My plea—" Layel hit the damned invisible wall again, knocking the breath right out of his lungs.

Brand's grin became smug. "What's the matter? Change your mind? Frightened?"

Calm. Do not show emotion.

"You're the coward, dragon," Delilah said, suddenly at Layel's side. Brand's smugness became fury.

"Can you move past this point?" Layel asked without

facing her, trying to quash the pleasure that came with her defense of him.

She bristled at his harsh tone. "Can you?"

"Woman."

"That is not my name." She kept her gaze on Layel; he felt the heat of it. A quick glance at her proved he was right, and that her hands remained fisted, as if she expected Brand to attack her at any moment.

"Can you move past this godsdamn point, *woman?*"

Silence.

He waited. Even Brand waited. Still she did not speak. Had he hurt her again? Did tears swim in her lovely lavender irises? Why did the prospect not please him as much as it should?

"My name is Delilah."

"I know."

Her shoulder brushed his arm and he hissed. "Say my name," she said, suddenly breathless, "and I'll consider finding out."

Something about her tone…pure challenge layered the wispy undercurrents, as if she *wanted* him to deny her. He was not sure what to make of that. "Why do you wish me to do this?"

"I want to hear my name on your tongue."

"Again, why?"

"Because." Stubborn as he'd come to realize she was, she said no more.

"Tell me why," he demanded.

"Just say it!"

"No," he said, while inside his mind he whispered *Delilah,* drawing out each syllable. The name was a prayer and a curse, both wonderful and evil. Unable to help himself, he looked down and studied her. So lovely, and yet so dangerous in a way she could not possibly comprehend.

A pause. A deep breath, as though she prayed for patience. "Have it your way, vampire. But if you won't say my name, at least tell me yours."

No reason to deny her. She would find out one way or another. "I am Layel."

Her eyes widened. "The vampire king?"

He nodded curtly. Was that admiration now sparkling in her eyes? Surely not. "Try and step past me. Please," he added reluctantly. It was easier to beg than to give her what she wanted.

Silent, trembling, she moved closer to Brand. Unhindered, unfettered. Irritation raced through Layel that she could do so and he could not. She did not remain there, however. She returned to Layel's side.

"Want me to kill the dragon for you while I'm here?" she asked, as casually as if they were discussing the weather.

Brand snorted, not the least bit fearful. Foolish.

Layel gave a clipped shake of his head. "Why?" he demanded of the sky. But if the gods heard him, they gave no indication. As usual.

"Maybe I'll do it for my own pleasure, then," she said to Brand, ignoring Layel as her eyes narrowed. "I haven't forgotten what was done to my sister."

The dragon scrubbed two fingers along his jaw. "What little was done, she brought upon herself. And anyway, I have a feeling we aren't meant to harm each other. Why else would our weapons have been taken?"

"I don't need any weapons to take you down." Layel stepped in front of Delilah. Not to protect her, he told himself, but to claim Brand's attention. "Why don't you try and breach the shield, dragon?"

"No, I don't think I will," Brand said. "I'm done with this conversation. Done with you, too, now that my anger has cooled. I'll leave you at the…tender mercies of the Amazon." Then he did the unthinkable. He walked away. *Walked the hell away.*

Layel's fangs cut into his lower lip, drawing blood. He tried to follow. Couldn't.

Delilah pivoted, in front of him again, blocking his view of the retreating dragon. "As I was saying, we have some things to discuss, you and I."

He popped his jaw before forcing his expression to relax. She was still geared for a fight, still seemed to crave one. "Poor baby," he said, unwilling to give her what she wanted. "Did I hurt your feelings when I abandoned you a moment ago?"

Her cheekbones pinkened, highlighting the freckles atop her dainty nose. Would she have a dimple when she smiled? *If* she ever smiled, that is. So far, the Amazon had only glared at him.

Susan had had two dimples, and she'd rarely been without a smile. One that had always entranced him. So why did Delilah's glare affect him just as powerfully?

Layel almost beat himself in the temples to dislodge that torturous thought. He would not compare another woman to Susan. There was no comparison. She had no equal, then or now.

"Why are you looking at me like that?" Delilah asked, now curious rather than upset. "In fact, why are you looking at me at all? You said you would not."

Because I am a terrible husband. "How was I looking

at you?" He stared past her, past the water to the crystal dome that was so close, yet so far away. *Like I want to draw you close and push you away at the same time? Like I want to both taste you and kill you? Like you're dangerous in a way you have no right to be?*

"Like I'm a disgusting demon," she said.

She wasn't a demon; she was far worse. Admitting it would have given her power over him, though. "Why did you approach me, Amazon? What do you want from me? And understand that I will not fight with you, no matter what you say. Not now. You will stop trying to provoke me."

"I wasn't trying to provoke you," she said, indignant.

"You succeeded nonetheless. I asked you a question. You will answer it."

At first, she gave no reaction to his words. Then her lips pursed. Those lush, beautiful lips. What would they feel like against his skin? What would—

With a hiss, she kicked out her leg, knocking his ankles together as he'd done to hers in the forest. At the same time, she pushed his shoulders, propelling him backward and giving him no way to balance or catch himself. When he landed, he landed hard, breathing a thing of the past.

You knew better than to allow yourself to be distracted in the presence of an Amazon warrioress, he berated himself, trying to suck in a mouthful of air. *Around any enemy, really, but especially one so volatile.*

Delilah hopped on top of him, pinning his shoulders to the sand with her knees. There was now another layer to her already complex scent, he realized. Arousal. The discovery shocked him. Hot, erotic arousal, and his mouth dried, his tongue desperate to lave between her legs, where she would be wet. If he moved, raised his head even a little, he would be able to quench his sudden, desperate thirst.

No. *No!*

"This is better," she said, practically humming with satisfaction. And disappointment? Did she *want* to be weaker than him? Surely not. To her, such a thing could bring only humiliation. "The king of the vampires, mine to command. Now you are going to answer *my* questions. Tell me why you didn't try to swim home like the rest of us. You know something. You must."

Fighting his need for her—just a touch, a taste—he snapped, "I will never be yours to command. Never be yours, period."

"We shall see." Baby-fine strands of her hair brushed his cheeks. A purr rumbled in the back of his throat, and he growled to mask it. "I have heard of your conquests, vampire king."

"Have you?" Slowly he raised his hands to her waist, pretending he wanted to hold her, be closer to her. Hating that it was not as much a pretense as it should have been.

She didn't protest. "Yes. They're impressive. You killed the demon queen, sucking her dry. You have slaughtered more dragons than anyone else ever to live. Combined. You torture ruthlessly just to hear your opponent scream."

"And yet you seem remarkably unfazed by such fearless feats."

"Have you, perchance, heard of *my* conquests?" She sounded hopeful.

"No." He hadn't, but wished otherwise.

"Liar," she said, unable to hide her dejection.

"About many things, yes, but not this." When she opened her mouth, perhaps to list her own feats, he added,

"I do not wish to hear about them, either." Proof that he did, in fact, lie whenever he wanted.

Fire blazed in her eyes as she licked her lips, baring that pink tongue again. "All I want to know is wwhhyy—"

With a flick of his wrists, he tossed her overhead. She landed on her back and rolled, but he expected the motion and rolled backward himself, pinning *her* to the sand with his body's weight. Behind them, a gasp sounded. Followed by a laugh, a cheer. No footsteps swished in the sand, however. Perhaps, like him, the others could not breach the shield. Or perhaps they were simply enjoying the show.

Delilah lay there a moment, stunned.

"You were saying?" he asked, one brow arched smugly.

"Release me, Layel. Now."

Her breasts pushed into his chest, her nipples hard and wanting. He was tempted, so tempted, to palm them. Was shaking with the need, he realized. "What are you doing to me? How are you making me feel this way?"

She blinked up at him, truly confused. "What way?"

He would not admit his desires aloud. They were wrong, unacceptable. Oh, he knew that men and women constantly fell in and out of lust. Knew that many who lost their lover grieved for a time and then found someone else.

He could not, would not do so.

Susan had been killed in the most painful, brutal way imaginable. She had been humiliated, used, spat upon and finally burned. She had felt her baby die inside her, the kicking gradually slowing until it ceased altogether. She had begged and she had pleaded for Layel's help, but he had not reached her soon enough. He had not saved her.

He did not deserve another chance at love.

He did not deserve another woman.

More than that, Susan did not deserve to have her memory overshadowed by another woman.

"What way?" Delilah insisted, reaching up.

What she meant to do, he might never know. He jolted to his feet with a roar. "Do not touch me. Ever. Just stay away from me, Amazon. Do you understand?"

He didn't wait for her reply, but stalked away from her. Stalked away before he looked at her, saw hurt in her eyes and apologized. Before he begged her to ignore his words and touch him anyway. Before he threw himself at her, sobbing for a chance at something he was not worthy of.

Sand was flung against his calves and he knew she'd stood. "I only approached you to ask if you knew why we were brought here," she called. There was no emotion in her tone. Merely a detachment he suddenly loathed nearly as much as he loathed the dragons.

Silent, he continued to stride away from her with a fierce determination he usually reserved for the battlefield. *One amorous glance from a woman and a part of you longs to forget Susan. You promised her an eternity, yet you only gave her a few hundred years. Pathetic.*

Cringing, he covered his ears with his hands. Dark, treacherous emotions were welling inside him, close to bubbling over. If they succeeded, Layel knew he would be lost to them forever. There would be no returning, no reclaiming his sanity. Vengeance would be forgotten, his own pain all he would be able to see.

"Do you know? Does anyone know?" Delilah shouted.

"I do," a booming voice answered, relish in every syllable. "I know."

CHAPTER FOUR

DELILAH FROZE. That voice…that power… In all her years, she'd never heard such a sound or felt such a presence. And yet, the shock of both failed to compare to the shock of having been face-to-face—body to body—with Layel, king of the vampires.

She had heard stories of the man's prowess, of course, of his dark nature, his unquenchable thirst for blood and power. Delicious qualities, indeed, and she couldn't help but desire all of his strength, all of his fervor, at her finger-tips again. He was a warrior to the core and would not care what her sisters thought of him. He would fight for what he wanted, damn the consequences.

He was the kind of man she'd secretly wanted for years, the need solidifying every time she saw a couple, no matter their race, cooing over each other. The kind of man she'd once thought she'd had, only to lose because he hadn't de-sired more than a night. But unlike the other, Vorik, who, at the height of passion, had claimed he would crave her forever, Layel said he wanted nothing to do with her. Should she believe him? His heated glances suggested otherwise.

She almost wished she'd spent more time with the male species. But with the exception of her ill-fated assignation, her tribe only consorted with them twice a year—mating season—when men were stolen from their homes, reduced to slaves, their bodies used repeatedly. When the Amazons finished with them, they were sent on their way. Because Vorik had not been one of those slaves, Delilah had foolishly hoped that, after all his tender promises and heated caresses, her man would fight to stay with her. Or, at the very least, fight to take her with him.

Not even a backward glance, she mused darkly.

So many times since then she'd wondered why none of the men—not just hers—had ever asked for more. After all, not one slave had even put up a fight when he'd first realized his destination and purpose. In fact, they'd seemed overjoyed. Willing and eager. And even though they were slaves, they were treated well, sex available anytime they wanted it.

But apparently, though Amazons were fun for a time, they just weren't worthy of forever. Not that any other Amazon but her wanted forever. *What's wrong with me?* Though her virginity was long gone, thanks to Vorik, she couldn't even use the slaves casually, as the sexual vessels they were meant to be.

Since taking her lover, Delilah had never experienced the urge to give herself to another, only to toss him aside later—or be tossed aside herself, his old life more important than the new one he could build with her. But Layel…she desired him, she realized. Desired his tongue in her mouth, hot and insistent. Desired their sweat-soaked skin slipping and sliding together. Desired his body arching and straining over hers.

Foolish girl. She could desire such things, but she could never allow them. Already she wanted Layel too fiercely. How much more would she want him if she learned the reality of his touch? The true bliss? She would give herself to him, wholly and fully, yet he would walk away afterward. Once again, she would be forgotten. This time, though, she suspected she would not get over the loss. She'd been given a glimpse of the man behind the legend and she'd liked what she'd seen.

Someone stepped on her foot, drawing her from her troubling musings back to the equally troubling present. What in Hades was going on? Everyone was inching toward the beach.

"Reveal yourself," the dragon with the braids was saying to the invisible being, his arms splayed wide as he turned in a circle in front of her. "If you have the courage."

Someone gasped. Someone pointed.

Wonderful. Another surprise. Delilah followed the direction of that finger, and her eyes widened. There, above the water, the air had begun to crystallize and thicken. A force of good? Or evil? She settled one foot behind her, ready to leap and attack at a moment's notice. The other creatures did the same, she noticed, each of them preparing for battle.

Unfortunately, the only weapons to be had were their own bodies.

Even Layel had stopped to face the swirling being. His expression was intent, though untamed, feral and savage, and somehow banked with undeniable sensuality.

"Oh, I have the courage. But do you, dragon? Do any of you? Only time will tell." Wind billowed and wet droplets sprayed. "Citizens of Atlantis, welcome to Paradise, created for the gods yet happily relinquished to you, our faithful servants."

Paradise? Servants?

The voice came from the water, but the air never coagulated completely. Just remained thick and dappled in the

shape of a human—large, probably male. Three mermaids—
a blonde, a brunette and a redhead—swam around the misty
form, cooing their admiration of his power and glory.

"Be not afraid," the being continued. "You have been
chosen to participate in a monumental event. All we ask in
return is that you show us your valor, strength and cunning,
qualities you have amply displayed on the battlefields of
your home." He paused, probably awaiting nods and mur-
murs of encouragement.

He got neither. The others were no doubt as perplexed
as Delilah.

A rumble of irritation sounded from the water.

"Why did you bring us here?" she demanded before the
being could speak again. So far, he had offered no answers,
only more confusion.

"There's going to be trouble," one of the mermaids
sang happily.

"You will not speak to me in that tone," the booming
voice announced, the jelly-air rippling violently.

"And you can't just—" Delilah began.

"Silence!"

A stream of water slammed into her, hitting with so
much force she dropped to her knees, gasping for breath.
Her mouth filled, and she gurgled and choked. *Even if you
are dying, show no fear.* The second commandment. She
might have broken most of the commandments this day,
but she wouldn't break that one.

Her gaze automatically sought Layel, the man who made
her feel both protected and hated. His beautiful azure eyes
were narrowed on her, his soft lips thinned. In displeasure?
She hadn't seen him move, but he seemed closer to her than
before. She forced her expression to remain neutral.

"Next time, Amazon, you will be *buried* in water," the being warned.

She didn't respond, even when the water spray ceased and she managed to suck air back into her lungs. As a warrioress, she had been trained in combat since the age of five. Every time she had failed at a lesson, she had been punished severely. A whipping most often, until her flesh was torn to ribbons. Sometimes a stoning. Sometimes a parade through camp, her faults shouted for all to hear.

She understood the need for such training, and didn't regret it. Her ancestors had been slaves to males of all races—just like the slaves they now took into their own camp those two months out of every year. Only their captivity had been eternal. Or had been meant for eternity. One day they'd risen up, attacked and escaped, determined never to suffer such a fate again. Determined no Amazon would. And so the commandments had been born.

Delilah bore both her internal and external scars proudly, for she had learned never to fail twice at the same thing. This god would not receive a second opportunity to best her.

"Impertinence will not be tolerated. We are Supreme Beings, your leaders, your creators. You will treat us with the respect we deserve, or you will suffer our wrath."

We. There was only one being here, yet he spoke of others. Were they all here, simply invisible? The thought didn't scare her; no, it infuriated her. An unseen, unknown enemy would be harder to defeat.

"Listen, all. You are our creations, meant for our amusement and protection, yet we have never made use of you. For too long, you were forgotten, our attention turned to the humans. But no longer must you endure our neglect. You have been remembered and now you shall know our favor."

The voice paused again, as if everyone should exclaim with joy that they'd been remembered. When no one did, there was another irritated grumble.

"Our greatest wish is to learn all about you. For weeks we have been watching you, studying, wondering who among you is the strongest. Those touched by Apollo's flame? Those gifted with Aphrodite's beauty? Those with Ares's thirst for war? And that is how you came to be here on this island, for after careful consideration, we plucked the most courageous, the most feared from the masses." Once more the wind blustered. "Faithful servants, it is time you put an end to our wondering, once and for all."

Delilah almost groaned. She could guess what the god—for what else could the force be but a god?—would say next. They were going to force the creatures here to fight one another. While she didn't mind fighting, she didn't like being jerked from her home, from Lily to—

Lily.

Damn this! What had happened to the girl after Delilah had disappeared? Had she made it home safely? Had she been captured again? Hurt? Delilah's hands curled into fists, itching to pound something. Someone. The tenth and most important commandment was to always protect the queen and her family. Had she left Lily at the mercy of the dragons?

"This will not be an easy undertaking, nor will it be swift. Not for you, and not for us. Time is required to sift through sand and find the gold. That is why you will remain on this island," the being continued, "where you will be divided into two teams. Every few days you will be tested, challenged, our way of dusting the sand from the gold. It will be up to you to prove your mettle and show us we were right to return to Atlantis."

"Every few days" would translate into weeks, if not months. Her nails dug crescents into her palm. *What did I do to deserve this?* Courage should be rewarded, not punished.

"Before you proclaim your joy at this great honor we have bestowed upon you, you should know that we conferred many days before bringing you here, one truth very clear to us all—the weak should feel the sting of our disappointment." There was another pause, laden with tension. "That is why the losing team will counsel with us. And why one member will be chosen…for execution."

Shocked gasps circled the beach. Delilah's jaw almost hit the ground. Executed? For losing a silly challenge? She could understand a beating—what Amazon wouldn't—but death? *Does it matter? You will win by whatever means necessary.*

"We have no doubt that all of you will try your best. But in the end, there can be only one winner."

"My lord," Brand said, stepping forward. "We—"

"For now," the god interjected, cutting the dragon off, "take this day for yourselves. You will find the elements no longer pain you." That seemed to be addressed directly to Layel and the other vampire. Had they been hurt? "Restore your vigor, build what weapons you think you need to aid you in your path to victory. I prevented you from killing each other when you first awoke, but I won't intervene any longer. Just know that to destroy another creature could very well be to destroy your own team—and so could bring you one step closer to facing execution. Welcome to Paradise, Atlanteans. Let the games begin."

The thickened air began to break apart, thinning to raindrops…then mist. But that soon dissipated, as well, curling toward the brightening blue overhead. A blue as clear and fathomless as Layel's eyes.

All three mermaids disappeared below the water's surface. A second later, their iridescent tails lifted and wiggled. Then those, too, vanished. Still, no one on the beach spoke.

Perhaps, like Delilah, they were shaken to the core, throats unworkable.

Nola was the first to move. She crossed the distance, grabbed Delilah's arm without slowing and tugged her into the surrounding palms. When they were far enough away that the others would not hear them, the warrioress stopped and whirled. "What are we going to do? Who *was* that?"

"I don't know." She massaged the back of her neck, hating the situation more with every second that passed. "I just don't know. Poseidon most likely, for he is the water god." She'd never interacted with a god before and hadn't ever thought to do so. As the being had said, the heavenly sovereigns had not bothered the citizens of Atlantis for thousands of years—and that had been just fine.

"The voice kept saying *we*," Delilah continued. "Others are involved."

"Did he? I didn't notice. All I could think about was the fact that I was looking at a creature comprised solely of water who wanted me to prove myself or die." Nola shook her head, dark hair flying in every direction. "We have never been friends, Delilah, but you are the only person I trust in this so-called Paradise. What if we are separated? Placed on opposing teams? Our first commandment is to always aid a sister in need. How can I aid you if we are suddenly enemies?"

"Nola, I'm just as confused as you are." Nothing like this had ever happened to her before. Most days were the same. Wake up, train for war, eat, train for war, sleep. Repeat. The only difference was usually *going* to war, something they did at least twice a year, whether provoked or not, to prove their continued strength. "Let me think for a moment."

Back and forth she paced, the trees blurring. Of the two of them, Nola was younger, less experienced. That meant the responsibility of keeping the girl alive fell on Delilah's shoulders. "We cannot leave, that much we know. And if we cannot leave, that means we must compete in the god's silly games or be killed." If they were forced to compete against each other, Delilah knew she would not be able to hurt Nola. Even if it meant dying herself.

She had been raised to protect her sisters, no matter what. That was her purpose, her privilege. A game was not going to change that.

Win by whatever means necessary, she'd thought only a few moments ago. Now she snorted. "We may not be separated, so let's not worry about that just yet. Right now we're going to gather all the sticks we can carry, as well as every sharp rock that we see. I want us prepared for battle by nightfall. Just in case."

Nola gave a stiff nod, but she didn't move off immediately. "Tell me we'll return home soon. Tell me, and I'll believe it." The vulnerability glowing from her expression was surprising.

"We'll return home," she replied without hesitation. Defeat was not something Delilah allowed. Ever. *What about Layel? He shoved you down, could have hurt you and you wouldn't have been able to stop him.* "You have my word," she forced past the sudden lump in her throat, her blood churning into liquid lightning. Damn that man, and damn the heavens! "Go. Before everyone else decides to make weapons, as well, and there's nothing left for us."

ENVELOPED BY SHADE, Layel had watched as each pair of creatures disappeared into the trees. To talk, he was sure. To plan. To arm themselves. At the moment, he was too furious to move. He'd been taken from his people and his war for the amusement of the gods. Intolerable!

"I will not stand for this," Zane snapped at his side.

"Nor I."

Zane blinked at him in surprise, as if he had expected Layel to chastise him rather than agree. "What can we do?"

"We can kill every creature the god brought to the island. That way, there are no players for his sadistic game and we can return home."

"What of the nymphs you so favor?"

A sigh slipped from him. "They are our friends. They live."

"What of the Amazons?"

Layel closed his eyes for a moment, drew in a shuddering breath. He'd thought to kill Delilah earlier, but had failed. Mistake. Now there was another reason to do so. A reason not so easily discarded. "They will not be so fortunate."

A slow smile spread across Zane's pale face. "The gods will regret bringing us here."

"Yes." A warm breeze slid against what little skin Layel had bared—the skin on his face, as well as a patch on his arm where one of the dragons had burned away his shirt. While he smelled salt and dew, flower blossoms, fruit and aroused female—damn, but he wanted to banish that scent!— this island lacked the scent of enchantment that Atlantis possessed.

In Atlantis, he could wander the halls of his palace, imagining Susan at his side, laughing up at him, green eyes sparkling. Here, he seemed to imagine nothing but the little Amazon. Even now, all he could picture was that blue hair fisted in his hands, that exotic face staring up at him in passion and need, those eyes hot, legs spread, feminine core wet and glistening, his tongue tracing those tattoos.

He craved her blood in his mouth.

His fangs sharpened, ready…so ready…

He would kill her first, he decided, hands compressing into fists. His nails were once again elongated into claws. They cut past skin and into the meat of his hands until warmth trickled and pooled in the creases of his fingers. *Why are you so upset? Why are you hurting yourself? Any more blood loss and you'll weaken. As the god said, you need your strength.*

"We'll wait for darkness to fall," he told Zane, the words emerging on another of those broken sighs. Why the reluctance to see his plan through? He didn't care about the Amazon. He hated her. Yes, hated. With nearly the same intensity he hated the dragons. "Then we'll attack them, one by one."

Delilah has done nothing wrong, his mind protested. *She does not deserve death at your hands.*

Logically, he knew that to be true. Yet logic meant nothing to him just then. He *had* to get that woman out of his head. She didn't belong there and was disrupting the only sense of peace he knew. A peace he desperately needed, for any distraction could allow the dragons to best him.

This time, when she was within reach, he would not look at her, would not smell her sweet fragrance. He would simply act. "Come, we need distance from the gods," he said, leading his charge deeper into the forest, not stopping until they reached a riverbank.

Zane bent down, palmed a stone and tossed it into the

pristine water. "I wonder what happened to our brethren after we were taken."

"If they assume we are dead and crown a new king, I will kill them all."

Zane snorted in amusement, as Layel had meant for him to do. He valued his people; they were his greatest weapon against his enemy. And though he had been teasing, knowing well how loyal his men were, he would not tolerate a new king. It was funny, really, since he'd once abhorred his crown. "If they are the warriors I trained them to be," he continued, "they finished slaughtering the dragons and are now celebrating the victory and planning a search for us."

"A celebration we are missing." A dark glaze spread over Zane's eyes, making the irises as black as onyx. He grabbed and threw another stone. "I hate this place. The demons here…"

"Are yours." When Layel had stormed the demon queen's palace to pilfer her treasury after he'd killed her, he'd found Zane waiting in her bed, naked and oiled so that he would be ready for her pleasure. Clearly he hadn't been forced by physical means to remain there, but his relief at her death had been palpable.

Layel didn't know why he'd been there, seemingly willing; he only knew the warrior's hate was as great as his own.

Zane's wide shoulders relaxed slightly. Until both men caught a glimpse of blue hair several feet away. The owner of that hair never came into sight, limbs and shrubs hiding her as she searched for…weapons? A place to stay? No, his first supposition was right, he mused, his traitorous heart speeding up. He would stake his life on it. Did she know he was nearby? Probably.

"What of the little Amazon you nearly ate?" Zane whispered fiercely. "I would like to finish her, as well."

Layel experienced a spark of anger. "She is mine. *I* will take care of her."

"That, I know. But do you plan to bed her or kill her? You looked ready to do both when she straddled your chest."

"What do you think?" he asked, because he did not wish to lie to a fellow vampire.

"I told you. I think you would like to do both."

"And I think you are in danger of unleashing my wrath." Truth.

"Nothing new there." Unconcerned, Zane tossed another stone. *Plop, plop.* "Perhaps you *can* do both."

Surely that had not been wistfulness seeping from his tone. "No." Layel ran his tongue over his teeth. One of his fangs stabbed into the sensitive organ, the resulting bead of blood reminding him that he'd gorged himself earlier, while battling the dragons, yet that hadn't stopped his cravings for Delilah. "No," he repeated for his own benefit. "Too cruel." For Delilah *and* himself.

"Have you ever tasted an Amazon?"

"No." Every race possessed a unique flavor. The dragons—sulfur. The demons—rot. Centaurs—sweet, almost like honeyed hay. Minotaurs—strong, tangy. Nymphs—ambrosia. But Amazons? What *would* they—she—taste like?

You will never find out, he vowed. He would die before he placed any part of himself inside that woman. It was time to change the subject. "Come. Time grows short. We'll make spears, daggers and arrows."

"And which do you plan to use on the girl?"

"My bare hands," he said. Even as he spoke, he longed to use his hands in a different way. For pleasure, not pain.

Satisfaction, not death. Neither of which he would allow. The fact that he *still* wished to do such a thing told him beyond any doubt he needed to rid himself of her, just as he'd planned.

Zane gave another of those eerie smiles. "Until night-fall, then."

Layel nodded grimly.

CHAPTER FIVE

POSEIDON, GOD OF THE SEA, towered inside the coral palace he'd built himself in the center of the ocean, staring into a large, mist-entrenched mirror. Beyond the mist, Paradise and its reluctant new inhabitants were visible, a feast for his gaze.

"They are confused," he said. He'd left them a short while ago, had told them not to worry—hadn't he?—yet their panic had only grown.

A murmur of "yes" arose, the timbres a mix of excitement, resolve and nonchalance.

Four other gods had journeyed through portals in Mount Olympus to join him here. Poseidon turned, studying them as intently as he'd studied the Atlanteans in the mirror. Ares, god of war, possessing a temper far worse even than Poseidon's own. Hestia, plain yet somehow seductive, whose spell-casting abilities were eclipsed only by her determination to make a name for herself by any means possible, fair or foul. Apollo, smile brighter than the sun he controlled, fiercely loyal to those he loved. And finally, Artemis, twin sister to Apollo, as wild as the flowers growing on earth—and as cold as ice.

Upon their arrival, Poseidon had been forced to drain his palace to accommodate lungs not as superior as his own. Now ocean water churned outside rather than in, lapping at the outer walls, the roof. Every few seconds, a droplet fell from the bejeweled chandelier and splashed against the ebony floor.

Hestia eyed those droplets with disdain.

If she wasn't careful, he would drown her.

For centuries, Poseidon had remained here in the water. King to his merpeople, forgotten by earthlings and utterly bored. Truly, nothing had entertained him. Not peace and prosperity. Not storms, famine and war. Then, a few months ago by the Atlantean calendar, two of his mermaids had told him of dissent in Atlantis. Atlantis, a place he'd forgotten completely over the years. A place they'd all forgotten.

A place that belonged to them.

He'd slipped inside, observed unnoticed for a bit, surprised to find the creatures thriving. Curious about their reaction to him, he'd finally announced himself. Still bored, he'd begun moving the citizens about like chess pieces, pitting the dragons against the nymphs and watching the strong, determined warriors resort to battle in their need to protect their females and homes. But in the end they hadn't killed each other as he'd anticipated. Hadn't really even argued. They'd reached a treaty, baffling him.

The unpredictability had been delightful. And just like that, all of his ennui had melted away.

Other gods, as bored with their routines as he had been, noticed the abrupt change in his mood. It wasn't as though he could hide it. The churning waters had settled into calm serenity. His four unexpected guests soon had arrived here, wanting to know the source of his joy. *I should have lied. Told them anything but Atlantis.*

That fateful day of their arrival was burned inside his head. *You can't just waltz inside,* he'd said after his confession—

and their subsequent desire to do as he'd done—wanting to keep his new favorite toy to himself.

Why not? Hestia had anchored her hands on her wonderfully flared hips. *You did.*

Yes, and we can't toss another surprise at them. That would be cruel.

Ares had snorted. *Like you're all flowers and sunshine. We're going in, and you can't stop us.*

His hands had fisted in frustration. *What do you hope to gain with this visit? Just as we once forgot the Atlanteans, they have now forgotten us. You will not be worshipped in their realm, nor will you be thanked for your reappearance.*

Apollo had shrugged, the dire warning of no concern to him. *I want to know how my nymphs have fared without me. I should not have abandoned them as I did and wish to make amends.*

His nymphs? His? *They were made with equal measures of all of us,* Poseidon had reminded him with irritation. But if he were honest, he would admit that some races tended to favor one god above the rest, as though a war had raged during their creation and certain characteristics had defeated all others. *Besides, they have flourished despite your neglect. They are happy now and would despise any interference.*

As they despised yours? Apollo splayed his arms. *Doesn't matter. They fared better than most, I'm sure.*

What's that supposed to mean? Artemis had asked. *If a creature resembles you, it's better than all those around it?*

Thus had begun a spirited hour-long debate about the strengths of each race, the weaknesses of each race and whom each race took after, finally culminating in an annoyed yet excited announcement from Ares. *Enough! Arguing solves nothing. Let's put them on trial, shall we?*

What do you propose? Hestia had asked hesitantly.

Simply that we put our opinions to the ultimate test with a little wager. We'll take two of every race—unmated, of course, or there'll be an uprising—and pit the creatures against each other. If your choice wins, you can enter and leave Atlantis unfettered. However, if your choice loses, you can never set foot in the dome again.

Poseidon had tilted his head as he considered the pros and cons. If he lost, his fun ended. If he ensured his creatures won, he could have Atlantis all to himself, just as he wanted.

A sound idea, but... Apollo frowned. *Why two?*

One powerful warrior could be an anomaly, Ares said. *Two powerful warriors will prove the race's superior strength and intelligence.*

And how will we choose the competitors? Artemis had asked, arching a brow.

Just the way our friend Poseidon chose the pawns in his little game, of course. Observation. We'll watch them and decide on the strongest, the bravest, the most resilient together. Then, we'll design challenges that will test their fortitude, wits and determination.

What will happen to the creatures who fail us? Artemis asked.

I think we should dispose of the losers, Poseidon had suggested. *That way they cannot sing tales of our actions to the people of Atlantis.* And he, the winner, would not have to deal with the backlash. *Besides, I'm sure the lot of you will be angry and looking for vengeance when your choice loses to mine. Killing the creatures who brought about your loss will surely be cathartic.*

Hestia's eyes had narrowed. *We'll see who wins, won't we?*

Two Atlantean weeks later, and here they were.

"The vampire will win," Ares said confidently now. "He has murder in his eyes. A look I know well."

Hestia peered out at the creatures moving through the forest, creatures who couldn't see them. "The vampire king or his warrior?"

"Does it matter? We were to pick a race, not an individual."

"I was merely curious." She shook her head, dark hair tumbling down her back. "But you're right. It does not matter, for the Amazons will win, no question. They are resilient, determined, unafraid to fight for what they know they deserve. A lot like me. The young one has been betrayed by everyone she has ever loved. There's bitterness inside her. Bitterness and hate. She'll unleash a storm of fury unlike anything you have ever seen."

"Please." Apollo laughed, the carefree sound at odds with the combatant he was. "She might be a smoldering cauldron of dark emotion, but she possesses the heart of an innocent. More than that, the nymphs carry my light inside them. Why do you think all creatures, male and female, are drawn to them? Your Amazon will be no exception and will end up bowing to them."

"The nymphs are indeed seducers," Artemis said, "but their beauty cannot compete with the fair-means-or-foul mentality of the demons. They would eat their own young to win a battle."

"Well, I say the dragons will eat *everyone* before the first game ends," Poseidon replied. "Their strength and hunger are legendary. Even the people of earth exalt them."

Ares rubbed his hands together. He was so tall, even Poseidon had to look up to him. He had dark hair and equally dark eyes, and radiated such intense wickedness he could have passed for Hades's twin. "We've all made our choices. It's past time to begin."

Another murmur of "yes" arose, this one dripping with exhilaration.

"The other creatures," Poseidon said. "Those we did not vote for. The minotaurs, centaurs, gorgons and formorians."

"If one of the unfavored wins, the contest is— What am I saying?" Ares chuckled. "The unfavored will not win."

"Well, I am ready to see who will. There can be no interfering from this moment on," Artemis said, eyeing each god until she received a nod of agreement. "What happens will happen. Whoever wins will win, and we will accept the outcome and the consequences with graciousness befitting our stations."

"Of course." Poseidon waved his hand in the air, hoping he appeared convincing. He would ensure the dragons won by any means necessary. He had no doubt his fellow gods would come to respect his actions in time. Hadn't Artemis praised the demons for just such ruthlessness, and Hestia admired the Amazons for a similar unyielding drive?

When the dragons won, Poseidon would win, and Atlantis would once again be his and his alone.

NIGHT HAD LONG SINCE FALLEN.

The air was warm, fragrant and fraught with danger. The insects were eerily silent, not a chirp or whistle to be heard. Only the wind seemed impervious to the surrounding menace, swishing leaves and clicking branches together.

Delilah's every self-protective instinct remained on high alert. No telling where the other creatures were. She'd spied a few here and there as she'd gathered stones and sticks. And then they had disappeared, hiding amongst the shadows. She could have hunted them down, could have challenged them to prove her strength, as was the way of the Amazons, but she hadn't.

The god's warning refused to leave her mind. What if she killed one of her own team members? To begin at a disadvantage would be the epitome of foolish. And she'd been foolish a little too often lately.

She and Nola had opted to sleep in the trees, making them harder to find, harder to reach. Right now she was strewn atop a thick branch, legs swinging over the side, handmade spear clutched tightly in her palms. Wooden daggers were strapped to her legs, waist and back. Thankfully, she'd been trained in the art of weaponry, learning how to create the deadliest of tools out of anything and everything she could find in the forest.

Sharp bark dug into her ribs, helping keep her awake, alert. What were the other creatures doing just then?

What was *Layel* doing?

Layel…beautiful Layel. She'd hardly interacted with him, yet their brief exchanges had been enough to utterly, foolishly fascinate her. There, an admission. He was like no one she had ever encountered. Constantly she found herself wondering what his body looked like underneath his clothes, what his face would look like lost in passion, what he would feel like, pumping and sliding inside of her.

He despises you. He's best forgotten.

Forget that his skin was pale and as smooth as silk? Forget that his eyes were blue like sapphires and fringed by black lashes that were a striking contrast to his snow-white hair? Forget that he was tall with wide shoulders and radiated a dark sensuality women probably salivated over? Impossible.

What kind of females did he enjoy? What type of females had he allowed into his bed? In all the stories she'd heard of him, not a word had been uttered about his preferred bed partners. That didn't mean he'd remained alone all these years.

Sparks of something sinister flickered in her chest. Jealousy, perhaps. She wanted to deny the emotion, but couldn't. *Mine,* she thought. He might want nothing more to do with her, but no way in Hades would he be allowed to have another woman. Not while they inhabited this island.

What's come over you? Men were no longer something she treasured, dreaming of love and laughter in the darkest of nights. To her, they were merely something for her sisters to use twice a year, something to destroy if ever they threatened her loved ones. Since her mating had ended so disastrously, she had not thought to ever again find herself possessive of a male.

How many times had she watched her sisters fight over a particular slave, as if he were a pretty trinket they meant to wear? *He's mine,* they would shout, commandments conveniently forgotten. *It's my bed he will warm this night.* A clash of daggers always followed, as well as cut and bleeding warrioresses. How many times had she watched those "prized" men leave when the loving was over? Without a backward glance at the females they were leaving behind? Not that her sisters had cared. But she had watched and wondered. How could they not want more from each other?

After Vorik, Delilah had thought herself immune to men, her secret longings buried. Until now. She'd straddled the vampire's shoulders and he'd looked between her legs with undiluted heat. The thought of giving herself to him had not been abhorrent. She'd wanted to command his hands on her, his mouth, something, *anything*. She'd wanted *him* to command *her*.

A shiver followed the thought, drowning her in another wave of that deep and inexorable desire. What would it be like to be bedded by him? Would he be gentle, taking her slowly? Or would his passion be as ferocious as his wild blue eyes promised? Perhaps even a little wicked?

"You're aroused, Amazon. Why?"

Layel's voice was so close, so husky, like a whispered entreaty, she wasn't sure if she imagined it. She stiffened, fingers tight on the spear as she searched the darkness for him. Only treetops and night birds came into focus. Not even where thin slivers from the golden ball high above seeped through the canopy of leaves did she make out the form of a man. Slowly she relaxed.

Why am I aroused? Because of you, she wished she could tell this fantasy.

"Well?" Chilled breath caressed her ear.

She gasped. Too real, too real, too real...

Before she had time to react, however, a hard hand settled over her mouth while another shoved her to her back. A heavy, muscled weight slammed into her body. She lost her breath, barely managing to remain on the branch.

In seconds, Layel had her stretched out, her legs restrained. Her eyes widened as her spear was torn from her grip and thrown to the ground. A mocking *thump* echoed in her ears. She balled her hand and moved to strike him, but he released her mouth to check the action. Next he caged her arms between their bodies.

"You will not hurt me," he said.

"And yet you feel free to hurt me. Besides, I'll do anything I want."

"Try."

One word, but it was so smug she longed to slap him. Sadly, below the urge for violence was also the need to kiss him. She didn't panic. Yet. Nola was nearby. Probably sneaking up on Layel…now. But no. A moment ticked by, then another.

Nola never arrived.

Delilah's heart began to drum erratically in her chest, a dazzling realization settling deep inside her. Her blood rushed through her veins with dizzying speed, and need quivered in her belly. Here was her secret fantasy, in the flesh. Hers for the taking. Part of it, anyway. There'd be no happily-ever-after with this man, but there could be pleasure, a moment of giving and sharing and taking between a man and a woman.

You're an Amazon. Act like one. Forcing herself into action, she raised her head and sank her teeth into his neck until she tasted the metallic tang of blood. He hissed in her ear, the sound a mix of pleasure and pain. *You're biting him to escape, yes? So why are you writhing?*

Mmm, so good…her tongue flicked against his racing pulse.

His hands now free, he fisted her hair and jerked her away. He was panting, anger and arousal bright in his eyes. "Think yourself a vampire, do you? Or are you half vampire? I know your kind consorts with all creatures and you could have been fathered by any of the many races."

She opened her mouth to respond but he shook his head, stopping her. "Scream and you'll regret it."

"As if I would scream," she muttered, offended that he thought so little of her abilities. *You did allow him to sneak up on you.*

Oh, shut up.

He blinked in surprise, as if he'd expected her to scream despite his threat.

Her irritation intensified, and she glared at him. "How did you get up here? Did you hurt my sister?"

"She was gone when I reached you. I did not touch her."

Where had Nola gone, then? "I suppose I will allow you to live. For now. But very soon I'm going to grow tired of letting you overpower me."

He snorted.

"I mean it. Be thankful I haven't already killed you."

"Do not fool yourself, Amazon. You would be dead right now had I not stayed my hand."

There was fury in his voice and hate in his expression. Stayed his hand? So he *had* come here to kill her? Bastard! Except, despite everything he had said, despite the genuine loathing directed at her, his legs were between hers and she could feel the length of his shaft hardening, growing, filling.

Just like that, her blood sizzled another degree. Blistered her veins. How did he do that to her? *I am callous, and I care for no one but my sisters.* If they were in Atlantis, she might agree to take him as her slave. If only for the two months males were allowed inside the Amazon camp. But here on this island with a competition in the works, they might very well be enemies.

A tremor slid down her spine.

"Afraid, Delilah?" he asked silkily, then muttered a curse she barely processed.

Then she realized why. Finally, he'd said her name. She wanted to grin. Spoken from those bloodstained lips…a hot ache bloomed between her legs, moisture pooling there. Earlier today, he hadn't wanted to say her name, but she'd *needed* to hear it and had tried to force his hand. Still he'd resisted. And every time he'd called her "Amazon," disgust had been evident in his voice. That alone should have caused her to lump him in the same forgettable group as every other man she'd ever encountered. But even then, underneath the disgust, there'd been a hint of husky satisfaction, as if he were already inside her, and she had only craved more of him.

"Of what?" The words emerged breathless. She wanted to point out what he'd done, what he'd said, but was afraid he would never do so again if she did.

"Dying. Pain."

"No," she answered honestly. Dying didn't scare her. Pain didn't scare her. But her reaction to this man petrified her. He made her feel vulnerable, as if she couldn't rely on herself. As if she needed him to survive. He'd already overtaken her thoughts.

"You should be very afraid," he said.

She stared up at him. His eyes were narrowed yet aglow with inner fire, drawing her in, mesmerizing her. *Do not let him best you. Again.* "My patience grows thin. Why are you here?"

"I thought I made that clear. I came to kill you."

He spoke so matter-of-factly, she was surprised by the statement. She should have fought him at that point. Damned *should*. She should have bucked him off, at the least. Dove for the ground or demanded…an apology? Reparation?

Instead, she remained still. Hating herself. But gods, she enjoyed having him on top of her. "So why didn't you?" Not that she thought he would have succeeded, even if he'd tried. Some part of her had to have known he was nearby. Some part of her had to have known he would not hurt her, and *that's* why she'd permitted him to get so close.

"You wield some kind of magic power over me, and I want to know what it is," he growled. That growl…it rolled along her spine, white lightning in a summer storm.

"Magic? Power?" she asked, wishing she sounded indignant rather than intrigued. "Me?"

"Do not pretend ignorance." He grabbed her shoulders, squeezing, shaking. "Tell me what you've done to me, curse you! I demand an answer."

"And I demand you take your hands off me before you lose them." The warning escaped automatically, but her mind screamed a denial: *Don't let go. Hold me. Want me the way I want you.*

"I will hurt you if I must, Delilah."

Once again, her name on those sensual lips was wholly erotic, somehow a curse, as well as a caress. Again she shivered. Her nipples pearled, reaching for him, abrading the leather top she wore. "Do it, then. Hurt me." She tilted her chin, knowing she was the picture of stubbornness.

What would he do, this warrior who had managed to sneak up on her? How would he react to her challenge?

His nostrils flared. The light in his eyes grew in intensity, casting an azure shadow over his wickedly eerie face. He stared at her mouth. For a moment, she thought he meant to kiss her. A bruising, punishing kiss. *Please…* But a minute ticked by, and he did nothing but glare.

Tired of waiting, she yanked one of her hands free, reached up and sifted strands of his hair through her fingers. "Soft," she whispered.

"Let go."

"No."

"Let go!"

"Make me."

With another growl, he snapped away from her hold. Away from *her,* severing any hint of connection. He perched at the end of the branch, his gaze tracing her tattoos with…longing?

No, he wasn't perched, she realized. He hovered, floating in place. When he realized he was perusing the war designs her commander had gifted her with each time she had proved invaluable in battle, his focus rose to her face, hatred once again gleaming in his eyes, a piercing red lance aimed directly at her.

Strange that it seemed to cut all the way to her soul.

"Do not touch me again."

"Then do not lie on top of me." Slowly she sat up, her gaze never leaving him. "Next time, I might not be so gentle with you."

"Next time, you'll be dead before you realize I'm nearby."

She *tsked* under her tongue, though his words struck deep. "I'm prepared now. You won't get this close again."

"We shall see."

Gods, his arrogance aroused her. Nothing he said was an idle boast. Anything he claimed he could do, well, she knew he possessed the power to do it. She admired that about him. Unfortunately, he admired nothing about her.

What about her upset him so? From the stories she'd heard, he treated only the dragons and their allies with anger. To everyone else, he was polite if distant. No, not true, she thought, playing some of those stories through her head. He loved the nymph king, Valerian, as a brother and had fought beside him on many occasions.

If she gave herself to Layel—*don't think like that, dangerous, you can't, it'd be the same as before*—would his face soften? Would he look at her with admiration? Mirth?

"Why do you hate me?" she asked him curiously.

His head tilted to the side as he studied her. "Why do you care?"

Argh. "Why don't you fly away and leave me alone?"

"Why don't you run from me?"

"Why haven't you kissed me?" The last escaped unbidden, but once said, she did not want to take the words back.

His fangs elongated as he glared at her, vibrant eyes following her tongue as she ran it over her lips, then dipping to her neck.

"Thinking about biting me?" she taunted, unsure why she did so. She had been bitten by a vampire before, a rogue who'd been starving and had ambushed her while she'd been training a group of younger Amazons, and it had not been pleasant. But the thought of Layel's teeth inside her vein… She shivered at the deliciousness.

His pupils dilated, his gaze dropping again and remaining on her chest. "Your nipples are hard."

Were they still? She didn't want to look away from him and was afraid to touch them. They tingled, they ached. For him, only him. "Thank you for noticing."

A muscle in his jaw twitched. "Incorrigible wench." He sighed. "A friend of mine taught me the power of bargaining," he said, "and now I will bargain with you. While we are here, I will stay away from you and, in turn, you will stay away from me. Agreed?"

She tamped down a wave of disappointment. "Decided not to try and kill me after all, then?"

"For now."

"Can't stand the thought of being without me?"

"Do you agree?" he insisted, ignoring her question.

"No." She didn't hesitate with her answer. "I never bargain."

One of his brows arched. "Never?"

"Never. Not for anything." Bargaining meant that she wasn't strong enough to take what she really wanted, and Delilah refused to show weakness. Well, she refused to show any *more.* "Now, I'm done playing. Leave, and I won't hurt you."

He was in her face in the next instant. "That sounds like a bargain to me."

His breath was warm, sweetly scented. His parted lips were close to hers...so wonderfully close. His pale skin glowed, nearly translucent in the light of those electric blues.

All of her body tingled, just like her nipples. Her stomach fluttered with a drugging, almost agonizing heat. She hadn't ever felt like this, not even with Vorik. She ran her tongue along the seam of her mouth again, this time imagining *Layel's* tongue in its place. Gods, she craved a taste of him. Just a small taste. Perhaps then her obsession would end. Curiosity only kept him centered in her mind.

Slowly, she leaned toward him. He didn't meet her halfway, but he didn't pull away, either. Anticipation swirled through her. Would he allow the touch? "Your lips," she said.

"What about them?"

"I want them."

His shoulders straightened with a jolt. "No?" He'd probably meant the denial as a statement, but it emerged as a question.

Closer...a little closer... Still he remained in place. His

breath hitched in his throat; she caught the slight sound and reveled in it. Closer… Just before their lips met, however, a harsh male curse echoed through the night—and it wasn't Layel's.

Whoever had shouted snapped him from her…spell, he would probably have said. Magic, indeed. How she wished she were capable of wielding enchantments. She would bind this man to the tree, keeping him in place until she at last knew the taste of him.

Layel straightened, fury once again falling over his mesmerizing features, overshadowing any hint of heat. "I let you distract me from my purpose this time. It will not happen again." And then he was in the air, flying away from her as hastily as if she were a gorgon, able to turn him to stone with a glance.

Delilah sat there a moment, shaken to the core. She would have believed she'd dreamed the entire encounter if not for the fire raging in her blood, infusing all her limbs.

What was she going to do about that man?

LAYEL SOARED through the trees, dewy branches slapping him in the face. He was glad for the sharp sting, for it helped calm his riotous, traitorous body. He was a bastard. Wicked, evil, wanting someone he should not.

Gods, that female…

She was a menace. Yes, a menace. Damn her! Why did she have to smell like rainflowers and look like a goddess? Why did her skin have to appear as smooth as golden velvet? Why did her eyes have to glow so vibrant a violet? She was violent, harsh, as bloodthirsty as any vampire. *Unworthy,* his mind shouted.

Yet he could not stop thinking of her. Could not stop picturing her, naked and straining against him. Wet, hot, tight. Eager. For him. For his possession.

He should have killed her.

But once again he hadn't been able to do that. Only the sound of Zane's curse had stopped him from kissing her, which would have been certain ruination. *I am sorry, Susan. So sorry. Not only did I fail you once, I seem to be failing you yet again.*

"—only because the gods might place us on the same team," a woman was snapping. "Otherwise I would slit your throat here and now."

"Try it and see what happens." There was fury in Zane's voice. But also... No, surely not. Surely not confusion. Zane usually revealed only two emotions: desire to kill and desire to maim. There was no uncertainty in his black-and-white world.

"As if you could hurt me," the female said. "You have only to look at your cage to see what happens when you attempt something so foolish."

"You will pay for this, woman."

The woman in question laughed, a sound of true glee. "Poor baby. All muscle and no brain."

Layel burst through a thicket and stopped abruptly, taking in the scene. Zane was trapped inside a makeshift cage, hanging from a tree. The second Amazon woman—Nola, he recalled—balanced on a branch, facing him and grinning.

When she sensed Layel's arrival, she lost her smile and whipped to face him. Her lips parted, and her hands fisted at her sides in preparation for battle. "Come to try and kill me, too?"

Though he concentrated on the female, Layel kept Zane

in his peripheral vision. The warrior's cheeks were bright red, stained with mortification. He'd been defeated by a woman. Layel would have laughed if not for the fact that Delilah had knocked him on his ass earlier.

"Well?" Nola prompted.

A moment later, Delilah appeared at Layel's side. He stiffened as her rain-kissed scent once more assailed him, as her body heat wafted to him. Could he never escape them?

This close to her again, he remembered the worst part of his encounter with her. She had desired him, had hungered for his kiss. Her nipples had begged for his touch. And he'd almost given her both. Teeth cutting into his cheeks, he stepped away from her, not even trying to hide the action. He hated that he was forced to act so cowardly, hated the weakness she caused in him. But he simply could not be near her.

She aimed a furious glare at him just as a moonbeam hit her directly, revealing dirt smudges all over her body. Sadly, they did not lessen her appeal. "So. You thought to kill me and your friend thought to kill mine," she said.

"Do not pretend surprise."

Her eyes narrowed to tiny slits, the top and bottom of her lashes fusing together. "Surprise? Ha! I'm merely thanking the gods you are both incompetent."

He had failed at so many things these last few years, her words struck all the way to the bone. He'd failed to destroy all of the dragons. He'd failed to numb himself to the pain of Susan's death. He'd failed to render the death-blow to Delilah, a woman who threatened the memory of his one and only love.

He wanted to strike at her. Hurt her. *Do not approach her. She's merely baiting you.* "The god told us that there will only be one survivor of this game. One. We shall see which of us is left standing."

"Do not threaten my sister," Nola shouted, stepping toward him. "I have decapitated men for less."

He did not doubt that.

Gaze never leaving him, Delilah held up a hand. The other Amazon stilled and pressed her lips together. "You have tried to prick my temper from the first," she said. "Well, now you have succeeded. Taking you down will be fun, vampire."

He studied her hauntingly lovely features. "I fear the pleasure will be all mine. But perhaps, at the end, I won't kill you," he replied. "Perhaps I'll let you live. As my dessert." The taunt was meant to infuriate her further, torment her, make her crazed—heightened emotions had ruined many a good warrior in battle—but the moment he realized what he'd said, *he* felt tormented. He longed to put his mouth on her, drink in the sweetness of her blood and savor every drop.

The same urge must have welled inside her, because her pupils dilated. Her mouth parted on a gasp of hunger. "I'm going to enslave you," she whispered fiercely. "You'll obey my every command, and all of Atlantis will know that Layel, king of the vampires, belongs to Delilah. You'll have me for dessert only when I permit it."

He thought, frighteningly, that she just might be able to do it. Without a word. Just a look, a breath in his direction. A touch, as when she'd held a strand of his hair between her fingers. Pathetically, he was reduced to a creature of sensation when around her. Even his scalp had become sensitized, each hair a thread of desire. For her. *Never again, never again, never the hell again.*

"The day I bow to you will be the day— No. Such a day will *never* come." There was barely a pause before he added, "Do you know why Amazons were created? Because the gods were trying to create males—and they failed."

He expected her to lash at him. She inched backward, instead, features so stricken his chest ached. "We are both mistakes," she said softly.

Cursing himself, he flew to the top of the tree that Zane hung from and slashed the rope with his claws. As the cage, suddenly free, tumbled to the ground, he hissed at Nola in warning.

Then Layel left the area and never once looked back. He had never hated himself more.

CHAPTER SIX

WHEN LIGHT CROWNED the land, Layel found himself whisked to the beach as abruptly as he'd been whisked to the island. The only difference was that he didn't feel as though he was falling through a tunnel. He'd been sharpening a rock into an arrowhead in the woods one moment, and standing on sand, his hands empty, the next. Without shade, his skin heated. Not painfully, just not comfortably. At least the sun was not as bright and hot as it had been yesterday. Perhaps he would not blister. After all, the god had promised the elements would not affect the Atlanteans adversely any longer.

A quick shift of his focus revealed that all the other creatures were lined up beside him, looking about in confusion.

Unable to stop himself—would it always be so?—he searched for Delilah. At first, he did not see her. Perhaps she had been spared, returned to Atlantis.

Good, that was good. What little sleep he'd gotten, she had ruined, for she had haunted every one of his dreams. Smiling at him, beckoning him to join her in bed. Nipples pink and hard, legs spread, feminine core wet and needy. Tattoos, his for the tonguing.

In his dreams, he'd been unable to resist. He had licked her, all of her, and she'd writhed against his tongue. He'd even bitten the center of her desire—something he'd never done to Susan for fear of hurting her tender flesh—and Delilah had begged him for more.

Even now, his body reacted instantly at the thought of her, tightening, hardening. Preparing. He should have spent the night hunting dragons and slaying his foes, but he had not. He had thought: *what if I destroy members of Delilah's team?* That would place Delilah in danger of losing and thereby in danger of execution.

When that woman died, it would be by *his* hand. No one else would be allowed to harm her. He had even commanded Zane, still sulking from his encounter with Nola, to abstain from hunting and killing.

Besides, Layel had decided to let her live. For a little while longer, anyway, and even though she tormented him. Even though she threatened his resolve. He did not know why he'd decided such a thing, did not want to think about it anymore. When he did, her exquisite face flashed inside his mind, violet eyes gleaming with hurt, the frequency pushing Susan out of his mind bit by bit.

Where was she? he wondered again. His gaze continued to cut through the masses, past Zane—*what kind of king am I, to concentrate on an enemy rather than a loyal follower?*—past Nola and Brand. Why would she have been returned to Atlantis? Unless someone had injured her after Layel left her. Or killed her.

A red haze swam over his vision. If someone had— There. He spotted her and relaxed. Then hissed. She stood behind the dragon named Tagart, who stood on the other side of Brand.

She was so tiny, he could barely see her face through the crack of light between those huge warrior bodies. Her blue hair gleamed, and her eyes were so vibrant that as the sun hit them they seemed to cast lavender beams in every direction. Layel's jaw clenched. He didn't like seeing her so close to his greatest enemy.

As if she sensed his perusal, her eyes swung to him and their gazes locked in a heated clash. This time there was no hurt on her expression. No emotion at all, really. That disappointed him when it should have delighted him.

Better this way. Waves echoed in his ears and salt saturated the warm breeze, but Layel would have sworn he could hear the shallowness of her breathing and smell the sweetness of her rain-scent. Perhaps she was not as unaffected as she appeared.

Tagart shifted, widening the distance between himself and Brand and gifting Layel with a better view of Delilah. She still wore the small leather coverings over her breasts and the tiny leather skirt that hung to just below the curve of her bottom. Her bootlike sandals were still laced up her calves, hugging lean strength and smooth skin.

She'd clearly taken a bath, though. Dirt no longer smeared her, and the tattoos on her upper temples, arms, waist and thighs gleamed brightly. Those tattoos…more than ever, he wanted to touch them. Trace the curling designs with his tongue. Did she have any more? Designs he could not yet see? What did they mean? Why did she have them?

Stop! Do not think of her like that.

His eyes lowered. He meant to cast his attention to the sand, but instead it latched on to her breasts. Even as he watched, her nipples hardened into tight little points, as if begging for his attention. Layel was ashamed for noticing, for craving, and forced himself to look down. Little bumps broke out over the flat plane of her stomach. Her navel dipped deliciously, he noticed, another spot for his tongue to enjoy.

You love Susan. And more, you are a king, a warrior. Act like one. Every ounce of his strength was needed to finally—

"Good morning, contestants. I trust you slept well, and that you are as eager as we are for the games to begin. So, without further ado…say hello to your teammates," a god-voice suddenly pronounced. This voice was deeper than the one yesterday, harder. A different god?

In the blink of an eye, Layel was whisked to the other side of the beach, standing in a new line—though this one was only half as long—and facing yet another row of Atlanteans. His teeth gnashed together as irritation flooded him. Being moved around like a puppet grated on his every nerve.

Zane stood across from him. He tried to snag the soldier's attention but failed. Following the direction of the man's gaze, he realized Zane was staring at Nola, who occupied the same side of the beach as Layel. Lust glittered in the warrior's expression. Lust and confusion and perhaps a little awe.

Delilah was in Zane's line.

Dread curled Layel's stomach as suspicions danced through his mind. Surely this god was not so cruel. Surely this heavenly sovereign would not pit friend against friend, man against woman.

"Yes, you will compete against your own kind. And, yes, you will compete against the opposite sex." A laugh, booming, strong, full of mirth, though edged in steel. Did the god read minds on top of all his other powers, then? "What better way to test your cunning, determination and survival instincts?"

Just as the water had done yesterday, the sand between the two lines of creatures swirled together, faster and faster, rising…rising…until the outline of a body formed. A few wayward grains drifted into Layel's mouth, and he spit them out in disgust.

"Who among you will place your allegiance with your own kind, rather than your fellow teammates, hmm?"

Layel twisted left, right, and eyed his team. A centaur, a nymph, Brand the dragon—bile rose in his throat—a demon, Nola the Amazon—he gulped—a minotaur, a formorian and a snake-headed gorgon.

All but the nymph had one thing in common. They were eyeing him with revulsion. Why? He shrugged, unconcerned. The only thing that bothered him at the moment was the fact that Delilah was not in his group.

He would be forced to compete against her.

"Great One, I would ask a boon." Brand stepped forward, his gaze still locked on Layel.

"Ask," the being said. "Though I cannot promise you will receive it."

Brand pointed to Layel, accusation in his eyes. "This… bloodsucker meant to kill us all while we slept. I ask that he be removed from my team."

Delilah had tattled on him, then. He felt betrayed by the knowledge, which was foolish. At least the revulsion of his teammates now made sense.

"And yet he did not kill you or anyone," the god said in his defense, surprising him.

"He will continue to try if given the opportunity. I ask that he be destroyed here and now," Brand continued.

"And I decline."

"But—" Before he could speak another word, Brand dropped to his knees with a grunt, as if he could no longer endure his own weight. He moaned, grabbing his stomach and falling the rest of the way into the sand. A trickle of blood escaped his mouth.

"You had your answer, and yet you dared to persist. Let this be a lesson to all who think to question the gods' wisdom."

No one rushed to the dragon's defense, and Layel smiled slowly. A more welcome sight he had never encountered. *Except for Delilah...last night...underneath you, panting... craving your mouth...* With a muttered curse, he blackened his mind.

"We are giving you a few more hours. Use it to strategize with your team. Tonight," the god continued, as if Brand's interruption had not occurred, "the first competition will take place. You'll need every ounce of strength you possess to survive. Because the challenge will be difficult, the winning team will be greatly rewarded. And do not think to rebel, keeping your team from victory. The losing team shall appear before me, and, as mentioned before, the weakest contender will be executed.

"Go now. Do whatever you must to strengthen yourselves and prepare for the challenge to come. Do not disappoint me." The last seemed to bullet straight to Layel.

He opened his mouth to say something—what, he didn't know—but a second later, the sand stilled, collapsed, the being clearly gone.

Then a dark cloud assaulted Layel, a single word whispering into his ears: *Gauntlet.* His eyes burned, some of the granules having worked their way under his lids. He scrubbed a hand over his face. Gauntlet? Confused, he held his breath until the cloud passed. It swept over several other creatures, and they coughed. But they did not act as if they'd heard a voice.

Finally Brand ceased writhing and dragged himself to

his feet with a dark scowl at Layel. Everyone else glanced around the island, as if unsure of what to do next.

"This is ridiculous."

"I'm not pairing with a demon."

"Or a vampire."

Layel blocked their chatter. Two teams. Competing against each other. Someone from the losing team would die. Tonight. Delilah? His fingers curled, nails cutting. *Don't think about her.* His focus settled once again on his *team.* How was he supposed to play nice with a dragon? A demon? He would rather die.

You just might.

He sighed. *Gauntlet.* Was that to be their challenge? Or was it a trick? He would soon find out, he supposed.

ZANE STALKED from the beach, through the trees and away from the harsh morning light and the creatures he despised. If he had stayed, the already-thin strand he held on his control would have snapped.

Bad things happened when he snapped.

But he could think of nothing to calm himself. The feelings the Amazon Nola wrought in him were too confusing, too similiar to what another female had once made him experience. Feelings that had changed him—and not for the better. More than that, he was hungry. Layel had ordered him not to kill last night, and he hadn't. Which meant he hadn't eaten, either.

Zane only drank from creatures he killed. That way, expressions of fear and pleas for mercy would not haunt him. And yet, those living creatures had begun to look tasty.

Also, taking a living being meant enduring hands and gazes on his body. He shuddered.

Last night he'd meant to feast on the Amazon, for she smelled sweeter than anyone he'd ever encountered. Even Cassandra, the woman he'd bargained away years of his life to save—the woman who'd then wanted nothing to do with him. In fact, he'd decided to destroy Nola even before the demons.

But she had bested him.

He'd gone in for that first slash of her throat, but she had anticipated his move and had struck first. Only, she hadn't hurt him. She had trussed him up like an animal. To do so, she had touched him. She had looked at him. And he had not wanted to run, hide, even die as he usually did when touched and gazed upon.

Actually, he'd wanted her to do both again.

What strange power did these Amazons wield? The blue-haired one had Layel tied in knots. Zane had never seen the king so confused. Soft, even. Layel lived and breathed death. Revenge. Two goals Zane admired. Yet neither of them had been able to hurt those women. Worse, both men now seemed to crave them.

Unacceptable.

Zane had avoided females since his release from the demon palace. Sex was not something he needed to survive, wasn't even something he wanted anymore, therefore he did not indulge. Ever. Even a hasty coupling gave a female power over a man.

No one would consume his thoughts; no one would dictate his body's feelings. Too many times over the years he'd had to… Bile rose in his throat. He swallowed it and scrubbed the memory from his mind.

But he knew it would come back. It always did.

Layel probably thought he'd been stolen, locked away

and forced. Layel was wrong. Zane had gone to the demons of his own volition. Every disgusting thing the demon queen had done to him, he had allowed. Begged for, even. He'd been cursed with a beauty most demons found irresistible, and the queen had craved him even though his heart belonged to another. A slave. *Stay with me until I tire of you,* the queen had said, *and then I will free you both.* But she hadn't, and Cassandra, a siren enslaved by the demons, had begun to look at him with hate.

Demon whore, he heard in his mind even now. *Demon whore, demon whore.*

Scowling, he flattened his hands over his ears. The taunts did not die. Only seemed to increase in volume. A roar ripped from him, and he slammed his fist into the nearest tree trunk. Bark cut past skin. Blood oozed down his arm. The vile things he had done…all for nothing.

"Are you hurt? Oh, I hope it's terribly painful!"

The feminine voice, soft and lilting, somehow managed to overshadow the din in his head. He whipped around and there, in front of him, was his tormentor, worse than any demon he had faced. Nola. She was so lovely, he lost his breath. She was tall, but not bulky. Lean, but strong. And yet, she appeared delicate, as if she would break in half with a good squeeze. Angelic, as if she had no other thoughts beside pleasure.

He knew those angel-looks were deceptive.

While he was not repulsed by her touch or her regard— why, *why?*—he found that he did not like *her.* She behaved like a demon, demanding, happily taking from others without giving anything in return. Taking his concentration, his self-protective instincts.

"Following me was foolish." If only he had his knives.

He could have thrown them, embedded each in her chest. But when the god had popped Zane onto the beach, the sticks he'd painstakingly sharpened had no longer been strapped to his body. And that made no sense. They'd been told to make whatever weapons they wished, yet still they weren't allowed to use them.

"We both know you cannot hurt me." Nola lifted her chin, her features smug. No, her features *attempted* a smugness she could not quite pull off. Too much vulnerability in her eyes, he noticed for the first time. Too much heartache. "You're not smart or fast enough."

Insults no longer affected him. Too many had been hurled at him over the years. Besides, while she sneered them at him, they lacked any kind of heat. "Last night, you surprised me. You will not have that advantage again." Of its own accord, his gaze lowered to her neck, where her pulse drummed wildly.

She flicked her dark hair over one shoulder, baring even more skin. Her hand was shaking. "Hungry, vampire?"

There was challenge—want?—in her tone, as if he could look but would never be allowed to taste. His eyes narrowed, the dare pricking at him sharply. "The thought of having your blood in my mouth sickens me."

He could not slay her; she was on Layel's team and Zane would never purposely hurt the man who had killed the demon queen, freeing Cassandra. And if he could not slay Nola, she would be able to touch him. What if last night had been an aberration? What if she touched him and he wanted to die, as he did with everyone else? Or worse— what if he wanted more from her?

"Sickens you, huh?" Unlike him, she could not overlook an insult. Fury and hurt flashed momentarily in those vivid emerald orbs, quickly replaced by determination. "I could make you beg for it. Many men have. Or I could make you a slave, just as Delilah will do to your king."

Every time she opened her mouth, he liked her less and less. How could he desire her, then? Even for a moment? "You are my enemy, now more than before. I am slave to no one." Would never be a slave again, willing or not. "The only thing I want from you is your absence. And believe me, as badly as I crave it, I am still unwilling to beg."

A tremor rocked her lithe body. "Oh? And you think your teammates will offer their blood to you?"

"Most likely." Not that he would sample a single drop. "They'll wish to keep me strong. They will not want a weak member dragging them down."

She raised her chin. "They know you considered killing them. I made sure of it."

"Yes, but you are now their enemy. They will no longer care what you say." He did not know if he spoke true. He only knew he wanted to wipe that haughty look off her too lovely face.

She ran the tip of her tongue over her teeth, and his cock jumped at the sight of all that pink and wet. He scowled in surprise. *True desire? Again?* That had not happened in years, yet now it had happened twice in two days.

Why did he want her? *Her* of all people? A cocky, irritating demon in an angel's skin?

"I'm going to feed," he said fiercely, quietly. "And then I am going to do everything in my power to make sure you lose tonight. *Then,* I will pray that you are the first to be executed."

She stepped toward him, hands fisted. "You are a bastard. No better than my mother. No better than my father, my brothers, men my mother abandoned her sisters to be with, men who helped her destroy me." Hate churned beneath the surface of her skin. Hate and fury. "Guess what I did to them?"

"Killed them?" Zane forced himself to remain in place, even though everything inside him screamed to back away before she could reach him. Not because he feared what she might do, but because he feared his reaction to her. She had suffered? Perhaps as he had?

"After I played with them a bit," she said silkily, "they begged for death. Still I waited days before I gave it to them." She stopped, turned away, but didn't move off. "Oh, and one more thing. If my team loses tonight, it might very well be your king who is killed. In fact, I'll make sure of it. Think about that."

DELILAH REMAINED on the beach, even though everyone else had left. Including Nola, her sister by race—and her new enemy?

She bit the inside of her cheek until she tasted blood. All her life, her only goal had been to protect her sisters. Those she loved, those she didn't. Now she was to fight against one.

And Layel…

What was she to do about him? She'd wondered all through the night, yet she still didn't have an answer. They were enemies now, more so than before. At least, they were supposed to be.

Last night he had said cruel things to her. At first, she'd been hurt and had by turns wanted to beat him senseless and cry in his arms like a weakling. But then she'd remembered something. *In battle, anything goes.* She knew that better than most, and last night they had been locked in a battle of fierce desire. Words meant nothing. Actions, everything.

He wanted her. Proof: just a little while ago he had peered at her with naked longing in his eyes. But while he did want her, he clearly did not want to want her. Proof: he always walked away.

Part of Delilah was ready to fight him until he changed his mind. Until he admitted that he craved her kiss as much as she craved his. And yet, the other part of Delilah insisted she do nothing, forcing *him* to fight for *her* and treat her as the prize she'd always wanted to be. She was confused by the conflicting nature of her desires. Fight for him—make him fight for her. Dominate him—be dominated *by* him.

She knew she would not do the first, even though she'd allowed herself moments of weakness and had almost given in to the thought of pleasure. To give herself to another man, she had to know she was the most important thing in his life. He had to want her more than anything. He had to need her.

Would Layel ever need anyone?

Someone approached her, and she stiffened. She heard the swish of sand against boot, the faint rasp of even breathing. Not Layel, for this man radiated heat and smelled like sex.

"Nymph." She pushed to her feet and turned to him, hands curled into fists. Just in case.

"Amazon." He was at her side a moment later. He faced the water, careful not to focus his decadent gaze on her, and locked his hands behind his back. "We are teammates, you and I," he said.

He was tall, forcing her to look up…and up…and up. He had pale hair and bright blue eyes. His body was stacked with muscle upon muscle, visible even through his clothing. Normally, she remained as far away from the nymphs as possible. After all, they were capable of enslaving a woman with only a glance.

Yet she felt no passion-flare for him. No compulsion to strip for him, kiss him, touch him. His eyes were not a clear enough blue. His hair wasn't white, completely devoid of color. His skin wasn't white-velvet and slightly chilled to the touch. His features were not haunted.

"Yes," she finally said. "We are."

"For us to win, I need to remain strong."

"Yes." Where was he going with this?

At last he faced her, his lips curling into a tender smile. "I am glad we understand one another." The words were casual, the tone joyful. "Do you prefer clothing on or off?"

She shook her head, positive she had misheard. "What?"

"Clothes on or off?" He fisted the hem of his shirt, ready to lift at a moment's notice.

Dear gods. He expected to bed her. "I don't even know your name and you expect me to welcome you into my body?"

"I am Broderick. And, yes."

Let's see. How could she respond without insulting a teammate she might need aid from tonight? "Gods, no."

"No?" His brow puckered for a moment before smoothing out. "Oh, you mean, no clothing." *Whoosh.* His shirt pooled at their feet. He was grinning now.

"No bedding." Why could she not desire him, though? Why did he fail to thrill her? He was handsome, as powerful as Vorik the dragon had been, might be able to talk her sisters into anything without having to fight them for her, hurting them. *With a nymph, you will never be number one. You will be exactly what you have never wanted: a convenience.*

Broderick lost his grin and blinked in surprise. "But to maintain my strength, I need sex."

"So go have sex." She braced her hands on her hips.

He breathed a sigh of relief and nodded in satisfaction. "Where would you like me to take you? Here?"

Were all nymphs so dense? "I don't think you understand what I'm saying, so I'm going to explain it a little better." In the span of a single heartbeat, she grabbed hold of his wrist, spun behind him and twisted, flipping him onto his stomach and giving him a mouthful of sand. "I'm not bedding you anywhere, anytime."

Spitting out those white grains, he rolled over and frowned up at her. "But we are teammates. If I am weak, we could lose."

"So you've said."

"If we lose, one of us will die."

Her blood chilled, becoming streams of ice. He was right. One weak link could drag down an entire army. She had seen it happen, had fought to make it happen, actually, her sisters sometimes seducing a warrior and enticing him to betray his own kind.

Losing had never and would never sit well with her.

But sleep with this man? This nymph? Just to win? She had once let a formorian fondle her while her sisters sneaked inside his home and searched for the young Amazons he had stolen and locked away, hoping to train them as his personal guard. He had repulsed her, but she had allowed his ministrations with a smile. Had even patted his head as if he were a favored pet.

Once the girls had been found, Delilah had sliced his throat.

That fondling had been for a good cause. This, too, was a good cause, yet the thought of letting anyone other than Layel pleasure her was somehow…abhorrent.

Broderick stood, and he did not appear pleased. Grains

of sand clung to his roped chest lovingly. Female sand? A pretty scar slashed from one of his nipples to his navel.

Women came easily, eagerly to him. That much was obvious. Delilah wondered if she was the first to ever have told him no.

"You will not find my touch distasteful, Amazon, I swear it."

"Step away from her, Broderick."

Both Delilah and the nymph pivoted to face their intruder. Layel. Her heart sped up, hammering so hard her ribs would surely crack. His voice had been devoid of emotion, as was his expression. Still, he was the most beautiful sight she'd ever beheld. Sensual, hard, determined. *Mine.*

Dangerous… Oh, yes, he was. In every way imaginable, maybe even some that weren't.

A needy whimper rose in her throat, and she barely managed to silence it.

"Layel," the nymph said, and there was genuine affection in his tone.

They were friends, and that friendship made her own turbulent relationship with the vampire seem so much darker.

"She is mine," Layel said firmly.

Broderick's lush lips dipped into a confused frown. "But you—"

"Mine," he insisted.

Hearing the vampire's claim was like being branded, the words fiery hot and reverberating all the way to her soul. She should have rebuffed him. Appearances had to be maintained. In front of others, especially her new teammates, she had to be cold, heartless. But she couldn't force the words out.

Mine, he'd said, mimicking her own thoughts. She wanted to smile.

The nymph sighed in disappointment, yet there was a sharp edge to the sound. "I never poach another man's property, you know that. If you change your mind…"

"I will not."

Wait. Property? Had Broderick just called her Layel's property?

Broderick shrugged and strode from the beach. His easy compliance confirmed what she had suspected. She would not have been important to the nymph. She would have been a warm body in an assuredly long line of warm bodies, forgotten when the loving was over. Not good enough for more than a few tumbles.

What would it take to be important to a man? To mean something? To mean everything?

For several seconds, neither Delilah nor Layel spoke. She didn't know what to say to him, really, too afraid to ruin this heady moment.

"Do not think I care about your welfare," he said, looking away from her and to the water.

Moment ruined. Still determined to fight her, was he? Disappointment rocked her, but she squared her shoulders and raised her chin. Words meant nothing, she reminded herself once more. Actions, everything. "Do not think I will deny myself a man if I want him."

A muscle ticked in Layel's stubborn jaw.

"So tell me. If you don't want me for yourself, why did you send the beautiful Broderick away?" she said.

Several seconds passed in agonizing slowness. "I will see you on the battlefield, Amazon," was all he finally said. And then he, too, strode away.

CHAPTER SEVEN

"LAYEL IS MISSING."

Alyssa, fierce soldier of the vampire army, stared up at the nymph king, gauging his reaction to her announcement. Valerian was the only man Layel truly trusted. The only man he counted as friend. Layel respected his warriors, of course, and he was fair and generous to his people. But he kept himself distanced, always distanced.

Still, ever since the nymph sovereign had struck an alliance with the dragons to maintain peace and possession of this palace, the friendship had been strained, and so Alyssa could not be sure of Valerian's innocence.

Had Valerian hurt Layel, the vampire king responsible for hundreds of dragon deaths, to appease his new ally?

The nymph king frowned over at her, concern lighting his brilliant blue eyes. "How long has he been gone?"

That concern appeared genuine, and Alyssa experienced a rush of relief. Layel shouldn't be made to suffer another devastating loss. He might not survive. *If* he even lived. "This is the second day," she said. "He disappeared amidst…" she swayed, her head suddenly swimming, her knees weaker than usual. Somehow she managed to remain on her feet.

"Woman?" Valerian inquired, concern shifting now to her.

"Forgive the disruption. I'm fine." But she wasn't. She

needed blood. Blood she hadn't been able to take in months. Much longer and she would collapse, no amount of determination or fortitude able to save her. "He disappeared amidst a battle in the Forest of Dragons."

Valerian was not easily diverted. "Are you unwell? We now have a healer in residence. Brenna will—"

Do not dare glance at the man beside Valerian. Eyes ahead. "I'm fine," she repeated firmly. "We were speaking of Layel…"

His frown sharpened around the edges. He was a beautiful man, probably the most sensually lovely creature the gods had ever created. He had golden hair, a hard, muscled body and an eroticism that radiated from him no matter where he was or what he was doing.

Females young and old constantly threw themselves at him, though there was only one woman he desired. And that woman was even now sitting on his lap, frowning just as fervently as he was.

"Layel has disappeared before," Queen Shaye said, patting her mate's arm in a bid to comfort him.

Alyssa's chest ached at the sight of their obvious love for each other. She wanted that for herself. Had thought, for a single night, that she had found it. How wrong she'd been.

Once again she had to remind herself to keep her eyes focused on something other than the soldier standing beside Valerian. Shivawn.

She'd hungered for him since the first moment she had spied him and the hunger had only grown. At that first sighting, she'd craved friendship, his fierce loyalty. As she'd grown into a woman, that craving had become sexual. To her absolute devastation, he'd never wanted anything to do with her. Except once…

After ignoring her for years, he had finally allowed her to entice him to her bed. For hours, she'd feasted on his body. She'd savored every sound he uttered, every move he made and every delicious beat of his heart. It had been the most exquisite night of her entire life.

But when the loving had finished, he'd left. No tender goodbye, no farewell kiss.

No hunting her down and sweeping her back into his arms the next day. In fact, he hadn't spoken to her since, even though they had stumbled upon each other several times. With his every glance, however, he'd conveyed his message perfectly: she was a nuisance. Beneath him. Unworthy. She wanted to hate him. Instead, she remembered. She desired. Still. Perhaps forever.

Her gaze moved of its own accord, landing on him, and her heart stuttered to a halt. He was tall; his sandy hair hung in waves to his broad shoulders. He was looking past her, just over her shoulder. His expression conveyed boredom, as though he could not wait for her to leave.

When would he learn? Leaving was the one thing she could never do, not with him. Pathetic of her, yes. But cruel as he was turning out to be, she now needed him to survive. Much longer and she would truly die. He just did not know it yet.

"My mate speaks true," Valerian said, claiming Alyssa's attention once more. "Layel often steals a few days for himself."

"Yet he has never abandoned his own people without word of when he would return. He has never left without placing a second-in-command. And you know as well as I that he would *never* leave during a battle with dragons."

"You speak true, as well." Valerian's tanned skin blanched,

his strong arms tightening around his mate. She was like new-fallen snow, with silver-white hair and skin so luminous it practically glowed. The only color to her belonged to her large, dark eyes. She was human, a child of the surface world, with blood that smelled pure and sweet.

Used to be, the gods had gifted the vampires with humans they didn't want tarnishing that surface world. Mmm, she remembered how delicious they'd been. No one tasted better.

Except Shivawn.

She had tasted him that night he'd allowed her to seduce him. The sensual power she had found with a single swallow, the headiness… Light-headed, she nearly lost her balance again. She had been unable to take a single drop of crimson nectar from anyone else since.

Oh, she had tried. But everything tasted like rot when compared to Shivawn and she gagged. Finally, she'd stopped trying to feed. She had lost weight, strength, and now spent more time in bed than she did out of it. She was becoming desperate for another taste of Shivawn.

"I will send a troop to scour the Inner and Outer cities," Valerian said. "We will find him."

"Another vampire disappeared, as well," she said. "Zane, a warrior. He is wild, even unpredictable, but he is loyal to Layel and would not have hurt him."

Pensive, Valerian stroked his chin. "Two vampires disappeared, you said?"

"Yes."

"No others?"

She shook her head.

"Two?" he insisted.

"Yes."

"That disturbs me, for two of my nymphs are unaccounted for. Two of my elite. I had thought they stumbled upon bed partners and simply lost track of time. But…"

Two vampires, two nymphs. "What could this mean?"

"I wonder if any other creatures are missing." Valerian flicked Shivawn a glance. "Go into the cities. Learn what you can and report back to me. I want an answer by morning."

Shivawn gave a stiff nod and turned on his booted heel.

"My lord," Alyssa rushed out, stepping closer to the king's dais. Had she been any other species, his guards would have attacked her. Because she was vampire, servant of Layel, the action was tolerated. "I must insist that I accompany your soldier."

Shivawn, who had not paused during her speech, halted abruptly. He kept his back to both Valerian and Alyssa. As he stood there, the braided hair at his temples swung back and forth, beads clicking together. "And I must insist I go alone, my king."

Her eyes narrowed on him, but she didn't direct her words to him. "Your man will get nothing done if he is forced to fight off every woman he encounters. More than that, he will enrage the men of those enslaved females and they will refuse to aid him."

Shaye sighed, a sound of feminine pique. "She's right. You nymphs and your damn mojo. It ruins everything!"

Mojo?

"Everything?" Valerian asked the queen huskily, as if he knew exactly what she meant. Just then, they were clearly the only two people in the chamber, everyone else forgotten.

The human chuckled and kissed his cheek. "Well, maybe not everything."

Another ache lanced through Alyssa's chest as Valerian gazed tenderly at his mate. Oh, to be loved like that.

"Shivawn," Valerian said, "take the vampire with you."

Pivoting, radiating outrage, Shivawn scowled. "My king, I—"

"Will do it," was the firm, sharp interruption.

A moment passed. Then another. The sudden silence was thick and oppressive. Hurtful. Shivawn wanted to argue. She knew that from the clench of his jaw, the tic below his eye and the fists he tried to keep hidden at his sides.

Alyssa pulled her gaze from him. Ultimately, he would not refuse his king. But his hesitation cut her so deeply she longed to sink to her knees and sob. He would have welcomed any other woman, she was sure. Why did he hate her so? *Clear your mind. Do not show him the depth of your hurt.*

Limbs trembling, she studied the palace throne room. The floors were white marble veined with silver, the walls black onyx studded with jewels of every color. From sapphires to rubies, from emeralds to diamonds, they winked at her, mocking her with their beauty and purity.

Why did he hate her so? she wondered again, unable to bury the question this time.

You know the reason, you simply do not wish to acknowledge it. True. To acknowledge the truth was to lose all hope of winning the man. *There* is *no hope.* To Shivawn, she was, and would always be, tainted, for he despised both demons and vampires—and she was equal measures of each. He didn't know it, no one did, but he must sense it on some level.

The demons he blamed for killing his father many years ago. A crime she had inadvertently been involved in, though he didn't know that, either. Would never know it, if she had her way.

The vampires he despised because of their need for

blood, for one had nearly killed him. That night, in bed, when she had sunk her teeth into his chest, he had almost slapped her. Had barely managed to stay his hand.

After he left, she had apologized and sent him invitations to join her again. Just as he ignored her when she was present, so had he ignored the summons. But…sometimes she could have sworn he was hidden nearby, his gaze boring into her. Wishful thinking, for she had never caught sight of him. Trained as she was, she would have found a trace. A footprint. A strand of his hair.

Even if she hadn't needed his blood, would she have been able to walk away from him? The answer to that was nothing new. No. To walk away was to lose all hope of winning him. *I'm not just demon, vampire and related to the men who destroyed his father. I'm brainless, too. Yet another defect.* As she'd thought before, there was no hope. Sometimes, though, she could fool herself.

"Very well," Shivawn finally said, his tone stiff. He strode from the room without another word.

Frustrated with him, Alyssa turned to the formation of vampire warriors behind her, lined against the walls. "Half of you will join Valerian's army in search of our king. The other half will return to the palace. I will report our findings in the morning."

Used to taking orders from her when Layel was gone, they nodded and filed from the chamber. Fighting another wave of dizziness, Alyssa followed Shivawn.

DARKNESS WOULD SOON FALL AGAIN, and when it did, the first challenge would begin.

Though he'd constructed weapons yesterday, Layel had spent several hours gathering the perfect limbs for a bow and arrows. The god had finally given permission to use them and wouldn't be taking them away. Again. Already he'd spent several more hours sharpening and honing. His hands were now raw, and his nails, which had healed soon after his encounter with the air shield, were once again coated with dried blood. He was weak from the loss of it and needed to replenish.

But he didn't. He hadn't.

In his foolish, hated desire for Delilah, he had abandoned his only purpose: death to all dragons. Nothing more, nothing less. The woman had occupied too many of his thoughts, tortured him with her femininity, riddled him with concern for her well-being, and nearly felled him with jealousy. *Jealousy.*

He would allow it no more.

She mattered not to him. Susan mattered. Always, only Susan.

I will prove it. Right now he hovered in a tree, concealed by branches and thick green foliage, looking down at Delilah's team. His bow was cocked, his arrow ready to sail into the heart of the beast.

"…work together," Tagart was saying. "That's the only way to win."

They were gathered in a circle, a fire blazing, some kind of fish anchored over the pit, roasting and filling the air with a sweet aroma. All of the creatures were listening intently, rapt gazes locked on Tagart. Except for Zane, who sat behind them, sharpening a branch with his claws just as Layel had done.

Delilah had her back to Layel, hair streaming wildly, like ribbons his fingers itched to caress. If she stood, Layel would kill *her* rather than the dragon. He told himself he didn't care. That he'd spared her one too many times already. Did he listen to himself, though?

"How can you know we'll have the chance to work together," Delilah asked, "rather than be called one by one to represent the group? The god didn't specify."

Her voice shivered through him, an embrace, a temptation. His fingers squeezed the bow tightly. *Relax, damn you. The wood will snap with any more pressure.* Gradually his fingers loosened their grip. He still had a clear shot of Tagart, could lose it at any moment. *Do it! Hurt him.*

"I *don't* know. Not for sure," Tagart said. "But we have to be ready for anything. If we aren't…"

"One of us will die," Delilah finished for the dragon, her voice now harsh.

The warrior nodded grimly.

You are facing a dragon. You have never hesitated before. Why now? Layel's hands remained steady despite his internal war, yet still he didn't release the blasted arrow. He ground his teeth together, ashamed and disgusted. He had come here with a purpose. To turn away from that *again* was disgraceful.

"But if we win, our brethren on the losing team could die," Delilah added miserably.

"You heard what the god said. They are testing us. Our mettle, our determination. We have to decide—who is more important? Them? Or us?"

Every muscle in Layel's body stiffened at that. *Them or us?* echoed in his head. Them or us? If he killed Tagart, would he ultimately condemn Zane? A warrior he had sworn to protect? Never mind Delilah. *Do not think of her, do not dare think of her.*

Whatever Layel did, someone was going to die tonight.

Zane…Tagart…Delilah… He wanted the latter two gone, but he would not be able to live with himself if he unintentionally harmed the first. But if his team lost, he would most likely be eliminated. After the way they'd looked at him this morning, knowing he had considered slaying them all…

Perhaps being the first to go was for the best. Perhaps then, he could finally join Susan.

No, he nearly roared. No, no. Not yet. More than he wanted to slay the dragons on this island, he wanted to slay the dragon king. Darius. Just the name caused him to growl. Darius should have stopped his warriors from hurting Susan, should have had better control of them.

Just as I was supposed to have control over my *men.* He brushed the thought aside. *His* crime had not destroyed Susan.

Once, about six months ago, Layel had nearly succeeded in killing the dragon sovereign. But then he had seen Darius with a human lover and had remembered Susan and his only days of happiness. In a moment of weakness, Layel had walked away.

Now Darius's woman was pregnant. Another dragon would be born. It was unacceptable. His fault.

I vowed never to walk away from a kill again, he reminded himself, eyes once more narrowing on his target.

Layel wanted so badly to join Susan. *All you need do is obliterate the entire fire-breathing race. One at a time…* His finger twitched, stilled. His teeth gnashed together.

An ashy breeze blustered past him, shaking the leaves. *If you do this, Delilah will view you as a coward. Unworthy, dishonorable.* Good. He was. His fingers tightened…tightened. The bow's string pulled taut. Almost ready…soon. He wanted Delilah to think poorly of him. No, he corrected, he *needed* her to think poorly of him. Another finger twitch. Tagart shifted, Layel's bow moving with him, maintaining the perfect shot. Straight through the man's blackened heart, slicing it in two as he'd done to countless others.

"There's something I must do. I'll return shortly," Delilah said, rising swiftly to her feet and blocking Tagart.

Layel froze. *Move, woman!* He'd finally convinced himself to act.

She remained in place. She was not as tall as the dragon, so Layel's arrow would nail her right between the eyes. Sweat beaded his skin. He could try and release the arrow into Tagart's face, catching an eye perhaps, missing the Amazon, but that wouldn't necessarily kill or even slow the bastard.

"We aren't done here," Tagart snapped at Delilah. "There's still much to discuss."

She flipped her hair over her shoulder and laughed. "Try and stop me and see what happens. Besides, you owe me a thank-you for this."

"A thank-you? What for? What are you going to do? Make a bed and seduce me?"

There was a shocked pause. "Something is seriously wrong with the men around here," she muttered.

The warrior's lips formed a thin line. Obviously he wanted to press her, but for whatever reason decided to quiet his objections. "Fine. Go. But don't cry for our forgiveness if you're the reason our team fails."

"You expect failure, then?"

He sputtered. "No."

The group's centaur rose on all fours and approached her. Ever the mediator, the horse-man said, "Tagart makes a fine point. Now is not the time—"

"Perhaps I wasn't clear," Delilah interrupted. "I'm not

staying here. I'm heading into the forest to think, alone. Don't you dare follow me." Quick as a snap, she palmed one of her wooden daggers and twirled it in her hand. Gave it a toss, caught it. "Understand?"

No one said another word.

Waning sunlight caressing her, Delilah stalked away from them. Her hips swayed, a mating dance Layel was not the only male to notice. All of her teammates watched her, lust blooming in their expressions. Layel battled a fierce urge to fly from the tree and slash each of their throats as she headed into the woods. Finally, she disappeared from view and he relaxed.

Now. Act now. There was no better time. Nothing else mattered. Revenge would be Susan's, rest would be his. *Focus, focus.* Damn him, the centaur blocked every killing shot, unintentionally protecting Tagart. Well, then, he'd just take out the centaur, too, he decided.

"I can't believe you," an angry female voice whispered fiercely.

Awareness slithered over his skin with all the finesse of a gorgon's reptilian hair. Hard, biting and undeniable. His shaft swelled, the hated traitor. But he couldn't deny that a part of him had expected her, had…hoped. Damned female.

Slowly he lowered the bow and arrow and floated from the tree, landing in front of Delilah. Her raindrop scent immediately invaded his nose, heady, erotic. Her lavender eyes flashed as if a lightning storm brewed inside of them.

"How did you know I was here?"

She arched a dark brow, and he could tell that his question offended her. As if he should expect better of her. Perhaps he should. "I smelled you."

He traced his tongue over the tip of one fang, simply

flicking it back and forth. She was *that* aware of him? As aware of him as he was of her? With the questions, there was an intensification of the ever-present arousal that plagued him every time she approached.

Hunger. Only hunger, he assured himself. Of their own accord, his eyes sought her neck. Once more, her pulse was hammering. Wild. Once more, his mouth watered.

She tilted her chin to the side as she studied him, her anger seeming to drain away. "You're paler than usual. Why?"

"Return to your new friends," he snapped, as waspish as Tagart had been. He didn't want her noticing things about him. Especially little details, the kinds of things a lover noticed. He didn't want her concerned for him on any level.

Her other brow joined the first in a stubborn race to her azure hairline. "I like where I am. You can walk away from me."

He didn't. His feet were rooted in place. This woman… drew him, held him, for reasons that had nothing to do with his thirst for blood.

There. He had admitted it without issuing an excuse. He still hated the knowledge with everything inside him, still planned to resist, but he could not deny her effect on him any longer. He wanted to be near her.

Why her, after so many years?

Why now?

"If you need blood," she said, choosing to overlook his lack of response to her demand, "take mine."

A more tempting offer had never been made. "Why would you offer such a thing?"

She shrugged, probably trying to appear casual, unaffected. Yet vulnerability darkened her violet irises to a deep purple-black.

"Why?"

Lush red lips pressed together in a mutinous line.

He gulped. So lush, so red, they were ripe for the plucking. "My answer is no, no matter the reason." But the need to drink from her and only her was strong, nearly uncontrollable.

Eyes slitted, she stepped toward him. "You came to kill me, and I offered my blood. I will not tolerate hatred from you now."

An excellent point. "I was not aiming for you," he admitted.

"Liar."

"Always you question the truthfulness of my claim when I'm not lying." He could not have silenced the admission for any price.

Surprise descended over her expression, coloring her cheeks a vibrant pink. "Who then?"

"Doesn't matter. I didn't do it." His self-disgust threatened to choke the life out of him.

Understanding dawned. Exactly what did she think she understood? "You should not even be here," she said. "Spying for your team is cowardly."

"Please. You only wish you were on the other side of the island, listening to my team strategize. Besides, I don't need to spy to defeat you. I've pinned you beneath me, remember?" The moment the words escaped him, the memory of when she'd pinned *him* flashed in his mind. Her legs straddling him, her core so close he had only to lift his head to taste her.

She clearly remembered, too.

Her pupils dilated and that rosy color spread from her cheeks, slowly overtaking her from jaw to collarbone. As she closed more of the distance between them, she dabbed at her lips with the tip of her tongue.

"Stop," he commanded, even as he inched toward her, as well. That tongue…

A moan escaped her, a whimper. "I can't."

What are you doing? Acting like the coward she had called him, he ceased moving toward his downfall and actually backpedaled—until he hit the tree.

Still Delilah advanced. "One of us could be the person to die tonight," she said huskily.

"We will not be chosen," he forced himself to say, even though he had thought the same only moments ago.

"You can't know that for sure." At last she reached him, was merely a whisper away. Her body heat radiated around him, into him, beckoning him all the closer. He'd always preferred the cold—or thought he had. This heat enthralled him, wrapping him in the inexorable threads of desire only she seemed capable of weaving.

Tiny as she was, the top of her head only hit his chin. Surprisingly her blue hair floated up with the breeze, sticking to his shirt and skin as if some part of her had to be in contact with him. He gulped, mouth going dry, blood roaring at a frantic speed.

Before he could stop them, his hands were on her waist, holding her captive. His nails were so sharp they had to be cutting into her skin, but she gave no protest. No, she leaned closer, until the hard tips of her nipples abraded his shirt. Until her legs fit between his, cradling his erection.

He couldn't think, didn't want to think.

"I know we are both strong and determined and we will not allow it to happen," he said, trying—so good, so damned good—to think of anything except possessing her.

Taking her. Hearing her cries of pleasure in his ears. Had he been talking about dying, or making love to her? He couldn't say for sure.

"I wanted you," she admitted. Her eyelids dipped to half-mast. "Before. In Atlantis. I told myself I couldn't allow it. I told myself it would be wrong. I told myself I needed to stay away from you. But right now, I can think of only one thing I will regret if I'm killed."

Push her away! "And what is that?" The words were broken, hoarse.

"Not knowing your kiss." She didn't ask his permission, didn't even give him a chance to respond. She merely rose on her tiptoes and meshed their lips together, her tongue thrusting inside his mouth.

He moaned, the sound more animal than human. The heat…the taste…the desperation… They filled him, consumed him, slayed him. Yes, something inside him died. Or broke. Whatever it was, sensation pounded through the numbness he'd forced upon his body with the ferocity of a winter storm, covering everything in its path, spreading… spreading so quickly there was no controlling it. He was not sure he *wanted* to control it.

Growling, keeping Delilah locked in his arms, he charged forward. Years of denied instinct surged to the surface, demanding he seize control. Too long. He'd been without a woman too long. Hadn't wanted one in two hundred years, and now all of his latent desires were suddenly revealing themselves, desperate, greedy.

When Delilah's back slammed into one of the trees, she gasped. His body trapped her and his tongue plundered deeper, taking everything and demanding more. She cupped his jaw, not to stop him but to hold him and angle him for even deeper contact. Her grip was so fierce she would have snapped the bones of a lesser man. He liked it. Liked that she was as lost to the passion as he was.

"More," she demanded.

"Ask," he said, because it went against the very nature of what she was. She might refuse, might deny him, and the madness might finally end. Perhaps she would even flounce away and he could regain his senses.

Her hands moved to his head and her nails dug into his scalp, as sharp as daggers. *"Please."*

He was surprised by the plea, even more surprised that he fell deeper into the passion. With a kick of her ankle, he spread her legs and meshed his erection against her, hardness to softness.

On a shuddering moan, she said, "Yes, yes. Like that. More."

"Ask." This time, it was a plea of his own. He was desperate to hear the entreaty in her voice.

"Please, please. Layel, please." With every beseeching gasp, her excitement seemed to increase.

She would let him have complete control, he realized with shock. This powerful Amazon would willingly submit herself to his demands. The knowledge burned inside him as he palmed one of her breasts. He felt the stiffness of her nipple through her clothing, but that wasn't good enough. He raked his claw over the material, ripping it in half and freeing her breasts. They were small and firm, perfectly tipped.

More…more…he needed more, felt crazy with the need. The sweet flavor of her skin was addictive, a drug. Her moans were like gateways to the heavens.

He pinched one sweet, pink nipple and rubbed his hard, aching cock between her legs. If only he could wish his clothing away. Skin to skin; he would die without it. "Hook your leg around my waist."

The moment she obeyed, she writhed and whimpered. "Layel. Oh, gods. So good."

As she tried to ride his cock through their clothing, his mind produced a single thought, everything else forgotten: penetrate her. Whatever he had to do to make it happen, he would do. He had to get inside her. Strip her. Throw her down…yes, yes. He tossed the tattered remains of her top aside and pushed her to the ground.

"You're going to take me. All of me."

"Yes."

Passion flowed through him, suddenly his only reason for living. He allowed all of his weight to settle atop her as he crawled down, inch by tantalizing inch. His tongue flicked over and laved her beaded nipple.

More…more…had never been like this. Had to have more.

"Don't stop. Never thought…so good."

"I'll stop if I decide to stop." The power was getting to him, urging him on, demanding he take more. "Understand."

"Please. More. Almost there…"

His hand delved under her tiny skirt, past the thin barrier of cloth between her legs. She was hot, wet. So wet. So tight. He experienced a surge of possessiveness as he thrust a finger deep—and she screamed, loud and long, piercing and sweet. Her inner muscles clenched around him, taking the ultimate pleasure.

More…more…yes, had to have more.

"Layel, Layel."

He surged up, teeth exposed, ready to take her blood while his cock took her body. But he had to release her to free his cock, and he couldn't force himself to release her. A moment later, the dilemma was taken from him. Strong hands settled atop his shoulders and jerked him away from Delilah.

"Bastard!" he heard.

Layel hissed in fury and launched himself at this new opponent. He needed Delilah. No one took her away from him. He was charged with so much passion—rage, dark rage, kiss, more kiss—it was like lava inside of him.

Tagart was knocked to the ground. Layel was there in the next instant, sinking his fangs into the dragon's vein. Blood filled his mouth, as hot as fire. Familiar.

More Delilah. More, his mind screamed. Kill the dragon, return to Delilah.

The warrior slammed a fist into his jaw, and he was propelled sideways. He was on his feet an instant later, warm blood dripping from his face. One step, two, he stalked, a predator locked on his prey.

Delilah stepped in front of him, panting, cheeks rosy from her climax. She didn't bother to cover her beautiful breasts as she held out her hands to ward him off. "Layel," she said, concerned. "Calm down. You have to calm down."

Not Susan, his mind suddenly shouted. *She's not Susan.* She had no right to be concerned for him. She had no right to kiss or touch him. He had no right to kiss and touch her in return. To drink from her, to rejoice in her pleasure.

The fire in his veins died swiftly, no longer even crackling. Leaving only ache and regret. He stilled, doing his best to catch his breath, as shame coursed through him.

Tagart stood in place, his expression gleaming with fury. "Come near her again, and I will not hesitate to kill you."

"Do not hesitate now, fire-bastard."

The dragon bent his knees to leap, but Delilah shook her head at him and he stilled.

"He wasn't hurting me," she said.

Tagart looked from Delilah to Layel, Layel to Delilah. "But you screamed."

"In pleasure," she admitted, bright stains of mortification climbing her cheeks.

Understanding lit his eyes, and Tagart scowled.

"Don't worry," Layel said, his tone colder than he had ever heard it. "I will never again approach her. She is yours." With that, he sprinted away as fast as his feet would carry him.

CHAPTER EIGHT

A GONG SOUNDED throughout the deceptively tranquil night, followed by the echo of a whisper. *Beach…*

Delilah almost groaned. No. Not now. Not yet. Layel had just finished kissing her. During that kiss, the world around her had faded, shattering everything she'd ever known, before another anchor had taken over: his tongue, his touch. *Him*. And then he had walked away from her, leaving her alone with the dragon. No, he hadn't walked. He'd run as if demons were devouring his skin. Leaving her half-naked, aching, wanting. Confused. He hadn't looked back.

He'd left her just as Vorik had left her.

Hands shaking, she bent down and gathered what was left of her top. She hastily pulled it around her, tying it in the center—which shoved her breasts together. Wonderful. If she ran, they would bounce. Perhaps, though, Layel would like that. *Silly girl*.

Tagart didn't turn away while she dressed. He watched her the entire time through slitted lids, golden eyes bright. Bastard. "The vampire king doesn't truly want you," he said.

She could have sliced his head from his body for that, for voicing what she feared most. *The vampire king doesn't truly want you*. Layel had left her and sworn never to come near her again, lending truth to Tagart's claim. But…that passion could not have been forced. More than that, Layel had fought the dragon like a man possessed. For her. She knew it had been for her.

Please let it have been for her.

When she failed to respond, Tagart sighed. "You know very well that Layel is the enemy. *Our* enemy, not just mine, right now."

Yes, she knew that. It just hadn't mattered. She could have claimed her actions had been for the good of the team. A kiss to soften, weaken the vampire. The boast wouldn't leave her tongue, however. She'd finally discovered magic in the arms of a man. She had no desire to taint that memory.

But damn him, she had never felt so raw. What had happened with Layel…what she'd experienced in the vampire's arms…it had been a possession. For that brief time, she had been the most important thing in his life— and she would have betrayed her tribe, not to mention her team, for him. Would have followed him anywhere, would have begged him for forever.

He had given her pleasure, wildness, freedom to simply experience. She'd climaxed around his fingers, his mouth on her nipple. She'd felt the rasp of his sharp teeth, but he hadn't broken her skin—something she should have been happy about, yet she would have willingly given him all the blood in her body, if only she could remain in his embrace.

In that moment, he'd had absolute power over her. Far from angering her as that should have, she reveled in the knowledge. *I could not have stopped him. Could not have escaped.* She shivered in remembered bliss. She had been his captive, had worried about nothing and reveled in the knowledge that she was safe, protected, cherished, and could give herself over completely without any type of rejection. With Vorik, she'd never lost her inhibitions and simply gone wild in his arms. She had worried about everything. *Am I doing this right? Does he like this? Should I do more?*

"Have you no reply, Amazon?"

"I know he is our enemy," was all she said.

"I expected better of you. A fierce fighter. The very woman who tossed me aside during battle only one day ago."

She blinked up at him in surprise. There had been so many opponents, she couldn't summon the image of a single dragon face. "We fought?"

He threw his hands up in disgust. "I'm so insignificant, you do not even remember."

"Fight harder next time," she suggested helpfully.

Far from being appreciative, he snarled at her in fury. "More and more, I am unsure as to why I'm concerning myself with you. Perhaps you and the vampire have been in league since the beginning. He *did* join you on the battlefield and every time I see you, you are near him. Or watching him. Is he paying you to topple your own team? A climax for every loss?"

She balled her fist and punched him, moving so quickly he had no time to protect himself. Her knuckles slammed into his nose, snapping it. He howled in pain, in outrage. He even stepped toward her, as though he meant to return her blow with one of his own. But he didn't.

He glared at her, blood dripping down his chin. "Do that again and you will regret it."

"The dragons incurred the wrath of the Amazons when they bound one of our sisters." Lily. Poor, sweet Lily. How was she doing? Delilah pushed the worry from her mind.

It was either that, or break down. "That we are teammates is the only reason you are still alive. And now that the gods' ridiculous game is beginning, let's see how long you stay that way." She blew him an unconcerned kiss, not surprised to see the puncture wounds on his neck were weaving back together and his nose was snapping back into place.

Dragons and vampires were swift healers. Unfortunately, Amazons were not. When it came to injury, they were as susceptible as humans. Recovery from a broken bone could take weeks, sometimes months. That was one of the reasons they trained so rigorously. Preventing injuries was necessary for survival.

Without another word, she leapt into motion. The gong sounded again. What would happen if she ignored it? Another blast of water in her face? Probably. Her steps increased in speed, and soon she passed a centaur.

What would the first challenge be? Sword fights? Hand-to-hand combat?

A naked branch slapped her cheek, and she reached up to rub the fresh wound. That's when she realized that she was still trembling from Layel's kiss. She was still hot, still achy. Tagart hadn't calmed her, the summons hadn't calmed her. By Kreja's Ax, the climax hadn't calmed her.

Worse, she knew that if Layel had been near her, if he'd shown the slightest bit of eagerness, she would have fallen right back into his arms. Anything to have all of his strength wrapped around her, under her palms, hers to lick.

Damn Tagart for interrupting! one part of her cursed.

Praise the gods he interrupted! the other part rejoiced.

Consorting with the enemy simply for pleasure—ridiculous! And utterly against Amazon code. Now she most likely had to face the vampire king on the battlefield.

Again. She stiffened her spine and drew on every ounce of resolve she possessed. Angry as he was, he might try and hurt her first.

If it came to that, she would have to cut him down.

She broke through the foliage and at last reached the glistening sand. Moonlight, such lovely moonlight, bathed the island in amber mist. Waves danced without a care, spraying droplets onto the shore with delightful abandon.

Several of the creatures already waited in front of her, and her eyes widened as she spotted the long, winding… *thing* in front of them. Made of wood, it stretched across the water. Multiple spiked bars swung from both sides. *Whoosh. Whiz. Whoosh.* There were holes carved into the bottom planks.

Anyone who walked the length of it would either be pummeled by the spikes or dropped into the ocean—where sharks already circled as though they sensed a tasty snack lingered nearby. And if she wasn't mistaken, mer-warriors were also in the water, spears raised, teeth gleaming as they smiled.

Confused, Delilah stalked beside… She searched her mind but could not remember the minotaur's name, even though he was on her team. He was tall, fur covering every inch of his bull face and humanlike body. Saber-teeth protruded from his lips down to his chin. Two horns rose on each side of his head in place of ears.

She'd invaded a minotaur camp once. The bull-men hadn't had a king in centuries, but one had risen among their ranks and tried to take the reins of power. To prove himself strong and unafraid, the foolish creature had insulted nearly every king and queen in Atlantis.

Kreja, Amazon queen then and now, had decided to

teach him the error of his ways and ordered Delilah to lead the army into battle. Delilah had chosen a sneak attack as she considered the weaker race unworthy of a full-on clash. During a rainstorm, she'd infiltrated their midst and simply cut the limbs from the bastard's body.

The next day, she'd delivered each of those limbs to a few of the kings and queens he had insulted. She wondered how Layel would have reacted to the gift, had he been among the recipients.

"What is that?" she asked the minotaur now, nodding at the monstrosity up ahead.

He turned his head and eyed her from top to bottom. Searching for weapons, most likely. She fluttered her lashes at him, projecting, *I'm harmless. You have nothing to fear.* If Tagart's accusations reached her teammates, they would most likely try and slay her in her sleep. They would believe him, too, because she had left their meeting so abruptly.

Gods, she was going to have to win their loyalty.

Slowly the bull-man relaxed. "I believe it's called a gauntlet. My mother used to tell me stories about brave warriors who attempted to defeat such things."

Gauntlet…the word played through her mind, finally snapping into place. Bedtime stories told of courageous soldiers forced to run the entire length to prove their valor. Trepidation bubbled in her chest, followed quickly by excitement. Danger always had that effect. Half of her hated it while the other half thrived on it.

Perhaps she had always been a woman divided. Perhaps she could not lay her dueling needs to conquer and be conquered at Layel's feet.

As if her thoughts had summoned him, a gliding black slash appeared down the beach. Layel had arrived. Her stomach quivered, and her knees weakened. Moisture flooded between her legs. Gods. He wasn't near her, yet she could almost feel his fingers inside her, pumping her to satisfaction.

His effect was even more potent than the thought of danger, for there was not a single part of her that hated it. *Come to me,* she projected. He didn't. And all of her willpower was required to remain in place—or, at the very least, not motion him over.

Should she call out to him? One glance at his eyes, that was all she needed. Hopefully, he had calmed, those invisible demons forgotten.

In the end, she didn't have to do anything. He faced her, a quick meeting of gazes before looking away. Usually he appeared cold, withdrawn. Sometimes, like a little while ago, feral. But now the hate had returned. Oh, had the hate returned. The heat and force of it was blinding.

Why?

She scoured her mind but couldn't recall anything she might have done to offend him. Could he, like her, be battling conflicting desires? She'd wondered before, but never had the possibility seemed more likely.

She knew why she did so. She wanted to be both woman and warrior, respected by her sisters and loved by a man. What was his reasoning?

"If you cause us to fail," Tagart said, suddenly at her side and blocking Layel from her sights, "I will kill you myself. Doubt me not."

She went rigid. In the past, no one would have been able to sneak up on her. Damn Layel and his strange pull on her! "Perhaps you haven't realized that your threats mean nothing to me."

Nola approached her other side, and Delilah turned away from the dragon. An insult, she knew. As if he were so insignificant he did not bear watching. She kept her ears tuned to him, though, in case he decided to strike.

He growled low in his throat, but never moved for attack.

"This cannot end well," Nola muttered. Strands of her dark hair brushed her cheek and whipped over her eyes. "I hate that we have been separated. My team leaves much to be desired."

Though they had never been close, Delilah's loyalty belonged to those of her own race. *Do not forget.* "No matter what we are ordered to do, I will not betray or hurt you. You have my word."

Nola's gaze fixed on the gauntlet. "I want to believe you. I do. But—"

"No. No god is going to change my allegiance."

"I cannot believe this is really happening. I want to go home. I want to hold Lily. I want my life back, riotous as it was."

"Everyone here wants to return to Atlantis, but we can't. So you're going to put those things out of your mind and concentrate on the task at hand. That's an order. It's the only way to ensure your survival."

Nola bristled, but a moment passed and she gave another nod. "All right. Yes."

Delilah's relief was short-lived.

"The time has come."

The god-voice came suddenly, without warning, and Delilah's already stiff body gave a jerk. This voice sounded different, deeper than the one yesterday had been, raspier than the one before. A third god? She faced the ocean, where the air and water beside the gauntlet mixed, thickening and dappling and already taking the shape of a man. Again, no face was visible.

"Citizens of Atlantis," came the voice again. "We hope that you have had sufficient time to prepare for this first test of your mettle. If not, you are not the warriors we thought you were and we will be highly disappointed."

Thunder suddenly boomed in the sky. A second later, dark clouds formed above the warriors and the gauntlet, and fat droplets of rain fell over the group in a hard pelting. Delilah didn't bother to wipe the water from her face; she wouldn't give the god the satisfaction.

"In life, as in this game, there are many obstacles. One wrong move and you could be destroyed. Remember that…"

Lightning streaked brightly, illuminating the god for a split second. Underneath the mask of water, Delilah thought she saw the visage of a gloriously handsome man. Eyes of bright blue, hair of honeyed silk. Perfect lips curved into a perfect smile of delight.

"Line up," he commanded. The rain mixed with ice, beating against them, bruising.

At first, no one moved. Were they, like her, disgusted by this god's behavior? What would happen if they continued to refuse?

Unwilling to find out, they finally trudged up three separate tiers one by one. Soon they stood on a flat platform. There were two identical paths in front of the scaffold, each leading to identical treachery. She was shivering, cold misting with her every breath, as she studied the gauntlet from this new angle. How had she gotten to this point? She might have devoted her life to mastering the art of combat, but never had she imagined being involved in something as sinister as this.

Tagart elbowed Delilah out of the way and claimed the first position for their team. She thought about protesting, then shrugged. Let him lead. He could be the first to fall, the first to be pushed.

In the other line, Brand assumed the lead and Layel floated to the space right behind him. His arm brushed hers, a slow stroke of fire. Unintentional? And why was he warm? He was usually as cold as the ice now falling from the sky. *Don't look at him, don't you dare look at him.* He would distract her, perhaps destroy her resolve.

"A successful team player will work to ensure that all members walk away from a battle, not just himself," the god said. "I suggest you use whatever means necessary to buoy your team along, for every one of you must reach the end." A crack of thunder boomed, and the god cleared his throat. "The first team to reach the end wins. Not only will you bask in the glow of our approval, but as a reward for your efforts, we will gift you with something you surely crave even more than another tomorrow. A glimpse of your home, your loved ones."

A glimpse of her loved ones…of Lily. She shook with the sudden force of her determination, all the while continuing to fight the desire to face Layel, gauge his reaction to the god's announcement. Was there someone at home, waiting for him? A woman, perhaps, snuggled in his bed?

Don't look, don't look, don't—she did it, willpower broken by need. She looked. Breath caught in her throat. The vampire was watching her, and their gazes clashed as sharply as the storm.

That quickly, her blood heated with renewed desire. Renewed? As if the sweet hum had ever left her.

Her nipples pearled again, her knees weakened.

Before he could turn away from her, dismissing her, *she* refocused on the god. Instantly her eyes mourned the loss of his decadent face.

"Before we begin, there is one rule I must mention. If one participant falls into the water, that creature must return to the beginning and start over. A little punishment for failing, if you will. Help your team or not. Hinder your team or not. The choice is yours. Just know that we will be watching, judging. Deciding." With barely a pause, the god added, "Go."

A moment passed before Delilah realized the contest had begun. Tagart, too, hesitated, even when Brand sprang forward.

"Go, go, go!" she shouted, shoving Tagart over the threshold. Her heart raced in her chest, adrenaline surging hard.

He tripped, sliding on the ice-covered wood. When he caught himself, he whipped into fervent motion. She stayed close to his heels, barely able to see past the pounding rain. The first spiked lance swung at her, and she ducked. *Whoosh.* One of the spikes sliced her shoulder blade. There was a sharp sting, a rush of warm blood, and she winced.

She didn't slow.

"Jump," Tagart shouted.

She did, a gaping hole suddenly underneath her, sharks swimming just below it, snapping up at her. Their teeth were long, white and jagged. As she landed, knees absorbing the impact, she threw over her shoulder, "Jump!"

The minotaur didn't react as swiftly as she had and failed to obey in time. He began to fall, down, down, swiftly. Not knowing if she would do more harm than good, Delilah stopped, spun and dropped to her stomach, grabbing for his arm. Their palms clapped together, and he latched on to her with frantic desperation. His heavy weight nearly slid her from her perch.

The team member behind the minotaur jumped and landed on Delilah's back with his hooves—a centaur—shoving the air from her lungs. The bastard kept galloping, obviously deciding she wasn't worth the effort. So much for buoying his team along.

"Pull me up," the bull-man screamed, his eyes darting between her and the hungry fish below him. Sweat dripped from his dark fur, and she lost her grip. Their fingers slipped.

"Hold tighter, damn it!"

A grinning merman swam to the bull and reached up, trying to grab his ankles. All the while she did her best to hoist him up. She was strong, but he was so heavy it felt as if her arms were being torn from their sockets.

"Kick him," she commanded through gritted teeth. She dug her booted toes into the wood planks and rolled her hips. Slowly, with every roll, she inched backward. "Don't let him latch on to you."

Another team member slapped into her back, and she nearly lost her hold again. So much for team players. Somehow she managed to maintain a solid hold this time, even as the minotaur flailed to avoid the laughing merman.

Layel appeared beside her, startling her. She glanced up, embarrassed that she needed help but happy to see him all the same. He didn't touch her or say a word as he kicked his leg into the hole. His foot slammed into the bull-man's face.

"What are you doing?" she shouted, rain filling her mouth.

The minotaur sobbed and grabbed for her wrist with his other hand.

"Let him go."

"No!"

Layel kicked the bull again.

Strong arms suddenly latched on to her waist, a thick leg whizzing past her temple and connecting with Layel's chest. The vampire soared backward and her helper gave a hard tug, pulling Delilah to her feet and the minotaur the rest of the way to safety. She glanced up, panting, and saw Tagart.

His eyes were grim, his face cut and bloodied. Water trickled from his cheeks in little rivers. "Let's go." He turned and was off, unwilling to wait for her.

She rubbed her shoulder and stumbled forward. As she moved, a flash of black drew her attention to the left. Layel had regained his balance and now kept pace beside her on his side of the gauntlet, watching her through eyes red with fury. Time seemed to slow, the dragon and minotaur racing toward the finish line and her other teammates rushing past her, her labored gait too slow.

Determined, she increased her speed. Every step jarred her shoulder and lanced her with fresh pain, but she didn't care. She dodged the spikes and jumped the holes without missing a beat.

Layel, she noticed, simply floated above the gaping holes. He never fell behind her, nor did he inch in front of her. Truly, what was his purpose? He could have maimed her, slowed her down and won, but he hadn't.

A pendulum swung at her and she ducked, soon realizing there was a rhythm to the game. Step, step, duck. Step, jump. Step, step, duck. Again, she quickened her movements. Twice, she skidded across the slippery ice, but both times she managed to stop herself before she slid straight into the water.

Where was Nola? Had the girl already reached the end? She looked, slipped.

Concentrate. Ducking nearly to her stomach as the lowest lance yet whizzed overhead, Delilah's gaze connected with Layel's as though tugged by an invisible chain. He'd already made it past the spike and was standing off to the side, next to a hole.

One of his teammates dangled under it, she saw, hanging on with only one hand. Gaze never leaving her, Layel stepped on the creature's fingers. There was a pained cry. Then nothing. Then a splash. Then another cry. Her mouth fell open in shock. Why had he done that? He had hindered his own team, sentenced them to lose.

To show her that he had no remorse when it came to killing?

To help her win?

The thought was heady. Shameful, but heady. She wanted to throw herself into his arms, feel him embrace her. Hear him proclaim to all the world that she was his, belonged to him, and he would stop at nothing to ensure her happiness.

Someone grabbed her arm, and she cried out at the renewed agony in her shoulder. Her attention skidded to her tormentor. Tagart.

He tossed her a dark scowl. "You're the last. Hurry!" With that, he jerked her forward.

She tried to pull back. Foolishly, she didn't want Layel to lose. But it was too late. In seconds, they were at the end. She saw every one of her teammates hunched over, gasping for air. But they were there, which meant her team had won. Cheers soon rent the air, louder even than the crashing thunder.

She turned as Layel reached his own team. They were hunched over and gasping, as well, but they didn't cheer when they saw the vampire. They snarled in rage. He was the reason they had lost, and they knew it.

"You'll pay," Brand snarled.

"You kicked him!" a centaur roared. "You kicked Irren."

Irren, the formorian in question, limped to the finish line a short while later. His only arm clung to its socket with thin strips of crimson flesh. Like all of his race, he possessed only one leg. That leg was missing hunks of muscle. Both of his wings were broken, barely able to flap, but keeping him upright. Injured as he was, he still attacked Layel from behind.

Frowning, Layel reached behind him, latched on to the creature and flipped him overhead. *Smack.* Irren hit the wood, causing the entire platform to vibrate. The formorian didn't rise. He just lay there, panting, tears streaming down his cheeks.

"You could have helped me," Irren choked out. "You could have helped."

"But I didn't," Layel replied coldly. He was peering at Delilah as he spoke, as if his every action was for her benefit.

Did he think she would turn away, repulsed by him? Did he *hope* that she would?

Violence was not abhorrent to her. She had done much worse over the years.

Not knowing what to make of him, Delilah tore her gaze away and searched for Nola. She found the girl in the corner, scowling over at her. Blaming her for the loss?

Having none of that, Delilah lumbered toward her. Just before she reached her target, however, everyone on the losing team disappeared. There one moment, gone the next. At first, Delilah glanced around in confusion. Then her stomach clenched as realization set in.

Elimination.

One member would not return from their counsel with the gods. And after the way the team had glared at Layel, she didn't have to guess who that team member would be.

IN THE SPAN OF A HEARTBEAT, Layel found himself sitting in front of a fire, trees surrounding him. The rain had stopped. Damn this! He was tired of being popped in and out of locations without warning. He himself had the ability but he rarely utilized it, not liking the sense of total exhaustion that always accompanied the transport. Still, he would rather deal with the weariness than with the god's seemingly unbeatable power. Freedom of choice was something he valued.

His *teammates* sat in a circle around him. They, too, had been popped here. How…wonderful.

"You purposely pushed the formorian into the water," Brand growled without preamble.

Layel arched a brow but did not verbally respond. He refused to explain himself to a fire-breather.

In truth, he couldn't even explain himself to himself. He didn't think he'd acted to prevent Delilah's team from losing. He despised that woman and her dangerous kisses. More than that, if they'd lost, Tagart might have been the one to die—a thought that pleased Layel.

Tagart.

Layel's teeth cut into his gums and blood flavored his tongue. Tagart obviously desired Delilah, obviously wanted her for his own. The dragon bastard was unworthy of her passion. All men were.

"He stepped on my hand," Irren cried, drawing him out of his dark musings.

Brand knifed to a towering stand. The fire crackled, amber light dancing over his harsh countenance. His hair beads slapped together in an ominous beat. "You cost us the victory, bloodsucker."

Rather than address the dragon, Layel eyed the formorian. "*You* cost us the victory, and you know it. You are simply too cowardly to admit it. Had you not fallen into the hole and slowed our momentum, I would not have been able to step on your hand, now would I?"

The creature's bruised cheeks colored in embarrassment, a rainbow of reds, blues and blacks. His glittering green eyes added to the rainbow effect. "Do not blame this on me! I would have climbed to safety."

"With your arm or your leg?" he scoffed without mercy. "You are the weakest among us and would have caused us to lose whether you climbed up of your own volition or not. You will cause us to lose *every* challenge, I have no doubt." He shook his head in disgust, though privately he admitted that disgust was not for the creature's infirmity. Rather his reaction stemmed from the desire he'd seen in Irren's eyes whenever the creature looked at Delilah. "You deserved to be hurt."

Surprisingly Brand had no response to that. None of them did.

Amid the silence, Layel's mind returned to Delilah and their kiss… His fangs elongated even more. He'd had his tongue and his fingers inside her. He'd rubbed his swollen shaft against her. He would have drunk from her and he would have bedded her if Tagart had not interrupted.

Not once had he thought of Susan.

Not once had he cared that it had not been his mate's gentle voice rasping his name, her soft hands clawing his back. No, Susan would not have clawed him. Their lovemaking had always been tender, as sweet as Susan herself. He had savored every moment with her.

Not once had he ever felt the desire to dominate her as he had with Delilah. He had wanted to possess the Amazon's very soul. Brand himself inside her, claim her every cell for his own. The need had been fierce, a rising tide of tangled darkness and light.

Because of that, he had betrayed Susan more than ever before. He didn't deserve pleasure. He didn't deserve happiness. And that he had experienced them, even for so short a time, made him as pathetic and shameful as the dragons. Yet…

When Delilah had reached for her teammate—nearly falling herself in the process—his first instinct had been to grab hold of her. Save her, keep her close. Guard her. He had refrained at first, telling himself it would be easier this way. She would fall, perhaps die, definitely be hurt. And he would stop craving her.

Finally, though, he had been unable to resist. He'd moved toward her. Rather than touch her, however, he had tried to dislodge the bastard holding her down. Stubborn as she was, she'd wanted to save her team member. Which Tagart had helped her do.

Layel blanked his mind as his teeth gnashed together. *It's done. Over. You can't go back and change what happened.*

As he focused on the here and now, he realized Brand had moved in front of him. Golden eyes were boring down at him, hot, wild. "I asked you a question, and I will be ignored no longer."

"What question?"

"You think to pretend ignorance?"

Annoyance swept through him, sure and potent. He'd

been lost in thought and far away from the conversation. He wouldn't admit to it, though. Instead, he withdrew one of his wooden daggers, moving with lightning speed to slash Brand's jugular. But the blade disappeared from his hand, causing Layel to hit the dragon with his fingers. Brand opened his mouth to spew fire.

"Sit down," a booming voice commanded. A *female* voice this time, though just as powerful as the male voices they'd encountered before.

He frowned. How many gods were pulling their strings? Watching them? Torturing them? This was the fourth. He glanced left, right, unsurprised that he could not see the being's form.

"Until next time, fire-bastard," he said.

"Next time, bloodsucker. If you survive the elimination, which I do not think will be the case." Jaw clenched, Brand stomped back to his seat.

Layel did the same, grimly suspecting Brand was right. This would probably be his last night alive. He deserved the death, yet he still wasn't ready for it. But not for his usual reasons, damn the gods. He found, in that instant, he regretted that he would die without tasting Delilah fully.

"Here we are, in the losers' circle, the first challenge completed. Some of you showed more courage than others. Some of you more weakness." There was a pause. The gods, Layel had noticed, did love their dramatic pauses. "In the end, you allowed your opponents to best you, and for that you have earned our displeasure. While the other team celebrates their victory, reaping its rewards, you are here before me, one of you destined to die."

Another pause, this one angry. "Because we could not agree amongst ourselves, we are leaving the vote up to you," the goddess said. "The creature with the most votes will be the one to face execution. May I recommend the dragon or the vampire?"

With her last words, a growl whipped around them as fierce as wind. Only sharper. Cutting. Layel thought he heard the words *No interference,* but he couldn't be sure.

The goddess sighed, then uttered a distinctly forced chuckle. "Just a little gallows humor, of course. Pick whomever you feel is most deserving of elimination, the warrior who will cause you to lose over and over again if he remains on your team."

Layel raised his chin, even as his heart shuddered. His death had never been more certain, for his teammates could never trust him.

"Brand." She said his name with...distaste? "You may begin."

"We need time," the warrior said. "Time to talk and decide."

"Actually, what we need is to be sent home." Layel figured he was about to die, so why not speak his mind? "This game is barbaric. We should never have been brought here."

"Brand," the goddess snapped, and Layel balled his fists at being ignored. "Vote. Now."

One by one, the members spoke their choice. Layel sat stiffly, and when his turn arrived a sword materialized and hovered just over the fire. Waiting...waiting for a target. And then the last vote was delivered.

"And so it is done," the goddess said.

Sharp silver twirled in the air and struck the first member to be eliminated from the game.

CHAPTER NINE

DELILAH SAT on the beach, the gauntlet no longer in place. A short while ago, every piece of timber had vanished like mist with the dawn. What surprised her most, however, was that she no longer blinked when strange things happened. Having been whisked from one place to another several times, having seen the gods appear and disappear in a heartbeat, she had reluctantly accepted that odd things were simply part of her life now.

Waves lapped at her feet and ankles as her mind whirled with realizations. When the losing team had disappeared, her first thought had been of Layel's welfare. Not Nola's, as it should have been.

Gods, what was wrong with her?

Perhaps the vampire's kiss had branded her, soul deep, and she was now bound to him for all of eternity. Possessed by him. A slave, his to command. Obsessed, hers to worship. She sighed.

Not even the prize her team received for winning the challenge had lessened her concern for him.

Less than an hour ago, a round, intricately framed mirror had appeared in front of her team. The god hadn't lied when he'd promised a reward. *Enjoy,* a voice had boomed. *You have done well and made us proud.* They had gazed at it simultaneously, but apparently each had seen something different: the person they missed most in Atlantis.

Delilah had seen Lily.

The delicate girl had been safely ensconced in the Amazon camp, but she had been wrapped in the queen's arms, crying. For Delilah. Both females assumed she and Nola were dead. They were in mourning, and Lily blamed herself.

Just as Delilah had reached for the mirror, determined to shake it until Kreja or Lily saw *her,* it had dematerialized as surely as the gauntlet had. She'd screeched and cursed to no avail. They all had. To calm herself, she'd had to close her mind and level her breathing, chanting under her breath that Lily was alive, Lily was well. Upset, but well. *One less worry.* And then, craving Layel's strong arms around her, Delilah had begun searching the island for him.

Every turn had led her straight back to this spot. Was Layel still alive? Had he been slain already?

Footsteps sounded behind her. She didn't turn, didn't acknowledge the intruder in any way. The heavy stride informed her it was a dragon; the scent of spice and darkness informed her it was Tagart. Maybe if she ignored him, he would go away.

He sidled right up to her. "Worried for your lover?" he asked, his words slurred.

Not her lucky night, after all. "You're drunk."

"I know. Isn't it wonderful?"

"Where did you find wine?"

"Every dragon possesses a mythical ability. Some can breathe underwater, some can travel from one location to another in the blink of an eye. Some can see anyone anywhere simply by speaking their name. Me, I can turn water to wine." Embarrassment and wisps of self-loathing drifted along the undercurrents of his voice. Why? "Where's your vampire?" he asked before Delilah could press him further. "Dead?"

Her heart lurched inside her chest, a vision of Layel lying motionless, blood pooling around him, flashing inside her mind. "Go to Hades, Tagart." She pushed to her feet, unwilling to give him any type of advantage. Even one as simple as height.

"You worry for him." A statement, not a question.

"We've already had this conversation, and I'm not having it again."

"You're right. I'm…sorry."

An apology? He must be drunk indeed to have offered one. Her eyes widened in surprise, and she studied the man responsible intently. He was as strong as Layel. He was dark, handsome, edgy. Resilient and capable. He wouldn't hesitate to destroy an enemy. And he had, she grudgingly admitted, helped her during the challenge. Why could her body not crave this man? She knew firsthand how lusty a dragon could be.

"You are courageous," he said, swaying slightly, "and unafraid. We would make a great team."

"We *are* on the same team."

He waved a hand through the air, swayed again. "I meant us. Together. We are the strongest of the group, the most competent."

All she could do was blink up at him. "I don't understand what you're trying to tell me."

"Silly Amazon." He chuckled, a sound of true mirth. It suited him, lighting his features and casting away the shadows that always seemed to hover around him. He reached for her shoulder, decided against touching her and dropped his arm to his side. "I will guard your back and you will guard mine. In the event that we lose a challenge, we will never vote to have the other killed."

"Vote? What are you talking about?"

"You do not know?"

"No," she said, and his expression changed to one of sympathy. "Tell me!"

"Delilah…"

She closed the distance between them, would have been nose to nose if she'd been taller. Waves washed over their feet, soon-to-disappear moonlight streamed in every direction, and the call of night-birds echoed. But nothing overshadowed the pounding of her heartbeat. "Tell me."

"The other team returned. They told us what happened, how they were forced to vote for the creature they wished off of their team." A heavy pause. "There *was* an execution."

Instantly panic and dread infused her blood, racing through her, cutting at her. She clutched Tagart's tattered shirt, wadding the material in her hands. "Did…Nola return?"

He nodded slowly, the grimness of their conversation clearly sobering him, and studied her features. "Do you wish to know if the vampire king returned, as well?"

She did. With everything inside of her, she did, but she was afraid of her reaction. If she learned that he was alive, would she smile? Laugh, dance? If she learned that he was indeed dead, would she cry? Sob? "I will consider your request for an alliance," she said, releasing him. She backed away slowly, desperate to be alone—and determined not to show it. "We will talk soon."

"He was not with the others when they returned," Tagart said anyway.

That means nothing, she tried to tell herself. But she

didn't respond to Tagart, just kept moving backward. Away. She had to get away from him.

His jaw clenched. "If you think too long about my offer, I will withdraw it and make it to someone else."

And she would be the first one they voted for, Delilah did not doubt. Still she remained silent. Finally she passed the line of trees. Their branches slapped in front of her, blocking the dragon from view. Immediately she turned and ran, arms and legs pumping furiously. Her skin was like ice, but sweat beaded anyway, trickling down.

Of course Layel's team had voted for him. He had hurt one of their own.

Tears burned her eyes, the very tears she had so feared. *You've only known him two days, and you suspected this was coming. Why are you upset?* He had caused her nothing but trouble and grief. And pleasure. Oh, gods, the pleasure. She would never again experience his kiss, his touch. Would never learn his secrets, ease the pain she saw in his eyes every time she looked at him. Never shine light into the darkness of his soul.

Foolish, she thought for the thousandth time. Where had that thought come from? Shine light into his soul? Hers was as dark as his was. Or rather, *had been.* A whimper rose in her throat.

Distracted as she was, she did not see the figure looming in front of her. Delilah slammed into him. He was as hard as a boulder, but unprepared for her momentum. They propelled to the ground, strong arms banding around her waist. He took the brunt of the fall, his breath gusting over her face. Metallic, sweet.

She was on her feet a moment later, ready for battle. But he never attacked her. He simply stood and wiped the grass from his clothing, saying, "I would like to say that was fun, but I told you I would not lie to you."

That voice…husky, sardonic. "Layel?"

He'd been glaring, his ocean blues hidden by the frame of his lashes, but that glare melted away as he studied her expression. "Are you…crying?"

He was here; he was alive. He had not been chosen for execution. Trying not to smile now, she wiped her eyes with the back of her wrist. "No."

"Did no one tell you Nola survived?" he asked softly. For a moment, only a moment, he looked at her with something akin to tenderness.

"I was told." Her heart already drummed erratically from her sprint, but now, as she drank in the sight of him, the silly organ wanted to pound its way free. "How are you alive?"

He *tsked* under his tongue, somehow conveying a wealth of pain and joy with the sound. "Disappointed?"

She raised her chin, refusing to lie yet equally unwilling to admit the truth. He would reject her again, and her emotions were too strung out to deal with another.

He sighed. "I want to be alone now," he said. He turned away from her and picked up a fat stick, then continued… whatever it was that he'd been doing before she ran into him. Was he…digging a hole? He pressed the stick into the ground to gather a mound of dirt, then tossed that dirt aside.

His muscles rippled as he moved, and her mouth watered. *I clutched those muscles once. I had them at my fingertips.* So badly she wanted to rake her fingers through his white hair. Even flatten her palm against his chest and feel the flow of life as he drank from her. "I'm waiting for an answer to my question," she insisted. "How are you alive?"

His broad shoulders lifted in a casual shrug. "My team decided I was not the one who would cause them to lose the next contest. So…" Another shrug, but this one was stiff, self-conscious. "Now, go away," he said, jamming a long stick into the ground. Then he popped it up, tossing a mound of dirt a few feet away.

"Who was chosen?"

"I love being ignored." Without pausing in his digging, he said, "The formorian who—" He pressed his lips together. Dirt soared over his shoulder as he heaved the stick upward.

"Who you helped into the water," she finished for him.

He gave a clipped nod.

To prevent herself from closing all hint of distance between them and burrowing her head in the hollow of his neck, she shifted and leaned her uninjured shoulder against the nearest tree. "You and Brand seem to hate each other. I'm surprised he didn't vote for you, no matter that the formorian was weak."

Layel laughed darkly. "Oh, he voted for me. Several members did. One more vote, and I would have been the one who lost his head."

Just how close had she come to losing him? "The gods actually decapitated him?"

Another nod.

Some part of her had thought, perhaps hoped, they would change their minds. "Why did you do it?" she asked after a tension-filled pause.

"Do what?" he asked, but she knew he only pretended ignorance.

"Hurt your own team member."

"Perhaps it amused me to hear him scream. Perhaps I

live for the deaths I cause, as rumors in Atlantis claim." Another mound of dirt flew over his shoulder.

This one was launched toward her. She hopped out of the way, barely escaping an earth-shower. He'd purposely aimed at her, the bastard. "That was childish," she said, crossing her arms over her middle.

"But satisfying."

"You remind me of Lily right now."

"Lily?"

"My sister by race, the future queen of the Amazons and the girl the dragons were carting in that cell." Only yesterday, she realized, though it felt as if an eternity had already passed. "When Lily doesn't get her way, she throws a tantrum."

"I'm not throwing a tantrum."

"No, you're throwing dirt. Is that any better?"

A rumbling noise escaped him, and she wasn't sure if he expressed amusement or irritation. He paused in his digging, though, keeping his back to her. "Go away, Delilah." He sounded weary.

Would she ever get used to the tremors of delight that shook her every time he said her name? "No. What are you doing here, anyway?"

"None of your concern. Go."

"Again, no." She'd almost lost him tonight. Part of her didn't want to be separated from him ever again. How had he engaged her emotions so strongly and so quickly? "I'm not sure if you treat me this way because you genuinely dislike me or because you're afraid of me."

"Wonder no more. I dislike you." Motions clipped, he slammed the stick back into the ground, and then another mound of dirt was sailing toward her.

This time, she remained in place. The grains pummeled

her calves and ankles, and she grit her teeth. "If you dislike me so much, why did you thrust your tongue into my mouth and your fingers into my—"

"Enough!" The stick snapped in half. Tossing the half he still held, he whirled, facing her. "I could tell you that I don't have to like you to bed you. Is that what you need to hear? Would you leave if I said it?"

"Would you mean it?" she asked in a broken voice she scarcely recognized as her own.

Silent, he swiped up another stick and began shoveling again. Wood and mud collided again and again, widening the hole clearly no longer his concern. Fury poured from him, making his motions frenzied.

The intense surge of hurt she'd experienced—*don't have to like you to bed you*—gradually drained. He couldn't say he meant it because he didn't feel that way. Not wanting to push him into lying, however, she let the subject drop. For now. For whatever reason, he wasn't ready to show her a softer side of himself. "Tell me what you're doing."

He stilled, panting, sweating. "Delilah."

"Layel."

"This isn't doing either one of us any good." He straightened, his profile to her. The elegant curve of his nose cast a shadow over his cheek. Seemed odd that such a ruthless man would possess such pretty features. Not that she was complaining.

"You would rather kiss than talk?" she asked, hopeful.

The tip of his tongue emerged, trailing over his bottom lip. Remembering the taste of her? Then he scrubbed a dirty hand down his face. Streaks of black remained behind. "I'm burying the body."

Body? As lost as she'd been with the thought of their

kiss, a moment passed before she recalled the formorian's death. She stared into the crowd of trees, searching. Sure enough, she found the corpse several feet away and frowned. Now why would the man who supposedly hated everyone around him concern himself with the burial of a stranger?

Guilt? A hidden sense of honor?

What a contradiction Layel was.

With a sigh, she gathered a stick and began digging alongside him, heedless of her injured shoulder. He didn't rebuke her, and they managed to work in silence. What seemed a lifetime later, the hole was big enough for a body. Somberly she helped the vampire place the formorian inside.

"So you know why I was fighting the dragons yesterday—to save Lily. But what about you? Why do you hate the dragons so much?" She threw her stick to the ground and peered over at him, determined to get at least one answer this night.

For a single heartbeat, his eyes pulsed a bright, fiery red, a look of such debilitating pain falling over his face that she almost dropped to her knees. Almost begged him not to answer. No one should suffer like that. No one. As though they were dying from the inside out, slowly, inexorably, and each cell that withered, each organ that failed, poisoned another, until there was only rot and disease left. Only agony. But then his expression cleared, and he said flatly, "They took something that belonged to me. And if you dare ask what, I will kill you here and now."

The warrior in her wanted to press; the woman in her never wanted to see that pain inside him again. So she said, "Perhaps you've failed to realize that threats only encourage me," in an effort to tease him. Then she eyed him nervously. Banter with a man was not something she had experience with. Was she doing it correctly?

His lips twitched into a semblance of a smile, causing her stomach to flutter and her heart to skip a beat entirely. "I've realized." He, too, dropped his stick. He offered no words of thanks for her aid. "Your team is celebrating their victory. You should join them."

Being here with him, talking to him, seeing that smile, thrilled her more than any celebration. But she did wheel away from him. "You're right." She didn't want to leave him, and that was precisely why she must. Slowly she walked away. Prolonging the contact was only sparking a desire for more.

When she thought him dead, she had mourned. *Mourned.* The more time she spent with him the more she wanted him. What would happen if he *was* killed? What would happen if she gave herself to him and he pushed her away afterward? Next time, she might not survive.

"Amazon," he called.

Irritation flooded her. He called her "Amazon" when he wished to put distance between them. That, she knew. But still she stopped. She just didn't face him. "Yes."

"I am…sorry. About the—about earlier. About what I said."

An apology from yet another man. Something must be in the water. "I don't regret anything about what has happened or been said between us." No, that wasn't true. She regretted that their time together had to end. Tonight, most likely forever. If she could stay away from him, for that would be the true battle.

Fortifying her resolve, she started forward again.

"Amazon," he called once more.

And once more she stilled, unable to help herself. "Yes."

"Do not approach me again. Your team will not like it, and next time it will be *you* who is voted for."

Concern? For her? Gods, she was as helpless against it as she was to resist him. "I can take care of myself."

"I have learned that in this game the opinion of your teammates matters more than your actual performance."

"You aren't the first to tell me such a thing. Tagart asked me to ally with him."

A heavy, crackling pause, then, he asked tightly, "Did you accept?"

"Not yet."

"You should." The last was grated, as if the words rubbed his throat raw.

Did he not like the thought of her with another man, as she'd considered before, or did he simply hate the dragons so much he loathed the idea of anyone helping them? "Have you seen the waterfall on the north side of the island?" she found herself asking. *Stop, don't do this. You're leaving to escape him.*

"Yes."

"I'll be there in an hour. Alone."

Silence. Then, "And you will remain alone. We cannot be…friends, Delilah. I'm sorry."

Another apology. Gulping, hurting again, she started forward for the third time. Part of her expected him to call her back. But he didn't. Not again. She reached the celebration a few minutes later. She was caked in dirt and sweat, but she didn't care.

Her teammates were dancing around a fire, drinking wine and laughing. All but the nymph, she realized. Broderick was gone. As was their team's other female. A gorgon.

So, he'd opted to risk a stoning to spend a little time between the snake-woman's legs. Layel, she suspected, would never do such a thing.

Speaking of Layel, his team sat several feet away. Their nymph female, like Broderick, was missing, as was… Hmm, all of the men were present—and each member was glaring with jealousy at Delilah's team. Even Nola.

Delilah met the Amazon's stare. Rather than a smile or a wave, she received a short, abrupt nod and almost sighed. Dissent within the same races already. Did Nola think she had betrayed her? Convinced Layel to lose? That, she would deal with later. At the moment she needed to approach Tagart. The dragon ceased his dancing, his smile fading when he spotted her. Sweat glinted from his skin, and he exuded a masculine musk every other woman on the island probably would have enjoyed.

Delilah found that she preferred the metallic sweetness of Layel's scent.

"I accept your offer," she whispered up to him. She didn't trust him, but she didn't mind using him. *You should,* Layel had said, as though he didn't care that she would forge an alliance with his enemy.

They would soon learn the truth of that.

Layel's obvious dislike of the dragons was the only reason she had hesitated before, she realized now. Subconsciously, she'd allowed him to begin affecting her decisions. No more.

Slowly Tagart's lips curled into a satisfied smile. "I knew you'd see reason." He reached for her, meaning to pull her into his embrace for a dance.

She backed up a step, not willing to take their alliance that far. Good or bad for her, Layel was the only man she wanted touching her. "Just tell me one thing."

Tagart's golden dragon eyes glinted like polished coins. "And what is that? You wish me to tell you the other team's nymph is out there right now, searching for your vampire, determined to have him?"

What? Why, that bitch! She had no right. *He's mine. No, no,* she immediately chastised herself. *Do not think that way.* "What did your brethren take from Layel to cause a war with the vampires?" The stories she'd heard of Layel's prowess had never said.

The glint in his eyes died. "He did not tell you?"

"No."

Guilt flashed, but he said starkly, "We took...his mate."

LAYEL BATTLED with himself for the entire hour Delilah had given him. He knew what he should do, knew what was wise. He could not go to her. Absolutely not. No. But she was slowly stripping him of his sanity.

Every minute he spent with her, he desired more.

Every minute he thought of her, he desired more.

Every minute he was *without* her, he desired more.

She drew him. If she had looked like Susan or acted like Susan, he would have understood her strange pull on him. But she didn't, so he didn't.

"I'm glad to see you survived," Zane said from behind him.

Layel had been expecting the warrior, and was only surprised he had not arrived sooner. What had he been doing? "I have a mission for you," he said, turning.

Zane floated in front of him. Layel could smell the sweet scent of fresh blood on the soldier. Female blood. His stomach knotted, for it was widely known the vampire only took from the dying. "Who did you feed from?"

Zane blinked at the fury in his tone. "That hardly matters."

"Tell me!" Layel was in his face a moment later. There were not that many females on the island. If he had sunk those fangs into Delilah…

"You had better back away, king. I serve you because I wish to, but that can change at any moment."

He'd heard similar words a thousand times before from the warrior. "Delilah is not—"

"The one I tasted, no."

Instantly Layel relaxed. Hatred—for himself, for Delilah—sprang free, never far from the surface. Always waiting to pounce. He shouldn't have cared who Zane drank from.

Zane shook his dark head. "So that is the way of things, I see."

"You see nothing," he growled.

"I see that you have staked a claim on her. Well, guess what? She is at camp right now, joining forces with that bastard, Tagart."

So. She *had* allied with the dragon. When she had told him of Tagart's offer, he had wanted to scream, *I will protect you. Me. Not him.* But he had held his tongue, knowing that was the wisest course. If he allowed it, Delilah would be his downfall. He would long to live with her, rather than join Susan in the hereafter. Unacceptable!

He studied Zane's sated expression. A single thought filled his head, overshadowing everything else. *I could have Delilah's blood in my veins right now. She would let me. I would not have to take her body, would not have to pleasure her or take pleasure for myself.* He gulped against a sudden onslaught of blistering lust. Oh, the temptation…

"I have a mission for you," he repeated past an aching throat. *Resist.*

"Let me guess. I am to protect the girl."

Yes. But… "Your arrogance displeases me."

"I am a warrior, not a bodyguard," Zane spit.

"You are whatever I tell you to be. I do not trust Tagart. If he aids her, fine. But if it appears he is going to betray her…"

A muscle ticked in Zane's jaw. "Is that all? *King*," he added after a tense pause.

"No. You will return to your team, and you will listen to what they plan. I will do the same. Tomorrow we will share what we have learned and decide our course of action. The gods think to divide us, but we will not allow them to succeed. Will we?"

A slight hesitation before Zane gave a stiff nod.

When the vampire stalked away, Layel glanced in the direction of the waterfall. His hour had passed. Was Delilah waiting for him? Perhaps she frolicked in the lapping water even now, naked and glistening. The stray thought arose, an image of exactly that forming, and he was halfway there before he realized what he was doing.

CHAPTER TEN

ALYSSA HAD SPENT the night searching both the Inner and Outer cities with Shivawn, flying from one to the other—or galloping atop a centaur, in Shivawn's case. Not once had he spoken a single word to her. Not in all their hours together.

Frustration rode her hard, sinking sharp claws into every part of her body. They were now on their way back to Valerian's palace. She could see it on the horizon, a towering stone and crystal monstrosity atop a steep cliff. Shivawn was still perched on a centaur and she kept pace beside him, floating rather than walking or riding. There were three benefits to this: he was always within her view. If she walked, she would have stumbled. And no centaur would have allowed her on his back without a fierce argument she didn't have the fortitude for.

A group of minotaurs and griffins raced past them, headed into the Outer City. They were laughingly chasing a pretty white unicorn. Had Alyssa any spare time, she would have joined them and tried to capture the horned stallion. A wish would come in handy right about now.

"Your king will not be pleased," she said, to break the silence and distract herself. No, that wasn't entirely true. She craved his voice as much as she craved his touch. Surely if she spoke first, he would follow suit. "All we learned was that two creatures of nearly every race disappeared in the blink of an eye. Nothing more. Valerian will desire the reason."

Shivawn gave no reply.

Sandy braids flapped around his temples. He appeared as cold in profile as he did from the front. But he was only cold with *her*. In the cities, he had flirted outrageously with the women. He had been charming, full of smiles and laughter.

Only one night had he been anything other than cold with Alyssa. Only one night had he been white-hot....

She shivered, remembering.

He growled low in his throat. "Wipe those thoughts from your mind, woman. Now."

The sound of his voice startled her, much as she'd been craving it. "Wh-what thoughts?" He couldn't know she was visualizing their night together, his body slipping and sliding inside of hers...sweeping her high, so high... Oh, the pleasure...

"Sex. Bodies. Straining." Pause. "Us."

Her eyes rounded. "How did you know?" Then her cheeks colored at what she had just confirmed.

"I can smell your desire," he said with disgust.

Disgust? "That offends you?" she all but snarled.

"You are not my mate, woman. Wanting me will bring you nothing but pain."

She would be wise to listen to him. Wanting him had brought her satisfaction only once and, as he predicted, pain many times. But... "You can't know that I'm not—"

"Yes," he said firmly, "I can."

Her pride meant nothing in the face of an answer. "How can you know? Beyond any doubt?" Surely she would not have desired him this strongly if they were not meant to be together. Surely she would be able to consume someone else's blood.

"I would sense it and be...unable to take another."

Unlike her, he was strong, so of course he had had other lovers since their night together. Nymphs weakened without sex. "You've had others?" she found herself asking anyway.

A terse nod.

She wanted to vomit. She had been with no one else, had hoped he would come only to her to renew his strength. "I would have helped you."

"I did not want you."

Her stomach churned with more of that horrible sickness. Did she like being hurt? It would seem so, as she continued to invite him to cut down her feminine pride. "I could kill every woman you've touched. You know that, yes?"

He stiffened, every muscle in his body going taut. And though she could only see his profile, she glimpsed the hatred rippling under the surface of his cheeks. Saw the furious onyx glow in his eyes. "Spoken like a true parasite."

Parasite? *That's* how he viewed her? Oh, that hurt. "I'm not asking more of you than you are willing to give, Shivawn. I'm only asking for a chance to be the woman to see to your needs. Just for a little while."

Finally he faced her, twisting atop the saddle. She could not read his expression. "Do you realize how pathetic you sound?" A deadly calm laced the words.

Yes, she did. Still she pushed him, refusing to be embarrassed by her desire. "I want you in my bed. That's all. I'll do anything to get you there. Usually you'll bed anything female. Why not me?"

The cliff seemed to tilt, its incline becoming impossible for the centaur. Silent now, Shivawn dismounted and shooed him away with a polite, "Thank you. You may return to the stable on your own."

The horse-man trotted off.

Shivawn watched until the last clop of hooves could be heard. If he knew she was still beside him, he gave no hint. What thoughts tumbled through his head?

"I want you in my bed," she repeated to gain his attention.

"You *had* me in your bed."

Strands of her dark hair whipped in her face, she shook so badly. Motions clipped, she hooked them behind her ears. "Yes, and I want you there again."

He pushed out a breath as he turned to her. His face was chiseled perfection, not a single flaw. "You are forcing me to say something you will not like hearing."

Again she felt sick, but she could not stop herself. She had to know, beyond any doubt, what was keeping him from her. "What? Say it."

"Are you sure you wish to know?"

Her blood chilled, ice crystallizing in her muscles and bones. "Yes. Tell me." Desperation dripped from each word. She hated herself for it, but it was too strong to hide.

"Bedding you was not…good for me. I did not even come."

"But…but…" Oh, gods. His proclamation echoed in her ears. *Bedding you was not good for me.* "You're lying. You have to be."

"No."

Her mouth floundered open and closed. The truth of his claim was there, in his hardened expression. She'd never experienced pleasure as she had with Shivawn and he had felt nothing? She'd known her bite had bothered him, but she hadn't realized his unhappiness had lingered all through the night.

Mortification consumed her, chomping her pride into little pieces before spitting out the bones.

"I'm sorry. I didn't want to tell you, but…"

Still reeling, she resumed her journey up the cliff, now desperate to escape him. To hide. How could she have been so wrong? She'd had a few other lovers over the years, yet none of them had complained. None had left unsatisfied.

That you know of.

For a moment she felt as if spiders were crawling over her skin, and she scratched at her arms. For so long she had dreamed of winning this man's heart. Her every action had been an attempt to impress or charm him.

She was not a warrior, not at heart, but she had trained as one, knowing Layel would not allow her to accompany him to the nymph stronghold otherwise. She had fought, she had killed. For Shivawn. Blood coated her hands. Always. Nothing cleaned them. For Shivawn.

She had risen through the ranks of the vampire army by any and every means necessary.

For Shivawn.

Yet he had never wanted her, not even the time he'd given himself to her. A nymph—a creature renowned for being more sensual than selective—found her so unappealing, he had left her bed still hard and aching. Had probably bedded another woman immediately afterward to relieve the ache.

"Alyssa," he said softly, and she heard him as clearly as if he were shouting. Damn it, she hadn't put much distance between them.

Her feet almost hit the ground, even her ability to float

trying to abandon her. *Keep moving. Don't slow.* "Did you come to me only because Joachim's human refused you? Did you not desire me for me, even a little?" Alyssa had caught him leaving Joachim's room one evening, the one evening they'd spent together, and he had reeked of human.

His eyes had been dark, haunted, and she'd later learned that Shivawn's human slave had chosen the other nymph warrior as her mate, leaving Shivawn without a woman. And because nymphs needed sex to survive there had been no better time for Alyssa's seduction of him. She had thought, *Finally. He will have me. He will desire me as I desire him.*

But I could not bring him to orgasm. Oh, gods, oh, gods. "Did you?"

"Yes, I used you. And, no, I did not want you."

"Did you—" *gods, why are you doing this to yourself?* "—did you think of her when you were inside me?"

There was a painful, tension-filled pause. "Does it matter?"

Oh, gods. That was answer enough, yet she still had to hear him say it. Maybe then her love for him would die. Maybe then her obsession would wane. "It matters. Tell me. Say it."

He uttered another sigh. "Then, yes. I did. But even then…"

Even then he could not come. Curse him! And curse herself!

Her nails elongated as she curled her fingers into fists, cutting past skin, drawing her own blood. She was panting, she realized. "You should not have used me while thinking of another."

"No, and for that I'm sorry."

She laughed bitterly, felt his eyes boring into her back.

"I must be like all the other women in your life, throwing myself at you, willing to accept any scrap of affection you toss my way. Not that you ever tossed me a moment to cherish. A moment to sigh over in the dark of night, to dream of for years to come and to giggle over with friends." If she'd had any friends.

"You could not help yourself. The allure of the nymph is impossible to ignore."

But no other nymph had made her crave things she could never have. "Do you laugh about us when you are alone?" she asked, striving for an unconcerned tone. Inside, she still seethed. What right did Shivawn have to hurt her like this? To use her and humiliate her? To treat her as beneath him? None. An idea took root in her mind and refused to leave. *No, I cannot do it.*

But he deserves it.

"Laugh? At who?" He quickened his step until he was beside her, obviously no longer content to lag behind.

She pushed the snow-white branch of a ghost tree from her path, taking a small bit of satisfaction when it slapped Shivawn in the cheek and he grunted. "At the women," she said. "At your females. At those of us who throw ourselves at you."

"I hope I am not so callous as that. I would die without those females. I need them as much as they want me."

Clearly, she wasn't part of the "they." Bastard. *No one else will give him what he deserves. Not the gods, not his king, not my king. I must do it.* "I wonder why I ever desired you." And why, despite everything, she still did.

"I have wondered that myself," he replied darkly.

"You are strong," she offered, not wanting to admit the real reason.

"So are others."

"You are handsome."

"Others are more so."

True, and yet…no one else had eyes like his. Most likely some shared the color, but not the pain banked there, the hint of, well, a man possessed by ghosts and dark passion.

Once, many years ago, she had glimpsed the beast inside him.

He didn't know it, hadn't seen her, but she had been mesmerized by him.

His father… She gulped, had sworn never to think of that terrible time again, lest it grow wings and fly from her memories, reminding him. But the dark images flooded her, images of that fateful day marking the beginning of her obsession, and she couldn't stop them.

Even though Alyssa was of mixed blood, both a vampire and a demon, she never allowed herself to think or act like a demon. Too many races despised them. As she appeared every inch the vampire, the deception wasn't difficult.

But that day—that week, actually—she'd snuck her way inside the demon camp, curious about the father she had never known, about his people. For days she'd watched them, beginning to despise them herself. They killed for fun, delighted by their victims' screams. They did more than drink blood; they ate flesh.

One day, several demon warriors—her brothers—ambushed Shivawn's father, an innocent, during peace talks. For sport, they had tortured the man in the most horrendous ways, and young Alyssa had stayed hidden in the shadows, cowering, too afraid to try and make them stop.

Shivawn had seen his father's limp body nailed to a tree

and attacked. A battle had been waged and he had ultimately triumphed, slaughtering the demons responsible. His love for his father had shown in every slash of his blade, in every roar of fury and helplessness that had left his mouth. That was what she'd wanted with her own father: loyalty, love. She hadn't gotten either, but by then, she hadn't wanted either. Not from him. Perhaps that was why her hopes and dreams had shifted so easily to Shivawn.

Afterward, with the demon pieces nailed to trees as his father had been, he had dropped to his knees and sobbed. He had gathered his father tenderly, reverently and begged the gods to awaken him.

Alyssa had ached for him, even as fantasies had begun spinning in her mind. Fantasies of Shivawn being her brother, standing beside her if anyone ever learned the secret shame of her dual heritage.

As the years had passed and she'd grown into a woman, her fantasies of hearth and home had taken a more sensual slant. No longer had she wanted him as her brother. She had wanted him as her lover. No one else would do, though she'd given several a chance. They hadn't compared to her dreams of Shivawn, not in any way.

Determined to experience the bliss of Shivawn's touch, she had journeyed to the nymph camp and sought him out. He'd taken one look at her and vomited.

She hadn't known why, still didn't, but she hadn't given up. *Should have. Should have given up.* Look where she'd ended up. Broken, raw. Physically doomed.

"I've seen the way the vampire soldiers watch you," he said now, slicing his way into her dark thoughts. "Choose one of them for your mate."

While she loathed the thought of him with another

woman, he could not wait for her to have another man? *Give him what he deserves...*

I am not like my demon sire. I am not vindictive and corrupt.

Nor are you a martyr. He will hurt others this way until he is stopped.

Yes, he would. "They do not appeal to me," she finally replied, not yet ready to act.

"I am nothing special."

"Perhaps I like the way you kill." She had seen him in battle, had even fought next to him.

His lips twitched, as if for once he was amused by her. "You try and act like a warrior, vampire, but I have seen you hesitate before delivering the death-blow. You might fight, but you do not like it."

He was the first to notice her secret revulsion during battle—a revulsion that stemmed, no doubt, from her desire to set herself apart from the demonlike acts of war—and she blinked in shock. Fought against a softening in her chest. "You know nothing about me, nymph." She uttered the last with as much disgust as she could muster. "You avoid me at every turn."

"True, but I know women."

Oh, that burned. Wiped away any hint of softening. She was one of a thousand others to him. *Give him what he deserves!*

Yes, she decided. Yes.

"I have always wondered why you fight when you so obviously hate it."

"You? Wondering about me? That's twice now you've admitted to such a thing. I'm surprised you haven't exploded."

Once again his lips twitched.

She ground to a halt. He kept moving, realized she'd stopped and turned, facing her. Looking at him, her heartbeat sped up. *Are you truly going to do this?*

"Nothing I've said has been meant to hurt you," he said softly. "But I had decided weeks ago to take a female as my own, even one who is not my mate, because I crave stability. That means I cannot be with you and you cannot…ask it of me again."

Any female would do but her, was what he was saying. *Yes, I am going to do this.* Slowly, so slowly, she closed the distance between them. "You do not want me to come around and bother her."

He gave a stiff nod.

"Then I will give you my word, Shivawn."

Slowly his features relaxed.

"I will not come around your woman."

"Thank you."

"But then, neither will you."

He frowned.

She launched herself at him with the last reservoir of strength she possessed, fangs bared.

VALERIAN CRADLED his mate in his arms, his skin sweat-slicked from the pleasure they had just shared. This woman never ceased to amaze him. She was beauty personified, softhearted, yet a tigress every time they fell into bed.

"If Shivawn doesn't return soon, I'll have to leave the palace and search for him. He is faithful, and would've sent word of a delay. If he could."

Shaye stiffened in concern. "Do you suspect foul play?"

"I'm not sure, but something isn't right."

"The vampire—"

He shook his head, certain. "Alyssa will not hurt him. She obviously loves him. Besides, nymphs and vampires are allies."

"Uh, I hate to break it to you, sugar, but a woman in love is an ally to no one but her heart."

"I know women, moon, and—"

"Stop right there. You don't know shit, big boy. Otherwise you would not be telling your wife how you learned about other women."

Softhearted? Had he seriously thought such a word in connection with his human mate? He pressed his lips together to keep from laughing. So fierce and possessive, his wife. She would slay anyone who "made a play for his bod," she had once said. And he would not have it any other way.

She placed a kiss on his chest, just above his heart, tongue flicking out and leaving a spark of fire. "Maybe I'll talk to Poseidon. He might tell us what's going on—if he's bored and looking to stir up trouble, that is."

Much to Valerian's consternation, Shaye and the fickle, annoying god had become friends. "No. Every time you speak with him, some kind of disaster happens."

"Hey, he brought us back together. Give the guy a break."

"I would like to break his—"

She slapped a hand over his mouth.

"I heard that," an irritated voice said.

Valerian reached for his sword, but it disappeared the moment his fingers curled around the hilt. Scowling, he glanced at Shaye to make sure she was covered, saw that a black silk sheet draped her from chest to ankle and relaxed. Barely.

The air crystallized in front of the bed, thickening until

the body of a man appeared. Some women had said Poseidon was the most beautiful male ever to walk under the sea. Lustrous hair, blue eyes. Muscles, power. Valerian did not see the appeal, but he covered Shaye's eyes anyway.

That amused the god, and he laughed. "As if that will make a difference."

Valerian bit the inside of his cheek to keep from responding. One wrong word, and the sea god might destroy the entire city. Almost had, in fact.

Shaye shoved Valerian's fingers away. "Welcome, oh mighty god of the sea. And since you have graced us with your presence, I wonder if you would be willing to help us. We seem to be missing two of our soldiers," she said. "Well, three now. Would you know anything about that?"

"Perhaps," was the unconcerned reply. Poseidon strolled to the far wall and traced his finger over the center. Valerian's sword finally reappeared—hanging upside down with colorful ribbons falling from the tip.

Not a word.

"Will you tell us?" Shaye asked sweetly. "Please."

Valerian squeezed her side in warning.

"I'll give the women here another lesson in women's rights," she added. "That will frustrate the warriors and provide much entertainment for you."

Valerian shuddered. Last time she'd done such a thing, his warriors had gone without sex for days and had become snarling beasts, picking fights with everyone they encountered.

Poseidon shrugged and then disappeared as if he'd never been. Valerian thought that was the end of it and was grateful. He didn't like the god. But then that unearthly voice whispered across the room, startling him.

"The first two are playing a little game. The third, well, he was just eaten alive."

The god's laughter echoed long into the night.

CHAPTER ELEVEN

LAYEL NEVER REACHED the waterfall that night.

Along the way, he had encountered Jada, the female nymph and Broderick's sister, and she had been determined to have him "for strength" because she "trusted him, friend to her king."

Over the years, many females had offered themselves to him. Unattainable as he was, he'd been labeled a challenge, a prize. He had denied them all, yet some had still claimed to have lain with him. In their anger over his rejection, the stories had not been kind.

Here, now, there were two beautiful females vying for him. One, a temptation. One, an annoyance, though Jada's beauty outshone even Delilah's. Or would have, to some. To him, Jada's hair was too fair, her sapphire eyes lacking any hint of purple. She was tall and slim with curves that should have been impossible, her nipples permanently hard.

Yet all he'd been able to think about when she pressed herself against him was the lean firmness of Delilah's body and how perfect it was to his palms. How he loved the way her nipples hardened right before his eyes.

He'd pushed Jada away, but in her ardor she'd taken the gesture as approval and had quickly stripped. He'd been unmoved. As unmoved as he'd been for the past two hundred years, which made Delilah's ability to tantalize him all the more undeniable. Thank the gods he had not gone to the waterfall, after all, but had hunted animals to distract himself.

Had he found her, he would have drunk from her. How close he'd come to talking himself into it.

And now, after an uneventful day by himself—without a run-in with his team, the other team or even the power-loving gods who had, for whatever reason, not forced a challenge on them today—Layel found himself stalking to the waterfall, unable to turn away this time. What was Delilah doing? Was she all right? Night had fallen again. He should have seen her, heard her.

To his consternation, she was not there. Even her sweet scent was curiously absent. There should have been a hint of it, at least a lingering imprint of her essence. Instead, it was as if she had not once neared the area. That didn't seem to matter to his body. Hard and aching, that's what he was, because she'd offered herself to him here in this location.

Thoughts of her played through his mind. Thoughts of her naked, writhing. *His.*

In his mind, every move she made was a sensual dance *for him.* Every sound that escaped her moist, ripe lips was a benediction *to him.* Every beat of her heart was a mating call.

The images were wrong, so wrong, but his mouth watered and his teeth sharpened. What would it take to purge her from his mind? Besides killing her, which he'd already admitted he could not do, there was only one thing left to try….

He would have to drink from her. No more resisting.

He'd told her that he never would. Yet the idea had been planted, had grown and intensified. Now, he realized he *must.*

He was a bastard for even considering it; he was lacking in honor and integrity. Truly, he was a monster. She wanted everything from him, but he only meant to take. He was going to fill his veins with her life's nectar, was going to reduce her to a meal. Finally he would know the taste of her and then he could forget her. His fantasies had built her up, but reality would tear them down. There was no possible way she could taste as wonderful as he imagined. No one could.

Sex would not enter into the arrangement. This time, when he placed his lips on her body, he would control himself. There was no better time to drink from her. Hunger did not ride him; weakness had not claimed him. He had gorged on the dragon yesterday and didn't need the blood.

Where was she? If she'd bathed in the waterfall or lounged on the moss-covered rocks, she'd left no trail. Layel walked through the forest, muted beams of twilight, hazy purples and pinks, illuminating his path. The lush emerald trees were different from those in Atlantis, yet somehow familiar to him after only two days. More moss covered the ground, soft against his feet.

Were he home, he would be training with his army and thinking of ways to thwart and slaughter the dragons. He would be torturing the fire-breathers locked in his dungeon, their screams his only real sense of peace.

Evil, he'd often been called. He did not deny it. *Couldn't* deny it. His heart was decayed. Rotted. His soul was black. No longer was he a man Susan would have loved. At the moment of her death, he had become everything his beloved mate had despised.

Yet there was no going back. No reverting to the man he'd once been. Not for him. Hate pulsed in his veins, thicker than blood. Revenge was the only thing he allowed in his mind.

Until Delilah.

Always his thoughts returned to her. Gods, how she haunted him. He should be searching for Zane, who had not yet shown up to report on his team. He should be planning his next move against Brand and Tagart. Instead, here he was, wishing for a taste of Delilah.

What was it about her that constantly drew him? While she possessed a breathtaking beauty, a sharp wit and an undeniable hum of energy, she would never hesitate to betray a lover to protect her sisters. That much was obvious every time she looked at Nola—a woman he wasn't even sure Delilah liked—with determined loyalty. There was no warm affection in her voice when she spoke to the girl, no softening of her expression. Yet she clearly felt responsible for her.

A flicker of jealousy sprang inside his chest, and he blinked in surprise. Jealousy? Over what? Delilah's loyalty to her tribe? Surely not, but he didn't want to consider the other option: that Delilah placed the welfare of another above him.

Made no sense, that line of thought. He didn't truly know her, certainly didn't like her and wouldn't even contemplate a future with her. *You're confused,* his mind explained. *That's all. Your life has been disrupted. When things return to normal, so will your emotions.*

Where was she?

He sniffed the air. The sweet scent of her, so at odds with her warrior personality, suddenly seemed to infuse every crevice of the surrounding area, yet he caught no glimpse of her. Still his cock swelled once again, the hunger he'd denied only moments ago suddenly upon him. His mouth watered. Blood…

She was near.

A tender side of him he'd thought as dead as his heart broke through mire and debris, shocking him. *You cannot do this to her. She will feel betrayed. She will hurt.*

His teeth gnashed together so sharply his gums were sliced. What was better? Delilah's betrayal or Susan's?

The answer was obvious. Or should have been. Delilah must be purged from his mind. Soon, very soon, she would be. For he would not stop hunting until he found her. The gods could summon them for another challenge at any time. The losing team would then be called before the fire, and Layel would be forced to wait. If he lived through another counsel.

"Eat this," he suddenly heard Delilah say. "You're pale."

Every cell in his body heated, sparking into small infernos. There was a muttered reply from a female. Most likely the other Amazon, Nola. Layel floated above the ground with only a thought, nearing the door of leaves arching in front of him.

Remaining in the shadows, he peeked through. And there she was, crouched beside Nola. His azure-haired, violet-eyed tormentor. The two teams were together, sitting around a fire, some kind of animal roasting in the center.

Tension swirled between winners and losers.

The teams might be together, but they were in no way unified. Glares abounded. Zane sat off to the side, sharpening a stick. Every few seconds, his narrowed gaze flicked to Delilah and Nola. His skin was flushed, his motions a dance of power, yet he pulsed with anger.

He *would* have to wait, it seemed. Layel broke through the trees with only the slightest rustle and approached the other vampire. As king, it was his responsibility to ensure no animosity grew between them. When he sat, Zane gave no indication he noticed Layel's presence.

Everyone else, however, did.

Conversations tapered to quiet. There was even an angered hiss from Brand. Layel ignored him, knowing it would rouse Brand's beast. Trying not to grin with the thought, his gaze shifted to the Amazons. Nola stared down at her food, flicking it with her fingers every few seconds but never actually eating. Delilah tipped back a coconut half, draining the milk inside.

Her eyes remained on Layel, ensnaring him, holding him captive. He could not have looked away had a blade been pressed to his throat. Her gaze was guarded, no hint of her emotions present. Why? What did she hide?

He bared his fangs at her and licked them.

Finally. Emotion. A flash of desire before she gulped and looked away. Only then, free of her powerful hold, did he realize something hard and tight had taken residence in his chest. Slowly it loosened, however, allowing him to breathe. His cock did not settle but continued to throb.

"All is well?" he asked Zane, noticing the bloodstained lips his friend still possessed. Blood always strengthened a vampire no matter its source, but blood overflowing with wine or medicines could cause a spike in aggression, anger and violence. Could that be the cause of Zane's current dark mood? Had he taken blood from someone inebriated?

"Yes." No pause in movement. Every time they were summoned, the god continued to remove their weapons, forcing them to make more at every opportunity. During their "off" hours, they had to be prepared for anything. "I am well."

Truth? A lie? "You do not like your new duties, then."

"I do not mind them." Flat tone, twitching muscles.

"Something is wrong with you, Zane."

"Yes."

At least he did not deny it. "Tell me."

"As king?"

"As…friend." The one friend Layel had allowed himself over the years was Valerian, and that was only because he'd known Valerian before Susan's death. They'd met in the Outer City and had become allies when they were too young to know better—the mixing of the species was most often frowned upon. They'd played together, discovered a passion for females together, and they'd fought together, guarding each other's backs.

After Susan, well, the nymph king had taken him in and cared for him until the emotional anguish gave way to a thirst for revenge.

Perhaps Zane needed someone to care for him. His time with the demons had probably razored his soul to tatters.

"Sure you want to know?" Zane inquired.

Layel nodded.

"Before, when you asked me whose blood I had taken…" Zane's fingers tightened over the rock and sparks erupted at the tip of the stick.

His stomach twisted into a knot. *Do not say Delilah.* If her name left the vampire's lips, Layel wasn't sure how he would react. Someone would die, he suspected. "You refused to tell me."

"I took from a woman."

No.

"From an Amazon."

No!

"From Nola."

First there was anger that Zane had strung him along,

most likely out of shame. Then relief. It nearly felled him, and he realized he'd been reaching for the dagger he'd sharpened only a few hours ago. Thank the gods. His hands fell into his lap. "She allowed this?"

"She did, though I doubt she remembers." Yes, that was shame dripping from the words.

He blinked in surprise. "Why would she not remember?"

"I went to her while she was sleeping."

"And she did not awaken?"

"No."

"How?" he insisted. The Amazons were highly trained; they would awaken the moment a man settled atop them. *That* he knew firsthand. And even if Nola had somehow failed to do so, she would have noticed puncture wounds afterward.

"I invaded her mind." The shame morphed into self-loathing.

Layel scrubbed a hand over his face. Some vampires were gifted with the ability to insert thoughts and images into another's mind. Most were not. Layel could not, though he'd always wished otherwise. How much fun would it have been to convince one dragon warrior to slay another?

"I filled her mind with dreams of making love to me, and when she opened her arms and spread her legs, I took what I needed."

"And how did you hide the marks from her? From others?" The moment he spoke, Layel realized what the answer had to be. With as little clothing as the Amazons wore, there was only one hiding place.

Zane glared at him for a moment. "If you were not my king and my friend, you know I would kill you right now, yes?"

"Yes."

"Still you wish me to say it?"

Another, "Yes." Without hesitation. Making him say it might prevent him from doing it again, the shame voiced, never to be forgotten.

"I bit between her legs."

Though he'd known what Zane would say, the words still managed to shock him. *Once again, I have lost control of my men.* Under Layel's rule, the vampires lived by a code. They could drink from dragon warriors anytime they wished, but never—never!—were they to take from another race without permission.

Some creatures enjoyed being bitten, but some refused to even consider it, mistakenly afraid of being turned into blood-drinkers themselves. Over the years, Layel had learned only humans could be turned. Most died, however, which was why he'd never attempted to turn Susan.

Suddenly a flood of his mate's screams bombarded Layel's mind, loud enough to crack glass if they'd been audible, and sharp enough to slice his soul. They were always close to the surface, but he usually could keep them at bay. *Shut up, shut up, shut up!*

It was only when his gaze locked with Delilah's that he was able to beat them into submission. How? Why? He was sweating. Panting. Frowning, Delilah turned to her sister. To escape her hold, he did the same. Thankfully, the screams did not return.

Earlier, Delilah had called Nola pale, but the woman was pallid, the blue lines of her veins evident. Dark circles formed half-moons under her eyes.

"You took too much," he told Zane.

"I know," was the gritted response.

"You will not touch her again. Do you understand?"

"She is your teammate. Of course you want her strong. What next? Will you demand I lose for you?"

Fire burned beneath his skin. "You had best watch your tongue before you lose it. She deserved a choice, Zane, a real choice, and you did not give her one." *Hypocrite,* he thought, for wasn't he planning to take the choice from Delilah?

"I know!"

"Trouble among the bloodsuckers?" Brand laughed, drawing Layel's attention and rage. "How sad."

Several creatures chuckled.

"Save it for the next challenge," Delilah said. At least she sounded angry rather than amused.

Tagart arched a brow, his golden eyes glaring. "An Amazon with a soft heart. Who knew?"

"A dragon with a bleak-looking future," she shot back. "I suspected."

His eyelids slitted. "Is that a threat?"

She pushed to her feet and squared her shoulders. "No. A promise. I will not tolerate insults. Especially from my supposed ally."

Layel was standing a heartbeat later, at her side before he even realized he'd moved. "Challenging a girl, fire-bastard? Perhaps you finally realized the big boys were too much for you."

Tagart's attention settled on him, pure menace. "I haven't forgotten the way you bit me."

"And I haven't gotten your foul taste out of my mouth."

A look of utter rage passed over the dragon's face and for a split second, his bones elongated, revealing a glimpse of snout, razor teeth and green scales. The beast was never far from the surface, apparently.

"I'm not going to wait for your team to vote you off,

vampire. Nor will I allow the gods the pleasure of killing you. I'll take care of you here and now."

Layel's blood boiled, turning his veins to ash. "Come and get me." *Please.*

"Enough," Delilah said, stepping between them.

Layel's gaze snapped to her. The length of her hair whipped around her on a sudden burst of wind. Wind—he suspected each breeze brought the gods closer to them, watching, always watching. She was tense, fingers arched into claws.

That she kept her back to Layel was telling, though he wasn't sure Tagart understood. The dragon was smirking now, as if the Amazon thought to protect him. *Stupid.* Delilah trusted Layel not to attack her while vulnerable.

Stupid, he thought again, this time directed at Delilah. She should not trust him like that. She should run from him. Fast and forever.

I would probably chase her.

Stupid! That curse had been for himself. She was not his, could never be his.

For that, more than anything, he suddenly wanted to launch himself at Tagart and eat him, organ by organ. The bastard's eyes would be the last to go, so he could see every terrible thing Layel did to him.

He fingered the hilt of his blade. "I'm waiting."

Delilah reached back and ran her palm over his stomach. He barely held in a shocked, aroused gasp.

Whatever look she gave the dragon had his cheeks coloring. He tossed Layel a final glare before stomping toward the trees, Brand close at his heels. They probably meant to plan his murder. He hoped they did. Foiling their attempts might prove to be a nice distraction.

Multiple sets of eyes watched as Delilah turned and faced him. Those violet irises framed in black climbed the length of his body, practically stripping him bare. He found himself stepping backward, away from the strength and heat and temptation of her.

"The waterfall," she whispered. "Will you meet me?"

"Will you be there this time?" he whispered back, hating the huskiness of his voice.

She shivered, her lips falling open in surprise. "You went?"

"Last night? No," he said. Truth. But obviously she hadn't gone at all.

"And yet your tone chastised me for not going. No, don't say another word. I was detained by my sister," she explained.

He would never admit to the relief he felt that she hadn't changed her mind.

The creatures around the fire leaned toward them, shamelessly doing their best to listen to the conversation. Layel hissed at them, and they quickly looked away. Someone even began whistling.

An eternity ticked by while Delilah studied him. No, surely only a few seconds had passed. "Did you pleasure the female nymph?"

Was that jealousy in her tone? He was not delighted by that. Really. Still refusing to voice the answer she seemed to crave, he said, "Would you care if I did?"

"No. Of course not." She lowered her gaze to the ground. "But I saw you in the forest. With *her.* So—"

He didn't owe her an explanation. He didn't. "What is to keep you from becoming distracted by your sister again?"

As she eyed the surrounding crowd, she said softly, "I want to talk to you. About the nymph. Did you—"

Would she never allow him to change the subject? "If you truly saw us, you would know what happened."

"I didn't stay and watch until the end. I would have killed her, and then your team would have been down two members."

So even though she'd thought he was bedding another woman, she'd been unable to commit a deed that might ultimately bring about his execution. The thought warmed him. "If you go to the waterfall, I will not be in a mood to talk."

Instant arousal banked her features. "What will you be in the mood for, then?" she asked in a wine-rich tone. "The same thing you probably did with the nymph?"

"If you show up at the waterfall, Delilah, I will bite you. Do you understand? I will drink your blood."

Her breath hitched. "But you swore never to touch me like that." She didn't sound upset by the possibility that he had changed his mind. "Did you bite the ny—"

"I lied, as you are always accusing me of doing. I *will* bite you."

Frustration darkened her expression. "What else have you lied about? The nymph?"

If she said that word one more time, he might…laugh. "You cannot trust me. Ever. That is all you need know."

"This is how you think to lure me to the waterfall? I may be an Amazon and not all that familiar with the ways of men, but even I know to expect a few tender words in a situation like this. You'd better rethink your approach if you really want me to join you. Because I doubt that ugly little nymph will be there."

His lips twitched and he felt a tickling in his throat. "I did not ask you there. You asked me. And I will go. Part of me hopes you will stay away."

Sparks lit her eyes, a blaze of fury and that seemingly ever-present arousal. "And what does the other part of you hope? That the sex-hungry bitch will go instead?"

"That you come, that I can rid myself of the thought of you."

She softened somewhat, as did the growing ache in his chest. "And if you can't?"

"That you'll be so weak from loss of blood that you fail during the next challenge and are chosen to die." There was stark truth in his tone, though he wasn't sure he meant a word.

"Liar." She arched a brow, not giving him the reaction he'd expected. "You want me, you're just afraid to admit it. Besides, you've told me time and again never to trust you," she said with utter confidence. "But you never told me if you bedded the nymph."

Do not give her the reaction she's looking for, either. "And I won't. Now, I've delivered my warning. That's all I can do. Come to the waterfall at your own peril."

"I'm not afraid of you, Layel," she said, raising her chin.

"Foolish."

"Confident in my abilities."

"Foolish," he insisted. But *he* was the foolish one. The world around them had long since faded. He was aware of her and only her. Anyone could have snuck up on him, and he would not have cared.

She stepped closer to him, cutting away at his prized personal space to gaze up at him in challenge. "Tell me one thing at least."

"Let me guess. The nymph?"

Irritation curtained her features as she snapped, "Do whatever you want with her. I don't care."

When she sounded ready to slay the other female? She cared.

"What I want to know," Delilah continued, closing even more distance, "is if you would mourn for me if I did get executed."

Any closer, and he might wrap his arms around her. Might press his lips to hers, and devour her. The thought of her death…hurt him, made him want to hold on and never let go. "No," he managed to squeeze past the lump growing in his throat. "No."

Surprising him still further, she grinned slowly. "Once again I'm forced to remind you that you told me never to believe a word out of your mouth," she said. "I think you would miss me greatly." With that, she sauntered off in the direction of the waterfall.

CHAPTER TWELVE

WOULD LAYEL COME?

And had he touched that nymph bitch? Delilah had the sudden urge to drive the length of her wooden blade through the nearest tree. Or heart. She wasn't picky. She'd spent more time worrying about him and his actions than about Lily, the next challenge and the frightening days ahead. Sadly, she doubted that would change.

All around her, water cascaded into a dappled pool of liquid crystal. Lily pads floated dreamily and lazy moonlight seeped from the sky. Everything around her evoked peace and romance, yet her heart pounded like a war drum.

Layel had stayed away from her for an entire day. *Pleasuring that nasty nymph?* How she'd hoped to see him, had looked for him in every shadow; she'd missed him terribly, dark temper, cruel words and all. She hadn't sought him out, though, lost in the wake of Tagart's sickening revelation. He'd had a mate. Obviously he still mourned her.

Delilah couldn't tolerate the idea of Layel thinking of another woman while he touched *her.* And the nymph?

"Argh!" She was taking a chance—a big one—just to appease her curiosity. At least, that's the reasoning she gave herself. Tomorrow, perhaps, she would believe it.

Right now, she wanted to experience possession. Utter, dream-about-forever possession. He wanted Delilah. On some level, he wanted her.

Oh, gods. Would he come?

Layel had considered her a fool for suggesting such a rendezvous, but then he had suggested one, as well. Perhaps she *was* a fool, but she had to know more of him. The compulsion to be near him, have his teeth in her vein, made her crazed. Wonderfully crazed, and that compulsion only intensified with every moment that passed. Actually, it was now buried so deep inside her she could not find and destroy it. Could only tolerate its ever-growing presence and follow wherever it happened to lead.

Would he never come?

Back and forth she paced, droplets of water splashing her calves. Tendrils of fear drifted through her. She didn't fear him. She was too much a warrior, too well trained, to let him conquer her completely and hurt her in the process. What she feared was liking everything that he did too much. Liking *him*. Wanting, needing, craving more and being unable to let him go.

That didn't drive her away. Oh, no. She doubted anything could drive her away right now. Nothing and no one had ever fascinated her as Layel did. All he had to do was show up and she would take care of the rest.

Another minute ticked by, then another. She had spent most of the day making more weapons, and now she fisted the two blades at her sides before tossing them down. The razored sticks crisscrossed at her back soon followed. They plopped against each other in the moss. Next came the arrows she'd painstakingly carved.

Without them, she felt naked. Not as naked as she wanted

to be, though. With a *humph,* she sat on the driest rock at the water's edge and unwound the laces of her boots. She tossed them aside as she had her weapons and dipped her toes into the warm, soothing water.

Where in Hades was he?

If he'd changed his mind, she would hunt him down and—

"I should not have come," he said, somehow behind her.

Gasping, she twisted. Not a single sound had given away his presence. Not so much as a blur of movement. But he was here now. Right in front of her. Beautiful, eerily so, those haunted, tragic eyes devouring her in a white-hot perusal. At least he wasn't eyeing her with hatred.

But seeing him, the first stirring of vulnerability overtook her. Suddenly she was unsure about what to do and say, and despised herself for the weakness. What did he think of as he looked at her like that? Perhaps nothing good. He still mourned the death of his human mate, after all. Still defended her honor.

Delilah, he threatened to slay at every opportunity.

"But you are here," she finally said.

He gave a stiff nod. "Here I am. I…did not touch the nymph."

Relief thundered through her, so potent she would have fallen if she had been standing. Thank the gods. Heads would have rolled had he delivered a different announcement. "As if I care," she lied airily.

Clearly, he was not so easily fooled. "You care. You shouldn't, but you do. I, however, only came for your neck."

"You need to feed," she said, and the answer suddenly didn't sit well. He hadn't come for her specifically, hadn't come for passion and satisfaction. He'd come for sustenance, nothing more.

"You knew that. I told you so. But need?" He shook his head. "No. I'll never need anyone."

What did that mean?

She hadn't voiced the question, but he answered her anyway. "I want your blood. I do not need it."

"Are you sure?"

He ignored her. "First, you will tell me why you are so willing to help me."

"I don't know."

He studied her, gaze probably taking in details she didn't like him being privy to. How badly she still wanted him, how much she wished she didn't. "You know nothing about me," he said.

She knew he was strong, loyal, resourceful. Kind when he wanted to be, sensual even when he didn't want to be. She knew his kisses were addicting, his body living art.

"And I know nothing about you," he added, stepping toward her.

A tremor slid the length of her spine. Close, so close. She had only to reach out to touch him, but she didn't. She turned back to the water and toyed with the ends of her hair. "No, you don't." Did he even want to? She hoped that he did, but she couldn't be certain.

Another step, and his knees brushed her shoulders. At both points of contact, her skin tingled.

"What happens here can only end badly." Awful words, yet hunger pulsed from his tone, slamming into her and fueling her own.

Sexual desire wasn't new to her. How many nights had she lain awake, sweating, panting, aching and wishing? Countless. How many times had she dreamed of a man to love her? Again, countless. This man didn't love her, but he was strong, beautiful, her secret fantasies come to sizzling life.

Gone was her pride. Gone were her self-protective instincts. With desire this intense, there wasn't room for anything else. They were burned away, rendered ash. She had no defense.

Weak, you are so weak. It was the same kind of weakness she had always despised in others. And for what? For a man. A man who might very well pretend she was someone else while he swallowed her blood. "If your mate were alive—" She felt him stiffen and forced herself to quiet.

"How dare you mention her to me?" he said in a low growl. "How did you learn of her? Who told you? I will rip their throat apart with my teeth." The ugly threat echoed around them. "I should not have come here."

"Wait." *I'm pathetic.* And yet, a hint of fury blended with her desire—fury and jealousy. Part of her hated his mate to the depths of her soul. *Mine,* her mind shouted. *He's mine.* "You're here now. Stay."

He curled his fingers atop her shoulders and squeezed. Cold as he was, she should have experienced a glacial chill. Instead, she burned all the hotter. "What were you thinking? Before?"

"That's none of your concern," she answered with a— gods, how mortifying—blush. If he knew, he would rebuke her. Perhaps try and kill her as he'd threatened.

"Your hands balled as if you were preparing to fight."

"And that frightened you?"

He snorted, and she could almost hear a smile in the sound.

Her chest gave a strange little ache. She wanted to see that smile with an intensity that surprised her. "Some people do fear me, believe it or not."

"I'm sure they do."

Feigning a casualness she didn't feel, she leaned her weight against his legs. He didn't back away, but accepted the weight as his due. She reached back and caressed his legs, up and down, soft and sweet. Her palms burned as she wrapped her fingers around his ankles.

Without any warning, she jerked his feet out from under him.

Caught off guard, he crashed to the ground without even reaching for an anchor, unable to breathe as his lungs emptied. She rocked to her feet, twisted and leapt. Before he could rise, she was straddling his chest.

"You were saying, vampire?"

There was a brief glitter of admiration in his azure eyes, quickly extinguished. "Nice move. Obviously a favorite of yours." No smile as she'd craved, but she could still hear amusement in his voice.

"Thank you. And, yes, I do prefer it."

Slowly he leaned up on his elbows. She flipped her hair over one shoulder, baring her neck, and tilted her head to the side. "Come. I'm tired of waiting for you to begin. Let's get this over with."

He shook his head. "I will not bite you there." Even as he uttered the restriction, he peered at her throat and licked his lips hungrily. "Your teammates will see the wound, and they will not like that you were with me." His voice was thick, almost slurred, as if he'd had too much wine.

"Then where?"

His gaze instantly lowered to her inner thigh.

Another shiver traveled through her.

"Do you like the thought of my mouth there?" he whispered fiercely. Before she could answer, however, he gave another head shake, anger dancing in his eyes. "Never mind. Do not answer. I find that I am more like my men than I thought and I don't want to hear about your desires."

She answered, anyway, for she would not allow him to reduce her to a thing, an object without feeling. When his mouth was on her, he would think of her, and no one else. Know she was hot for him, eager. "Yes. I love it. Dream of it. Crave it."

His pupils dilated, and he sucked in a breath. Against her thigh, she could feel the swift beat of his heart. She blinked her eyes, nothing more, and suddenly she was on her back. He loomed over her, white hair falling like a curtain to brush her cheeks.

"We shall see if you like it after."

"Plan to purposely hurt me?" His scent wafted to her, and there was power in it, something spicy and male. She inhaled deeply, savoring, and their chests brushed, hardness to softness. Her nipples instantly pearled, desperate for contact.

"Spread your legs," he gritted out, ignoring her question.

A command. Though she'd once claimed she would never obey him, she found herself doing exactly as he'd ordered. Her blood was so blistering it had already liquefied her bones.

His heavy weight settled more firmly atop her.

Warm water lapped at her feet, rising higher and higher up her legs, her sides, her shoulders, as if it wanted to caress her. Several strands of hair swished and waved around her, ribbons against her sensitized skin.

"I warned you. Told you to stay away from me. But here you are." Layel crawled backward to his knees. He stared down at her, his face now unreadable. The rest of him, well…there was banked strength in every tensed muscle.

Her stomach quivered. "Here I am. Delilah. Yours." For now. The thought saddened her.

His nostrils flared. His hands hung at his sides, the nails elongated. She imagined them on her body, raking. Stinging a little. Then, of course, he would lick away the pain with a hot flick of his tongue. She would beg for more, so he would turn his focus between her legs, touching… Oh, gods. She shivered as moisture pooled there.

He gave an animalistic growl, pure predator. "Tell me true. No lies. Have you ever before been bitten by a vampire?"

"Yes. It was not pleasant."

His hands moved to her waist and squeezed. In jealousy that he wasn't her first bite? "So you are not addicted to our…ministrations."

"Hardly."

"You say that as though it isn't a possibility—but I assure you that when done right, it can be pleasurable. I wonder, though. Why let me do this here and now if you hate it so?"

Somehow he radiated more of that delicious heat. It surrounded her, dangerous, overshadowing everything in its path and leaving only…a woman. The warrior inside her had long since said goodbye. Would Layel bite her the right way? Make it pleasurable for her?

"Well?" he demanded.

"Curiosity," she told him, giving him the same answer she'd given herself.

"I don't think so."

"All that tells me is that you should think less." She didn't want to tell him the truth, that she couldn't bear the thought of him going to someone else. Possessiveness was as new to her as this all-consuming need.

"Do you want my teeth inside you or not?"

"You talk too much, too."

"Probably," he said, but made no move toward her.

Indecision played over his expression, his first hint of emotion since rising above her. Battle-trained as she was, she suspected he hoped to talk himself out of this. Probably hoped her answers to his questions would aid him in that.

He wasn't going to walk away from her, not after she had humbled herself like this, something she had never done for anyone else, even her sisters. Even Vorik. "If you fail to bite me in the next three seconds, vampire, I'm going to rise. I'm going to leave you here and nothing, not even curiosity, will bring me back."

He gripped her shoulders, pinning them to the ground. But he did not lean into her. "Don't make threats you do not intend to keep. They give your enemy an edge over you."

"One."

He gave her a little shake. "You will not manipulate me, and you will not rush me. Do you understand?"

"Two."

"Look at you." His hands moved slowly, purposefully to her breasts. He kneaded them. Gasping, she fell back and closed her legs against the sudden sharp ache pulsing there. "You can count."

Her jaw tightened. "Three."

She made to rise. He pressed down hard, holding her in place. Riding a crest of fury, she bucked her hips, dislodging him. She worked one of her legs between their bodies and kicked. Her strength must have surprised him, because he propelled backward and landed on his back.

She was on her feet in the next instant. Half of her hair was soaked and dripped down her back, cold, yet doing nothing to dampen the heat of her anger and ever-present arousal. "We are done. I have had—"

She never saw him move.

One second he was on his back, the next he was crouched in front of her, his strong grip banded around her ankles and tugging. Now *she* was propelled to the ground and when she hit, she hit hard. For a long while, she couldn't breathe, couldn't think, dizzying clouds inside her head.

There was no time to recover from it, either. Layel's sharp teeth sank into her thigh without warning. At penetration, he jerked, moaned. She cried out, fell all the way back. Her hands fisted in his hair—soft, silky—not to push him away but to draw him closer.

He did it right.

He drank and drank and drank, her entire existence centered on his mouth.

"Layel," she found herself chanting. A prayer? A plea? Oh, gods. So good. So damned good. It was as though ambrosia flowed from his teeth into her body, heating her up, stroking her nerve endings to a fever pitch.

"Should not...be so...heaven. Heaven." His tongue laved her skin while he continued to suck.

She arched and she writhed, her head thrashing. "More. Take more." Her neglected leg curled over his shoulder, down his back. His hands gripped her hips again, and this time the nails cut deep. She didn't care. Actually reveled in it. His passion was as fierce as hers.

"Don't want... Can't take...too much."

"Take more."

"Shouldn't." He gave one last, strong pull, and then his teeth slid free.

She moaned in disappointment and realized she would have let him suck her dry. Anything for a continuation of that sweet pleasure-pain. Her legs fell limp, boneless. She was gasping, that rush of whatever it was still in her veins. "I said…take more."

He licked his lips and closed his eyes in an expression of absolute ecstasy. "Any more and you would have been unable to rise for hours."

"Don't care."

"Should."

Oh, gods. She was floating. Desperate, needy. She couldn't force her hips to still. They moved up and down, left and right, seeking completion. "Your fingers, then." If he didn't touch her… Damn it! Her arousal was too intense to control or forget. "Touch me. Please."

There was a long, tense pause. "No."

She gripped her breasts and squeezed, just as he had done earlier. Her nipples throbbed all the more, wanting *his* hands. A whimper escaped her. Normally she would have hated herself for making such a sound, but now, this moment, she was owned by her passion.

She was used to taking what she needed, when she needed it. Right now, she needed release. Would die if she didn't get it. "Touch me!"

"No!"

"But I hurt." Mewling, pleading.

"I'm sorry," he said, and he once again sounded drunk. His hot gaze locked on her dripping core. "Has a man ever tasted you there? Tongued you deep?"

In my dreams, you *have.* "A man? No." Vorik had stripped and entered her in seconds, and there'd been nothing but thrusting at that point.

His eyes flared deep, bright blue. "A woman?"

"No. Dreams…" She arched her hips up, up. "Touch."

"Did you like it? In your dreams?"

"Yes." She had. But she wanted more, wanted reality. Many Amazons expounded about the act. *My turn,* she thought. "Need you. Please."

"Only me, or will anyone do?"

She caught a note of jealousy. Perhaps even, dare she hope, possessiveness. "You. Only you." She slid her hands down her stomach, and her navel quivered. Her fingers pushed past the leather waist of her skirt and dabbled just above the place she needed to be touched. She bit her bottom lip. Would he do it?

With a moan, he brushed her hands aside and replaced them with his own, tunneling under the patch of material. Two fingers slid into her wetness, spreading the moisture. His eyes closed, as if he was savoring everything about her.

"Yes, yes!"

His thumb circled her swollen clitoris. "You're so tight. Have you had a man, Delilah?"

Delilah. He'd said her name. He was here with her, not imagining himself with another woman. She nearly came.

Her gaze lowered to his huge erection, straining so proudly against his pants. She had to touch it, had to taste the head peeking from the waistband, had to taste the seed glistening there.

"Have *you?*" she asked him, hoping her sarcasm hid how much power he had over her just then.

His lips twitched. "How many have you had?"

"One," she finally admitted.

"I think I hate him."

What a sweet thing to say. She did not allow herself to

consider the fact that Layel truly would hate the man when he learned she'd given herself to a dragon. Perhaps he would hate her, as well. Even more than he already did.

"Did you love him?"

"I thought I did. No, not true. I thought I could." How could she broach the subject of his mate without infuriating him again? "You have loved before."

He nodded. "Yes. Two hundred years ago, she was my everything." The moment he spoke, all hint of drunkenness left him. His color remained high, but was no longer soft. Every inch of him hardened. He jumped away from her as if she were poisonous. "*Is* my everything. Is still."

He said that while Delilah's arousal glittered on his fingers.

Her own sense of possessiveness sparked with renewed life, even while her fervent arousal chilled. "She is dead."

Though he had just fed, his fangs descended over his bottom lip. A lip stained red with her blood. "You will not speak of her. Ever."

"And if I do?" Delilah challenged, jumping up. Boneless as they were, her knees almost gave out. Somehow she managed to remain standing.

"I have dealt with you gently so far. Do not force me to change that."

"Gently?" She laughed, the sound bitter. "You have hurt me at every turn."

He flushed. With embarrassment? Regret? "Speak of her again and I will not only kill you, I will slaughter your entire race."

Far from cowed, Delilah refused to back down. The man had grieved for two hundred years. He might wish he had died with the woman, but he hadn't. And as far as

Delilah was concerned, it was past time he began living again. "Like you've done with the dragons?"

He was in her face a split second later, breath hissing over her nose and lips. Despite everything, she wanted to jerk him closer, shove her tongue into his mouth and taste more of him. *She* might even bite, so fierce was her need.

"You have no idea of what you speak, so shut your mouth. I did not lie. I did not exaggerate. All of you, even the child queen you spoke of so fondly, will die by my hand."

Fury and disbelief fought for control inside her. "My blood is even now coursing through your body and you dare threaten me and those I love? That is low, even for you."

The electric spark in his eyes died. "I am a king. I do whatever I wish, whenever I wish."

A mirror of her earlier thoughts, but she didn't like them coming from him. "Even a king can be made into a slave."

"So you hope to enslave me, do you? Now the truth is revealed. An Amazon to the core. Give the vampire your blood and watch him beg for more. Is that it?"

"That's not—"

He cut her off with a low snarl. "Know now that I will never beg you for anything, Amazon."

Finally she allowed herself to step closer to him. Still she didn't grab him, didn't kiss him. "That's what you said about drinking from me. How did I taste?" she finished with a smugness she wished to the gods she felt.

His eyelids narrowed to dangerous slits. "I think it will be best if we avoid one another. As I've suggested all along."

"I was about to say the same—" Her knees buckled. She collapsed on the ground, her head seeming to fly to the heavens, an ache in her temples. Groaning, she massaged them. What in Hades had just happened?

Layel cursed under his breath and scooped her up.

"Let me go," she managed to say, though it was breathless, insubstantial.

"You don't really want me to let you go, Delilah."

A mortifying truth. "What's wrong with me?"

"I must have taken too much." He might have added, "I've never tasted anything so rich, so good," but she couldn't be sure. The words were more of a rumble than anything.

"Bastard. I've never fallen before." And she did not like that she had now. With this man watching. And though she might like being in his arms, she couldn't forget the hateful things he'd said to her. "Put me down. Now!"

"Whether or not you've fallen before, if I put you down, that is exactly what you'll do. Again."

"That's a chance I'm willing to take."

He dropped her legs first, and she immediately regretted her demand. Until a cool caress of air hit her bottom half, she hadn't realized how warm he'd made her. Still. She planted her feet on the solid foundation and locked her knees, determined to remain upright no matter the cost.

That's when Layel released her completely, *tsking* under his tongue.

Like a wave in the ocean, she glided forward without the strength to stop herself. Silent, he wrapped his arms around her and held. Simply held. When she heard the strong gallop of his heart, she relaxed. Didn't try to pull away. Just listened. Slowly, so sweetly, his hands stroked up and down her spine.

She'd expected him to push her away. At the very least to say he'd told her so. That he did neither… Would she ever understand this man?

His arms tightened around her, nearly crushing the

breath from her lungs. She didn't complain. She liked it, felt safe. The man now holding her was not the same man who had insulted her.

"You confuse me," she said softly.

"I know. I confuse myself." His breath fanned the top of her head, and then he was resting his chin there. "I still think it would be wise to remain at a distance."

"I—" *Want you to kiss me. I want you to make me forget what we were fighting about. Convince me we have a tomorrow.* "You're probably right."

"Well, well, well," a voice said behind them. "Isn't this nice?"

CHAPTER THIRTEEN

LAYEL DIDN'T YET HAVE his desire under control when the dragon's voice invaded his thoughts. *This is a good thing. Really.*

Delilah stiffened in his arms.

Delilah…her blood was the nectar of the gods, surely. One sip, and he'd been transported to the heavens. One gulp, and he'd experienced more sexual ecstasy than he'd ever experienced while pumping his cock inside of a woman. *Shouldn't have tasted her.* He'd expected to find her ordinary, to reduce her to a meal.

He had failed.

Now he knew the truth. Now he knew that nothing compared to her. Not a rich, aged wine, not ambrosia.

Slowly he lowered his hands to his sides and turned, surprised by just how relieved he was to see the pair of dragons. Surprised the two warriors were standing together as allies when most of the races had already divided against each other, thanks to the gods' cruel game. A moment more, and he might have done something irrevocable. *As if you haven't already.* Something…tender, then.

Gods, this woman challenged him. Angered him, drew him. Tormented him. Cut him up and left him bare. She'd had a lover once, had welcomed the bastard inside her sweet body, and he despised the man with his entire being. *Not a good time for these thoughts.*

He studied his new opponents. Seeing those golden eyes roused every spark of hatred banked inside him. Better. The emotion was a constant part of him, fused to his bones and flowing through his veins. And yet, tonight he felt no urge to attack or kill. Why?

Delilah couldn't be healing the wounds inside him, he assured himself. There was nothing to heal. Some injuries caused irreparable damage, so complete there was nothing left to sew back together. She wasn't making him forget; he could never forget. Perhaps it was that odd sense of relief that held him in place and dulled his rage. The dragons had prevented him from doing something stupid.

More, Delilah had panted earlier, and he'd been very close to giving it to her. He'd been close to giving her everything. Sex, promises…forever. Was still close. Gods, she was no longer in his arms but he could still feel the softness of her body. Worse, that sickening feeling of tenderness lingered. For her.

No one had spoken a word for several seconds—minutes?—he realized. Each of them had been standing in utter silence. Layel knew why he had done so; he'd been lost in thought. Why had they?

"So nice of you to join us," he said to break the quiet, his tone smooth.

Brand and Tagart both blinked at him, as though they couldn't believe what he'd said. They didn't relax, though, clearly still expecting him to attack. Both kept their hands poised over the wooden hilts of their daggers.

"Was he hurting you?" Brand asked Delilah. Though his words were addressed to her, his eyes, narrowed and filled with menace, never left Layel.

Layel wasn't sure what he expected the Amazon to say in response—or what he wanted her to say. Part of him wanted to hear the woman whose blood now flowed through his veins praise him. Stand with him. The two of them against the world, united, two halves of the same whole.

The other part of him yearned to hear her tell them that, yes, he had hurt her. That would be easier to deal with later, when he was alone with his shame. He might be able to convince himself that he hadn't kissed her because he craved her more than he craved vengeance, that he hadn't, for that terribly beautiful moment, treated her as lovingly as he'd once treated Susan.

If only he could convince himself of that. Because, had Susan risen from the dead and been the one to interrupt them, Layel wasn't sure he would have been able to pull away from Delilah. He would not have regretted where his arms had been. Or where his mouth had been earlier.

Right then he felt divided, like two separate beings tugged in different directions. Sadly, both entities had one thing in common: they both hated him. He decided to blame the island. Not only was it dividing brother against brother, it was now splitting him in half, confusing him, causing him to war with himself.

"I'm well," Delilah finally answered the dragon. "There's no need to fret."

You are disappointed.

"There was so much screaming…"

"I am well," she insisted, cheeks blooming with bright color.

"As am I," Layel said, though he highly doubted the dragons would care.

Tagart leaned one shoulder against a tree trunk, a deceptively casual pose. "We have had this conversation before, have we not?"

Without a word or a glance, Delilah stepped away from Layel and closer to the dragons. His enemies, he reminded himself. A growl rose in his throat, but he quickly cut it off. He did not want her near them, wanted only to jerk her back against him, hold her tight, protect her. *This is for the best.*

"Before you ask another question," she continued flatly, "know that I do not have to explain myself to either of you."

"Don't you?" Tagart asked softly, fiercely.

Layel looked between them, from one to the other. Delilah's cheeks again heated, this time with what looked to be guilt. Guilt? He knew she had formed a partnership with the dragon, but he had not thought emotion existed between the pair. Were they… Could they be… He didn't want to consider it, but couldn't keep the question from drifting through his mind: *what if they worked together to destroy him?*

"Walk me back to camp," Delilah told the dragons.

Layel's hands curled into fists as the woman damned herself further. Why ask *them* for an escort? Why not Layel? *Because she* does *care for Tagart,* his mind answered, *and wants him safe.*

She doesn't matter. She's nothing to you. Her blood and her taste and her strength and her sweetness and her soft, warm body, soft, warm moans meant nothing.

His gaze bored into her back. Her spine was elegantly ridged, her thighs strong—tiny droplets of blood caked the inside—and her feet submerged in the water, the very place he'd laid her down. The place she'd writhed and groaned and fisted his hair.

Her white-hot passion had not been faked. Whether she cared for Tagart or not, she *had* desired Layel. Perhaps she, too, felt as if she were two people.

She wavered suddenly and had to brace her legs apart to maintain her balance. "Come, dragons. Let us return to camp. I'm hungry." She sounded frightened, impatient.

Layel frowned. Where was the confident woman who had begged him for more? *Weakened, because of you.* He realized suddenly that of all the things he hated most about this experience, the worst was that he had taken too much of her blood and reduced her to this. He was no better than Zane, whom he'd just lectured on this very subject. The Delilah he knew would have stomped away from them all, unconcerned about who followed and who didn't.

You know her so well, do you?

His frown pulled tight into a scowl.

"Well?" she snapped to the dragons. Again, she wavered.

Layel barely stopped himself from reaching for her.

Tagart bristled at her tone. Brand looked as if he was fighting a grin.

"If you want to keep your internal organs, I would suggest you take her to camp," Layel said. *You trust the dragons to keep her safe?* In her condition, she wouldn't be able to defend herself.

Ask her to stay.

No. No! *Who are you? What kind of man have you*

become? Susan's mate would not act this way. He would protect above all else; he would place a female's safety over his own needs.

Brand's gaze snapped to him, his earlier amusement gone. "I doubt you care about my organs, vampire."

"You're angering the Amazon, which puts you at risk. And if she cuts them out of you, what will I have to eat later, hmm?"

Fury blazed just behind that golden gaze, but it was not Brand who stepped forward, challenging him. It was Tagart, one dagger raised. Delilah whipped out her arm and curled her fingers around his wrist, stopping him.

"No," she said. A single word, but effective.

The man's attention shot to her, as did Layel's. His teeth ground together at the sight of them touching. Better this way. So much better, he told himself again. How many times would he be forced to think it? His teeth were so sharp they cut his gums. His own blood mixed with Delilah's, trickled onto his tongue and down his throat, fiery hot.

Tagart's arm lowered. His gaze did not leave Delilah as he said, "We won't stand for your threats, Layel."

"As I am a king, you should only address me as Your Highness," he said. "What will you do if I refuse to stop, hmm?"

"Sure you want to know, *Layel?*" was the reply.

"Come!" Delilah shouted, her voice trembling. "This has grown tiresome."

You can't protect the dragon from me, he thought, red shuttering over his vision.

Tagart slammed his dagger into the sheath at his side. "We never killed you, vampire, because our king ordered us to leave you alone."

"Tagart," Brand growled, a warning.

A warning that was ignored.

"You hunted us, and we let you because of our king's desire for peace. He knew what had been done to you and your mate, and he regretted it, hoped to make amends. Well, I don't, and the dragon king isn't here. We are. And if there's one positive thing to come of this wretched game, it's going to be your demise. I was stopped last time. I won't be again."

At the word *mate,* Layel's rage intensified to an uncontrollable degree. He launched forward, intending to knock the dark dragon on his ass and slice through his neck with a single cut of his teeth.

Expecting him, the dragon opened his arms and grinned.

But Layel didn't slam into him. He slammed into Delilah, who'd thrown herself in his path. They hit the ground, battering against rocks as they rolled. The fullness of her breasts pressed into his chest, her riotous heartbeat a mirror of his own. Her hair tangled around his face, a cerulean shield.

His teeth were in her neck before he realized what had happened, his mind not yet accepting he'd missed his target. Her sweet, sweet blood filled his mouth once more. But he wasn't gentle this time, wasn't caring. She cried out in pain and fear, knocking sense back into him. He gave a startled gasp and jerked away.

Warm, delicious blood trickled down his chin. He stared down at her, the woman he had just savagely attacked. She lay under him, eyes closed, breath sawing in and out. Not in pleasure, but in pain. Red coated her skin, bathing her. Her eyelids cracked open, her eyes dry, not filled with tears. Not filled with hate, either. Just blind panic that her life might now be over.

And for what? Trying to save an undeserving dragon?

"Why did you do that?" he snarled, rage draining from him and leaving only guilt. Remorse. More of the hatred—for himself. "Why?"

She didn't answer. Probably couldn't. Her eyelids slowly closed again.

Brand gripped Layel's shoulders just as he was leaning down to scoop her up—gently, gently—and he was thrown backward, jostling her. Layel hissed at him. The two dragon warriors hovered over her. Brand caring for her—*that should be me!*—and Tagart glaring at him, daring him to approach.

"…going to be all right," Brand was saying. "I've got you."

"No. I've got her." Layel sprang forward, grabbing her as gently as possible and flying into the air. The warriors could have morphed into their dragon forms and followed him, but they didn't. Why, he didn't know or care.

In his arms, Delilah was limp.

I did this. Me.

Unlike him, she wouldn't heal quickly. Or would she? He didn't know much about the Amazons. *Please let her heal quickly.* But with all the blood he'd taken from her earlier—and now…

"You will live, Delilah, if only to punish me for this."

When he saw a moss-covered bank by another stream, he floated to the ground and slowly laid her down. He ripped the shirt from his chest and wrapped it around her neck to stanch the flow of blood. Careful, so careful.

Her eyelids fluttered open again, brushing away the shadows her lashes had cast.

He almost didn't have the courage to look at her. But he did, forced himself, and his chest lurched. She was so pale, paler than Nola had been.

"You are going to drink my blood," he told her. Not a question. A command. He hadn't shared his blood in two hundred years, but he didn't hesitate to do so now.

She opened her mouth to respond, but only a pained gasp emerged. Using one of his nails, he sliced into his wrist and held it over her mouth. She turned her head away and pressed her lips together.

With his free hand, he grasped her chin and turned her. Two of his fingers anchored on her jaw and pried her mouth open. Blood dripped past her teeth, but she didn't work her throat.

"Drink."

She glared up at him. The thought of ingesting another's blood had to be abhorrent to her. Pagan and disgusting. Only vampires were forced to do so to survive; demons did it just because they liked the taste. Most everyone else despised the act.

"You don't have to worry about becoming a vampire. It only happens to humans." So far, to the best of his knowledge, that is. Saving Delilah was worth the risk, however. "Now, if I must, I will work your throat for you. Drink!"

She swallowed.

"Why did you take his place?" he asked to distract her from what she was doing. Perhaps he craved the answer, as well, but he would never admit it aloud. "Why did you save him?" Only one answer made any sense, and he liked it less now than he had earlier. A mere alliance would not have prompted a woman to willingly take a death-blow meant for another. She would do it for a lover, however…

He'd suspected. Now all he could do was imagine Delilah in Tagart's arms, naked, writhing, gasping the bastard's name as he pumped into her. The way *Layel* wanted to pump into her.

Susan—

No, do not think of her. Not now. Later, he could regret. Later, he could scream and rail and curse. He could hate himself all the more. Later.

Again, Delilah tried to turn her head away. He tightened his grip on her jaw. "You will drink until your color returns."

Her violet eyes flashed with ire.

She was still too pale, lines of tension around her mouth, bruises under her eyes. "You helped me. Now I will help you." The wound on his wrist continually tried to heal itself, and he had to cut himself three more times to keep it open. She never again attempted to turn or close her teeth.

Finally he was satisfied that she'd had enough.

Twin pink circles now dotted her cheeks, and the lines of tension had faded, the skin plumping before his eyes. His relief was too profound to dismiss. Hands trembling, he gently unwound the shirt from her neck.

The teeth marks were still there, still deep, still wrong, but they were no longer gushing. He pushed to his feet, not surprised to find that his legs were shaking, as well. He strode to the water, bent down and cut strips of cloth from his pants. He dipped them into the liquid, soaking them, before striding back to Delilah.

"I've had worse," she said, her voice husky, rough.

The fact that she could talk, astonishing. Her words,

earth-shattering. He had hurt her, yet here she was, trying to comfort him. Why? "I did not mean—"

"I know."

"If you begin to feel sick," he said gruffly, "let me know. With humans, there is always a chance of vampire blood trying to consume the body like a ravaging sickness, making them weaker than ever. I have never heard of such a thing happening to a creature of Atlantis, though."

"Humans can transform into vampires?"

"Some can. Most die."

Delilah pushed out an angry sigh, her first show of negative emotion. "Still. You shouldn't have had me drink. I'm Amazon, not vampire."

"You are alive. That is all that matters."

"Yes, and when I return to Atlantis, I will be even more set apart from my sisters. They will despise me if I am forced to drink their blood to survive."

She considered herself different? Why? "Have they never taken vampire slaves? For that matter, which race was your father?"

She glanced away from him, looking anywhere but in the vicinity of his body. "No, we've never taken vampire slaves. And as for the other question, I'm not telling."

"Please."

She blinked in surprise. "I think that's the first time you've ever asked nicely for something."

"Please," he repeated. "Whichever race he is, he's the reason for your blue hair, yes?"

"No. Several Amazons have been born with unusually colored hair."

He was left clueless, then. "Delilah…tell me."

"You'll laugh."

"I won't. I swear it."

"Centaur," she said, cheeks as red as twin rubies. "And if you dare call me Horse Girl, I will slay you."

Others had called her such a name? He yearned to punish them. "You are too pretty to be called a horse girl."

The color in her cheeks deepened. "I— Thank you. He was not their king, nor was he a warrior. Just a commoner with an irresistible smile. That's all I know about him."

From her tone, he could guess that she did not like those facts. Had probably been forced to prove her strength time and time again because of her father's lack. The need to punish her sisters grew stronger. Which was silly. Time to change the subject. "Why did you do it?" He dripped water onto the injury, trying to clean it without actually touching it and hurting her further.

She didn't have to ask his meaning. "Doesn't matter." She looked away.

"It does."

"Why?"

"You saved him."

Her brow puckered. "I saved you."

"No." What did she mean by that? "You saved Tagart."

She waved a hand through the air. "What if I did? He is on my team."

"And that makes him worth more than your own life?" Layel snapped.

"A team must—"

"Work with him to destroy me if you must, but tell me this. Is he your lover?"

She studied Layel, considering, a bit hesitant. "Would that matter to you?"

Yes. "No."

"Then you wouldn't care if I allowed him to touch my breasts and lick my nipples? You wouldn't care if I guided his fingers inside me and—"

"No! Now, not another word from you." He fisted the material, wringing out the last of the moisture. Clear droplets blended with red, creating a pink river as it slid along the slope of her neck and onto the emerald moss. "If you take him to your bed," he found himself adding, unable to stop the words, "I will eat his heart in front of you."

He could have been mistaken, but he thought he saw a flash of delight in her violet eyes. "There's only one man I crave in that way," she admitted softly.

Thank the gods. *You grow more dishonorable by the second.*

She tried to sit up, but he gripped her shoulders and pinned her down.

"Not yet. Rest."

"Don't order me around."

"I'll order you if I please. I'm stronger than you are."

"Only when I allow you to be."

He crouched beside her and rested his hand on her stomach, needing to feel her heat, her life. Her belly quivered. "You truly think yourself stronger than me?"

"Think?" she snorted. "Your ass has seen more dirt than mine these past few days."

That wrung a surprised laugh out of him. He blinked. Laughter? Now? That hadn't been part of his life in so long he'd forgotten such a thing was possible.

Delilah was staring at him as if mesmerized. "I thought your smile lovely, but...you should laugh more often. You're breathtaking."

He looked away, proving that she was indeed the

stronger of the two. "This madness will have to end soon," he said on a sigh. "We will find a way to end it."

"If we don't kill each other first," she muttered.

How close had she come to death this day? Sadly, he couldn't even blame the gods. "I am...sorry."

"For what?" she asked, sounding genuinely confused.

"Is your mind addled now? Why do you think?"

"For biting me, yes, I know. But explain yourself, explain why you're sorry."

"You were hurt, Delilah."

"By my own actions, Layel, so there is no need to apologize for the bite. I deserve an apology for the other thing, however."

His name on her lips was paradise. "What other thing?"

"You stopped kissing me. You left me...needy."

Heat, so much heat. His muscles twitched in response, his cock hardening. Again. "I will not apologize for that."

She lifted a hand to her neck and traced the wound there. "I would have liked to finish," she said with a pout.

He allowed his fingers to dabble at her navel—pretty, smooth skin, lovely tattoo—his blood flowing faster and faster in his veins. Stop. *Can't.* He moved his fingers to her neck and flattened his palm to the back of her hand. "Your willingness to absolve me is surprising."

"Back to the bite?"

"Of course."

She sighed, loud and long. "Why surprising?"

"You don't strike me as the forgiving type."

Her wrist twisted so they were palm to palm. "What do I strike you as, then?"

He peered down at her, snared in a spell he didn't like but was helpless against. "Lovely. Strong." He grinned slowly. "Vindictive. You were ready to slaughter the dragons for taking your sister."

"That was different."

"Why?"

"My sister could've been hurt."

"You *were* hurt."

"I believe I mentioned that I caused it."

"Which you should not have done and will not do again. I'll have your word."

She shook her head, blue hair dancing around her. "No, you'll not get it. You can try and force me, however."

There was relish in her tone. A dare, a challenge. His eyes narrowed. If she'd been his woman, he would have— Nothing, he told himself. He would have done nothing. She would never be his. To even consider the possibility was a betrayal. "Are you not worth as much as your sisters?"

"I was born to protect them."

Hmm. Did she see herself as worthless when compared to them? *As worthless as you tried to make her feel earlier?* Using his free hand, he scrubbed his face wearily. "If I had hurt you purposely, would you have retaliated?"

"Yes," she answered without hesitation.

"But this time…"

"I don't know." She uttered another of those sighs. "I only know I didn't want you to fight. Not me, not the dragons."

"They would not have bested me."

"I know."

She did? And why did he find such pleasure in the knowledge? "Then why—"

"Your questions will never stop, will they?" She didn't sound upset, just resigned. "Any man who can pin me cannot be easily bested. I know that, yet the knowledge didn't stop the worry that you could have been hurt."

Him. Not Tagart. Satisfaction filled him, as potent as bloodwine. "I have lost several battles over the years," he admitted.

"Then you didn't really wish to kill your opponent," she said simply.

He blinked in surprise. He had known that, but no one else had ever suspected. He'd allowed his own people to think he'd merely been weak in those moments, rather than let them know the truth. Pride had not concerned him on those occasions.

Every battle he had lost, he'd lost because he had walked away after seeing his opponents with their mates. They'd been so deeply in love. His chest had ached, as it was doing now. He hadn't been able to deliver that final blow, separating the couples for eternity. It was either kill them both or not at all. In recent years he had erred too much on the side of not at all.

How could Delilah realize that, after knowing him for so short a time?

He opened his mouth to say something—what, he didn't know—when a trumpet reverberated in the distance. He whirled around, searching through the trees. The trumpet sounded again.

"What is it?" Delilah asked, pulling herself into a crouch.

"I think," he said, dread flowing through him, "we're being summoned for our next challenge."

CHAPTER FOURTEEN

SHE MIGHT NOT SURVIVE the night, Delilah thought. She'd spent her life fighting one battle or another, had gone weeks at a time with barely any food or rest. But she had never been this drained. Literally.

Twice Layel had drunk from her. One encounter she'd enjoyed a little too much. One had been necessary to save him. If he had killed Tagart, her team would have killed *him*. So she'd taken the force of his fury herself. There had been pain in the savage bite, but there had also, unexpectedly, been pleasure. His weight pinning her down…his strength… his ferocity…

He'd told her many humans had died after drinking vampire blood. How would it affect her? As strongly as the man himself did? She shivered as she remembered the way he'd hovered over her, determined to keep her alive, protective, focused only on her, everything she'd ever dreamed—and almost fell from the log she currently balanced upon. Becoming vampire would ruin her. But she couldn't deny the fact that she liked the thought of having some part of Layel inside her. Even his blood.

Mind on the task at hand.

The gods had indeed decided it was time for another challenge. Every member of the two teams had been told to choose a log rising from the water. One team on each side, opposing members facing each other. They were to stand on the tiny planks while the waves danced at their ankles.

Last one standing won.

A worthy warrior can endure heat, exhaustion, hunger and inactivity for long periods of time, one of the gods— a female this time—had said before the game commenced. *And so you will stand and endure, proving by your tolerance that you have earned the right to call yourselves warriors.*

Once again you are working as a team. Encourage each other if you must, distract your opponents if possible. But above all else, your mission is to be the last one standing. Your team will then know the glory of our delight—but since I suspect you will not fully comprehend just how great a reward that is, you will also be granted a more tangible prize. The other team, the losing team, will say goodbye to another member. I wish you all the strength you are surely going to need.

Those words ringing in her ears, Delilah peered down the opposite line and eyed Nola. Her sister seemed fine, anchored and steady. Thank the gods. Assured of the warrioress's stamina, Delilah shifted her gaze. To Layel. She couldn't help it. They were facing each other. He'd made sure of it, shoving Brand out of the way when the dragon tried to take the stump opposite her. She had experienced a stirring of pride as she'd watched her man—*is he?*—fight to be near her.

They'd been standing here for over an hour, moonlight keeping them cool. With every minute that passed, her head swam with more dizziness, becoming lighter, as if she were floating in the clouds.

"I know the goddess told us we were doing this to prove our endurance, but really. What's the point of this challenge in the big scheme of things?" she muttered.

"The warrior who can stand firm against any obstacle to meet his objective is the warrior who will prove victorious in the last battle," Layel said.

"Do you mean *bite* any obstacle?"

Layel didn't laugh as she'd intended. As she reflected upon her words, she realized they weren't funny. They were cruel. He had not meant to hurt her. He'd even apologized. Gods, what was wrong with her? Why was she—swaying…falling. Her eyelids popped open—when had she closed them?—and she planted her feet firmly on the stump, maintaining her pose.

"Look at me," Layel demanded fiercely.

Black spots winked over her vision as she sought him. A long, dark tunnel greeted her. Where was he?

"Delilah," he snapped.

"What?" she snapped back. Lashes—closed. Damn it! She pried them open again. Feet—planted. Layel—glaring at her.

"Do not fall asleep, woman. That will only irritate me."

Her lips twitched. "Are you commanding me because you hope I'll jump in the water just to spite you?"

His eyes sparkled like freshly polished sapphires, and he slowly smiled.

She loved his smile. Loved the way his eyes crinkled at the corners. Loved the light that seemed to illuminate his entire face, chasing away the somber memories. But every time he showed her the barest hint of genuine amusement, she fell a little deeper under his seductive power and that was foolish.

"I'm going to beat you." Hopefully by speaking the words she gave them the power to keep her upright.

"Me, perhaps." His broad shoulders lifted in a shrug. "I doubt you will defeat my...*team.*" He said the last with disgust. "They are determined to win this time."

If they didn't, they would go back to the execution circle. Her blood chilled. To lose another man meant that Layel's team would be two members short. Worse, Layel might be the player to go.

Another bout of dizziness hit her, and she swayed.

"Damn it, Delilah."

Her legs shook and her neck ached, but she stood her ground despite her body's obvious need for rest. "Yes, cursing helps," she said dryly.

"What will it take to make you concentrate?"

Several others glanced over at them, frowning. At the moment, she didn't care what anyone thought. "How about if you jump? That ought to get my attention," she said, half-fearing he would.

"Besides that." He scrubbed a hand over his face, wiping away the beads of sweat glistening in the golden moonlight. "How do you feel?"

"Fine."

"Liar."

She liked that he knew her well enough to sense when she spoke true—or not. "How much longer until people start to fall?" she wondered aloud.

"Hours. Days."

She nearly groaned. "Surely someone—"

"Quiet!" a centaur snapped.

"If you desire peace," Layel told him sharply, "jump from your post and swim to shore."

Silence met his solution.

Why did that excite her? What kind of woman had she become? He had only to exude his prowess on *anyone* and her body reacted. Her nipples were hard, and that moisture once again pooled between her legs despite her weakness, despite those around them, despite the circumstances.

Broderick the nymph inhaled deeply and sent his gaze down the line. His pupils were dilated, and when he spotted her, he licked his lips. There were tiny puncture wounds all over his face, neck and arms.

Her gaze shifted to the gorgon on their team. A beautiful woman—a rarity among the race—she was tall and lithe, with elegant features. Her eyes were wide and dark, flecked with silver and filled with satisfaction. Long, thin snakes slithered atop her head, hissing in every direction. Broderick must have sated himself with her, over and over again, for he appeared stronger than ever, his skin rosy with color, his muscles firm, his stance solid. And yet he still wanted Delilah? Nymphs! They were impossible to please.

Layel growled low in his throat, drawing her attention, the nymph forgotten.

"Something wrong?" she asked him.

"I told you to focus, yet you were staring at the nymph."

Jealous again? How had he treated his mate? Had he smiled at her often? Tenderly loved her each and every night? Given her everything Delilah wanted for herself? Or had he been fierce, as he was now? Delilah wished she had known him then. Except, well, she might have killed his mate in a wee bit of jealous rage, so perhaps meeting now was for the best.

"Preparing to chop someone to bits?" Layel asked, catching her expression.

"Perhaps."

"The nymph, I hope."

"You?" She'd meant it as a statement, but it emerged as a question, the thought of feasting on him tantalizing.

"That would be wise," he said, and there wasn't a hint of anger or amusement in his tone.

Her head tilted to the side as she studied him. "Why?"

He was silent for a long while before shrugging as he had earlier. "Remind me never to attack you again. You become annoying."

A gasp escaped her. "Annoying?"

"You continually ask questions and repeat what I say."

"What questions have I asked?" she demanded, then felt color heat her cheeks as he gave her a droll look. With the color, however, came strength, her limbs trembling less. Had he purposely baited her to help her retain her balance?

Dear gods. Now she was questioning herself. "Never mind. You are not as evil as you would have the world believe," she told him, neither asking a question nor repeating something he'd said.

"You're right."

He was agreeing with her now? That was a first.

"I'm worse."

She rolled her eyes. "I don't believe you. Tell me the worst thing you've ever done."

"I can tell you that," Brand said, suddenly speaking up.

Layel bared his fangs at the dragon.

That man and his hate. He was eaten alive with it, had condemned an entire race for one woman's death. *You would do the same had it been one of your sisters.* That would have to change, she thought. For both of them. She didn't like the thought of Layel being consumed by anything save desire. His touch—and his smiles—were simply too wondrous.

She leveled a narrowed glance at Brand. While she wanted Layel's secrets, she wanted the vampire to be the one to tell them to her. "Keep speaking, and I'll tell the entire assembly something about *you*. Something you wish I didn't know."

Nola, who stood at the far end, leaned forward. "Speak louder. I want to hear this."

Zane stared at the girl, his expression dark. Brand, too, looked over at her and tilted his head to the side thoughtfully. Nola caught his look and blushed. Actually blushed like an untried girl, though Delilah knew she had once been given a captive male as a reward for demonstrating unparalleled bravery on the battlefield. Perhaps, though, she had left the man untouched and spent the night alone. Perhaps she'd wanted something more than mere capitulation from a lover, as Delilah did.

If she kept looking between them, Delilah mused, she was going to fall. She carefully replanted her heels on the log. Heard a splash in the distance. Her back straightened, and she gazed down the line, searching.

The demon on her team had fallen. He came up sputtering. The two centaurs, who'd twisted to watch the creature swim to the beach, fell next, unable to balance their hooves any longer. Delilah shook her head—dizzy, stop!—and sighed.

"Amazon," Brand called suddenly.

Delilah blinked at him, but he wasn't watching her. His gaze was still glued on pretty Nola.

"Stop glancing between your sister and the vampire. You'll fall," he said.

Nola raised her fist at him before glaring straight ahead.

"Ah, look at that. An Amazon who obeys a man's command without question. A novelty indeed," Layel said.

Delilah turned back to him, pulse jumping at the sound of his husky voice. Gods, he was beautiful. Striking and full of verve. A protector in a predator's skin. "Are all vampires angry, snarling beasts?"

He inclined his head. "Just me. Thank you."

"That wasn't a compliment."

"You're sure?"

"Look who's asking questions now," she told him smugly. A swift survey of the contestants had her noticing the other vampire's gaze was once more on her friend. "Your warrior watches my sister with dark intentions in his eyes, as though he wants her for dinner."

Layel's gaze slowly perused Delilah's face. "That displeases you, I see. Jealous?"

There was so much anger in the question, she was momentarily taken aback. And then, gods help her, she was smiling. "Are you?"

He didn't answer. He even looked away as if dismissing her. But he didn't dismiss. He merely said, "I am not jealous," his tone quiet, calm. "But I think I would kill even my own brother, if I had one, if you decided to take him as a lover."

Water splashed. There was a vile curse.

The other demon had fallen.

"How do you feel?" Layel asked before she could respond to his angry—wondrous—announcement.

Tired, weak, shaky. Unsure. "Fine."

His gaze slid back to her in another lingering perusal, hot, stopping in all the places she wanted his mouth to travel.

He licked his lips as if remembering the taste of her. For once—twice? A third time?—nothing around her mattered but a man. Her weakness was forgotten. The game was forgotten. Consequences were forgotten. Only Layel existed.

"You never told me the worst thing you ever did."

A muscle ticked below his eye. "Why do you wish to have such information? What purpose could it possibly serve?" There was genuine perplexity in his voice.

"I want to know you better. That's all."

A warm blast of sea-kissed air blustered about them, whipping his hair around his face and causing her mouth to water. He didn't have a shirt on and his pants were ripped. Every hard rope of muscle and sinew he possessed was bared to her view. She couldn't help but marvel at the sight. *I held this powerful man in my arms.*

He didn't have any scars. She'd always thought she'd desire a man with scars—proof that he did not back down from a fight. Proof that he'd fight for *her.* Vorik had possessed many. But she wanted Layel far more than she'd ever wanted the dragon—who hadn't fought for her after all. The vampire's skin was velvet-covered steel, smooth and strong, and tempted her as nothing else ever had.

"Have you ever killed a woman?" she asked, inclining her head.

"Oh, yes." He didn't hesitate with his answer. "I held Marina, the former demon queen, in my arms and killed her the way I almost killed you. I drained the life out of her with my mouth. And I have never regretted it."

"I suppose she hurt you in some way." Had they been lovers? Delilah wondered, fists tightening. That small action upset her balance, and she swayed again.

Layel kicked out his leg, preventing her from toppling.

The movement was as swift as a blink—gliding up, then back down—that no one could have noticed, but it saved her.

Her heart pounded in a staccato rhythm of gratitude and embarrassment. "Thank you," she muttered.

"I warned you. Pay attention. Next time, I may let you fall."

"My sweet hero." Feeling a hot gaze boring into her, she glanced around. Brand and Nola were staring straight ahead, Zane the vampire was watching Nola again and— Tagart. Damn. He was glaring at her.

"You have to stop helping me," she grumbled to Layel. "Saving me will only get you killed."

"At least you don't deny needing aid. And before you tell me that you wouldn't have needed aid had I kept my teeth to myself, I know. You are strong and capable when your veins are fully stocked."

He acknowledged her abilities as a warrior? Shock nearly felled her. One of the reasons the Amazons so often had to prove their abilities was that the men they fought so often lied, claiming victory they had not warranted, too embarrassed to admit they'd been defeated by mere women.

"Sometimes I feel weak around you," she admitted quietly, lowering her voice so only he could hear, "and it has nothing to do with blood loss. The things I want you to do to me…they shame me, and yet that never seems to matter when I'm with you. I crave them."

He gulped. "They should not shame you."

"And why is that?"

"Because it has been my…pleasure to fulfill some of your needs. Because it's all right to allow another to see to your care."

"Would you? Allow another to see to your care, I mean?" *I want to be that woman.* She desired him so badly. In her bed, in her life—there, she had finally admitted the second. They should have been enemies; he would probably hate the woman who made him forget his precious mate, even for a second, but… If he would look at Delilah with tenderness just once, it might just be worth any hardship.

"I— No. If I were not mated…"

But in his mind, he was. Would always be. Much as the knowledge hurt, it was the most he'd ever offered her and so she took heart. Seemed she grew more foolish with every day that passed. "Why did you kill Marina?"

One corner of his mouth curled upward. "She was breathing the same air as me."

Her heart skipped a beat at the sight of that half smile. "And?" she prompted when he failed to elaborate.

"That…offended me."

She couldn't stop a grin of her own from forming. "I never liked her. She was a thief and a liar."

"And lies disgust you?"

"Of course." Trust was a sacred thing, and lies mocked it.

"*I* am a liar."

A moment passed in silence as she digested his words. Liars didn't usually admit to their sins. Which meant he must *want* to elicit her disgust. Why? "You've said that before." Had she ever sounded so shaky? So…female?

"And you did not believe me. Yet, look what happened to you." His gaze flicked to her still-healing neck. "I said I would stay away from you and then I stole your blood."

Perhaps this was his way of keeping her away from him, she thought. Perhaps she was proving too much a temptation to his peace of mind. Perhaps he hoped she would treat him horribly so he could then hate her. "I like everything that comes out of your mouth," she said softly, huskily.

His breath hitched at the implication.

She wanted to laugh—*am I right?*—but added, "You may tell me anything you desire without fear."

Water splashed, signaling that someone had just fallen, but she didn't look away from the vampire. "Tell me—" She stopped, frowned and peered down at her feet.

The stump seemed to be shrinking. *Was* shrinking, she realized with shock. Her toes and heels were now hanging off the edge. She shifted, trying to discover a new sense of balance.

"Be still," Layel snapped.

Someone else fell, followed quickly by another. From the beach, she could hear cheers and shouts of warning as fallen teammates encouraged their brethren.

A rock suddenly flew past her face and into Layel's. He teetered, cursed, but thankfully stayed put as a trickle of blood flowed from above his eye.

"Who threw that?" she demanded. Her gaze moved over the challengers. Several mermaids were swimming around Broderick's ankles, some reaching out to caress his thigh, cooing as they did so. Mer*men* were swimming around the female nymph, who appeared frustrated by the attention. Every time they touched her, they caused her to wobble. How would Layel react if she fell?

"By any means necessary, the gods told us," Tagart said, drawing her attention. Eyes narrowed, he withdrew another stone from his pocket and launched it.

"No!"

Expecting it this time, Layel managed to catch it with a movement so swift his swinging arm was nothing more than a blur. "Coward."

"What did you call me?" was the hissed reply.

"You heard me, dragon. Hitting me while I was unaware is the act of a coward."

"No, it is the act of a smart man."

"Tagart," Delilah snapped. "Stop."

"Whose side are you on, Amazon?" Tagart pointed an accusing finger at her. "I thought you had already chosen. But every time I turn around you are with *him*."

She opened her mouth, but no words emerged. Were she to say that she was indeed on his side, Layel would hate her. Again. Were she to declare allegiance to Layel, her team would soon vote for her to die.

In the end, she didn't have to say a word. A shark suddenly flew from between the center stumps, large jaws and fearsome teeth snapping at them. Its fat gray tail slapped at the female nymph, who screeched and fell. Layel didn't seem to care. Maybe that was why Delilah suddenly felt sorry for her. Thankfully the mermen swam her to safety.

One of the shark's fins nailed Nola in the stomach, but she managed to remain standing. For the moment.

When the shark hit the water, disappearing from view, everyone stilled, quiet.

Nola's eyes closed and she rubbed her temple. "I do not feel so…good." Her knees suddenly collapsed and she toppled.

Brand dove for her. When he surfaced, he had her wrapped in his arms. She was pale, teeth chattering as he dragged her toward the beach and laid her gently on the sand. That's when Layel tossed the rock he'd caught. It slammed into Tagart's groin with a thud.

"You're right," he said when the distracted dragon doubled over and yelped. "Smart."

Tagart propelled straight into the water. He didn't rise

for a heartbeat, two, and then the water began to swirl, brighten. There was a huge spray when Tagart emerged as a dragon. He unleashed a fiery roar, his wings spreading, scales already replacing skin, tail twitching.

A stream of that fire launched at Layel. He ducked, the flames singeing his back. Vampires were quick, faster than any other race, but Layel had nowhere to go—and fire was a vampire's greatest weakness. She knew because Amazons made a point of studying every race, looking for ways to defeat them.

"Stop, Tagart. Stop!" Brand called from the beach. "Innocents are in the way."

Tagart was beyond listening. He spit another stream of crackling flames, cutting past everyone still standing—Zane and Broderick jumped into the water to avoid impact—and then the fire hit Layel, who had stubbornly refused to budge. Delilah screamed and found herself leaping to take the hit herself.

Just when the flames were about to engulf her, Layel's arms banded around her, jerking her down, down, down, twisting, landing in the water, his body the first to hit. But his feet had been the last to leave the stump. Which meant his team had won. She swallowed a mouthful, choking. The salt stung the marks on her neck, her lungs seized and she fought to get to the surface.

Layel's grip tightened. Her eyes widened as she realized why. The shark was swimming toward them, mouth open, teeth gleaming hungrily.

CHAPTER FIFTEEN

SHIVAWN AWOKE with a jolt and moaned. Gods, he ached. Was weak, drained. Too much sex play, he suspected. Had happened before, and would probably happen again.

Grinning, he cracked open his eyelids, the world around him blurry, out of focus. There was darkness with only the slightest hint of gold. A few feet away, water dripped a slow, steady rhythm. The walls closing in at his sides were…rocky, he realized, not the ivory and onyx he was now used to.

Where was he?

Not in a bed. The ground beneath him was as rocky as the walls, the air damp and musty. A cave? And why did heavy weights pull at his wrists and ankles? His grin faded, amusement replaced by anger, as he turned his head and saw the heavy chains that bound him.

Bound? He was bound?

A lovely female face flashed in his mind, teeth bared, fury in her blue eyes. He remembered. "Alyssa!" he snarled.

One of the shadows in the corner shifted. Then, suddenly, she was beside him, staring down at him. Never had she looked lovelier. Her skin was flushed a healthy pink, her cheeks filled out, her lips bloodred. She wore a black robe, and it covered every inch of skin except for her breathtaking face and delicate hands. "So. You're awake."

"Unchain me. Now!" He jerked his arms and legs, but the thick links held strong. His weakened state was no match for them.

"You had best be quiet, nymph."

"Alyssa."

She traced her fingertip over his bare chest. So. She had removed his shirt. What else had she done to him? His teeth ground together, his body unresponsive.

Most of his life, his cock had been an asset. It had reliably risen for anything female. Except her. He didn't know why. The night he'd spent with her, he'd had to think of others to stay hard.

He hadn't lied to her. He'd left her sleeping in bed, sated, while he had wallowed in dissatisfaction, frustration and confusion. He wasn't eager to repeat the experience.

What was it about her that so turned him off? Every time he looked at her, all he could see in his mind was blood. All he could hear were screams.

"Let me go and we'll pretend this never happened."

Her nails, still resting on his chest, grew to sharp little points, slicing into his skin. "Oh, no. There will be no release for you. Not yet."

"Alyssa," he gritted out again.

"I brought you here to punish you, you know. To give you what you deserve. I wanted to hurt you, destroy you, but as I watched you sleeping I realized I couldn't do it." She laughed bitterly. "What I can do, however, is pleasure you. Pleasure you so fiercely you'll never forget what happened in this cave, never forget the woman responsible. And most of all you'll wish, desperately, for more." The more she spoke, the more determination dripped from her tone.

"The nymph army will search for me. They'll find us and you'll be killed for this."

A cold smile hovered at the edges of her lush mouth. She shook her head, hair dancing. "They'll assume we disappeared like the others."

His stomach tightened with dread. She was right. "This isn't going to make me love you, Alyssa. This is going to make me hate you."

Her gaze lowered, and she traced circles around each of his nipples. "I know," she admitted softly.

"Then free me. Now."

"It seems I've wanted you forever," she said as if he had not spoken. "I know I've dreamed of us together, over and over again. And the one pure, perfect memory I had, you ruined."

He could not, would not soften toward his captor. When he gained his freedom, and he would, he would ensure she was unable to harm another warrior. "I told you that was not my intention, but you wanted the truth, so I gave it to you."

"I was not finished," she said, jaw firmed. "You left me and you were unsatisfied."

He could not deny it, so did not reply.

"As I said before," she rasped, long lashes rising. Her eyes glittered dangerously, filled with a determination so complete he'd never seen its equal. Stronger, even, than her tone. "You will be completely sated when I'm through with you. You'll think of me constantly, recall the bliss I gave you, and you'll want more the way I have wanted more all these years. But I will never give it to you. After this, we will be on equal ground. And I will be done with you."

Dark rage seethed through him. He was a warrior. Being captured like this—and by a woman—was humiliating. What's more, he was a nymph. He should be able to charm her into doing anything he wanted. More, he should want this, should merely consider it play.

Not desiring a woman was almost…sacrilegious. "That will be rape," he found himself saying, and could not believe the words had sprung from his mouth. No other nymph would have uttered them. Ever. They would have reveled in any pleasure this woman gave them.

A strangled cry left Alyssa, and she jerked her hand away from him.

He used the reprieve to think. Why had he stopped her? Nymphs needed sex to survive. Without it, they grew weak. Might even die. With it, though, they grew impossibly strong. He should let her ride him, restoring all of his strength, and then he should break these chains and strangle her with them.

Yes, that was a sound plan. He would grit his teeth and bear it. He only hoped he could fool her and actually respond to her touch.

He popped his jaw—*calm, stay calm*—and forced his expression to soften. "I'm sorry. That was cruel of me to say." And difficult to apologize when he did not mean a word of it. "You want me, and I want you."

The woman was going to suffer for bringing him to this point.

She blinked in surprise, then suspicion. "What game do you play?"

"No game. I simply wish to bed you."

Unconvinced, she shook her head. "You suddenly want me before I have even begun? Just like that?" She snapped her fingers. "Only a moment ago it would have been rape."

"Yes. Just like that." He'd had to swallow his fury to choke out the words.

"Liar." But her hands returned to his chest, as if she wanted to believe him despite her doubts. She dipped a fingertip into his navel, leaned down and kissed him there, gaze never leaving his.

He inhaled sharply, then had to grit his teeth as he'd supposed, his father's screams suddenly exploding in his head. His ears rang, and the scent of death filled his nose. Every muscle in his body tensed. This was what happened every time Alyssa neared him. Regaining his strength was not worth this. "You...you... I can't stand the smell of you," he ground out, not knowing what else to say to make her leave. "You have to back away from me."

Alyssa uttered an embarrassed yelp and stood. "You're a cruel man," she rasped out, "yet I convinced myself otherwise, lapping up every scrap you tossed my way. Enough! No longer will I do so. You want me to bathe? I will. I want nothing to diminish your enjoyment. And you will enjoy. Not that you deserve it.

"You never noticed, but I've been unable to drink another's blood since our joining. I was literally dying for your blood, damn you, but now I've had it. Now I'm strong. And soon we will be free of each other." She stalked from the cave, leaving him alone.

His head fell against the rocks, those terrible memories fading from his mind in the wake of her heated accusations and departure. She hadn't drunk from another? She loved him *that* much? It was almost...humbling. But surely she had exaggerated. Surely she hadn't truly been dying because of his refusal.

Right?

He thought back to how pale she'd been lately, how sunken her cheeks and eyes had become. Now, after having his blood, she glowed. He was ashamed to admit it, but he *hadn't* noticed her decline.

He frowned, concern overshadowing every hint of his anger and freeing his mind from thoughts of revenge. How would he feel if she were to take her last breath? If he were never to see her again, as she'd vowed?

He'd come to expect her presence. She was Alyssa, the female who constantly sought him out, who watched him with lust in her eyes. Who did everything in her power to seduce him. The same as most females, were he honest. But she wanted more than sex. As many times as she'd invited him to bed, she'd asked for his aid in devising battle plans, beseeched him to join her for a stroll through the Outer City and sent him books she'd enjoyed so that they could one day discuss them. She wanted conversation, to know his thoughts and have him listen to hers. She wanted to know him as a man, not just a lover.

There wasn't a single spark of satisfaction at the thought of her demise, as he would have guessed. There wasn't even relief. The thought of being without her actually saddened him. Yes, saddened, he realized.

Despite what she made him feel when he looked at her, she was lovely. He even liked arguing with her. A few times, she'd even made him smile. She was smart, witty. Lusty. But somehow he'd come to equate her with the suffering of the past, and that had tainted his feelings toward her.

The first time he'd seen her, as a woman, no longer a

little girl, he'd been consumed with lust for her. He'd wanted her more than he'd ever wanted another. But the moment he'd approached her, gazing into her eyes, that lust had turned to disgust, the screams of the past consuming him. That had never changed. *Why* had the past interfered? Did it matter? Escape should be his only concern right now.

For an eternity, he tried to fight his way free of the chains. All he did was cut his skin. *What kind of warrior am I?* he wondered.

Finally, she returned. Her hair was wet and she was wearing a different robe. A blue one, to match her eyes. Prettier than ever, he thought and closed his own eyes. Instant arousal, but he knew it was only a matter of time before it withered.

"I should now meet even your lofty standards," she said.

Alyssa climbed on top of him, straddling him. She flattened her palms on his chest, the heat of her core, covered though it was by her robe, pressing against his cock. Where she touched, a small blaze kindled. Odd. That had never happened before. Not with her. Why had it now?

"There is much we need to discuss," he said, mind still churning. She hadn't looked any different, and she certainly hadn't endeared herself to him. But for once, there was no flash of blood in his mind, no screams. She stroked his chest like a favored pet. There were calluses on her hands, calluses that evoked a delicious friction.

Suddenly he didn't want her to stop touching him.

"Alyssa," he began, not really knowing what to say.

"Stop talking." Her fingertips never ceased their determined movement, tracing the line of his jaw, his ears, the slope of his neck and collarbone.

His blood heated with a shocking amount of desire. "You are…this is…" His frown deepened. How was she doing this? He opened his eyes to study her, heard a scream inside his head, lost his arousal and quickly closed his eyes again. Silence.

Her face, he realized. Something about it must send him back. But what?

She scooted lower on him, rubbing him once again to readiness. He hissed in a breath as she leaned down and licked him directly on his nipple. It hardened, reaching for more of the hot perfection of her mouth.

"Are you thinking of another woman?" she asked huskily.

Her sharp little teeth scraped the skin surrounding his other nipple, so the only noise that escaped him was a moan. Of pleasure.

She hadn't been this aggressive before. She had bitten him last time, yes, but it had been accidental. Even knowing it, he had nearly slapped her for it. Only his quick reflexes had stopped him.

He'd nearly been drained once, and it had been as painful, horrific and humiliating as having a limb severed. Alyssa had nearly drained him to get him here, and that hadn't been pleasant, either. So the thought of being bitten again should have disgusted him. Except...

Gods, he didn't want Alyssa to stop. He wanted some part of her inside him, taking nourishment, living because he gave her life.

What was happening to his mind, his desires?

She nibbled harder. "Are you?"

"Am I what?" He had forgotten the question, was too busy arching up to meet her mouth.

"Who are you thinking of, Shivawn? What woman's image is in your mind when I do this?" She licked her way down, not stopping until she reached his navel.

His cock reached for her, craving her mouth. Hot, tight, wet. Pumping in and out. Hard. Fierce.

"Tell me and I'll be gentle with you," she whispered before blowing a warm puff on the moisture her tongue had left behind.

"You," he replied honestly. "I see you." And he did. Her heat infused his skin, her silky hair tickled his chest, and he liked it.

Her fingers curled around his cock. Squeezed. His hips surged up, a groan splitting his lips. Where had this tigress come from? Mostly she had been still last time, as if savoring every touch, every sound. He'd thought at the time that he might have been a wee bit charmed if he hadn't been so busy wondering why his body wasn't responding as it should.

He tried to lift his arm to fist her hair, force a kiss, but the chains rattled and pulled tight. "Release me."

"Of course." She released him—just not the way he desired. His cock was suddenly free, hard and aching on his belly. Satisfied she had his attention, she continued, "You don't give the orders here."

She probably meant the words to sound harsh and commanding. She sounded breathless.

"Then touch me again. That's why I'm here, isn't it?"

Before she could reply, he cracked his eyelids open. He did not focus on her entire face, but on one feature at a time, trying to figure this out. He saw the pink tip of her tongue emerge, darting over her lush lips. The sight was amazingly erotic, and rather than losing his erection, his arousal was ratcheted another degree. Her lips weren't the problem, then. He watched her wrinkle her nose. Again, his arousal remained. He gazed into her eyes. The screams returned.

Her eyes, then. What about them transported him back to that bloody field?

She peered down at him, hair hanging over her shoulders like damp velvet. Her eyelids were at half-mast, her expression soft and luminous. Needy as he now was, the screams were a nuisance rather than a hindrance.

"Touch me," he commanded her again, but there was a plea to the words. He flattened his palms against the cool rocks beneath him.

"Not yet." She reached up and tugged at the shoulder strap of her robe. The sapphire material floated to her stomach, revealing full, proud breasts with sweet, pink nipples.

His mouth watered as though he were starving and had just been offered a banquet. "Release me." He could barely work the words past his thickening throat. "I want to touch *you*."

Her eyes narrowed. "You're lying again."

"Look at my body. I'm not lying. Desire beats through me."

Her gaze remained locked on his face. "I can feel it," she said, her cheeks growing bright with color.

A blush? From this fierce warrior woman? Even that fueled his desire.

"But it's there because you're thinking of another," she added. "I know you lied."

"Only you, I swear it."

"What's changed?" she demanded. She traced her fingertip over the head of his penis, which was sticking out from between her legs, and spread a sheen of moisture on his stomach.

Sweet heaven. He opened his mouth to reply—how, he didn't know—when she stopped him.

"Never mind. It doesn't matter. As I said, you will find

pleasure with me this time." She scooted farther back and then—sweet gods, then—she took his cock into her mouth, sucking him all the way to the base.

Every muscle in his body went taut, his blood molten. "Alyssa," he gasped.

The sound of her name must have been startling to her, for she stopped. With her mouth a mere whisper away from his cock, she stared up at him. He saw pleasure in those lovely eyes, but only a little. There was too much hurt and determination standing in the way. The screams increased in volume in his mind, but still they didn't affect him. Just then, something else mattered more. That hurt...

That didn't sit well with him. He wanted her wild. Out of control. Not so that he could regain his strength and escape, he realized, but because...with his private admission that he liked having her in his life, that he liked her, with the flashes of blood and screams overshadowed, he was beginning to sense something else...something shocking. Wondrous. Unbelievable.

Something that swept through him, infusing his cells, his organs, imprinting her essence inside him.

He closed his eyes and pictured Twila, a female nymph he liked to bed. His penis withered as it used to do with Alyssa. He pictured Helen, a siren he had spent a month pleasuring. Nothing, not even a twitch. He pictured Brenna, the human he'd wanted above all others. Again, he remained flaccid.

"Shivawn?" Alyssa asked hesitantly.

Just like that, he was hard as a rock, her voice the fuel needed to spark his desire.

Dear gods. She was his mate, his one and only. No other would do. She was it for him. She was a part of his life, always had been. He could no longer deny it—why had he ever?—for all he could suddenly think about was her pleasure. Her protection. Her smile, her laughter, her body. Him, inside of her. Her, and no other. All these years, and he'd allowed painful memories, memories that had nothing to do with her, to cloud his judgment. All these years, he'd pushed her away, treated her horribly, hurt her deeply.

She was a vampire. That no longer mattered.

She would have to bite him to live. He was glad.

She had stolen him. Merely loveplay.

My mate, he thought, shocked to his very core. How he'd mixed his past with her, he didn't know, but he would act the fool no longer. Besides, now wasn't the time to figure it out. He'd ponder it later. Much, much later. "Alyssa," he said.

Something in his tone caused tears to spring to her eyes. He knew women well enough to know they were not tears of happiness. What had brought them on? "Unchain me, love. Please." His tone was gentle. He had to caress her face. Perhaps lick those tears away. Hold her. Apologize for all he'd done to her.

She wiped the moisture away with the back of her wrist and shook her head. Her chin trembled, her gaze lowering once again to his cock. "No."

"Strip for me, then." There would be time later to convince her of his new feelings. Right now, anything he said would most likely be dismissed as a lie he told to ensure his escape. "Let me taste you while you taste me."

Again, she shook her head. But there was intrigue and passion blended in her eyes now. She nibbled on her lower lip, something he suddenly wanted to do. "Last time, I found fulfillment and you didn't," she said. "This time, you will find it and I will not. Equal ground, Shivawn, remember?"

"Alyssa." Oh, yes. He had hurt her, and he hated himself for it.

"No!"

"Keep me chained, then. But at least allow me to kiss you. Somewhere. You may choose where. Your mouth… your breasts…between your legs… I will not find pleasure unless you allow me to do so."

Her pupils dilated, delighting him. "You don't really want to pleasure me," she said, even more hurt drifting from the undertone.

"You and no other," he assured her. He could not explain this change in him, even to himself. All he knew was that he *was* changed. Later, he told himself again. He would reason it out later, when their mutual passion was sated. "If you want me to beg, I will beg."

She looked away from him, as if his gaze was too much to endure. "All I have ever wanted was you. Everything I did, I did for you. Learning to fight, so that I could be close to you and so you would know I could take care of myself."

"That, you will stop doing immediately."

One of her delicate brows arched. "Trying to please you?"

"Fighting." He wanted her safe. In his bed. Away from the war-torn life she lived. He liked the thought of protecting her.

She traced his navel with her tongue. A tear ran down her cheek and splashed onto his pelvic bone, glistening. The sight nearly undid him. "Alyssa…"

"I should not have placed you above my own needs and desires. Silly of me."

"You are not silly. But your happiness *is* more important than mine," he said. "Always. Soon, I will prove it."

Another tear.

"What else have you done for me?" he asked gently.

Her fangs elongated with an angry hiss. "Will that stroke your male pride, hearing what poor little Alyssa, hopelessly in love with you, did to make you notice her?"

"No. In the telling, I will begin to understand what I must now do for you in return and how I might make up for my negligence. Equal ground, as you said."

Shock flashed over her expression. Her mouth fell open, but she quickly closed it with a snap. Eyes gleaming fury, she snarled, "You want to know? Fine. You refused me time and time again. After a while, I lost hope. I took another lover. And another. And another. Can you make that up to me? Return me to my untouched state?"

Oh, now that he did not like hearing. He did not like the thought of this lovely woman in the arms of any man save himself. "No," he admitted softly. "All I can do is try and make you forget. Brand you with my touch, for though I did not have the privilege of being your first, I promise I will be your last."

"You courted thousands of women," she said bitterly, "enjoying yourself, laughing. I cried every time I saw you with another, every time I gave myself to a man. Can you make that up to me?"

His stomach twisted so painfully he would have sworn knives were slashed through every knot. "I am sorry, so very sorry. I wish I could go back." She would never have reason to cry again. Whatever he had to do, this woman would know only joy and laughter from this moment on.

What if, tomorrow, the blood and screams are no longer dulled?

That no longer mattered. They could storm through him,

lightning and thunder, but he would not leave her. She was too important to him. He would endure anything for her. Hadn't she endured all but death for him? "Somehow, some way, I will make you forget those experiences. I swear it."

"The lovers I took," she continued as if he hadn't spoken, "I had hoped they could teach me how best to please a man. I thought if I only knew how to pleasure you, you would want me." She laughed bitterly again, a tear-filled choking. "But that didn't work, did it? You finally took me to bed and you hated every moment of it."

"Alyssa," he began, then stopped himself. How could he explain that she had always reminded him of the worst day of his life without hurting her further? "That night I spent with you…I was in a dark and dangerous mood. No one would have been able to please me."

"Your mate would have."

An hour ago, he would have agreed. "I followed you for days afterward," he admitted.

Eyes widening, she shook her head. "No, you didn't."

He nodded. "I did. I couldn't understand why I had been unable to respond to so beautiful a woman. So I watched you, more intently than ever, trying to reason it out."

Again, she shook her head in denial, though there was a gleam of hope in her eyes.

That hope spurred him on. "I'm responding to you now," he reminded her. "I want you, Alyssa. Let me have you. Please. Your pleasure will be my own."

Her features hardened as though she'd stared at a gorgon a little too long and had been turned to stone. "Oh, you'll have pleasure."

"That's not enough. I want you to have pleasure, as well."

"Like I said, I already had my turn, didn't I?"

He never should have told her the truth. "I promise you I will find greater pleasure if I know you are enjoying this, too."

"The same was true of me. Once." She didn't give him a chance to say anything else. Her mouth once again lowered to his cock, taking him all the way inside, sucking…sucking… Her tongue swirled around the swollen head with an ever-upward glide. He tried to resist the headiness, wanting to see to her climax before he took his own.

"Let me lick. Between your legs," he worked past his constricting throat. "Need to taste you."

Up and down she sucked him, her teeth scraping, ignoring his plea. Her fingers bit into his hips, released him, then wrapped around his testicles. His body was tensing, readying. Power was surging through his bloodstream, unstoppable and inexorable. He'd never wanted anything as much as he wanted her. Couldn't stand the thought of leaving her unsatisfied.

"Alyssa. Please."

She increased her speed, and his passion spiked. Consumed him. He roared loud and long, his hips pumping his cock down her throat. He couldn't stop the motions, couldn't stop the momentum of his release.

"Drink from me," he commanded. "Take my blood."

"Already did."

"Do it again. Let me feed you."

"No!"

The hot spike of her tongue swirled over the head of his shaft, and he lost control completely. His muscles clamped down on his bones, endlessly spasming.

The pleasure… Oh, gods, the pleasure. More intense

than anything he'd ever experienced. He couldn't speak, could only gasp, groan and pant like an animal.

When he got inside this woman again, he might not survive. The thought almost made him smile. But as he shuddered and calmed—would his erratic heartbeat ever slow?—Alyssa straightened, pulling away from him. She refastened her robe, shielding her nipples from his view. Her color was high; she, too, was panting.

"Now you have found release with me. You can't deny it this time."

"Alyssa."

She moved swiftly to his wrists, gave a tug, and the chains fell away. She followed suit with his ankles.

Free, he sat up, already reaching for her, needing her in his arms. He could smell her sweet desire, had to sate her, had to…now. Forever. But she backed away from him, shaking her head.

"Come here, Alyssa." He gave a gentle swipe of his fingers. "Please."

"Return home. Tell your king what I did. Send the entire nymph army to kill me. I don't care."

"This is between us. No one else. I will go nowhere without you." He pushed to shaky legs. Gods, where was his strength? He should be completely energized now. All he wanted to do, however, was lie down with his woman.

"Very well," she said, and stopped, studying him bleakly. The jagged walls of the cave were at her back, a harsh frame for her fragile beauty. "It is I who will go. This is goodbye, then."

He frowned. "No. Never goodbye. Come—"

She disappeared.

A roar rushed past his throat and he stumbled from the

cave, searching for her. As his eyes adjusted to the light, he found himself in the Forest of Dragons, fat trees towering all around him. What he didn't find was Alyssa.

She was gone as if she'd never been.

CHAPTER SIXTEEN

BRAND PICKED UP THE Amazon, Nola, and carted her away from the beach. She was bleeding, but refused his aid because of their audience. One of the sharks had decided her leg would make a tasty snack and had chomped on her calf. Blood had swirled in the water and now dripped onto the sand.

"I have you," he assured her.

Her cheeks were a stark white, but she was shaking her head. "I can walk. I'm fine."

He tightened his grip on her. "Be still, woman."

"Put me down. I have to find Delilah."

Chaos was behind them, but Brand didn't fear for Nola's friend. Even though Tagart was responsible for the trouble and no one could cause more damage or carnage than a pissed-off dragon changeling, the other Amazon would be fine. He'd seen the way Layel looked at her, the way he'd held her earlier, an expression of both torture and pleasure on his face, the way he'd dove to save her from sharks and dragon. The vampire would ensure her safety, no question.

Brand had never liked the vampire king. From his earliest memory, they'd always been at war, striking at one another in every way possible. But Layel had walked away several times, allowing defeat. All in the name of love. Now Brand was going to walk away from Layel. In the name of love.

"The vampire will take care of her," he assured Nola.

"They are enemies."

He noticed she didn't have to guess *which* vampire he'd been speaking of. "As are we," he reminded her. "Your people attacked mine just before we were sent to the island. I haven't forgotten."

"Yet another reason for you to put me down." But she stopped struggling and allowed him to carry her past the line of trees, away from the other creatures lying on the beach. "Bad things happen to my enemies."

"And you do not wish anything bad to happen to me?"

"No, of course I do. I just… I—"

He laughed. "I will accept the consequences. All right?" When he felt they were well enough away from prying eyes, he finally set her down and lifted her leg to study the damage. The flesh was torn in several places, and a sharp tooth was embedded deep. "This will hurt."

"What?"

Not giving her time to tense, he pinched and pulled the sharp white tooth out of the savaged skin and muscle. "You must be in great pain." But she hadn't even gasped when he'd slid his fingers inside her wound.

"I've had worse." Absolute truth sang from her tone.

"I will not think less of you if you cry."

She snorted, as far from tears as a creature could be. "Why do men act this way when a woman is injured?"

"What way?" He had seen worse injuries, true, but this one actually made his stomach churn with sickness. Bone seemed to be glaring up at him.

"You are protective. When my sisters and I fought your army, the men pushed us away rather than slice at us."

His gaze lifted to her face, and he wanted to smile. She

reminded him of the sister he'd lost long ago to humans. Confused by him, exasperated. Actually, she could have passed for his sister's twin. Same turquoise eyes, same pert nose. Same stubborn chin and sun-kissed skin.

"We do so because women are softer," he finally replied, his chest aching for what he had lost. "They *need* protection."

She gave another snort and lay back on the moss. "I have endured more pain in my life than anyone should be forced to endure in seven lifetimes. I've had to look out for myself, trust only myself. I don't need anything from you or anyone else."

"Who hurt you so terribly? I will slay him for you."

She waved a hand in dismissal. "No need. I took care of it myself."

His lips twitched. Though she was tall and leanly muscled in the way of the Amazons, she was a tiny thing compared to his massive size. Would reach no higher than his shoulders. "You think yourself hard?"

"Think? When I have killed more soldiers than I could possibly name, warriors of every race living in Atlantis?" There was no pride in her tone, only fact. Perhaps a little sadness. "How many have you killed?"

"More."

Now her lips edged into a smile.

"Are you in pain now?" he asked.

"Yes."

Still, not by word or deed did she reveal it. He thought, had their places been reversed, he might have been cursing the heavens. He couldn't help but admire her fortitude— and be dismayed by it. To shrug at this pain, she truly must have suffered over the years. "Seems you and the other, Delilah, are constantly being injured."

Nola's brow puckered. "When was she injured?"

So. Delilah hadn't told her of Layel's bite. Guarding the vampire already, was she? Interesting. Though he doubted Layel would be any more grateful for the protection than Nola had been. "I thought she was. My mistake," was all he said.

She anchored her hands behind her head and stared up at the muted sky. "Men always make mistakes."

That haughty tone would have set him on edge had anyone else used it on him, but again, she reminded him of his sister and he could only shake his head and grin. He returned his attention to her poor leg. "Does your race heal quickly?"

"None of your concern, dragon."

"I'm not going to use the information against you."

"So you say."

So distrustful, she was. "So I swear."

"Would you give your enemy knowledge about *your* race?"

Excellent point. "Right now, I am not your enemy. We are teammates, you and I." The bleeding hadn't stopped. The wound was so deep, it probably wouldn't. Without help. "Close your eyes."

"No."

Damned woman. He shook his head in exasperation. "Keep them open, then, but know that this is going to hurt."

"What are you—"

He sucked in a deep breath, held it a moment, then pushed the air from his mouth. Air that was now blended with orange-gold flames. Those flames licked her skin, the now sizzling flesh cauterizing over each bite mark.

Nola screamed. "Bastard! Son of a demon! Centaur's ass!"

The sound of that tortured scream echoed from the trees, filling his head, making him cringe. "Had there been another way, I would have taken it." He grabbed the shoulder-length mane of his hair and squeezed the cold water from it, dripping liquid over the blisters, calming the remaining embers. "The pain will end soon, I swear it."

She continued to curse him. He didn't look at her face, too afraid he would see tears. That, he would not have been able to tolerate. When a woman cried, he became a babbling fool, stumbling over his words, desperate to escape. And this strong woman's tears would be even more powerful than most.

"There will be scars," he told her. "I'm sorry."

"Scars are…nice," she panted, cheeks flushed. He suspected she was more embarrassed by her reaction than still drowning in pain.

Behind him, the leaves clashed. Someone approached. As he stood, a roar sliced through the air, a dark shape propelling toward him. Almost there… He tensed, ready. They collided with a grunt.

Zane chomped for his throat, but Brand swung a clawed fist, connecting with the blood-drinker's jaw and knocking him to his back. Unencumbered now, Brand sprang. A few kicks and punches the vampire was too wild and crazed to duck and he was able to pin his opponent to the ground.

He didn't like the way the man had watched Nola out there in the water. Darkly, possessively. But rather than spew fire all over the warrior, killing him—Brand would not have it said he was afraid to face the vampire during the challenges—he punched Zane in the nose.

Snap.

Blood squirted, and there was a howl of rage and pain. All too soon, the blood-drinker recovered, shoving Brand off with enough force to throw him into a tree.

"Mine," Zane snarled, hopping up and kicking him in the stomach. "You do not touch her. You do not touch me."

There was a feral, animal glaze in his eyes. Brand was on his feet a moment later, scales crawling up his arm as rage filled him. He'd always been a dragon who preferred peace to war, and just then he suspected there would never be peace on this island as long as the unpredictable vampire lived. Brand forgot his pride, forgot what the others might say if he did this deed, and spit a stream of fire.

Zane dodged quickly, only a single flame touching him, burning away his shirt. He leapt forward, makeshift wooden dagger suddenly raised. Brand spun, his tail sprouting and nailing the vampire in the face, drawing blood.

Finally fully dragon, he used his wings to soar high, higher, then he descended, nose facing the ground. Faster, faster, he plunged toward the vampire. When he opened his mouth to spew more fire, he spied Nola limping into the stream. He snapped his jaw closed and allowed himself to slam into Zane. They rolled to the ground in a tangled, violent bid for dominance.

A jagged branch suddenly sailed into Brand's shoulder, knocking him down. He hissed. Saw the same thing happen to Zane. Both men panted, looking between the lances and each other when Nola limped between them, hands on her hips. Her face was pallid, and there were dark circles under her eyes.

"Do I have your attention now?"

She was a fearsome sight. Despite her weakened condition, rage radiated from her in powerful waves. Her lips were thinned in displeasure and her hands curled into weapons.

"First, I am not yours," she said to Zane. "Second, I can defend myself," she said to Brand. "If I could not, I would not be worthy of my tribe. Were we in Atlantis, I would be punished for allowing you to tend me."

"I know your taste," Zane growled, startling Brand. "You are mine."

Must have startled Nola, too, because she paled all the more as she studied the vampire. "You do not know my taste. I have never given myself to you."

"You have dreamed of me." Zane threw the words at her as violently as if they were weapons.

She stumbled backward and shook her head. "How can you know that?"

"Because—"

"How!"

"Because they are not dreams! I came to you last night and you welcomed me with open arms."

Again, she stumbled backward, eyes wide, dazed. She glanced from Zane to Brand, Brand to Zane. "I—I—"

Brand jerked the stick from his shoulder, grimacing at the torn muscle and skin. There was a sharp burn, but it swiftly dissipated as his skin and tissue wove back together, healing.

"I would never have let you do those things…" she gasped out.

"You did." Zane stepped toward her, the stick still protruding. "Eagerly."

"Liar! I do not want you."

"You do. You did."

"No, no. It was a dream."

Brand's rage sparked to new heights. "Go to her again, and I will linger over you when I kill you," he told the vampire.

"I will kill you," she corrected, tears beading in her eyes. Gods, the sight nearly undid him. "I might have desired you in my dreams, vampire, but I don't want you now. I can't."

Zane frowned, confusion lighting his eyes. "But I don't want to die when you touch me. That makes you mine. That has to mean you are a gift for all I've endured."

"No, it doesn't." She bent down, grabbed another branch and launched it at him. "I am meant for no man."

He was too startled to move—or perhaps he chose not to move—and the limb sank into his other shoulder. He did not make a sound. Just stood there, both sticks protruding from him.

"Leave me alone," the Amazon choked out. "Both of you."

"Nola," Zane called.

She turned on her heel and limped away.

"Nola!" the warrior screamed, the sound echoing from branches, causing a flock of birds to take flight. "Don't leave me as she did. Please."

Suddenly not knowing what to do, Brand watched as the vampire crisscrossed his arms, gripped the sticks and jerked them out. Watched as the vampire stepped forward as if to follow the girl, stopped and emitted a sound unholy in its intensity and pain. Zane had truly desired the Amazon, was truly confused that she didn't want him in return.

Brand's dragon form retreated, leaving him in the guise of man. Naked, his clothes having been ripped away.

"Nola," Zane whispered now as he fell to his knees.

Brand slowly, quietly, receded into the shadows. Still, Zane's head snapped in his direction and their gazes clashed in heat. In hate.

"I won't let you hurt the girl again, Zane," Brand told him calmly. He hadn't protected his sister all those years ago. This girl, he would protect with his own life.

"I did not hurt her," Zane growled.

Brand's jaw set in a mutinous line. "The coming days

should be interesting, then, wouldn't you agree?" With that, he stalked away, determined to find Nola and guard her the rest of the night.

But he knew that he and Zane would have a reckoning. Soon. Oh, yes, soon.

CHAPTER SEVENTEEN

LAYEL DIDN'T KNOW what to do.

He had Delilah in his arms. Hungry sharks and blood-thirsty mermen swam around them and a volatile Tagart flew above them, spraying streams of white-hot fire. Every single one of them wanted Layel. Unfortunately the Amazon was caught in the crossfire.

Several times he'd dared break the surface of the water—only to be met with more of those molten beams. Now, he and Delilah were underwater again, spears jabbing at them, teeth snapping at them. She had slipped in and out of consciousness and had yet to awaken from the last time. Was she all right? He didn't know. What he did know was that she needed air. Soon.

He kicked a merman in the face and fought his way to the surface, maintaining a strong pinch on Delilah's nose to prevent her from breathing in the salty liquid. As his head broke the surface, he released her face, sucking in air and praying she was doing the same. If not, he'd give her every molecule in his lungs once they went under again.

Another river of fire. A quick dodge, barely avoiding contact. Through it all, Layel knew where to lay the blame for this travesty. Delilah was weak because of him. *Him.* She was a woman who prided herself on her skills and resilience, yet his actions had reduced her to a helpless damsel.

He could have transported himself to the beach, but he wouldn't have been able to take Delilah. He, too, was weak. Without him, she would sink, be eaten, stabbed, burned. She would die, like Susan.

Susan. Once more he heard his mate screaming inside his head, dragons abusing her, using her in the most terrible way. Part of him wanted to crumble under those screams, to finally give in. But just as before, thoughts of Delilah muted them to quiet whimpers, keeping him focused, able to fend off his opponents.

Delilah. What should he do? How could he save her? A few days ago, he truly might have left her here and saved himself, thinking *to Hades with everyone else.* After all, he was a killer, not a savior.

Today, that moment, for whatever reason, he didn't want to whisk himself away. Didn't want to put his life above another's. Delilah's life was more valuable than his own.

Another blaze of fire launched at him, but this time he was too slow and it slammed into his shoulder, sizzling the skin and half of his hair. Plumes of black smoke wafted around him. For once, his mind was not on retaliation. He didn't care that Tagart was breathing the same air he was, didn't care that Tagart was alive. Delilah was still all that mattered to him.

Was she breathing? Not a single sound emerged from her. She was so still, so lifeless. Damn this! She couldn't take much more.

Something sharp cut into his leg. A shark. He kicked with his other leg, knocking the creature away and diving under just as another blaze of fire rained. Eyes open in the murky liquid, he saw a smiling merman grab Delilah's waist, trying to pull her away from him. Enraged, Layel wound his legs around her. Crimson liquid swirled out of him and around them.

The merman stopped grinning and jerked. "Mine!"

Layel managed to latch on to the fish-man's hair and tug him forward, body gliding smoothly through the water. Never breaking momentum, Layel chomped down on his neck. The merman flailed, his tail hitting Delilah.

Finally, her eyelids popped open.

Immediately she began flailing for freedom, panic blanketing her expression. If he lost his grip, Delilah would swim unknowingly into the fire above. Though he had a hard time holding her and fighting his opponent at the same time, he managed it, too desperate to do otherwise.

The merman thrashed so fiercely, a small whirlpool formed below their feet. Only when the creature went limp did Layel release him, watching as he floated down…down…

Another shark darted past.

Layel's arm snaked around Delilah's chest, cupped her breast and jolted her into the hard line of his body. She stilled on contact. Softened as though she recognized him. As the shark turned, darted past again, mouth opening, teeth gleaming, she punched it in the nose. That quickly, it swam away.

And then Delilah was gone, and Layel was grasping only water. Wild, he scanned the murky liquid…. A shark hit him from behind and he spun. Another merman sprang forward, tackling Layel and flipping him over.

Where in Hades was Delilah? How had she disappeared like that? Only the gods could—the gods, he realized. Elimination. He roared through the water, dread coursing through him. Dread and panic, followed by shock at the knowledge that he cared. But he did. He cared and he couldn't deny it. Didn't want to deny it just then.

Delilah could be voted off. Killed. Her teammates didn't like her association with him, after all. Layel didn't waste any more time in the sea. He pictured the crackling bonfire in his mind, the moonlight, the rocks and the moss. A moment later, he was there, the ocean a distant memory.

He collapsed into a dripping heap, suddenly unable to support his own weight. His strength—gone. All of his limbs shook so forcefully, he wouldn't have been surprised if he caused some kind of quake.

Delilah. Had to find her. He barely managed to lift his head. His eyes roved the area. There were the rocks, the moss, the circle where the bonfire had once crackled, but there were no people. No, wait. There *were* people. His team. Not who he'd been looking for. They strode through the far bush, all of them frowning in confusion as they surveyed their surroundings.

"…summoned here, I think," someone said. "Why are we back at the counsel circle? We won. Our team was the last standing."

"For our prize, perhaps?" another replied. "Perhaps we are to come here after every challenge, whether we win or lose."

Damn this! Where would the gods have taken Delilah? Helplessness settled heavily on Layel's shoulders as no answer presented itself. *Think, think!* Off the island? Back to Atlantis? No, no. She was here, had to be.

"I bet so," the conversation continued, distracting his muddled mind.

"I can't wait!"

"Wonder who will be killed from the other team."

"Dear gods. Look!"

There were gasps, excited whoops, and then the sound of plates and bowls rattling, teeth chomping. Layel's gaze lifted. There, in place of the fire, was table after table piled high with food. Scents of sweetmeats and spice wafted to him as his teammates gorged.

Delilah. She was here, surely. Somewhere. Layel wanted to find her, see her, make sure she was all right. Make sure she was not the one chosen to die.

What he would do if she was, he didn't know. He only knew it would be his fault. Because of her...relationship with him. Relationship, yes. Not just an association, as he'd thought earlier, but a true relationship. There was no denying it. Not any longer. They searched for each other while standing among a crowd. They each wanted something from the other—blood, passion. They were intimate only with each other. They talked, they shared, they looked out for each other.

Panting, sweating, bleeding, he labored to his feet. Swayed just as Delilah had done while standing on that stump. He tripped forward and had to seize the base of a tree to hold himself upright. Breath in, breath out.

He sniffed the air, suddenly hating the smell of that food because it saturated everything, blocking Delilah's scent. No, wait! He sniffed again, catching a trace of her innate perfume—woman and strength, waterfall and sweetness— and forced his heavy legs into motion. Each step was agony.

An eternity passed, surely, as he stumbled through vines, over thick roots, across crystalline pools and around the animals that usually hid from him. Pigs, birds, some type of cat. They watched him curiously, as if realizing he was too weak to hurt them but unsure what to do about him.

Why are you doing this? Why do you care? This is wrong. He had no answers, didn't even want to think about it just then.

Finally he heard the sound of a crackling fire, could almost feel its tantalizing heat. He stopped, black spots winking in front of his eyes. Murmurings floated to him.

"…will have to choose."

"But who?"

"The weakest or the betrayer?"

He crouched as best he could, considering his condition, and moved forward, determined to remain unseen by the god. He might be sent elsewhere if he was spotted. When he reached the edge, a group of leaves blocked his path. He pushed them aside—quiet, steady—and then he was looking directly at Delilah.

His heart stopped beating. The world slowed, fading to her. She was as soaked as he was, what little clothing she wore plastered to her like a second skin. Her body was cut and bruised, making her look like she'd just returned from a vicious battle—and lost. But she was awake. Alive. Shivering. And the most beautiful sight he'd ever beheld. Ever. Even Susan had not compared, and he felt evil for even thinking so terrible a thought.

She'd anchored her hair on top of her head. Several stubborn strands refused to stay in place, however, and cascaded down her temples and past her shoulders. Tagart sat beside her in human form. Someone had given him a pair of pants, so his male parts were covered at least. The pants were too small, however, and hugged his thighs.

The bastard reached over and hooked one of Delilah's

tendrils behind her ears, brushing her cheek with his knuckles in the process. Layel's stomach twisted and bloodlust roared through him.

Delilah angrily slapped the dragon's hand away, and that saved Tagart's life. For now. Layel relaxed slightly.

Tagart scowled and whispered to her—Layel couldn't make out the words.

"Has a decision been reached?" a disembodied voice suddenly asked. Harsh, edged with steel. "And do not think to beg for mercy as the team before you did. I have none. Not for you. You had only to stand in one location and demonstrate your endurance. Yet you failed, every one of you, allowing yourselves to be distracted, forgetting there were consequences if you lost sight of the goal. Had one of you lasted a single minute longer, you would have been the last standing. You would have won."

Everyone sitting around the fire stiffened. The flames stroked upward as though stoked, mingling together, swirling, almost raging, then forming into the body of an amazingly tall, thick-chested man.

"May we have more time at least before we cast our votes?" Delilah asked through her chattering teeth.

"No," was the firm reply. "You did not earn it."

"Then I guess we are ready." She closed her eyes, opened them, and determination fell over her features. Layel longed to wrap his arms around her, hold her close, fill her with his warmth. Keep her safe. "My vote is for the demon. He was the first to fall."

"I second the motion," Tagart said, shooting Delilah a pointed look.

The demon in question hissed at them. "I vote for Delilah," he said, his horns sharp and glistening with poison.

"I had planned to choose the vampire, but you just changed my mind."

Layel's hands tightened into fists. He'd promised the demons to Zane, but he might take this one for himself. Or perhaps not. Zane's turn had come and the fierce vampire gleefully said, "My vote is for the demon."

"I vote for the Amazon," the centaur who'd shouted for quiet in the water said.

"That is three votes for the demon and two votes for the Amazon," the god said dramatically, as if everyone present had forgotten how to count. "A close race, indeed. Formorian, who does your vote belong to?"

The one-armed, one-legged creature scanned his teammates. His small, gossamer wings fluttered erratically as his mind swirled with what to do. The demon or the Amazon. Layel returned his attention to Delilah. She was stiff, unemotional. Waiting and expectant. She thought she would die.

The desire to hold her intensified as his gaze shifted to the dragon who had tried to kill him only a short while ago. The warrior was currently staring at the formorian with murder in his golden eyes, a silent command to vote as Tagart thought he should. Or die painfully. Ironic, Layel reflected, that he would feel grateful to a dragon.

The formorian gulped audibly, ruddy skin paling. "The demon. I vote for the demon."

And just like that, the others voted for the demon, too.

"No, please no," the demon was saying, shaking his head with violence. "Don't do this. I'm strong. I will take us to victory."

"Enough. The verdict has been rendered." The silver sword Layel now saw in his nightmares appeared in the center of the fire. Round and round the weapon spun, lethal, macabre.

With a shove, the demon was on his feet, backing away, gasping out, "No, don't do this. Please, don't do this." He stumbled over a thick root and fell.

Before Layel could blink, the sword descended.

There was a sickening whoosh, followed by a thud. A roll. A feminine scream echoed through the trees, powerful, ear piercing. Godly? The sound blended with Zane's laughter.

Then absolute silence enveloped the bonfire, even the flames quiet. Layel was glad for the death, would have rendered it himself if possible, and so he didn't flinch at the violence.

Delilah didn't flinch, either, though there was sadness in her eyes.

Layel had done so much to cause her pain, and even this could be laid at his door, yet she deserved only happiness. *I almost lost her.*

He was going to have her, Layel decided. Just once. He would know her taste, her scent and her body. He would keep his emotions separate from the act, of course. He wouldn't tarnish Susan's memory by doing otherwise. But he had to have Delilah, every inch, every breathless moan.

So far nothing else had pushed the Amazon from his mind. And he was tired of trying. There was no telling how much time they had left on the island—or alive, for that matter. In two hundred years, he'd known nothing but hate, pain and sorrow. He'd never minded that—had welcomed it, even—because he didn't deserve better. Still he did not deserve better, but he could no longer welcome the suffering. He ached.

Susan had loved him, for their too-brief time together. She would not have wanted this horrible life he'd built for himself. Had she known he was hurting, she would have smiled, traced her fingers through his hair and told him to be happy, to enjoy.

Were the situation reversed, Delilah would have threatened to attack anyone he encouraged, he thought with a half smile. The smile grew as he imagined her in his bed, spread and wet and eager.

One night together. That would have to be enough.

How long will you destroy anything and everything close to you because Susan cannot be here? His smile gradually faded. Forever, he knew. He wouldn't allow himself a happily-ever-after. One night, yes. But no more. Susan hadn't died happily, so neither would he live as such. No matter that she would have wanted him to. She *would* be avenged.

But for today, this one time, he would forget everything but Delilah. And passion. Oh, yes. Passion. He would be a man worthy of love and tenderness. He would be Delilah's man, giving her everything she craved, and perhaps more. If she would have him still…

Tagart stood, drawing his attention. "Let us return to the beach," he told his team. "We must do whatever it takes to win the next challenge, even if that means training the entire night. We cannot afford another round of…this. Understand?" His voice was hoarse, laden with undercurrents of shock.

Had they not expected the god to kill? Had they expected him to laugh and send them on their way?

There was more murmuring as the creatures lumbered to shaky legs, looking anywhere but at the still-bleeding, twitching body. Only Delilah remained seated.

"Come," Tagart commanded her, motioning her to him with a jerk of his fingers.

Appearing dazed, numb, she shook her head. "I need…a moment alone."

She had hesitated. What had she really wanted to say? Layel wondered.

Tagart's jaw clenched. "You shouldn't stay here. The god could return. He could—"

"Hurt me no matter where I am on the island," she interjected. "I need a moment, Tagart. Please. I won't be long."

The *please* softened the harsh contours of his expression, yet he remained in place. "Remember what I told you, Delilah?"

She gave him another of those absent nods, but there was a sudden blaze in her eyes. "I won't forget, I assure you."

Curiosity rose inside Layel. What had the dragon told her?

"Good. See that you don't." He looked pointedly at the lifeless demon body and stalked away.

The others followed quickly, obviously not wanting to be parted from the man they now saw as their leader. Layel was content to wait, doing nothing, saying nothing, simply staring at the woman who had fascinated him so deeply these past few days.

"I didn't expect it to be like this," Delilah said, gaze lifting. She found him, even hidden in the darkness as he was, and he blinked in surprise. "I've killed, seen others kill, but this just seems…cold."

"Yes."

"All I could think was that it could have been me. Probably *should* have been me."

A denial instantly roared through his mind—*not you, never you*—but he tamped it down. "It wasn't." He straightened, dislodging the leaves that covered him. Tried to glide forward, but he did not have the strength to float. He stumbled to her and thudded onto the log beside her. Their shoulders brushed, and there was a zap of something hot between them.

She gulped, said brokenly, "I didn't thank you. For—"

"You owe me no thanks."

"Yes, I do."

"No, you do not."

"I fell from that log like a damned untrained *man*."

His lips curled at the disgust in her voice. "Actually, you jumped. Do you not remember? And anyway, you wouldn't have done so if not for me. I weakened you, mind and body."

"I have been weaker, yet I've never reacted that way before." Now she was speaking as if to reassure him of her strength.

"I don't think poorly of you, Delilah. I…" *Don't tell her, don't say it aloud, that will make it real.* But he couldn't help himself. "I liked taking care of you."

For a long while, she remained silent, the crackling fire and song of the surrounding insects the only sounds. Then she sighed. "I liked hearing you say that, even though I shouldn't. An Amazon's only purpose is the protection of her sisters, and she cannot protect them if she is weak or if a man is stronger than she is. But…"

"But?" He wanted to hear the rest. A part of him *needed* to hear it. He was just a man tonight, and she was just a woman. This was allowed.

When she gave no response, Layel stood to mask his disappointment. "Wait here. I will bury the body."

"I will help."

"You're still weak."

"We do this together, Layel. Remember?"

He nodded, foolishly happy with her insistence.

The task lasted an hour and they were exhausted by the

time they settled back in front of the fire, sweaty, dirty and struggling to calm their breathing.

"Your strength pleases me," she finally blurted. "That is what I was going to say before."

Hearing it was as wonderful as he'd imagined. And yet… "I am not strong," he found himself saying bitterly.

She tossed a stick into the flames, watching as it burned to ash. "How so?"

He was here when he should have been anywhere else. He hadn't saved Susan, and he wouldn't have been able to save Delilah had she been chosen tonight. "Too many reasons to name."

Delilah looked over at him, studying him in the firelight. Whatever she saw amid that flickering gold she must have liked, for she reached out and traced a fingertip along the curve of his jaw, over his lips. Gentle, so gentle. "You're pale," she said.

"I'm always pale."

"More so than usual. Are you injured? More than I can see, that is?"

"I'm fine." His strength pleased her. No way in all of Hades he would admit to weakness now.

"Do you need more of my blood?"

"No," he lied, unwilling to risk taking more from her for any reason. He captured her hand and placed a soft kiss on her wrist, where her pulse suddenly leapt to erratic life. Blood was rushing through her veins, a sweet scent drifting from her skin.

His mouth watered.

"Wh-why did you do that?" she asked.

"What?"

"Kiss my hand?"

"I wanted to." Truth. "Did you not like it?"

"I liked it, more than I should, but you've never touched me willingly before."

A crime. "I have wanted to," he admitted.

The long length of her feathered lashes lowered to half-mast, shielding her vibrant gaze. "I'm supposed to stay away from you."

Unable to stop himself, he leaned toward her. He would not kiss her lips—couldn't, wouldn't succumb to this attraction so deeply, intently—but he needed his lips on her. Somewhere. He pressed softly into the line of her jaw, her chin, inhaling her sweetness. "Why?" He knew the answer, though. Tagart. *Remember what I told you,* the dragon had said.

A shiver moved through her. "Why what?"

"Must you stay away from me now?" Out flicked his tongue, tracing the same path his mouth had taken. Smoothness, sweetness, heat. His cock hardened painfully.

"My team," she breathed, arms wrapping tentatively around him.

They would kill her next if she was seen with him again, he realized. "We won't let them find us, then. Not tonight." She needed him as much as he needed her. That was clear with every heated breath she took. "Tomorrow...tomorrow we can act as strangers."

Her fingers glided up his back, over the ridges of his spine, then she stopped, her nails digging into his shoulders. She arched forward, meshing her breasts against his chest. He hissed in a breath.

"You will not mind?" she asked.

Now *he* could not recall where the conversation had left off. "Mind what?"

"Loving tonight, being strangers tomorrow."

Her words should have delighted him. That was what he wanted, what he needed to return to his cold, isolated world. It was exactly what he'd just told her had to happen. Hearing her easy acceptance and even willingness to forget his touch, however, irritated him. Caused every possessive bone in his body to roar.

"No," he said through clenched teeth. A small protest from her would have been nice. Wouldn't it? "I will not mind."

"Unlike my sisters, I've never wanted the short-term from a man." She swung her leg around and hefted herself up so that she was straddling his waist, her hot core poised directly over his straining cock. He hated their clothing. "But I can't seem to stop. You, I will have, if only for the night. So, tell me. What do you plan to do with me?"

What had she wanted then? Forever? His chest lurched, because a tiny part of him would have loved to give it to her. "First we will bathe." He would be nothing less than perfect for her. When she thought of him in the years to come, and he hoped that she did, he wanted it to be with fondness, perhaps arousal.

She nibbled on her bottom lip. "Considering what we just endured in the water, are you sure you want to go back in?"

"Oh, yes. We'll go to our waterfall."

She offered him a half smile. "And after? What will you do to me?"

He studied her. Dirt streaked her bruised face and her partially dried hair was in tangles around her arms, curling, a bit frayed. Yet she suddenly pulsed with vitality, as if the thought of being with him gave her all the energy she needed. Her lips were soft and red, her violet eyes luminous, sensual. Erotic. The sight of her always made his chest ache. He didn't like it, but he craved that ache, grateful for the reminder that he was still alive, not dead and buried.

"Well?"

Rather than answer her, he asked a question of his own. "Are you nervous? Is that why you wish to know?"

"Not nervous. Curious. Excited."

"Then I will explain and hopefully increase your excitement. I will taste you here." He circled her nipple with the tip of his finger.

She gasped in ecstasy.

"And here." He inched a bit lower, staying atop the tiny leather skirt that shielded her feminine core from his gaze.

"I— Yes. That's an excellent plan." Licking her lips, she leaned toward him. Almost, almost…she would taste so good, so very good. "Tonight you will love me," she whispered.

Love her. The words trembled through him and he turned his head away before he drowned in her, sinking deeply, sinking completely, losing himself. Her kiss landed on his cheek, and then she pulled back and blinked in disappointment.

Once more, he'd hurt her.

He pushed to his feet—*don't fall, don't you dare fall*— and she slid down his body. Pleasure speared him, lancing him more surely than a weapon ever had. "Come," he said roughly, harshly, holding out his hand. *You can walk away,* he found himself projecting. *You do not have to do this.* "Unless you've changed your mind?" *Do not change your mind. Please, do not change your mind.*

Her fingers curled around his. Without a word, they walked to the waterfall.

CHAPTER EIGHTEEN

A THOUSAND EMOTIONS SEEMED to swirl through Delilah—excitement, joy, sorrow, tenderness, passion, anger, regret, confusion, even the nervousness she'd told Layel she didn't feel. She wanted this more than she'd ever wanted anything. Would have killed for this moment with Layel, harshly and without remorse.

She was going to be with the man who'd captured her interest. Would know him as intimately as a woman could know a man, allowing him inside her body, perhaps her soul. For once she would be the prize and not the conqueror. And yet...

She wanted to cry.

He would walk away afterward without a backward glance. Once again she would be nothing more than a pleasurable encounter, easily forgotten.

She had shed tears only once in her life: the day her mother sent her away to begin training as a warrior. Her first tutor had beaten her for those tears. Since then, she had not cried. Not in pain when her body was abused beyond recognition, not in sadness when she buried several of her sisters after battle, not in shame when Vorik left her. Tears were a sign of weakness. But weakness had mattered little when Layel turned his face away to avoid her kiss.

He had turned his face away exactly as her sisters turned their heads when their slaves tried to kiss them.

As if she wasn't good enough for more than a quick tumble—she'd known that.

As if she meant nothing—she'd suspected.

As if he would remain distanced from the act, while she gave everything she had to give—that, she had not expected.

The knowledge had burned hotter than dragon fire, scraped deeper than a demon's claw and slashed harsher than a vampire's teeth. He was willing to take her body, but not her mouth, even though he'd kissed her before. Why? Had the first been a mistake? No, his actions were fueled by loyalty to his mate, she suspected, and that just intensified the hurt. But she couldn't bring herself to halt what they were about to do.

Just once, she told herself. Just once, she had to know what it was like to be utterly possessed by a man. Vorik had taken her body, but he had not consumed her. She and Layel remained in the shadows, careful not to allow anyone to see them. They remained quiet, careful not to allow anyone to hear them. After an eternity, they broke through the trees and the waterfall came into view, dripping cool liquid into a decadently fragrant pool.

Her hands began to sweat, her body to tremble.

"Bathe," he said, his tone flat. "I will check the area to make sure we are truly alone." He didn't give her time to respond, just released her and strode out of sight.

"Now there's another emotion to add to the ever-growing list," she muttered. Bereavement.

With a sigh, she stripped and padded into the water. Her skin seemed to soak up every drop, drowning, muscles softening. She washed her hair with the flowers blooming at the edge and cleaned the rest of her body with the glistening white soap-sand. At least the gods weren't denying them nature's sweetness.

Scrubbed from head to toe and unsure how much time had passed, she eased up onto the bank and sat upon a smooth silver rock, knees drawn up to her chest. Where was Layel?

As if her thoughts had summoned him, he appeared beside her. She hadn't heard him, which meant he'd floated, and she hadn't smelled his scent, which meant he'd bathed with the same sand and blooms she had. He wasn't naked, though. Actually wore his pants. But they were unfastened and sat low on his lean, sinewy waist.

His hair hung in dripping chunks, white and glorious. There was a smear of blood on his lips.

"You fed." Frowning, she pushed to her feet.

"Yes." His gaze slowly raked over her, lingering on her breasts—nipples hard and straining—and between her legs.

"On who?" She meant to snap the words, but they emerged breathless. His eyes were so vibrant with arousal it was palpable. The nymph?

"No one. An animal."

Her jealousy melted away, leaving only an arousal equal to his. Her stomach fluttered, her skin heated and her limbs shook. "You could have taken mine."

"Pretty," he said, reaching out and rolling one nipple between his fingers.

She bit her tongue to silence a guttural moan, a plea for more. "Why not use me? For blood, I mean?"

"You've lost enough." His eyes never left her breasts; they were glazed, as if he were entranced. "I need you strong."

"Aren't you afraid I'll beat you at the next challenge?"

He chuckled, but it was a harsh sound. Strained. "If I

cannot beat you fairly, I don't deserve to be here with you."
The moment the last word left his mouth, he stiffened.
Stepped backward.

He was going to leave her, she realized. Why, damn
him? Because he didn't feel he deserved her now? Her eyes
widened, her anger mutating into tenderness. Yes, that was
exactly what he thought, but she would have none of it.

She closed all distance between them, leaving only a
whisper that was conquered every time she drew in a
breath. They were body to body, skin to skin. Only his
erection and thighs were covered. And that wasn't good
enough. She wanted to feel them, too.

As if he couldn't tolerate brushing against her with his in-
halations, he stopped breathing, becoming as still as a corpse.

"Did you come here to reject me?" she asked. "Again."

He flinched. "No."

"Do something, then. Before I change my mind and leave."

His nostrils flared. "Don't pressure me, woman."

Rising on her tiptoes, she pressed their lips together. His
were soft, moist. His eyes never closed, only narrowed. He
allowed the contact briefly before turning his head away.

"No kissing there," he said. "I have to keep some part
of me removed from this. That is the only way I can allow
it to happen."

"You've kissed me before."

"That was a mistake. A mistake I will not make again."

No hurting, she told herself. "All right. No kissing you
on the mouth." She pressed her lips to his cheek next.
"What about here?" Then his jaw. "And here?"

Once again he began breathing. Choppily. Harshly.
Sweat broke out over his skin. "Fine. Those are fine."

The hard tips of her nipples rubbed against his chest,

creating a dizzying friction. Yes, oh, yes. Lowering, she concentrated on his neck, laving her tongue over the graceful column.

He inhaled sharply as his arms banded around her waist, clutching, the nails digging into skin.

"Take off your pants," she commanded fiercely. "I want you naked."

His fingers slid to her bottom and cupped, spreading her a little to hold her up. "Do you think to be in charge?"

"Yes." She arched forward, grinding herself on the massive erection straining so proudly from the waist of those unwanted pants.

"No." His grip tightened, holding her in place, keeping her still.

"But I ache," she told him before licking one of his nipples. The hard tip abraded her tongue deliciously.

A groan of pleasure sprang from him, the sound echoing in the night. "Lay down."

"You first. I would—"

"Lay down, Delilah."

His tone was hard, uncompromising. She should have bristled. She didn't. She tingled, her knees going weak. Breathless, she obeyed. He didn't move, just stared down at her.

What did he think of her?

Did he compare her to his mate?

Former mate, her mind supplied on a jealous burst. Tonight, he belonged to Delilah, only Delilah. "Well. Do you plan to join me?"

"Spread your legs. I want to look at you, all of you."

Cradled by moonlight and moss, she slowly…slowly… moved her thighs apart. She drew up her feet, bending her knees and anchoring her weight against her elbows. She was as vulnerable as a woman could be and surprisingly thrilled to be so.

His hot gaze raked over her thoroughly and soon those crystalline irises were glowing, practically surrounding her in a cerulean halo. She could feel the heat of it invading every inch of her needy body, blanketing her.

"You're wet," he said.

The reverence in his tone stroked her as expertly as a caress, and she shivered. "Yes."

"You want me."

"Yes."

"What do you want me to do to you?" As he spoke, he gripped the waist of his pants and slid the material down…down…then stepped out of them, leaving him bare.

"I—I—" Dear gods. His raw masculinity enthralled her. He was lean, yet so muscled he could probably have crushed her with his strength. There was no hair on his body, just mile after mile of perfect skin and sinew. His cock was long and thick—*mine*—and his testicles were drawn up tightly, heavy and proud.

"Like what you see?" he asked huskily, almost sounding drugged.

Unable to speak past the heated breath blistering her throat, she nodded. The length of her hair tickled her now sensitized skin, her beaded nipples, and she tore her gaze from Layel to study herself. To see what he saw. A thick blue lock of hair was curled around one hard, pink tip, stroking lovingly with the breeze. Her stomach was flat, her thighs firm and tattooed, quivering.

"Look at me," he commanded.

She did. Oh, gods, she did. Need was like a storm inside

THE VAMPIRE'S BRIDE

her, his every command hers to fulfill. Here was everything she'd ever wanted, dreamed about, craved, offered to her on a night of moonlight and bliss, starlight and dreams.

"What do you want me to do to you, Delilah?"

Took some coaxing, but she finally found her voice. "Touch me." A broken plea.

"Where?" He fisted his cock and moved up, down, in a measured stroke.

I want to be the one to pleasure you. "Everywhere."

"You asked me before what evil things I had done, if I had killed a woman."

Her gaze snapped up, clashed with his. "That—" *hardly matters now,* she was unable to say.

"Not only did I slay Marina, I slayed the wife of a dragon," he interjected. "He was there…that night…he was there. He escaped before I could take his heart and hack it to bits. But I followed him. I watched him. He had a family. A wife, a child."

"Layel—" She made to sit up but he was suddenly on top of her, pushing her back into the moss, his knees pinning her shoulders, his cock rising just in front of her face. She yelped in surprise, but didn't protest. She simply peered up at him, silent, beckoning him to finish. For he had sounded torn, part of him thinking—hoping—she would reject him, part of him…afraid? Afraid that he would die if she did? "Tell me."

His eyes glazed with the darkness of his memories, a darkness still infused with passion. "I was infuriated. Crazed. The bastard had violated my woman, had laughed while she screamed and fought and then returned to his own woman for comfort."

Delilah bowed her wrists and caressed as much of his thighs as she could, offering her own comfort.

His fangs lengthened, sharpened.

"And?" she prompted softly.

"I snuck inside his home that night. I drank from the two of them to weaken them and then I tied them up. I meant to take her, use her, as he had done—as he—" Layel drew in a labored breath, released it. "But I couldn't. She was crying, pleading. So I killed her instead, right in front of him. I didn't give him the same courtesy, though. I dragged him back to my palace and locked him up, letting him live with the image of what he'd done, what I'd done."

As Layel had had to do, she thought, aching for him.

"But as the days continued to pass, his life…offended me. I couldn't tolerate breathing the same air as him. So I called my people forward and let them drink from him, tear him limb from limb, his screams of agony in my ears. I laughed, but his pain wasn't enough, not nearly enough."

"I'm sorry."

"I burned him until there was nothing left but bones. And then I used those bones to make my throne, and every time I sit on it—him, all of them responsible—I pray he is rotting in Hades."

When his words faded, silence enveloped them, laden with tension.

"Do you still desire me? Do you still want such evil inside of you?" Again he sounded as if he was at war with himself, wanting two different things from her. Exactly as she had felt when she'd first met him.

"You're not evil. But, yes, I do." And that was the truth. She wouldn't have thought it possible to desire him more, but she did. The fierceness of him, the darkness…they called to her, drew her. They represented the very thing she'd always craved for herself: to be loved so inexorably, no act was too vile when it came protecting her—or avenging her.

But because of that ferocity, Layel would never be an easy man. He would always be brutal, savage. He was conflicted and complex, hurt and broken, would probably never be whole. He wasn't misunderstood, and there could be no deluding herself about who and what he was. There was no denying he'd done an evil thing. Many evil things.

"Yes," she repeated, confident. "Yes. I still want you inside of me."

He jerked as if she'd punched him. Not the reaction she'd expected. "What did you say?"

"I still want to be with you. Release my arms now. Please. I need to touch you, Layel."

A play of emotions danced over his features. The same bombardment she had experienced earlier, a combination of a thousand different feelings, both wonderful and terrible. "You…want to touch me still?"

"More than anything I've ever wanted before."

As if he feared moving too quickly, he gradually moved down her body until his knees straddled her waist. Shoulders finally free, she reached up and flattened her palms on his powerful thighs.

The muscles underneath jumped.

"I love the feel of you," she whispered.

"Delilah," he said, and it was a broken cry. "I will be careful with you." It was a vow. "Tonight I will be careful. You will experience nothing but pleasure."

She studied him through the thick fan of her lashes, shadows twining around him like midnight phantoms who meant to carry him away. "I don't want you careful. I want you inside me, hard and demanding."

He leaned down, this beautiful dark warrior, and laved at her neck, his tongue a hot brand. "You are so lovely. So strong and brave."

"Again," she gasped, hips arching. "Lick again."

While he obeyed, his body covered hers, his legs between hers, his cock rubbing against her belly. She rocked into him as he palmed one of her breasts, unable to remain still. The pleasure was simply too great. "Good?"

"Yes."

"I could lick you forever. Want to lick all your tattoos." His mouth soon replaced his fingers and he sucked her nipple gently, so gently. "What do they mean?"

"Victory."

He chuckled softly, and she shuddered at the exquisite bliss the sound wrought. "Should have known," he said. "Tell me if I do something you don't like. It's been a long time for me."

Heat was building inside her, a fire her blood could not seem to put out, only seemed to incite as it rushed through her veins. The fire raged like a warrior, insistent, sure, strong. She could not fight it, didn't want to fight it. Only wanted to be consumed by the flames.

"More," she begged.

Still unhurried, he moved to her other breast, gave it the same hot, moist attention. Her hips writhed, riding wave after wave of sensation. Layel kissed just above her heart, as if trying to absorb the beat. One of his hands glided down her stomach, swirled around her navel, then dabbled at the small tuft of hair between her legs.

"Yes, yes. Touch there."

"Like?"

"Like. More." She clutched his back, nails scoring deep. "Will you… Can you… Please. Hurry."

Two of his fingers slid between her hot, aching lips and straight into her core. A groan of ecstasy burst from her. In and out. Another finger joined the play. She was stretched in the most delicious way.

"So very wet," he praised.

She undulated against those expert fingers, her vision going black.

"That's right. Ride them, take what you need." In and out he continued to pump.

She thought his voice sounded strained, wanted to tell him to replace his fingers with his shaft, but the words caught in her throat as wild passion slammed through her, a battering ram intent on destroying her every defense. She spasmed, jerked, arched, silently screamed.

"I want to taste your release."

He kissed a path down her body, tracing her tattoos with his tongue as he'd promised. And then he was between her legs, lapping at the wetness there. Hot, so hot. He tongued her, sinking deep, just as his fingers had, riding the waves of her orgasm and pushing her right into another one.

Her legs locked around his neck, her hands fisted in his hair. Too much…too much…but she found that she wasn't shoving him away. She was pulling him closer, seeking more of him. Needing all that he had to offer.

"Never this sweet," he said.

He was infinitely careful not to lick her with his fangs, but she thought she might have liked that. Would have liked his teeth there, so intimately taking what he needed from her.

As her tremors subsided, he kissed his way up her stomach, leaving a trail of aroused, sweet fire. *I'm ready for more,* she realized shockingly. Far from sated after those two climaxes, her body only seemed to be primed.

He wasn't so careful now, perhaps was close to losing control, and one of his fangs nicked her. She hissed in surprised delight.

"I'm sorry, I'm sorry."

"Don't be. More."

He was at her neck in the next instant, not drinking but kissing, licking, tonguing, and his arousal was probing for entrance in a rough forward-backward dance.

"Tight," he gritted out.

"I can take it."

"Don't want to hurt."

"Hurts without you. Need you." To prove it, she arched up, up, drawing him deeper.

Sweat beaded on his face and dripped onto her, lava on her skin. "Almost…just…need a moment."

"Now."

"No, I—"

"Yes!"

With a roar, he slammed all the way to the hilt, as if he couldn't hold himself back a second longer. Stretched, burned. It had been a long time for her, too, and then only for that one night. Yet… Oh, gods, oh, gods. Nothing had ever felt so wondrous, so perfect. He was inside her. Layel was a part of her, touching deeply, so deeply, filling her up with all that he was.

"Sorry," he chanted. "Sorry. I'll be still. Give you time. Can't leave. Long time, sweetheart?"

Sweetheart. "Layel, kiss me. Please." She needed it, would die without it.

He nibbled on her ear, his warm breath fanning the lobe and ruffling her hair. But he denied her demand. "You feel so good. I think I could happily die here, in your arms."

She grabbed his face, palms flat on his cheeks. Their gazes met in a heated tangle. There were lines of strain around his eyes and mouth, passion blazing from his expression. Passion and pain and need, tenderness and self-loathing.

"Kiss me. On the mouth."

"No," he said, shaking his head. "Told you. Can't."

"Kiss me. Take me the rest of the way. *Please.* I'm giving you everything. Do the same for me. I'm not asking for something you haven't already given, mistake or not."

He shook his head again, pumped inside her once, twice, slow and measured. His lips drew tight over his teeth. "You're heaven, sweet. Feel just like heaven."

She arched back, almost lost, drowning. Her head thrashed from side to side as he continued to pump. *Important. Concentrate.* She pulled herself from the eroticism of the moment. There was something she wanted, something she needed. Something she— A kiss! Yes. Her eyes narrowed on him, taking in the blood dripping from his lip where he'd bitten himself. He would not hold a part of himself back. She wouldn't let him. He could hate her later, could resent her forever, but she didn't care.

She was a warrior and she would fight for all he had to give.

"Kiss me," she commanded once more. She lifted her head and bit into his jaw. "Kiss me now, like you did before, with tongues rolling together, teeth scraping."

He stilled, his muscles taut. He was growling low in his throat, an animal. Needy. "I can't!"

She almost gave up, that cry was so tortured. More than that, she was desperate to have him moving again. Without the friction of his body sliding in and out of hers, she felt lost, adrift. "Kiss me. I need your tongue in my mouth, tasting. I need your flavor. I need you like I've never needed anyone else. I want you so badly, I feel like I've been waiting for you forever and will think of you, dream of you, every night for—"

Her words were cut off as his mouth smashed into hers, tongue thrusting deep. With that one touch, that one melding of their mouths, it was as if his control snapped completely. No tether, no reining him in.

He jerked from her only to slam forward, hard, rocking her and even scooting her backward, from moss to twig-laden bank. A few rocks cut into her skin, but she didn't care. This was it, the kiss she'd remember all the days of her life, more powerful than even the first. "Yes. More."

He tongued her deep, probing. Their teeth scraped together with a ferocity that surprised her. His fangs even dug into her lower lip. He sucked and he thrust and he growled, all the while hammering inside her.

This wasn't sex. This was possession. This was…magic.

Release tore into her with the same intensity as his thrusts and her inner walls clamped down on him. He roared loud and long, and she swallowed the sound. His body heaved, the force of his climax so strong he was nearly convulsing.

He gripped her tightly and she thought her bones might snap, but she didn't stop him. She held him, cradled him, cooed to him as she'd never done to another.

A few minutes passed, maybe an hour. His spasms eased and he was left shuddering…shivering… Her own limbs were weak, her body utterly sated, but still she held on to him. Every feminine instinct inside her was screaming for her to do so, to never let go.

He was hers.

Only tonight...foolish girl.

She wanted forever. Wanted more nights like this, wanted to wake in his arms and talk with him, eat with him. Every morning.

Mine, she thought.

"I'm sorry," he said brokenly. "I'm sorry."

She tangled her fingers in his silky hair. "I'm glad we did this. I loved everything that happened. I—"

"I'm sorry," he repeated as if he couldn't hear her or just wasn't listening. Perhaps he was trapped inside his head, his thoughts consuming him.

Her chest ached for him. For herself. "Layel—"

"So sorry." He wrenched from her, separating them completely. His half-hard shaft was covered with her climax and glistening in the moonlight.

She shivered from the sudden cold. "Talk to me. Tell me what's going on."

He turned from her without a word and ran. Just ran. Delilah watched, feeling more helpless than she had in the whole of her life. Even the time she had been captured by the demons after she'd been wounded in battle, she hadn't experienced this sense of despair.

What should I do?

She pushed to shaky legs, almost fell as she tried to move forward. Then something cool and wet slid from her collarbone and down, down her stomach. Confused, she wiped at it and held up her hand. Clear, glistening liquid.

Tears.

Layel's tears.

LAYEL HUDDLED against the base of a tree, raw, alone, destroyed. Hot tears streamed down his face, and he laughed bitterly. What kind of warrior was he? What kind of king? Sobbing like a godsdamn infant?

He wasn't a warrior, he decided. He was a nothing. Worse than nothing. He had betrayed Susan in every way possible now.

He'd thought to hold a part of himself from Delilah, to prove to himself, he supposed, that she was different than his beloved mate. But in the end, he had given Delilah everything. His body, his mouth, his desire, his seed, perhaps even his soul—because he wanted to give her even more.

Shame coursed through him. Shame and—no, surely not. But it was there, undeniable. Pride that he had satisfied a woman such as Delilah, that pleasure had blanketed her features, that she'd clutched him tightly, gasped his name, wanted more. That she'd given herself to him, precious gift that she was.

Never again, he vowed. He'd had his night, and that would have to be enough. Any more, and he would forget Susan altogether. And if he forgot her, he would not be a man worthy of Delilah. Delilah, who he wanted to return to, take again, hold. And love. Should have been Susan he craved.

"Susan, I'm sorry. I'll do better, I swear it." Scowling, he grabbed a jagged rock from the ground and jabbed the sharpest end into his wrist. Tissue broke apart, veins split, revealing a pool of blood.

He carved two words into his flesh, a reminder: *Never again.*

CHAPTER NINETEEN

SHIVAWN WAS NEARING panic.

He had searched the Outer City, but Alyssa hadn't been there. So he had gone to the Inner City. No sign of her there, either. Next he'd traveled to the vampire stronghold, where she lived. No one had seen her. He believed them, because they'd immediately launched a search party of their own.

Shivawn knew of no other place to look.

No matter where he'd gone, he'd caught no trace of her scent—and nearly two days had passed since he'd breathed her in. Almost two days since he'd spoken to her, enjoyed her wit, tried to convince her of his love.

She was his. He needed her. Would die without her.

Already he was weak, but no other would do. Not anymore. He couldn't even consider *kissing* another woman. The thought was abhorrent to him. This must have been how Alyssa had felt, needing his blood and no other's. He deserved this suffering, he realized. This and a thousand times more.

Alyssa was the only female for him. The one. The forever. No longer could he get hard for anyone else. During his search, many had tried to change that and had failed. A fact he was glad for. He didn't want anyone else, didn't want his body reacting to them. That would be a betrayal to Alyssa and Alyssa was more important to him than breathing.

He just had to find her.

What if she was hurt? What if another man tried to claim her? An unholy fire sprang to life inside him. When mated, a nymph female would desire no other man, but he wasn't sure how vampires handled mating. He didn't know of a nymph who had ever taken a vampire as wife.

Where in Hades was she?

I caused this, he thought darkly. *I should be gutted.* He had hurt her deeply, and he planned to spend the rest of eternity making up for his behavior. If only he could find her.

There was a sudden bang. A crash. His eyelids popped open. When had he closed them? Shivawn frowned and studied his surroundings. All he could see was nymph warrior after nymph warrior. His frown deepened.

Valerian had the lead and scowled down at him, sword in hand. "Where have you been?"

Better question: where was he now?

His tired gaze moved from the warriors, up, up, to a thatched roof. The scent of hay and horse filled his nose. A rented room, he remembered. He was inside a centaur stable, on the outskirts of the city and as close to the vampire fortress as he could get without actually being inside it.

Just in case she returned. Or her brethren found her.

Damn it. Where was she?

"Shivawn?"

His attention snapped to Valerian, and he eased to a sitting position. Scrubbed the sleep from his face. "Have you seen Alyssa?" he asked without preamble.

"No. Is she missing?"

"Yes. Damn it, yes."

"Where have you been? What have you been doing? You didn't report to me as ordered, and I've been worried."

"I'll tell you." He leveled a pointed glance at the men. They didn't need to hear of his shame. "Once we are alone."

Valerian's jaw clenched and for several seconds he said nothing, did nothing. He loathed being thwarted. That Shivawn knew well, for the king usually killed such offenders.

"Please," Shivawn said.

Finally Valerian nodded and the army pounded from the chamber without hesitation, their boots clomping heavily. "Talk."

They were alone now, but Shivawn suddenly couldn't find the words. He dropped his head into his upraised hands and anchored his elbows on his knees. The sheet covering him slid to his waist and pooled over his flaccid cock. Would he ever be hard again? Alyssa…it twitched.

"Did you learn anything about my soldiers?" Valerian asked, trying to get them started.

"No. They have disappeared, along with two creatures from every other race. No one has seen or heard from those warriors, either. A few even disappeared in front of witnesses, there one moment, gone the next."

"So Poseidon is responsible," Valerian muttered. "Who else could conjure such mischief?"

The gods had ignored them for hundreds of years. But Poseidon, the sea god, had remembered their presence a few months ago and now evidently thought to make up for lost time, subjecting them to all manner of hardships. Bastard. "Do you think they are…dead?"

"If they are, there will be a heavenly war such as even the gods have never seen. But no, I suspect they are being used for something. The sea king's amusement, perhaps."

"Bad things happen when he is bored, I've noticed."

"Yes." Valerian closed his eyes for a moment. "I want to hate the bastard, but I cannot."

"He gave you back your woman," Shivawn said, wishing Poseidon could do the same for him.

The nymph king nodded. He sheathed his sword and strode to the room's only table, a small square wooden mass with low seats that allowed the centaurs to stretch out comfortably. Valerian sat, somehow managing to still appear regal, sprawled out as he now was.

"I will have troops patrol both cities and keep watch."

"Good."

"Now, tell me the rest." Valerian's stare became penetrating.

"The rest?"

"Why you look like—" Valerian's hand waved over him "—death."

"I found my mate," he said. Just like that, Alyssa's image formed in his mind. Silky hair tumbling, face softened in pleasure—face tight with pain—body soft, eager. Body stiff, dejected.

"Ah, that explains it," Valerian said with a chuckle. "You had me worried for naught. The right woman always makes her man suffer, Shivawn. Shaye did the same to me when we first met, as you probably recall. Took me a while, but I finally realized working so hard to attain my prize was a very good thing. Never will I forget how blessed I am to have found and won her. Never will I take her for granted."

If only Shivawn could be assured of a similar outcome for Alyssa and himself. "You worked for Shaye, yes, but she always wanted you. My woman despises me." And gods, she had every right to do so. He had pushed her away time and time again. Year after year. He had hurt her, insulted her, smashed her pride, her femininity. Her heart.

That precious, beautiful heart. A heart he was supposed to protect.

"Talk to her," Valerian advised. "Apologize. Women like that."

"I tried. She ran." He pinched the bridge of his nose. "What am I going to do? I have prayed for a mate forever, it seems. I would watch my friends fall and wish it were me. But I never sensed her, and finally I gave up, only to learn she had been in front of me all along. Now Alyssa has—"

"Alyssa the vampire?" Everyone knew of Shivawn's dislike of the species.

He gave a stiff nod.

"I should have guessed, as...fierce as you were with her." Valerian *tsked* in sympathy. "She is a warrior, not easily conquered."

"No. She isn't a warrior. She doesn't want to be. Perhaps never wanted to be." But for him, she had fought. Oh, yes, he owed her more than he could ever repay. Forever wouldn't be long enough to pamper her.

Valerian didn't look as if he believed the claim. "Still, she has known battle. If you desire her as you say—"

"I do." With everything inside him. He wanted her more than he'd ever wanted another.

"Then you must now fight for her, with her. It will probably be the bloodiest battle of your life."

But the reward would make any injuries worth it. "I will do whatever's necessary. I just have to find her." She was hiding from him, he knew that. Might assume he meant to search for her just to kill her. Punish her at the very least.

He'd vowed to do so, after all.

Had any man ever been so foolish? She could chain him, hold him prisoner. If he was with her, he wouldn't care about anything else.

"Does she have family?" Valerian asked.

His brows furrowed as he pondered that. Did she? She never spoke of them if she did. "I do not think so."

Valerian was frowning, scrubbing his jaw with two fingers. "Brothers," he said, then nodded. "She had brothers."

Shivawn hated that he had not known that. He wanted to learn everything there was to know about her. Then one of Valerian's words got caught in his thoughts. "Had? They died?"

"I believe Layel mentioned they were unruly, cruel. They must have been, for they were killed, their heads removed, their bodies nailed to trees." He nodded as if the vampire king's words were echoing in his mind. "From what I gathered, they were demons, though Alyssa had no idea Layel knew that about her, and their queen never found their murderer."

Everything inside of Shivawn went still, his blood chilling to ice. Not because he hated what Alyssa was—he could not hate any part of her—but because of what he'd just realized he might have taken from her. If she truly was half-demon, and if her brothers had been killed in that manner…that meant… Shivawn thought he might vomit.

Once, long ago, he had decapitated three demon warriors and nailed them to trees. "How many were there?" he croaked out. "Brothers, I mean."

"I do not recall their exact number. Two. Perhaps three. Evidently their horns had been cut off, along with their heads."

The ice burst into millions of tiny slivers, cutting his every organ, felling him. Three. There'd been three. "I killed them," he managed to work past the hard knot in his throat. "I did it. Took their heads. Removed their horns. Strung them up."

Valerian straightened. "They were the ones…"

"Yes." He felt like such a fool. That was why Alyssa had always reminded him of that horrid night. Those demon eyes had stared up at him as his sword struck, in reality, in his nightmares—eyes just like hers. Only, hers were kind and loving. Maybe he'd smelled her demon blood, as well. Maybe she had been there, and he'd subconsciously sensed it.

Of course she'd been there, he thought, though she wouldn't have participated. She'd probably been hiding and scared. He had caught her watching him soon after, ducking whenever he glanced her way.

He had wronged her far more than he'd supposed. He had despised all demons for what had happened to his father, yet Alyssa had had every reason to despise him. That she didn't was a miracle. That she had looked at him with tenderness and desire in her lovely eyes was even more so.

Until two days ago, when he'd ruined everything.

"What are you going to do?"

Shivawn thought he knew where she was now. The one place he'd never thought to go again. The one place he'd *vowed* never to go again. The site of his father's death.

"I'm going to get my woman," he said determinedly. Whether she wanted him or not.

THE GLOWING ORANGE-YELLOW BALL of fire rose in the sky, higher and higher, burning Zane's skin but not truly harming him, as the gods had promised. He wished it would. He welcomed every sting.

Nola had rejected him.

She didn't want him, didn't crave his touch as he craved hers. That was not supposed to have happened. She'd been wild in his arms; she'd even cried his name. He'd been so sure of his reception, once he declared himself. The gods owed him. He hadn't expected her to run from him, hate him, as Cassandra had.

She'd looked at him as if he were the very demon he'd just watched die. Demons—how they sickened him. They thrived on pain, screams, agony—the pain, screams and agony they inflicted on others. They loved to hurt their partner while fucking. And he'd endured it. Had hated himself, but he'd let the cruelest of them all do whatever she wanted to him. He wouldn't think about that. Too painful. When he'd left, Cassandra done with him, he'd thought—hoped—to never have sex again.

But Nola…the beautiful Amazon had made him want to try, to have the simple pleasure he'd enjoyed a lifetime ago. Before…just before. But no. She loathed him.

Somehow she must know, deep down, what he'd been. What he still was. He closed his eyes against a too-bright ray, the burn intensifying on his face. What had he expected? Her to fall at his feet? Beg him to pleasure her?

He had forced her to want him as surely as the demon queen had forced him to her will.

With that thought, Zane leaned over and emptied the contents of his stomach. He heaved and heaved and heaved until there was nothing left. Until he was empty. Until every ounce of his energy seeped away.

If Nola was not the female for him, why did he still want

her? He had no answer. Did she desire the dragon? *That,* he thought he knew. Of course she did. Brand was strong, untainted, and honorable.

Zane's entire body tensed, a surge of fury giving him momentary strength. Nola had indeed seemed attracted to the dragon warrior—as she wasn't to him. Was Zane not allowed to even experience that sweet, basic attraction?

Was he to suffer forever and still another lifetime?

Probably. He wasn't worthy of anything else. He was nothing, no better than the stinking, bile-laden sand he now lay upon. After all, he'd willingly done those things with the queen for all those years. For his woman, yes. For her freedom. But he had still willingly bedded the bitch when he could have found another way to save his loved one.

But maybe, just maybe I could *be worth something.* If he won this ridiculous competition, became the last warrior standing, thereby proving he was stronger than all the others. Maybe…

Yes, maybe.

NOLA HAD HAD ENOUGH.

She wanted off this island of torture, away from the men. Just…away.

Had she been in Atlantis, she might have explored the flutters in her stomach that appeared every time Zane the vampire looked at her. But not here, not now.

She just wanted to go home.

She would have searched for Delilah because she needed her sister right now, but she didn't bother. Most likely Delilah was with the hated vampire king, a man who would betray her, ruin her. Men always did. So did women, for that matter. People simply couldn't be trusted. The moment you turned your back, they would hurt you. Her own mother had taken her to the Outer City and sold her to any creature who wanted an Amazon but didn't want to be enslaved in the Amazon camp. She'd fought them—at first. But they'd held her down, allowing more and more people to witness her humiliation.

Nola's teeth pulled back from her lips as she strode past a thick grouping of trees, daggers clutched in both of her hands. Vampires. How she was beginning to despise them. Zane had no business making her feel this way, confused and achy, unsure and hopeful. So many times throughout her life she'd hoped for something better, only, always, to be let down.

I should kill Zane and his king. Delilah had never acted so…soft before. Clearly all Delilah could think about lately was that bastard king. Every time Nola looked at her, she was looking at him. Why? Delilah was hard, reliable, caring to all of her sisters. Nola had always been a little jealous of her. Everyone loved the warrioress, thought she could do no wrong. She'd never known any hardships that Nola could tell.

As for Nola, she'd always existed on the outskirts, afraid to be a part of the tribe. Afraid they, too, would use and hurt her. That hadn't stopped Delilah from trying to protect her, both in battle with the dragons and on this island. Despite the distance Nola kept between herself and the world, Delilah had truly thought to help her.

For that, I owe her. And there was only one thing Nola could think to give the warrioress. Freedom. As long as the vampire king lived, Delilah would be ensnared by him, a victim who accepted everything her man did to her in the name of love. "Love," she scoffed.

"A weak and treacherous emotion," a soft voice whispered.

Nola stiffened, spun around, searching for an intruder. There wasn't one. "Who are you? *Where* are you? Show yourself, coward."

"Kill the vampires, my beloved," the soft yet somehow powerful voice continued. "They deserve it, as you know, and you will be handsomely rewarded. I'll even help you in your quest. Bespell you to heal as the other creatures heal, fast and without any lingering discomfort. Surely your leg is paining you even now?"

"What kind of reward?" she asked, realizing she could only be speaking to one of the gods.

"Should you succeed, I shall grant you a boon. Anything of your choosing…"

Anything? Nola licked her lips in growing excitement. More than anything, she wanted her mother brought back to life—so that she could kill the bitch again. *I'll kill the vampire king for Delilah, as well as for the reward.*

Zane she would simply destroy for fun.

CHAPTER TWENTY

DELILAH SPENT MOST OF the morning contemplating what to do about Layel. Once she'd thought—hoped, tricked herself into thinking—a single night with him would be enough.

It hadn't been.

Now she wanted more. More of him. More of everything. He'd touched her body, but he had branded her soul. She thought she might even…love him. Love who and what he was, who and what he'd been. Who and what he would be. The darkness of him, even. And she wanted him to love her in return, to desire her as a mate. To make love to her and hold her afterward, not run away as if she were poison.

She wanted him to cherish her as he *still* cherished the other. *I am a prize, damn it!*

Delilah was jealous, she admitted that. And even though she craved Layel all to herself, she would not ask him to forget his first love. Provide Delilah with a place in his heart, yes. She suspected a small part of his heart would be better than the complete devotion of a thousand others.

Had Delilah been less of a warrior, she might have said the task of winning him was impossible. Already her teammates were turning on her, thinking of her as the helper of their enemy. And Tagart had warned her. To engage the vampire king was to nullify their alliance. More than that, Layel himself seemed determined to push her from his life.

He had cried, for gods' sake. *Cried.* Thinking of those hot tears knotted her stomach painfully. How broken and raw he must have felt to do such a thing in front of her.

How broken and raw *she* felt, remembering. He hadn't shed a tear when he'd been hurt. He had not even grimaced. Why, then, had he done so after making love to her?

If only she knew more about men and their ways. But she didn't, had only her limited experience with Vorik to lean on, so she was just going to have to fight for him blind. "The most important battle of my life, and I'm practically weaponless," she muttered to the trees.

After she bathed, hating to lose Layel's scent on her skin but knowing it was necessary, she dressed, wrapping thin strips of leather around herself. The less material she wore, the less her opponents had to grab.

With a sigh, she made her way to the beach. Above, the orange globe shone brightly, its heat dotting sweat beads on her skin. Yet both teams sat around a crackling fire, she saw when she reached camp, eating from the body of a roasted pig. She spotted Nola, who was soaking wet and bleeding, but the wound was weaving itself together even as Delilah watched. How was that possible?

Nola spotted her, too, studied her, frowned and motioned her over with a wave of her fingers. She crossed her legs, hiding her swiftly healing wound.

Delilah blushed as she walked. *Do I look different to everyone? Satisfied?* She sat on the log beside the other Amazon, a spicy aroma wafting to her nose. Her mouth watered. "Your injury is—"

"Not important. We lost another member of our team

this morning," Nola said, handing her a thick green leaf topped with blackened meat.

"What?" Eyes wide, she balanced the leaf on her knees. "How? *My* team lost the challenge."

"Silly fool tried to escape. Swam toward the dome." Nola shrugged, uncaring. "He was eaten by the sharks. Probably a merciful death compared to what the gods would have meted out. But I won't ask where you were or why you weren't here to help me as you swore you would be."

Delilah's blush intensified to a sizzling burn. "Hopefully the number of teammates will not matter during the next challenge."

Nola popped a bite of yellow fruit into her mouth, chewed thoughtfully. "Do you truly care if my team fails?"

"Of course."

"For me, or your vampire?"

Her vampire. She liked the sound of that. "Why can I not be concerned for you both?"

"The vampire king despises you, you know. He's using you to win."

Delilah stared down at her plate, tendrils of fear whispering through her. "Why are you doing this?" She'd come here hopeful of a future with her man. Her sister had, with only a few words, sliced her up inside and exposed all the fears she'd tried not to dwell on. "I'm not allowed to find happiness? Is that what you're trying to tell me? Just because I'm an Amazon?" She pinched a bite of meat into her mouth, her fingers shaking.

"Happiness?" Nola laughed down at her, but the sound had a sharp bite to it. "With a man? An enemy? A warrior who will ultimately betray you? We have never been the best of friends, Delilah, but even I would not wish such a fate upon you."

Delilah knew that, and the food she'd just ingested turned to a lead ball in her stomach.

"You're willing to leave our tribe for him, aren't you?"

If he would have her, she thought she just might. Men were not allowed to live among the tribe outside of mating season. To even ask for such a thing was to invite punishment.

Layel would be worth it, though she doubted he would want to live with her sisters. Still, she suspected he would do it if she asked—and if he loved her, of course. He would do anything to protect and soothe the woman he loved. She sensed it with everything inside her. He would not be happy until his mate was happy. He would love her so fiercely, the rest of the world would vanish.

She could do no less.

Could he love her, though? Those tears…and he'd asked only for one night. *But so did you.* True. Perhaps, like her, he now regretted that decision. Perhaps he was thinking of fighting for her. Slowly she grinned.

"You're smiling at the thought of betraying your race? You truly are demented," Nola grumbled.

Funny that the Amazon thought so, since Delilah had never felt more levelheaded. Nervous, yes. Unsure, yes. But the thought of being with Layel just felt right.

Was he worth anything? Worth everything?

The questions besieged her just as Layel stepped from the forest and toward the fire. He winced against the bright light overhead, his movements slow, his expression unreadable. He'd found a shirt, probably stolen it from one of the other creatures. The black material covered his chest—and the scratches she'd probably left there. He wore the same pants he'd donned last night, though they were now clean, as if he had meticulously washed them.

Her heart skipped a beat at the hauntingly lovely sight of him. Awareness rushed through her veins and a sense of possessiveness rose inside her. *Mine.* She didn't like other women even looking at him, she realized. Last night, she'd fisted that white hair. She'd kissed those red lips. She'd caressed that hard body. *Definitely mine.*

See me, she silently beseeched. *Come to me.*

Layel didn't look in her direction.

Just one glance, that's all she needed. A moment between them, stolen and knowing. Private. But he gathered a leaf and meat and sat as far away from her as possible. As far from *everyone* as possible. Vampires could eat solid food? She hadn't known.

Evidently Nola hadn't, either. "Why is the vampire eating real food?" she asked, head tilting in thought as though she were outlining battle plans.

"I'm not sure. Perhaps he just wants to blend in." She hated that she didn't know. She wanted to learn everything about her man and his race. *Look at me, Layel. Please.* What was he thinking? Did he even know that she was here?

Delilah also hated that she had to war for his affections in private when everything inside her screamed to go to him, sit in his lap, wrap her arms around his neck and kiss him breathless. To put her brand on him so that everyone would know who he belonged to.

Belonged to? She frowned. The mighty warlord would never belong to anyone. That, she knew. He was too proud, too stubborn.

"I'm ashamed of you," Nola said, dragging Delilah from her thoughts. "Deeply ashamed. You are looking at him as if you would strip away your pride, turn your back on your family and give up all that you are if he offered the slightest encouragement."

Those words echoed in her mind, and Delilah pushed to her feet, leaf tumbling to the ground unnoticed. Anger was a hot poker inside her. Anger with Nola, anger with herself. "I'm ashamed of myself, too," she said, "for allowing the opinions of others to sway me." She'd wanted to go to him, and so she should. She should not care what anyone else—her sister, her teammates—thought. She was not ashamed of her feeling for the vampire and she would not act as if she were.

That was weakness at its finest, and weak she refused to be.

Was Layel worth anything, worth everything? Even risking her life? Yes. Oh, yes.

Determined, she kicked into motion. His gaze lifted, clashed with hers as if he'd been attuned to her from the first and had known her every move. His eyelids narrowed to tiny slits, shielding the brilliant blue of his irises.

He gave a harsh shake of his head, a single movement meant to stop her.

She continued forward. This was a war, after all. Besides, his dominance might be welcome—and enjoyed—during lovemaking, but anywhere else she would not obey.

Several gazes followed her, watching, intent.

Only when she reached her target did she stop. They were toe to toe, almost touching. Up close, she could see his hair was damp, his skin glistening like freshly polished pearl. He smelled of man and power. Dark, energetic.

"What do you think you are doing?" he demanded quietly, fiercely.

"Giving you my support." She could feel Nola's gaze boring into her back, hotter than anyone else's, but she did not back down. The outcome was too important.

"I don't need your support, woman."

"Still, you have it."

"Let me rephrase. I don't want your support."

"You're lying." *A battle, remember?* She could not give up. "Last night—"

"Was not supposed to be repeated. Was not supposed to be talked about."

Delilah anchored her hands on her hips. "Well, I changed my mind."

His nostrils flared. "You cannot do that."

"I did. I have. Last night—"

"Was clearly a mistake," he finished for her.

The claim wounded her, but she had fought hurt and bleeding before. "No. I enjoyed myself. I liked having you inside me, and I want you there again."

His focus snapped behind her, to the creatures surely still watching them. Tagart wasn't here, she knew, but he would hear of this. She didn't care.

"We agreed," Layel growled. "Once. No more."

Stripped of pride, Nola had said. If that's what was required, well… "I want more. I need more."

He shook his head in denial, though his pupils dilated. "You can't have more."

"I can. I will."

"Then you'll have to find someone else to give it to you." He said it flatly, as if he didn't care and almost hoped she took his advice. But there was something in his eyes, a gleam of absolute murder. So ferocious, she shivered.

One of her brows arched. "Shall I disprove your words right now?"

"Delilah." A warning.

"I'm willing to risk everything for you, Layel. My sister is back there, hating me, but I came to you anyway. My team thinks I mean to betray them. I *am* risking everything."

"Which shows only that you are foolish."

A red haze washed over her vision. She had not thought winning his heart would be easy, but a little cooperation would have been nice. "I'm not asking you to give me everything. I am asking you for time. A chance." *Don't push me away. See me as a prize worth fighting any battle for.*

There was a long pause, but his expression gave nothing away. "Delilah…" He stopped, whatever he'd meant to say destined to remain forever unheard. "Listen closely, for I do not wish to have this conversation again." He stood, towering over her. Then he leaned down, placing them nose to nose.

She bit her bottom lip, wishing he would kiss her as he had last night.

Breath caught in his throat—she heard the hitch—and he backed a step away. "I had you and now I am done with you," he croaked out, staring at her lips.

Another lie. She knew it. "Layel," she said, reaching for him. "Don't do this. Let me—"

"No." Another shake of his head, this one nearing violence. "I don't want you. Nothing you say or do will change that."

The sharpness of the latest rejection slapped her, cut her, made her bleed on the inside as she'd never bled on the outside. And still she fought. "Layel—"

"No! Look at my arm, Delilah. Do it!" he growled when she hesitated. "Look and see what I was willing to do when I left your embrace last night."

Dread filled her, because she knew, deep down, that what she would see would change her somehow.

"Do it!" he shouted, and all of the forest quieted.

Gulping, she lowered her gaze. He had rolled back his shirt's sleeves, showcasing deep, deep grooves in both of his forearms. Dried blood, scabs. "I don't understand."

"I've had to carve this six times already because the wounds keep healing. I even rubbed dirt, moss and salt into each slice to slow the process. Read the words. Read them!"

She focused, tracing each scab with her gaze. *Never. Again.*

"Do you understand now?" he asked, his voice suddenly quiet.

Her mind emptied of thoughts, and her emotions numbed. The warrior instincts she'd been so sure would win him vanished as if they'd never been. He absolutely and unequivocally did not long for a future with her.

Never again. Never again would he kiss her, touch her, love her. She was not a prize to him, she was a nuisance. She was everything she'd never wanted to be, forgettable, unimportant, unworthy. Once again, she'd chosen the wrong man. Craved something that could never be. This time hurt far worse than the other. Far worse.

"I understand," she said softly. This time, he did not have to put space between them. She did. Inch by inch she backed away. Her legs were shaky, she realized vaguely, near collapse.

I was willing to give up everything for him, yet he doesn't want me. Oh, gods. He didn't want her. The numbness began to crack, lances of pain trying to shoot through her.

The more distance she gained, the more emotion Layel showed. Regret flashed over his beautiful features, followed by sorrow. "It has to be this way," he said with so much self-loathing it even managed to saturate the air. "I have a mission. I have a mate. I cannot forget that."

"You had a mate," she said, wanting to hurt him as he'd hurt her. "She died. You didn't save her and you feel guilty. I had thought, hoped, you'd done enough penance. Clearly you will never do enough."

A muscle clenched in his jaw, but she wasn't finished.

"No matter what you've done, it's who you are today, tomorrow, that matters. You deserve to be happy. I wanted to be the one to make you happy. I can't, I see that now. No one can. You don't have to worry that I'll bother you anymore."

"Delilah."

Well, he remembered her name at least. Another step. "You don't have to say anything else. I saw only what I wanted to see, blind to…other things. I will not be so foolish again."

He ran his tongue over his fangs. "You are hurt. Do not think to fall into the arms of another. That will only make things worse for you."

"Only one way for me to know that for sure, isn't there?" she asked bitterly.

He was panting shallowly as he rubbed a finger over the carved reminder on his arm. "You are better off without me."

"Yes. I am. That's one point on which we absolutely agree." Another step. She wanted to spin around, flee, but refused. He would know how thoroughly he'd destroyed her. She laughed. What did it matter if he knew? He could not think any less of her. Oh, wait. He could. "My first lover, he was a dragon. Do you know what that means, Layel? It means you claimed the castoff of your hated enemy. You took a dragon's leavings. I hope the knowledge sickens you the way you have sickened me this day."

One of his fangs peeked over his bottom lip.

"I didn't ask you to give up anything for me," she told him, "but I would have given up everything for you." *The war is over, and I have lost.* War. Ha! As if she could have fought a dead woman. The battle had been over before it began. "Until the end of forever, Layel."

With that, she did spin. She did flee.

And for once she did not hope he would follow her.

CHAPTER TWENTY-ONE

TWO WEEKS PASSED. Several new challenges were forced upon them. Several more creatures were ruthlessly executed, leaving only a few members of each team. That's when the gods decided to dissolve the teams so that it was every man for himself. Unfortunately, the game itself hadn't changed. It was still life and death.

Though he had no right, Layel had kept a sharp eye on Delilah. She had survived the challenges. A simulated battle with swords and spears—to prove their skill in combat. A seemingly endless hike without food or water—to show their ability to forage for their own provisions while weakened. A quiz, taken while leaping through fiery hoops—to test their memories while under stress.

Through it all, Delilah had never looked at him, never spoken to him, never betrayed any concern for his survival. And he found that he...missed her. He wanted more of what they'd shared, hated how he'd hurt her. Again. He didn't care who or what her first lover had been, only that he himself was no longer allowed to worship that sweet body.

And he could have had it forever. She would have given him more, for as long as he'd desired. They could have been together without reservation, for now they could spend time together without having to do so in secret—not that she cared.

Never again, he reminded himself as he surveyed the pool where he'd taken Delilah. He was alone, even the animals wary of him.

At least Delilah wasn't trying to kill him. Nola, on the other hand, had attempted to slay him twice. The first time, she had almost succeeded, sinking a stick into his stomach and twisting his organs while he was distracted. By Delilah. The second, she'd gone for his neck with a dagger while he appeared to be sleeping.

That time, he'd been waiting for her and had managed to subdue her without hurting her. He didn't know why he cared, except that Delilah might have been angry if her sister were hurt.

Delilah.

You got what you wanted. She is no longer a part of your life. They were now the enemies they should have been in the beginning. Yet he had never been more miserable.

Layel wasn't sure how much more island life he could tolerate without snapping, flying into a rage. Something. Two nymphs and both dragons had survived, as had the Amazons. Brand had, for whatever reason, stood beside Layel each and every time they entered council and kept the others from voting for his death.

Layel was too stubborn to ask him why.

Zane was still alive, as well. He fought each challenge now with a ferocity that was astounding. Layel suspected Zane would fell even him if the gods decreed it. Once, during a race through a maze, Zane had pushed Delilah to the ground in his rush to the finish line and Layel had nearly beheaded him. *What kind of king am I? What kind of friend? What kind of* mate *am I?*

At the word *mate,* it was not Susan's image that flooded

his mind, but Delilah's. Blue hair, violet eyes, lush lips, tattoos. Spread, eager for him. Shock filled him. Delilah... his...forever. The past forgotten. It was almost too much to take in.

What was she doing?

He knew she was not sleeping enough. Every time he saw her, there were dark circles under her eyes. Her body was always taut, as though she were an injured predator, afraid, ready to strike. Tagart was always at her side, ever the protector, glaring at Layel in a silent warning to keep his distance.

Layel no longer knew what to do or what he wanted. He knew he hated seeing Tagart near her. Knew he should be the one guarding her. The woman had given him pleasure— peace—for the first time in hundreds of years. That meant she was his. Or would have been, if he hadn't purposely destroyed her.

Oh, gods. The look on her face as she'd backed away from him those weeks ago...the things he'd said... He was a monster. She hadn't deserved that. Had only deserved his utmost care.

You didn't save her, she'd said, devoid of emotion as she spoke of Susan, *and you feel guilty. I had thought, hoped, you'd done enough penance.*

Had he? It was almost too wonderful to believe.

I would have given up everything for you, she had added.

He'd nearly caved then, had nearly forgotten his vow, his past. His only love. Because, for a brief moment, he'd seen his future in Delilah's eyes and it had been a sight so beautiful it was beyond his comprehension.

Susan used to look at him like that, but back then he'd been worthy. Now, after the things he'd done, he'd known that Delilah was simply fooling herself, wanting him to be something he was not and could never be again: pure.

One day soon she would realize that and leave him. After everything he'd said, perhaps she had *already* realized her mistake. And it was better this way, he reminded himself for the thousandth time. He stared up at the heavens, the moon shooting golden rays in every direction. She deserved someone else, someone better. Someone who wasn't…tainted. Tagart?

Glowering, Layel anchored his weapons on a rock at his feet and ducked under the waterfall. He didn't bother to undress, just let the cool water run down his body, drenching him. Unfortunately, it didn't wash the dark thoughts from his mind. Tagart wasn't any better than Layel and if the bastard touched Delilah—

Don't think like that. Those were the thoughts of a mate. Was that so bad, though?

Layel slammed his fists into the rock stretched in front of him. They throbbed as he braced both palms flat, just above his head. As he stood there, Delilah's image filled his mind—she was never far from the surface—and overshadowed the darkness. This time, she was smiling at him, beckoning him to join her in a bath.

Instantly he was hard. Aching.

He would have given anything—yes, anything, he realized—for the chance to pump inside that luscious body one more time. Stroke her inner walls, feel the heat of her desire. Gods, she'd been wet.

The water continued to pound at him, reminding him of all that they'd shared. His fingers were shaking as he unfastened his pants. His erection sprang out, long and hard and thick. He gripped it, nails cutting into skin.

If Delilah were here, she might have fallen to her knees. Might have taken him inside her mouth. If he'd begged. "Oh, gods," he panted. He would have begged, happily and without hesitation. Anything for her. His hand moved up and down, slow, so slow. She might have cupped his testicles and pulled. He might have gripped her blue hair, fisted it, guided her down further and further, until the tip of his shaft hit the back of her throat.

His body was on fire now, pulsing with need and coiled tight. So damned ready for her. He increased the speed of his pumps, up and down, up and down, over and over, faster and faster. His lips drew back, peeling over his teeth in a snarl. Every muscle in his body clenched…preparing…waiting…

He could almost hear Delilah pleading for his come, could almost feel her pleasure-moans as he gave it to her.

With a deafening roar, he climaxed, hot seed pouring from his cock and straight into the water. As the water continued to rain, that seed washed away as if it had never been.

An eternity passed as Layel struggled to breathe. He hadn't thought of Susan, he realized. He'd thought of Delilah. He should be ashamed, yet…he already wanted Delilah again. Only Delilah.

A hum of power suddenly filled the air.

Layel straightened. He righted his soaked clothing as his attention slowly flicked to the wooden daggers he'd placed on the rock at his feet. Stupid of him, with Nola somewhere on the island, but he hadn't wanted them to float away. He began to bend for them, projecting his senses in every direction, searching for the intruder…finding nothing out of the ordinary. That didn't mean anything, he supposed.

In a quick, fluid motion, he grabbed both weapons and whipped around, ready to launch them if necessary. But as

his senses had perceived, there was no one nearby. Except…
the pool below him swirled like the ocean did every time a
god made an appearance. No, not now.

Layel remained still as dread speared him. Was he to
be singled out? Punished? The water thickened, rose,
kept swirling, churning, forming a clear dappled body.
Steady, stay calm.

The body began to glow with multihued colors: pinks,
blues, yellows, greens. Those colors soon began to glitter
like nighttime stars and then, in a burst that nearly blinded
him, everything died away, leaving only—

Layel gasped. Fell to his knees as if struck in the
head. Surely not. No. *No!* Couldn't be. But he found
himself reaching out, arm shaking, mouth dry, heart stut-
tering to a halt.

Susan stared over at him.

Logically, he knew it wasn't her, couldn't possibly be
her, was only one of the gods playing some cruel trick, but
he was struck speechless with his first glimpse of her in two
hundred years. She was as beautiful as he remembered.
Shoulder-length brown hair, soft and wisping. Eyes the
same rich, vibrant color as dewy moss. Skin a lovely cream.

Her lips curled into a small smile.

"Oh, gods," he gasped out brokenly. That smile…he'd
never thought to see it again, had held it inside his chest,
his only warmth some nights.

She looked away from him, her body turning grace-
fully, her long white robe dancing at her ankles. She
laughed up at…someone? something?…her graceful hand
covering her mouth. Layel had prayed for this so often,
would have given his soul for it. Now, here she was.

Susan turned back to him, then, eyes alight with amusement. She motioned him over with a crook of her finger, and he was on his feet before he realized what he'd done. Was stepping toward her, desperate to wrap his arms around her. Desperate to gaze into those adored violet eyes as he held her close.

Layel stopped abruptly. Susan's eyes were green. Delilah's were violet. *Delilah.* Water lapped at his feet, cold reality in contrast to the beloved vision.

Susan motioned him over again, the action a little forced. *Why are you still standing here? Why aren't you moving toward her?*

"Do you hate me?" he asked her. He'd wanted to ask her so many times. "Do you blame me for what happened?" He didn't expect her to answer, but the words tumbled from him anyway.

Frowning now, she dropped her arm to her side.

"I hate myself. I blame myself."

Her head tilted to the side, as if she understood what he was saying but still didn't know how to reply.

"You died, our unborn child died, and I was left with nothing but memories and pain. If I had been stronger…if I had protected you better…"

For the first time, she spoke. "I love you," she said in that soft voice he remembered. "I need you. Come to me."

His chest ached, hearing the sweet timbre after so long, but not for the reason he'd always assumed it would if he saw and heard Susan again. He ached because, as he continued to study his beloved, he realized the deep sense of possession he'd always felt for her was no longer there.

He blinked, unsure of his thoughts. Surely they were wrong. Surely he still craved her as much as he always had. But…no. He didn't. His hands didn't itch to tunnel through her hair. His muscles didn't jump at the thought of her touch. His stomach didn't quiver at the thought of claiming her.

He did love her, that would never fade, but the passion, the *need,* were gone. Every ounce of his passion belonged to Delilah. His hope for the future—Delilah. His reason for living—Delilah.

With the shocking revelations, it was as though a weight was lifted from him, a weight that had dragged him down, kept him in the dirt, unable to rise. Not *wanting* to rise.

"Please, Layel." She beckoned him with a clipped, almost angry, wave of her hand. "Come to me."

Layel found himself on his knees once again, tears pouring down his cheeks. Still he knew this was only a trick, but what both saddened and thrilled him was the revelation that even if this had been the real Susan, he would not have gone to her. That would have been a betrayal to Delilah, and he just couldn't force himself to do it. He loved Delilah. Dear gods.

He had been punishing himself for two hundred years and he didn't want to do it any longer. He wanted freedom from the hate. He wanted to live. Truly live.

He wanted the Amazon. Now, always.

He still didn't deserve her. Nothing he did would make him worthy, but he wanted her. He wanted the chance to make her happy. He wanted a chance at forever with her, pampering her all the days of her life.

"Susan," he groaned. "Susan, forgive me yet again." He was finally going to let her go when he'd vowed to fight for her for eternity. "Forgive me."

DELILAH HAD WATCHED as Layel moved toward the empty pool, talking to himself, crying again. She'd been unable to budge, brought here by the gods, beings so great they'd been able to plant her feet in place and hold them there. Why had they singled her out? Hadn't she suffered enough?

"Susan. Susan, forgive me yet again. Forgive me."

There was so much pain and suffering in Layel's voice, tears burned in *Delilah's* eyes. She saw him, saw the sheer torture on his face. *I need to comfort him—if he'll let me.* But she tried to move and only managed to fall to her knees, scraping her skin.

"Why did you show me this?" she whispered brokenly. "Why?" For weeks she'd given the vampire the space he'd said he wanted. And she'd been miserable, missing him, craving him.

He had missed her, too. She knew it. He'd watched her. Every day, he had watched her, and sometimes he'd even followed her. Hope had renewed inside her, and this morning she'd decided to try yet again. She was a warrior. She shouldn't have given up so easily, anyway. Before she could find him on her own, however, she'd been whisked here.

He isn't the man for you, a quiet voice whispered. *He loves another.*

She stiffened. One of the gods, definitely. The voice had belonged to a female, soft and lilting, one she'd heard before a few of the challenges. "No. I don't believe that."

Even seeing him, you refuse to believe? was the confused response. *Even hearing him?*

Even then. She'd come to know him, his stubbornness. He was holding on to the past, not because he still desired his mate, but because he felt responsible for what had happened to her. "He needs me."

There was a crackling pause. *Why do you still want him?*

"I love him." And she did. He was a part of her. He was

a man of devotion and passion, darkness and light. He was loyal and strong, a warrior to his core. He was the other half of her, the piece she'd always been searching for.

Your sister has failed me, time and time again. That leaves you, and I will not be kept out of Atlantis because you have fallen in love, Amazon. This time, there had been no confusion in the voice. Only anger. *He is distracting you, a distraction neither of us can afford.*

Be kept out of Atlantis? How could such a powerful being be kept from anything she desired? "Yes, he's distracting me from your cruel game, but I don't care. I love him, and I'm not giving him up. Just take us home. Please. We don't deserve this. Whatever's keeping you out of Atlantis, I'll help you find a way in. I swear it."

A cold laugh. *You should care. I will not lose. Which means* you *cannot lose.*

Lose? Lose what? As far as Delilah knew, only she and the other creatures were participants in the challenges, not the gods themselves. But there was no time to reason it out as she doubled over in pain. Intense heat invaded her, every muscle in her body constricting. She felt as if something were being pulled right out of her, the thing scratching at her organs, her veins. Then, suddenly, she was…free of it. Completely free.

Her emotions—gone. Her feelings for Layel—gone. She didn't love him, didn't hate him, she simply felt nothing for him. Nothing for anyone. She frowned, waiting for confusion, anger, or even relief to fill her; her obsession with him was over. Still nothing.

One day you will thank me for this, for I have just assured our victory, the goddess said.

Something's wrong with me, she thought, but she couldn't find the will to care.

Layel was still at the pool when her feet were freed, but she didn't walk to him as she'd planned. She simply turned on her heel and ambled away. She was tired. Perhaps it was time for a nap.

CHAPTER TWENTY-TWO

"YOU HAVE INTERVENED for the last time, Hestia," Poseidon growled as he materialized in the forest, mere inches away from the goddess in question.

The dark-haired goddess cast him an innocent glance, not the least ashamed of her actions. Or fearful because she'd been caught. "Me? What have I done?"

"Cheated, that's what." Ares appeared in a blink. "Again and again. I should strike you down."

Apollo quickly followed, a blinding light surrounding him. Artemis was beside him a second later, ice to the sun god's heat, seeming to drain his power and diminish the aura around him. Interesting. Poseidon had never noticed that before.

Hestia gave up the innocent act and glared at them. "Like any of you are blameless. I've watched each of you save your chosen contestants and lash out at their enemies. And don't try to deny that some of you have even offered your players tips. Besides, I grow weary of waiting for the finish line. I want this game over and done, the winner declared."

Poseidon crossed his arms over his massive chest. He agreed. Evidently the other gods had the same fickle attention span and restless need for constant amusement as he did. The game had begun to lose its appeal, the weeks dragging by. He wanted back inside Atlantis, its citizens his and his alone to enjoy, and he wanted to ensure these gods remained out of it.

"How about one final challenge?" Artemis said. Her demons had been eliminated, therefore she had lost the competition already. Atlantis would not be hers, yet she hadn't left the island, apparently too curious about the end result. "A winner could be declared today."

Excitement saturated the forest. Poseidon fairly shook with it. One final challenge…surely he could help a dragon win. Somehow, some way.

"What shall the challenge entail?" Apollo asked eagerly.

"And what should we do with the losers?" Hestia added, rubbing her hands together.

"I have an idea," Poseidon said. They huddled closer to him, each grinning with anticipation.

LAYEL WAS STILL RAW an hour later, when the gratingly familiar challenge horn sounded. He stiffened in dread but pushed to his feet. Once Susan's image had faded, he'd dressed and begun tracking Delilah's footprints. He'd been hunkered on the ground, following her trail, but her prints had seemed to disappear.

He needed to find her, talk to her, hold her. He just… needed her. If necessary, he would beg for her forgiveness. He should have fought for her, should not have driven her away. Hopefully it was not too late.

She'll be at the challenge, he thought, quickening his footsteps, dread shifting to anticipation. *I will* make *her talk to me.*

These past few weeks, he hadn't drunk any blood, hadn't slept, hadn't really eaten. He'd been tortured with thoughts of Delilah and Susan, with need and want and pain and bone-deep suffering. All he'd wanted was Delilah, he realized now, but he'd hidden the need with memories of the past. A curtain, a shadow.

Finally he'd allowed the light inside. Nothing and no one would do but Delilah.

I've been such a fool. He'd wasted all of this time. Time he could have spent in Delilah's arms. *I'll make it up to her.*

The sky was brightening as he broke through the forest's trees, and his heart was pounding. Everyone was already in place. Delilah was there, too, and his breath caught in his throat at the sight of her. *Mine.* Her back was to him, and that blue hair he so adored hung to her waist in silky waves. He wanted his hands in it, fisting it, jerking her face to his for a kiss. Never again would he deny himself those delectable lips.

My mate. My love. He needed her to love him, which meant he needed her to give him what she'd offered before: a chance. And once he had her, he was going to get them both the hell off this island and safely back to Atlantis, where they could be together in peace. He'd go wherever she wanted, live in the Amazon camp if necessary.

His focus stayed on her as he stalked to the beach. She didn't stiffen when he drew near her side, didn't act as if she cared at all.

Tagart, who stood guard at her other side, was less nonchalant. He hissed at Layel with the feral intensity of a hungry predator.

Layel paid him no heed. All he cared about was Delilah. "Delilah," he said, savoring her name on his tongue.

She flicked him a bored glance. "Go away."

I deserve that. Once, she would have turned to him with

longing in her violet eyes. Once, her arms would have opened for him and she would have proudly embraced him. "Delilah, I want you to know I care nothing about the dragon you were with. My past has hardly been perfect. I—"

"Will leave," Tagart growled. "You aren't wanted here. By any of us."

Brand strode to the warrior's side and gripped his arm, probably holding him back from a sure fight. A fight Layel would have craved only hours ago, with blood, with death and staggering amounts of his enemy's pain. Today, there was only one thing Layel wished to fight for and it wasn't the death of a dragon.

He breathed in Delilah's scent, a fragrance of femininity, the essence of pleasure, and savored every drop in his lungs, his mind accepting his adoration without protest. Peace truly was his for the first time in centuries.

"I need you," he told her, and they were words straight from his soul. "I need you more than I've ever needed another."

Her gaze finally returned to him, but her eyes were devoid of emotion. Violet yet…blank. Gone was her warmth, her laughter. "I'm sorry, but I'm no longer interested."

Again, deserved. She'd once asked him to reveal the worst thing he'd ever done. Now he knew. It was causing this, this change in her. She looked colder. Harsh. Hard. He battled despair. "You should never be sorry. Not to me. It is I who owe you a thousand apologies. I know a thousand will not be enough, but however long it takes, whatever I have to do, I am willing. For you, anything."

"Go away," she said again, just as bored.

Never. "All I ask is that—"

There was a screech, high-pitched, infuriated, and then

a spear was sailing toward him. Lightning fast it happened, yet he watched as if the world had slowed to a crawl. He heard the whistle of air and managed to reach out and catch the limb just before it penetrated his heart. A second longer, and he would have been dead. As it was, the razor-fine tip managed only to slice his skin.

There was no time to search out his attacker. No need, either. Nola was shoving him down before he could drop the weapon. He allowed her to pin him, punch him and claw at him. He had vowed never to let anyone hurt him without retaliation. But her, he let. She was avenging her sister.

Delilah watched, her blank expression never changing.

A hard right was delivered to his nose, and the cartilage snapped out of place. Nails scored his cheek, drawing blood. Another right, then a left.

"That's enough. Stop!" Brand had issued the command with enough force to halt the Amazon's fist midair.

She glanced at him, murder in her eyes. "Don't interfere, or you'll be next."

Then someone was lifting Nola off Layel, and she was cursing in outrage.

Zane, he realized. The warrior held the now struggling Nola, and released a roar the likes of which Layel had never heard. "Be still, woman! And be quiet."

Zane, willingly touching a female?

"I warned you what would happen if you neared her again!" Brand launched himself at the vampire.

Layel scooted back, out of the way. A war had erupted, it seemed. The three rolled on the sandy beach in a tangle of fists and kicks. Both Brand and Zane tried to shove Nola aside as they punched and bit at each other, but she kept returning, going for Zane's throat every time.

Her fury was like a living thing.

I was like her, Layel mused. He'd been filled with hatred and anger, not really living for anything but death. Susan would have been ashamed of him had she met the man he'd become. But Delilah had found a way to love him, anyway.

She was a gift. A treasure.

And she was striding toward the bloody trio, he realized. He popped to his feet and dashed to her, grabbing her arm and pulling her back. She turned to him, still expressionless.

"Release me," she said.

"Stay here. Please. *I* will help your friend." It would be his pleasure, giving her something she desired.

She opened her mouth to reply, but another voice stopped her.

"Actually, *we* will stop them."

Layel's stomach clenched as the trio was frozen in place. How he despised these gods and their seemingly all-consuming power.

In a blink, the fighters were on their knees, bowing, blood trickling from their wounds. They were panting as a clear jellylike being materialized in front of them. No, not one. But five. Five beings. Layel's eyes widened. He'd known there was more than one god pulling the strings, but hadn't expected so many.

"I admire your vehemence, vampire," one of them said, solidifying into a tall, muscled, dark man. Fire blazed in his eyes, fierce and war-hungry. Ares. Ancient scrolls and portraits of the gods had once filled his palace. After Susan's death, Layel had removed them. He'd felt forgotten, abandoned, and had wanted no part of the beings who seemed more concerned with their own selfish pleasure than with the well-being of their children.

"Enough is enough," another added, solidifying, as well. Hestia. She was plain of face yet somehow so sensual she would have made any other man hard as a rock in seconds. Any but Layel. His body existed only for Delilah.

"The time has finally come to end this." Another female. Dark-haired, lovely. Dressed in a bright yellow robe. Artemis.

"I, too, am tired of waiting." A man. Blond, muscled, casting an aura so vibrant Layel had to squint. Apollo.

"Vampires, Amazons, dragons and nymphs. At last we come face-to-face. You've become predictable, the lot of you. My amusement with our little game has rapidly waned. You were to prove your strength to us, as well as demonstrating which race is superior to all others." Dark hair he sometimes changed to gold, male, tall and muscled, with eyes as blue and fathomless as the sea. Poseidon. "We could not decide, you see, and fought amongst ourselves. You were brought here to settle that argument, but all you've done is prove you are as weak and foolish as the humans, placing your hearts above your own survival."

"What more do you want from us?" Layel asked them, inching in front of Delilah to shield her. He didn't trust these beings, and wouldn't tolerate their attention being turned to his woman. "We've done everything you've asked."

He was on his stomach a moment later, writhing in pain beyond imagining. Dirt filled his mouth as he gasped for breath.

"No questions are allowed, vampire," Ares said. "Damn, but I'm disappointed in you! You should have slayed them all by now."

"And you." Hestia looked at Delilah and *tsked* under her tongue. "I had such high hopes for your independence and strength, yet you focused on a man and lost sight of the true prize."

"I know you," Delilah said, frowning. "Your voice. You were there. In the forest. You—"

"Enough from you," Hestia rushed out, and then Delilah, too, was on her knees. At least she wasn't writhing.

"Enough from all of you. You had your chance, yet here you are. While we admire your fortitude, your continued refusal to remove the threat of your enemy has been… disappointing," Ares said to the still-bowing trio. "The time has come to narrow the combatants to only one creature per race. That means you three are no longer needed. Brand, Zane, Nola, rise."

Hestia stepped forward as they obeyed. All three blanched, opened their mouths to protest, he was sure, but no sound emerged. "Dragon, vampire, you fought over the Amazon, and so you shall soon be surrounded by them. We are sentencing you both to be their slaves."

Zane roared with fury and terror, leaping backward, away from the crowd. "No." Finally, sound. "No!"

"I'm begging you not to do this," Brand gasped out. "I never wanted the Amazon. She is like a sister to me."

Their cries went unheeded. Each of the gods waved their hands through the air, an eerily synchronized movement, and the two warriors disappeared, only the imprints of their feet left behind. Layel had been reaching for his soldier, trying to grab hold of him. Beside him, Delilah remained unmoved. With his other hand he grabbed her calf, stroking, offering comfort though he could see she felt no fear.

"Great Ones, please," Nola said on a shaky breath, backing away. "I beg you, do not—"

"Silence!" Artemis bellowed.

And so there was silence, even the insects ceasing their songs.

"Better." Hestia relaxed, her expression softening. "I don't like the thought of a woman being enslaved, nor do I like the thought of destroying you when you have not yet had a chance to truly live. And so you will not be given to the vampires or the dragons."

Gradually Nola, too, relaxed. Until…

"Therefore, because you failed time and again to kill your targets," Hestia continued, her tone cold, "you will be sentenced to watch them live, unable to be seen or heard by those around you." The goddess paused. "Let this be a lesson to you. When a goddess demands a favor of you, promising a reward beyond imagining in return, see it through. Had you done so, you would have known a different outcome this day."

All color leached from Nola's cheeks. Shock and terror filled her eyes, and tremors rocked her body so forcefully even the ocean's waves undulated. "No. Please, no. I didn't pit them against each other. I didn't. And I tried to kill the king. I did, but he—" Nola disappeared, her words gone with her.

"Return her. Now." Delilah stood and strolled forward, the casual movement at odds with her words, as if she was doing what she knew she should but couldn't bring herself to care about the action.

Layel latched on to her ankles and jerked. She hit the sand face-first and came up sputtering. Though still in pain, he pushed to his feet and moved in front of her. The few creatures left standing were pallid, quiet. He wanted to tell Delilah there would be time to save their friends later, but kept silent, unwilling to incite even more divine punishment.

Hestia dusted off her hands, a job well done.

"You." Ares pointed to the female nymph. "You appear weak."

Gulping, she took a trembling step backward. "Me?"

She appeared strong to Layel, healthy, her color good. He frowned.

"You're being eliminated, as well. There is no place for weaklings here. However, I have decided to be lenient and restore your strength to full capacity. That is why you will wait in my heavenly chambers. I will join you shortly."

Her fear turned to eagerness as she realized what he wanted from her, and she vanished with an excited gasp. Now Layel understood, as well. The war god wanted the nymph for his own.

Poseidon frowned. "That wasn't fair. I wanted her."

Ares shrugged, unconcerned. "He who hesitates does not deserve such beauty. But do not worry. Who would know better than you, Poseidon, that there are plenty of other fish in the sea?"

The sea king glared, but didn't issue a rejoinder.

"Finally, the four strongest contenders remain," Apollo said, rubbing his hands together. "Delilah, the stubborn Amazon. Broderick, the loyal nymph. Layel, the fierce vampire king. Tagart, the determined dragon. Which of you will survive, though? Which of you will fall?"

"Soon you will face the greatest challenge yet, and only one can win." Hestia splayed her arms wide. "What will this winner receive, you ask? The answer is as simple, or as life-altering, as you want it to be. A boon. Anything you wish of us, we will do. Anything you desire shall be yours."

"And what of the others?" Layel asked. "What will happen to the losers?"

Rather than scold him for asking a question, Poseidon

eyed him sharply. "That, too, is a simple but life-altering answer. They will die."

Die. The word echoed in his mind, an ominous threat that overshadowed the physical pain still beating through him. Gods. He was going to have to win this competition. His boon—sparing Delilah's life. Once he would have used such a favor to obliterate the dragons. No longer. Delilah came first.

"Before the prize can be awarded, the challenge must be met. Heed our words well, for things are not always what they seem. Each of you will travel up the mountain behind you," Artemis said. "There you will find something the likes of which even the bravest of men would run from. Something you fear above anything else. You are to face it, defeat it."

There hadn't been a mountain on the island before, but Layel was willing to bet that if he turned, he would see one.

Poseidon grinned, a wicked edge to his amusement. "But fear not, creatures of Atlantis. I'm returning all the weapons you crafted, for what better way to prove the true depth of your might than to utilize such instruments of death on your fellow opponents? Although...perhaps you have all you will need without them, hmm?"

Layel was suddenly weighed down with swords, daggers and lances. And then, one by one, the gods vanished.

"May the best warrior win," whispered on the breeze in their wake.

His pain instantly ceased. Panting, sweating, he straightened, squared his shoulders and looked at Delilah. She was watching him. Unemotional. Unreadable. They stood there in silence for several seconds—an eternity.

"One of us will die," she ventured, but she didn't sound as if she cared who lost their life.

It would not be her, he vowed. He would die himself before he allowed any harm to fall upon this woman. "No." He shook his head. "One of us will win a prize. Anything we desire, even the life of the other."

Her head tilted to the side, thoughts swimming in her eyes. "Or the life of someone else. Your mate could live again."

For one moment, he was overjoyed by the possibility. Susan…returned to him. He couldn't catch his breath, saw white lights behind his eyelids. Then, with a glance at Delilah, the joy shifted. Susan's return wasn't what he wanted anymore. It was time to let her rest in peace, as he'd realized at the waterfall. He wanted Delilah. She was his present, his future. "I want you."

She shrugged.

Tagart approached Delilah's side, eyes narrowed on Layel. "Come," he commanded the Amazon. "We'll work the mountain together."

All of Layel's possessive instincts surfaced with a roar. *Mine!* "You will not touch her. You will not aid her. I will."

Delilah, ever emotionless, shrugged off Tagart's hold. "You have issued ultimatum after ultimatum, dragon. I was to follow you or risk death. Well, I am tired of following you. Our alliance ended when the teams were dissolved. I think you now *want* me to die. Anything to punish the vampire. So I'll work the mountain on my own. Besides, I'm an Amazon. I don't need a man."

She turned and strode away from them, Layel's gaze tracking her every movement. She approached a— His eyes widened. There was a mountain, huge, towering, dark and surrounded by foreboding shadows. *Even the bravest man would run from what's up there,* the gods had said.

Tagart took advantage of Layel's distraction and attacked, claws raking Layel's chest. Rather than engage, Layel simply dematerialized. Only one thing mattered right now—and for once, it wasn't the dragon.

DELILAH FELT DEAD inside as she increased her speed, going from a stroll to a run in seconds. She dodged trees, their limbs slapping at her, jumped over thick roots and ignored the eerie animalistic purr that reverberated through the air. Soon she was panting, didn't know where she was or where she was going, and didn't care.

Her sister had been sent away to be mentally and emotionally tortured, and she hadn't been able to save her. Layel was toying with her for some reason, offering her everything she'd once desired. *I want you,* he'd said. She still couldn't bring herself to care—not even if he'd meant every word.

I should care. But in the void that was her heart, there were no regrets. No happiness, no concerns.

"Delilah."

One second she was running, the next she was soaring through the air. She struggled until she drew in the scent of man, strength and blood. His arsenal of weapons pressed into every point of contact, abrading her skin.

"Put me down," she said flatly.

"Hold on to me." Layel's voice was strained. Sweat beaded every inch of his face, and lines of fatigue etched his eyes and mouth. Never had he appeared more exhausted.

"Put me down." There was a spark of awareness inside her, arousal about to bloom, but it was quickly snuffed out as if it had never been. What was wrong with her?

"I hurt you," he said into her ear. "I am sorry for that, so very sorry."

"As sorry as you are about your mate's death?" she found herself asking. She didn't care about his answer, but something compelled her to ask, anyway.

"Yes," he replied without hesitation.

"There's no reason to lie. You're nothing to me now. I was merely curious."

Pain glowed in his eyes, deepening the blue to a sorrowful black. "I want to be everything to you."

A few hours ago, she would have rejoiced. Now… "I told you, I no longer want you." Truth. There was nothing inside her to give him. Or anyone, for that matter.

"I want you. You are all that I desire, and instead of cherishing you as you deserve, I was cruel. I beg your forgiveness for that, and will do anything to get it." When she said nothing, he added, "I hate that I hurt you, that you now look at me as if I'm invisible."

Wind ruffled her hair across her face as she studied his features. She saw what she'd wanted to see all these many days: tenderness, kindness and caring. She saw… love? In that moment, she *did* regret the numbness. "You were calling her name. You told her you were sorry."

His brow furrowed in confusion. "When— Oh. Yes, I was. I was telling her goodbye."

"Telling her—" Delilah couldn't form the words, couldn't comprehend what he was saying.

"Telling her goodbye," Layel repeated. "Susan is no longer my mate. She is gone, and I am here. I want you. I want to be with you, have a future with you."

"Layel—"

"You asked me for a chance, but I didn't give it to you. Now I am begging you for one." He shifted her in his arms, forcing her to wind her legs around his waist and lock her ankles to maintain some sort of balance. "Please. I will do anything for it. Anything at all."

They were hovering in the air, over the trees and inside delicate puffs of white. She braced her arms around his neck, staring deep into those bright eyes. "I'm sorry. I have nothing inside me to give you anymore. Besides, there's no time for this. Tagart and Broderick are searching for the monster, or whatever it is the gods wish us to slay."

"We will make time. Nothing is more important to me than you. Not even the win."

"But without the win, one of us will die."

He sighed at the reminder. "Much as I wish otherwise, you are right. But…" He nuzzled her cheek with his nose. "The blankness still lingers in your eyes and that tears me up inside. What can I do? Tell me what to do to help you?"

"I wish I knew. One of the goddesses came to me earlier. Hestia, I realize now. She wanted me to forget you and focus on the game so she…she…" Delilah's eyes widened, the truth crystallizing. "She took my love for you so that I would no longer place you above victory."

Layel's arms tightened around her, anger flashing over his countenance. "I don't understand."

"I have no emotions. She took them, all of them." Delilah should have been infuriated by that, but again, there was nothing inside her, not even a single spark of the fury that was so warranted.

"You love me?"

"I did." She could think of no reason to deny it. "Yes."

"And the goddess made it so that you felt nothing?"

"Yes," she repeated.

"Oh, Delilah, sweet Delilah. I am so sorry. It seems I have more to apologize for than I knew." His warm breath fanned her ear, a drugging caress she should have enjoyed. "I will have to feel enough for both of us, then, because I love you, sweet. I love you so much and I cannot let you go."

It was everything she'd ever longed to hear. Here, now, a strong, powerful man was looking at her as if she were a prize, talking to her as if he would fight anyone or anything for her honor. As if he would hold her tight and never let her go. But still *she did not care*.

"I will find a way to heal you," he vowed.

Could he, though? Whichever of them won could ask the gods for the life of the other as their boon. But then the prize could not be the return of her emotions.

It seemed that no matter what happened, they were doomed.

CHAPTER TWENTY-THREE

SHIVAWN CROUCHED on the patch of land his father had died on. He'd expected memories to swamp him, pull him under a wave of misery, but surprisingly they didn't. He felt remorse, of course, for the strong male influence he'd lost. But stronger by far was the swell of anticipation for what would be. Alyssa was nearby. He hadn't yet seen her, but he'd at last caught a hint of her delectable fragrance.

A fragrance he planned to surround himself with for the rest of his life. Though he'd blamed her eyes for triggering his nightmares, all this time it had been *his* eyes that were the faulty ones. He hadn't seen deep enough to the wonderful woman she was.

And, to be honest, he was glad her eyes reminded him of what he'd lost. Glad, because he would never forget how quickly someone he loved could be taken from him. He would not take her for granted again. Besides, those eyes were a part of her and he wanted every part he could get. She was his. His demon, his vampire. His love.

He scanned the area, an area vastly different than he remembered. A village had been built here. Once there had been forest, now there were homes with thatch roofs scattered in every direction. Minotaurs and centaurs worked together in harmony, gardening, pruning, drawing water from wells. Children frolicked and played, laughing in carefree abandon.

Shivawn leaned against the wall, trying to appear inconspicuous. But several females had already gotten a whiff of his nymph scent and were lingering, trying to catch his eye. Lust colored several of their faces, and in turn fury colored several of the men's.

He was a nymph. That was business as usual for him. He was only astonished he hadn't picked up a trail of females on the daylong journey here. Perhaps his scowl had scared them all away.

He'd been forced to self-pleasure what seemed like ten thousand times just to garner enough strength to get here—and for the fight he knew was to come. But he was ready now. He had thoughts of Alyssa in his mind, thoughts that kept him aroused and strong enough. At least, he hoped.

Alyssa rounded the corner of a far stable, kicking stones with the tip of her boot. She wore a long yellow robe, the hood draping her face. He recognized her sensuous stroll, the sweet tilt of her head. More, he knew it was her, sensed it with everything inside him.

His joy, lust and love returned in full measure, stabbing at him fervently. His body shook as he drank her in. Did she think to hide her heritage from the creatures? Most races feared vampires and demons alike. Or had she heard of his arrival and assumed he wouldn't know her if she hid her face?

That was not something he could allow his woman to do.

Her gait never slowed, and she drew closer and closer to him. Was almost within reach…almost…he pushed deeper into the shadows as she stilled, raised her head. The hood fell back and she sniffed the air. Horror blanketed her features, and she stumbled backward.

Unwilling to give her a chance to run, he dove on her, rolling them midair to take the brunt of the fall himself. She was gasping and sputtering, but managed to pull a dagger and hold it to his throat when they finally stilled.

"Stab me if you wish, but know that I'm here because I care for you," he said, holding her tightly to prevent escape.

"You're here for revenge," she spat.

"No. For you."

She pressed the blade deeper and he felt a bead of blood trickle. Around them people watched, no doubt unsure of what to do. "Go about your duties," he called, not removing his focus from Alyssa. Gods, she was lovely. How had he resisted her for so long?

"I won't accept punishment for what I did," she told him. "It was necessary."

Her weight was delicious atop him, but he rolled them over, inserting his legs between hers for better leverage. Her eyes narrowed, and she kept the blade balanced. Thankfully she didn't try and scoot away.

"Why did you come here?" he asked. "To this place?"

"I won't discuss that with you, either. Now get off. I *will* kill you."

He cupped her chin with one of his hands, tender, gentle. "Sweet, I know who your brothers were. I know you were here that night."

When his words registered, she gasped. Tears sprang into her eyes and she shook her head.

He groaned, hating the pain banked in every hollow of her face. "Do you hate me for killing them?" he asked softly.

Her mouth floundered open and closed. "I should."

"That doesn't answer my question."

"No." She sighed, a troubled sound. "Even then, I understood."

His relief was a palpable force.

"I would have done the same," she admitted. "I didn't know them, was only there to watch them, learn about them. So many times I've wished my mother hadn't told me about my family. But my father raped her, and I guess she was afraid there were pieces of him inside of me."

No wonder she had reacted so badly when he'd accused her of trying to rape him. It must have seemed as though he were comparing her to the demon her father was. How she must have suffered, knowing she was the product of such a violent, horrific crime.

"You aren't evil, Alyssa. You're perfect." Pinned like this, he could feel all of her curves, all of her femininity. He'd been with her twice, but he had not savored her. He would never make that mistake again. "Remove the blade, love," he told her gently.

At first, she gave no indication that she'd heard him. Then, with another of those labored sighs, she tossed the weapon to the ground. It landed several inches away, close enough for them to grab if another creature made a play for it. "I'm too tired to fight you anymore."

The glowing dome cast her in reverent light, making her appear otherworldly, a phantom that might slip away from him if he wasn't careful. He could tell her what he felt, but he doubted she would believe him. Most likely she would view every word as an attempt to lure her to relaxation so that he could better punish her. Strike.

He reached for the knife at his back. She cringed. He

didn't say a word, just pulled from her and sat on his knees, legs straddling her waist.

"Is this the part where you kill me?" A question without any heat or emotion. "You owe me, after all. For what my family did to yours."

Slowly, so as not to scare her, he lowered the blade and held it to her, hilt first. "Take it."

"Wh-what?"

"Take it."

Suspicions darkened her expression. "Why?"

"I wish you to have my weapon."

"Why?" she repeated, still unsure of his purpose. "Why have me toss mine if you wanted me to have yours?"

"So you realize that what is mine is now yours. We are on equal ground now, as you wanted."

No part of her softened. "I doubt this is your only weapon."

Very true. "The gesture is symbolic then," he said drily.

"I'll reach for it and you'll laugh and then stab me." She shook her head, hair grinding into the dirt. "Sorry."

He *tsked* under his tongue, trying for a nonchalance that he didn't feel, and stood. He placed the blade beside her and stepped back, holding his arms wide. "If you wish, I will strip here of everything. Know that I don't want to, don't want to place you in danger and not be armed to protect you, but if you wish it, it will be done."

Her slitted gaze circled the growing crowd around them. At the women eyeing him, even inching toward him, reaching out for a touch of his skin.

With a hiss, she grabbed the blade and leapt to her feet. She also snatched her own and held both in her hands when she faced him. "Shall we fight?"

"No. We shall enter that home." He pointed to the small hut he'd been crouched beside.

That gave her pause. "Why?"

"Alyssa. Please. You are armed, I am not. You are warrior enough to subdue me if I do anything you dislike. All I desire is a few moments of your time. Alone."

Indecision played over her delicate face. Once, twice, she opened her mouth to speak but no sound emerged. She glanced at the house, taking its measure, then at Shivawn. Finally she found her voice. "Fine," she said, stomping to the hut and disappearing inside.

He eyed the rapt crowd. Damn, but the females were closing in fast. Like Alyssa, he stalked to the home—a home he'd purchased just a few hours ago—and called over his shoulder, "Stay out no matter what you hear. Enter and you will regret it." Nymph warriors were slow to anger, but when their tempers were roused, all of Atlantis suffered the consequences.

When he closed the door behind him, he wasn't sure what he'd find. Alyssa, ready for battle. Alyssa, ready for loving. What he ended up finding broke his heart into thousands of tiny pieces. She knelt in front of the fire he'd built several hours ago, poking it with a stick. The weapons were forgotten at her feet. Her shoulders were slumped, tear streaks on her cheeks.

"Don't cry, love," he said. "There's nothing to be afraid of. We're here, together, and I own this house, so do not worry about being disturbed."

The only bed was draped with chains, the very chains she'd used on him. He'd put them there, hoping he would not be forced to use them. Had she seen them?

"Now you will chain me, humiliate me and leave me once and for all. Right?"

He sighed. She'd seen them. "No. That is not how this will progress."

Her head snapped up, and she was blinking in surprise. "How then?"

He reached back and tugged his shirt over his head. As he tossed the material aside, a shocked gasp escaped her. "Now I'm going to love you," he said. He unwound the ties at the waist of his pants, loosening them.

Alyssa pushed to shaky legs, scrubbing her face with the backs of her hands. "Wh-why?"

"If you ask that one more time, I just might punish you."

"Aha. So you—"

"No. Hurting you is not my goal." His pants fell, leaving him bare except for his weapons. His erection sprang free, hard and achy. "But if I were to punish you, it would be with a tongue-lashing, then perhaps I would tickle you a bit, then lash you with my tongue again."

She gulped, her eyes impossibly round. "But—but—I don't understand."

One by one he removed his weapons. The blades strapped to his chest and back. The poisoned arrows glued to his side. "What you did to me was deserved. We are even." Not even close. But perhaps, after an eternity of seeing to her needs, they would be. "Do you agree?"

"Yes, but—" She was staring between his legs as though entranced.

He would have laughed if he hadn't been so aroused. He wanted her hands where her gaze was. "What I told you before was true."

"You've told me many things," she said with a tremor.

Gods, he hated to bring this up. "The first time we were together…"

Her cheeks heated to a bright crimson, as if she'd been slapped. From softening female to scorned witch in seconds.

"That was not because of you, Alyssa," he rushed out. "I know that now."

"I don't want to hear this." Stiff, she spun away from him, back to the fire. Imagining him roasting inside it?

He moved to her, placed his hands on her shoulders. He'd thought her stiff before, but she proved him wrong, every muscle she possessed turning to rock. At least she didn't jerk away, even when his erection rubbed the crevice of her bottom. "Every time I was near you," he said into her ear, nibbling on the soft lobe between words, "I saw that terrible night here. I couldn't figure out why, only knew that you were a reminder of it. And with the reminder, my desire was buried under regret. Do you understand?"

She nodded slowly, and he thought he saw a fresh tear glisten on her cheek.

"What do you understand? Tell me."

"That I will always remind you of that night. That you can never truly desire me."

Leaning down, he kissed away her tear. Breath caught in her throat—he heard its cessation. He slowly glided his hands down to cup her breasts. "Wrong. I desire you now more than I've ever desired another." He kneaded, gently pinched at her hardened nipples.

A moan slipped from her. Her hips arched back, rubbing more fervently against his erection.

Shivawn experienced a wave of hope. "Once I knew why, I knew what battle I was fighting."

"Wh-what battle?"

"Thinking of you and that night together, when I should not have. I've separated the two now. All I see, all I desire, is you. And I know you aren't even close to believing me. I know you think I'm merely playing with you to hurt you, but I'm going to do everything in my power to prove otherwise." He was going to have to use the chains, he realized. There was no other way.

Slowly, giving her time to protest, he unhooked the shoulder latch that held her robe together. The bright material floated to their feet. She trembled, but didn't try to stop him.

"Step out of it."

After a slight hesitation, she did. He allowed his fingers to dip into her navel before fanning through the soft curls between her legs. Her stomach quivered.

"Do you feel how hard I am for you?" he asked, his erection nestled against her bottom.

Nibbling on her sumptuous bottom lip, she nodded.

"You know I am a warrior, yes?"

Another nod. She spread her legs, silently asking him to delve deeper, to touch her where was she already wet and hot. His desire was so fierce, he almost caved, almost sank his fingers inside her sheath, but knew he would be lost if he did. So he held steady.

"And a warrior would never willingly bind himself in the presence of an enemy."

At the word *enemy,* she stiffened again.

He placed a soft kiss on the side of her throat. So pretty. So sweet. So his. Then he moved away from her—gods, the agony—and strode to the bed. Her hot gaze tracked his every movement. Facing her, he sat on the mattress and clasped the chains in his hands.

"Shivawn," she said brokenly. Nervously she rubbed her palms on her naked thighs.

"I'm trusting you not to leave me and lead me on another chase, love."

Careful not to look away, he shackled one of his wrists. With a tug of his arm, he proved it was anchored to the wall. Then he bound the other wrist, motions just as measured, just as precise.

Once again, her mouth floundered open and closed.

"There is no other I would bind myself for. Do you know why, Alyssa? You are my mate. I want no other but you. I would give my life for you. I...love you. Your wit, your smile, your determination, your stubbornness, the light in your eyes when you look at me. The way you move, the timbre of your voice, the curves of your body. Everything. I worship it all. Yes, I once hated vampires. Yes, I still hate demons. Yes, your family destroyed mine. But I'm here, offering myself to you, proof of my devotion."

Those tears free-fell down her cheeks now and she hugged her arms to her stomach.

He'd hoped, been so sure of success...until now. "Am I too late? Is the hurt too great? I know I made you feel less than a woman. That will haunt me for the rest of my days. But I *have* found pleasure with you, love. That night in the cave, I had never experienced so much. I want to satisfy you now. I want—"

She was in his arms a moment later, placing kisses all over his face. "I love you. I've always loved you."

Thank the gods. Their lips met in a fierce, drugging kiss. Her hands were all over him: his chest, his neck, his arms, his cock. He banded his arms around her, lay down and rolled, tucking her securely underneath him.

"Let me make you feel good." He licked at her neck, careful not to wrap the chains around her delicate skin.

She spread her legs, welcoming him into the curve of her body. "You are."

"I want to give you more. So much more." Because of the chains he could not trail down her body as he wanted. "Scoot up for me, love. I need to lick between your legs. Don't deny me the honor this time. Please."

She was pulling at his hair, trying to get his lips back to hers. "Kiss."

"Soon. If I don't taste you, I'll tumble straight into insanity."

Unsure, she inched upward. Her sweat-soaked skin slid, abraded deliciously against his own. And then her feminine core was right there, his to devour. He did. He licked the pink lips apart and sucked on the sweet little center.

Her hips writhed, her knees dropped further apart and she moaned. "Shivawn."

"This is mine. All mine."

"Yours."

"This is what's going to keep me alive from this day forward." He pumped his tongue into and out of her tight little sheath, taking more of her sweetness down his throat. "And then you're going to bite me and take what you need to live."

She gave a violent shake of her head. "You hate being bitten. I'll find nourishment elsewhere. Oh, gods." Her muscles were tensing, gearing for release. "Shivawn! Don't stop."

"This is heaven, sweet. This is heaven. And I will take great pleasure in giving you my blood. Great pleasure." He sucked her, hard. "There'll be no one else for you. It's my blood for you. I *want* to give it to you."

She fell right over the edge, screaming in ecstasy, chanting his name. While she hung in the balance between satisfaction and a new flood of desire, he scooted her back under him and entered her, filling her up.

"Mine," he gritted out through teeth clenched in absolute abandon. "All mine."

Her arms wrapped around him as he began pumping. "You're mine, too."

"Always. You feel so good," he praised. "I never want to leave you."

"Don't." She pressed a kiss into his neck, where his pulse fluttered wildly. But she didn't bite him.

"Do it. Please."

"No. Not with you. Already this seems like a dream. I don't want to awaken."

His strokes never slowed. "Do it. Please, love. Please. I'm desperate. I want those teeth inside me, sucking deep and hard."

"Are—are you sure?"

"Beyond."

A moment passed. Her teeth scraped at his skin but didn't penetrate. He increased the fervency of his thrusts, pounding, slamming. "Do it, love! I need those teeth in me like my cock is in you. I need—"

With a growl as fierce as any warrior's, she bit him. Deep, hard. A cut that would mark him for eternity. On and on she drank, and the sensation of her hot tongue on his neck, her teeth in his vein, combined with the knowledge that they were joined in every possible way, sent him over.

He shouted with his release, spurting his seed straight to her core.

Her teeth pulled out abruptly as she, too, cried out in

release. Their bodies strained together, spasming. "Never leave me," he gasped out, half-fearing she would bolt afterward. "Never."

"Never," she swore.

Shivawn collapsed on top of her, content and smiling.

VALERIAN STEPPED into the fire-lit hut and glanced around. It was bare except for a straw bed, which Shivawn lay upon. He was on his back, sleeping, naked. Chained. There were teeth marks all over his neck.

Valerian frowned. The vampire, Alyssa, was curled into Shivawn's side, her hand resting directly above his heart. She, too, was naked and asleep. And if Valerian wasn't mistaken, there was a love bite or two darkening her neck, as well. Frown deepening, Valerian strode to the bed, boots thumping against the twig-laden ground.

Shivawn's eyes fluttered open, as did Alyssa's. Shivawn growled, Alyssa screamed and scrambled backward as he raised his sword.

"Valerian, stop! This—" Shivawn threw himself on top of the woman as best he could with the chains pulling at him.

Valerian smiled but didn't stop. As if he would have hurt the woman. He hit the chains, snapping the links in half. "I see you took my advice and apologized. Good man. Now I will offer an apology of my own for not being able to give you more time with your woman. The army waits outside. We have need of you."

Once, Shivawn would have jumped up and obeyed. Now he growled, "Turn your back. Now!"

As king, Valerian wasn't used to being ordered and did not like it now, but he obeyed instantly. He understood the need to keep a mate's nudity all to oneself. If anyone were to look upon his Shaye in such a state, well, they would lose their eyes.

There was a rustling, some cooing, and Valerian rolled his own eyes. Then there was even some kissing. "Sometime today," he said.

"You may turn."

He did. Shivawn was draped by a blanket and the pretty vampire was covered with a dirty yellow robe, only her face and hands visible.

"We have news of the disappearance. Two of the warriors have been found. Rumor has it they are locked up at the Amazon camp."

"Who was found?"

"A dragon and a vampire," he said, flicking a glance to Alyssa.

She squared her shoulders, plans to retrieve the warrior already swirling in her eyes. "Is my king—"

"No. It is the other." Valerian's attention shifted back to Shivawn. "I want to talk to them and find out what happened, if they know where the others are. If the others are… I want to hear firsthand that Broderick and Jada are alive and well."

"The Amazons never allow armies near their holding," Shivawn said, but he was gathering his weapons.

Valerian smiled smugly. "As if they could turn a nymph away. As if any woman could."

"I'm going with you," Alyssa said, standing.

Shivawn pulled her to him for a deep kiss. "I wouldn't have it any other way, love. We're together, now and always."

CHAPTER TWENTY-FOUR

LAYEL FOUND a cave as far away from the unearthly growling as possible. Whatever creature was producing the eerie rumble, he wasn't ready to approach. Only when Delilah had been well cared for would he even *think* of battle.

Delilah.

His chest ached for her. He laid her down gently, peering at her beautiful, expressionless face. Hestia had taken her emotions from her, and he hated the goddess for that. Yesterday he would have hated himself, too, for allowing it to happen. But he wasn't that same man anymore. He refused to wallow in pain and pity.

Today he was a man who took action, who kept his eye on the prize and did what was necessary to win it. In this case, the prize was Delilah's heart.

"We should find and kill the beast," she said, sitting up.

He kissed her softly. Her skin was cold, and she did not respond as she once had. "I love you," he told her, words he'd never thought to utter again.

She opened her mouth—to rebuke him, he was sure, so he placed a finger over her lips. "Shh. Don't waste your strength."

She shrugged as if she didn't care one way or another,

but there was something in her eyes…a spark of something hot. Was she feeling? Was it possible?

"Close your eyes and rest, sweet." He draped an arm around her, surprised when she obeyed. "You're safe."

"I *am* tired," she said with a sigh. Just like that, her body sagged into unconsciousness. There were no fears to keep her awake, no desire to cause her to ache. Only a void to tug her under, into nothingness, as if she had lost even her will to live. Had he imagined that spark?

Layel swallowed the hard lump in his throat and stood. Darkness was thicker than a blanket as he strode forward, pushing through the trees, not noticing as the branches slapped and cut him.

When he was far enough away that Delilah wouldn't be able to hear him if she awoke, he dropped to his knees. He jerked the shirt from his torso and tossed it aside.

Hestia, the bitch, clearly wanted Delilah to win. And though it angered Layel to agree with her, his wishes now aligned with her own. Layel had thought to win the competition himself, but now knew he couldn't do it. If Delilah won, she would keep her life and could demand as her boon the return of her emotions, her will to live. But he would die. There had to be a way to save them both.

"Hestia, goddess of hearth and home," he cried. "I come before you as your humble servant, my heart heavy and my greatest wish to beg an audience."

A minute edged by, then another. There was nothing, no pickup in the wind, no dancing of the trees, no singing of insects.

"Please," Layel gritted out. He had hated the gods all these years. After Susan died, he had begged like this, pleaded for her life, and he had been ignored. Now he had

Delilah and he intended to keep her for as long as he lived. As far as he was concerned, the gods owed him one. "Show yourself!" he shouted then, respect and decorum forgotten. "You want victory? Well, you will not get it. Not without my aid. You will lose. You will—"

"I will not lose," an angry voice said from behind him.

Layel was on his feet and spinning in an instant. His heart hammered erratically when he saw that Hestia stood before him, draped in a white robe and holding a spear. The goddess glowed with the force of her power, obviously no longer content to hide behind a veil of secrecy. But though her might had never been more evident, Layel was encouraged by the fact that she had heeded his call.

"Forgive me for my outburst." He forced his head to bow. *For Delilah.* "I was desperate to reach you."

The goddess sighed and was suddenly right in front of him, her sandals pressed against his boots. She smelled of the sea. "What do you want from me, vampire king?" Though he never saw her move, she was behind him again when the last word was spoken.

His jaw tightened. "I ask that you return Delilah's emotions to her."

"Why would I be so foolish as to agree to that? With them as her guide, she chose you over victory. An intolerable decision."

"Yes, but without them, she chooses nothing. She is no use to you now. She doesn't want victory. She wants only to sleep."

His knees were suddenly kicked from behind and he found himself kneeling again. He didn't fight, didn't complain. He simply ran his tongue over his teeth, the sharpness of them slicing. A pity it was his blood rather than Hestia's, but he knew he could not hurt the goddess without severe consequences.

"Better. I like you like this, vampire. Even a king should learn to show proper respect to the gods."

I hate you. What have you ever done to earn my respect?
"Would you be willing to consider a trade?"

A crackling pause that seemed to stretch into eternity. Then, "What are you offering?"

"For the restoration of Delilah's emotions, I will promise to lose this competition. Not only that, but I will do all I can to ensure that she wins."

Another bout of silence. "A novel idea, but you cannot assure me beyond any doubt that you can acquire the victory for her. The dragon or the nymph could swoop in and stop you both. What's more, you cannot assure me that once her emotions are restored she will use them wisely to secure her own triumph. She could very well fight for *you* to win."

Very true. Stubborn as Delilah was, she just might try to aid him. "I'll stop her." Somehow, some way. "Upon my honor."

"You have no honor, vampire." Her head tilted to the side as she considered him. "But your proposition intrigues me nonetheless. What if I agreed to return her emotions for a single night? You would have one night to convince her of the merits of winning, no matter the cost. Even though she will lose her emotions again in the morning, the logic you plant inside her mind will still remain. And victory will once again be her concern." An excited laugh. "If I do this for you, you will not tell her about our bargain. Understand? You will tell no one."

A minute with Delilah's love was better than a lifetime without. "I would agree. To all your terms." Of course she wouldn't wish the other gods to know of her intervention. Layel stored that information, to be pondered later. "And as winner, she will still be awarded the boon. For aiding her, would I be given one, as well?"

"*This* is your boon. Now, have we reached an agreement? Will you help her solve our riddle?"

A single word caused Layel's mind to spin. *Riddle.* What kind of riddle? He racked his brain to remember what the gods had said earlier. *You will find something the likes of which even the bravest of men would run from.* He'd thought the answer a beast. His brow furrowed as he pondered further. If those words were indeed a riddle, could that mean there wasn't really a beast in the mountain? But he'd heard the snarling, hadn't he?

"Killing me will cause more harm than good," Layel said, forging ahead despite his confusion. "Surely you—"

"Enough," she interjected. "Answer. Now. Do we have an agreement?" Such sudden impatience. Either she'd realized she'd said more than she ought or she sensed his inner turmoil.

"I agree to everything," he said. "Return Delilah's emotions for one night. In turn I will purposely lose while doing my best to ensure that she wins by whatever means necessary." He wanted it spelled out, so there could be no question later what he had agreed to. "And I will not tell her or anyone what I've done."

Hestia was in front of him again, kneeling, placing them nose to nose. Her lips brushed his in a soft kiss that shot wave after wave of electricity through him. There was nothing sexual about it; this was just her way of proving her power, he supposed. "Then go. Your woman feels again."

Suddenly a scream echoed through the night. Delilah's scream.

Layel was on his feet in the next instant, running back to her, desperate to reach her, the goddess already forgotten. He broke through the final layer of trees. Saw her. She was curled in a ball, sobbing.

"I'm here, I'm here." He flew to her and gathered her in his arms, holding as tight as he was able without hurting her.

She didn't protest. No, she clung to him. "Oh, gods. Oh, gods. I feel… There's so many… They're so strong… Can't process all of them. What's wrong with me, Layel?"

"You've been given back what was taken from you," he said. He hadn't broken the pact, either, though he knew he skirted a dangerous edge. "In the morning—" he said, then stopped himself. As he watched, her eyes began to grow cold again, as if her emotions were once more receding. Her sobs quieted. Hestia was watching, he realized, and subtly conveying to Layel that she would reclaim Delilah's emotions if he broke his word. Layel clamped his lips together.

As quickly as it had appeared, the coldness vanished and her sobs returned.

"Shh, shh. I've got you now." He ran his hands down her spine, then up, under her half-shirt. Her skin was blazing hot. "I love you. I love you so much."

"I—I— Layel, Nola was taken and I didn't fight for her. You told me you loved me and I didn't care. Oh, gods. I should have fought. I should have told you I loved you, too, and would do anything to stay with you."

Joy burst through him, hearing that heartfelt proclamation, and he knew he'd lived these past two hundred years for this moment. This moment, and no other. Not revenge, and not to become worthy of Susan. Everything he'd done, everything he was, was for Delilah. All his torment had led him to her.

Softly he brushed her trembling lips with his own. "There's nothing we can do for your sister now. Once we leave the island—" no matter what the goddess said, Layel would not allow himself to be killed "—we will retrieve her."

"But you—you—"

"I love you, warrior woman. I love you. I am only sorry it took me so long to realize it. I am sorry for hurting you, sweet. So sorry."

He pressed their lips together and thrust his tongue deep into her mouth, feeding her a kiss that scorched even him to the bone.

"What of your mate?"

"You are my mate now. But if you wish to know of Susan, I will tell you anything, everything." He drew in a breath, slowly released it. "You know the gods used to exile unfavored humans to Atlantis, hoping we would annihilate them. Well, some of them survived and Susan was their descendant. As she grew they kept her hidden very well. But vampires sense human blood as no other can. We're drawn to it. The taste, the sweetness. Though nothing compares to yours," he hastened to assure her.

She snuggled against him, listening intently, urging him on.

"My men and I sniffed her out," he said, pleased to discover that talking about the past was no longer like ripping open a wound. "I meant to keep her chained in my room, mine to drink from anytime I desired. Remember, those were much different, much harsher times. Anyway, I grew to love her smile, her gentle nature. She…softened me.

After she finished scolding me for trying to hold her captive, that is. We had two wondrous years together before she conceived. The baby was due just after the dragons came, killing both Susan and my unborn daughter."

"You knew the child was a girl?"

He nodded. "We were going to name her Bianca."

"I'm so sorry, Layel. Truly, I am. I ache for you, and would return all that you've lost if I could."

Oh, no. There would be none of that. "As I told you, it is you I desire, Delilah. No one else. Not even Susan. Now, tell me of your dragon," he said, before she could protest his words.

"Vorik?"

Vorik. He played the name through his mind before nodding. "I know of him. Strong, fierce. A charmer, or so I heard."

"Oh, yes. A first-rate charmer. But then, I was ripe for the plucking. I'd always longed for the kind of I'll-die-for-you love all other creatures but Amazons embrace. When he expressed desire for me, I thought I could make him love me that way. But I was wrong. He left without saying goodbye the moment the mating was over."

"Shall I kill him for you?"

"No," she said with a chuckle. "I punished him already. A few weeks later, my army marched through dragon land in one of our bids to prove how strong we are, and I ensured all the females in his village knew of his…shortcomings."

Layel barked out a laugh. "That's my Amazon."

Her smile was warm, lighting him up inside. That smile quickly faded, however. "I'm glad that we're both able to talk about the past like this. Do you think… What if—would you like another child, Layel?"

He cupped her cheek, his eyes suddenly burning with tears, a hard lump in his throat. "With you, I would like as many as we can make."

"Me, as well." She turned in his arms, placing her lips just above his. "I want you, Layel, I want you so badly. Now, forever."

They were words he had never thought to hear again. His joy intensified, blending with his arousal. "We don't have a lot of time, sweet. There's much to do. And we can't risk Broderick or Tagart beating us to the monster." Whatever the monster was—beast, a riddle to be figured out or something else entirely.

"It's dark. They won't risk fighting the unknown in the dark. And I need you. Please. Don't make me beg. Don't make me—"

He tried to be gentle as he swooped down and claimed her lips, he really did, but his need was too fiery. He'd nearly lost her, would probably lose her again when her emotions drifted away with the daylight.

As he tongued her, he ripped the leather top from her and tossed it aside. Her tiny skirt was given the same treatment, leaving her bare. His gaze cut through the dark and drank in the tattoos he so adored. *I've licked them. Will again.*

"Layel!"

He snapped out of the momentary lust-daze and attacked her breasts, flicking his tongue over the hardened pink berries he found there. Her hips writhed; she moaned.

"I'm burning up for you," she gasped out.

"You and no other."

"You and no other," she agreed. "I love you."

"Oh, gods, Delilah." So beautiful, those words. They

would define the rest of his life, for they changed him, turned him from beast to man.

He laved her face with nips and kisses, then licked away any sting he might have delivered. All the while his fingers explored her body until finally sinking deep into her wet core.

She cried out.

"Love you," he said, working a third finger into her.

That was all her desire needed. Her inner walls clenched around him, drawing him deeper. Moisture flooded his hand, hot, slick as he pumped, taking her higher. So high. "That's it. Give me everything."

Her hands clutched at his back, squeezed the muscles so tightly he would carry the bruises for weeks. "More," she said on a broken breath. "Do that again."

"My pleasure, though I plan to use something else on you."

He kissed her then, and her eyelids popped open. Their gazes met in a tangled web of desire. She must have seen his desperation because she pushed him to his back, worked his pants off and straddled him.

Her blue hair fell around them like a curtain as she positioned herself at the tip of his mighty erection. Shaking, he reached up and cupped her cheeks, fingers gliding easily over her sweat-soaked skin.

"You arms are cut," she said. Arousal morphed into concern, and she traced a fingertip over his brow.

"They'll heal."

She wrapped her fingers around each of his wrists and brought his arms to her mouth, one at a time, kissing his injuries. "I don't know why I'm feeling again, but I'm glad that I am."

"As am I." The gesture warmed him, body and soul. "As am I."

Her face was soft, glowing with love. She sank an inch…then another… "You really love me?"

"Gods, that feels good! More than I could even say. You are my strength. You are my joy. My peace."

She nibbled on her bottom lip. "I like the contradictions of you, you know? You are light and dark, brute warrior and gentle protector."

He squeezed her hips, grinding his erection another blissful inch.

"I was drawn to you from the first," she said, head falling back. "Have thought of nothing and no one since."

"I fought my desire for you with all my might, but in the end there was no denying it. You are the woman for me. You are my woman. Take me all the way inside, Delilah."

"Let's take each other."

"Always." He rolled her over, spread her legs as far as they would go and pounded all the way home. They cried out in unison. He fit her perfectly, sublimely, for she was the piece of him that had been missing all these many years.

"Bite me," she commanded him.

"Not yet. Need you strong." She was going to win this challenge and he was going to help her, just as he'd promised.

"Please."

"Delilah," he said, glancing at her neck. Her pulse hammered wildly, and his mouth watered.

"Layel," she moaned. "Please."

"Not yet." He would take too much. In and out he continued to pound. He hooked his elbows under her knees to spread her even wider. Her head arched back, gifting him with a better view of her neck.

Her nipples rubbed his chest, and he released one of her legs to roll a sweet berry between his fingers. "Yes!"

She was meeting his thrusts with her hips, driving him deeper. Deeper. So good. He kissed her mouth, plunging his tongue just as deep. Her inner walls squeezed him, his testicles slapped at her, and then he was coming too, pouring into her. Shuddering.

She groaned, massaging his neck, and he realized his teeth were in her, drinking the sweetness. Rather than draining her, he gulped back a mouthful and gently pulled from her. Even while enthralled, he couldn't hurt her.

When the aftereffects eased, he fell beside her. She kept her arms around him and rolled onto his chest. Both of them were panting and sweating, and never had he felt more content.

"Will you be my mate?" he asked her, his joy sobering in the face of what was to come. The return of her coldness, her lack of emotion. He needed to lay what groundwork he could to guarantee they remained together when this was over. "I vow to love you, now and forever, see to your comfort, now and forever, and protect you with my own life. Now and forever."

She raised her head, eyes sultry, and peered down at him. A slow smile lifted her lips. "Yes. Yes. All that I am, all that I have, is yours. I will love you, comfort you and protect you. Now and forever."

"Swear to me you will not forget that we are mated. That no matter what you feel inside, you will not forget this moment, this promise." He cupped her cheek and stared up into her eyes. "Don't ask me why, just swear it."

Her smile faded, but she nodded. "I swear it. I will not forget."

He squeezed her tightly. And when she rested her head in the crook of his neck, he sighed, praying the night never ended.

"I can't believe we are together at last."

He could. He only hoped it lasted.

CHAPTER TWENTY-FIVE

ONLY A FEW HOURS of darkness remained, Delilah thought, more sated than she had ever been in her life. She and Layel had made love several more times in several different positions. He couldn't seem to get enough of her, his need almost…desperate.

He'd made her promise all kinds of things. To always love him. To always forgive him. To kiss him every morning for the rest of her life. To be the one to win the challenge, no matter what she saw or heard, no matter what happened. She had been more than happy to agree to everything but the last—which had only made him work harder to convince her of the rightness of her taking victory for herself. Finally, she'd given in and promised. She would win, and she would demand Layel's life as her prize. But she didn't want Tagart or Broderick to die, either. Was there a way to save everyone?

Miracles were indeed possible, she now realized. *He loves me,* she thought with a shocked grin. They should be up, finishing the challenge, but she cherished this time with him and couldn't stand the thought of it ending. He had said goodbye to his old love; they were going to be together. She didn't know how they would leave the island together—the prize perhaps. But never again would she push him away.

"I could happily lie here forever, sweetheart, but time is running out for us to find the answer to the gods' riddle," Layel said as he rubbed a hand down her spine. Confusion, determination and dread layered the announcement.

She shivered and propped her head on her hand, looking down at him. Just catching a glimpse of his eerie beauty caused her chest to constrict. *He's my man.* What an exhilarating concept. "What makes you think it's a riddle? We were told there was something up here that even a brave man would run from. And we have heard the creature's cry, so we know they weren't lying."

As if it had heard their conversation and wanted to reaffirm its presence, the unnamed creature howled, the unholy sound rending the air. Judging by the volume, the beast wasn't close to them, but it was closer than it had been a few hours ago.

"The goddess Hestia called this challenge a riddle."

"No, she didn't. I would remember."

His glowing blue eyes focused on her, and never had they appeared so grave. Secrets churned in their depths. "Trust me on this."

"All right. I do." She trusted him with her heart, so there was no reason to doubt him in this.

He leaned up and kissed her, and just like that she felt him grow hard against her thigh. Reaching down, she curled her fingers around his length and squeezed. His eyelids closed in ecstasy as he hissed in a breath.

"Are you always this insatiable?" she asked with a laugh.

"I could ask the same of you, sweet. But to answer your question, yes, but only with you."

No wonder she loved him. "I'm glad, because I would slay any woman who tried to take you from me." And it was the truth. As she stroked him, loving the feel of velvet over steel, she said, "What would a brave man turn away from, I wonder."

"I don't know. I can't think right now."

After moistening her lips, she moved above him, scattering kisses over his chest and delving her tongue into his navel. "I like when you can't think." Lower still. Her mouth sank down on his erection, her tongue playing the head.

"Delilah, I—I—we should be figuring this out. This challenge, this—" Her tongue swirled over the plump head. "Oh, gods."

"Has a woman done this to you before?" She'd heard talk of it among her sisters and knew men relished having it done.

"No. Never."

She would be the first, then, and the knowledge filled her with possessive pride. "I've never done this for a man, but it's my honor to do it for you." Without another word, she sucked him. Loving the moans and groans he made, reveling in the gyrations of his hips, the feel of his hands fisted in her hair.

Up and down she worked, taking him so far down her throat she couldn't breathe. But she loved it. Couldn't stop. Rode his erection with her mouth until he collapsed, spent.

Smiling, she curled beside him. Gods, she loved this man. There was nothing he wouldn't do for her, she knew that now. Battle her sisters—yes. Walk through raging fires—of course. Kill Vorik—she had only to name when and where.

"You were saying something about a riddle," she prompted.

He chuckled.

"I'm not sure why the gods would give us a riddle rather than test our battle skills. Didn't they mention they wanted the strongest warrior to win? If so, why not give us another, more straightforward challenge?"

"Strongest warrior, yes, but also the best warrior. They've already tested our might, our endurance, our memory. Perhaps intelligence is the only thing left." He sighed, loud and long. "We'll figure this out. And if necessary, we'll destroy the creature, whatever it is, as well as that blackguard Tagart. Broderick, I would like to save, if only there were a way. As for you, you've managed to distract me again. I believe I owe you a very special kiss. And while I'm tasting you, I want you to remind me of everything you've promised me. If you stop talking, I stop kissing."

And with that naughty threat, he bent and made good on his word.

SHIVAWN HAD ALYSSA behind him on the centaur as they pranced toward the edge of the cliff. The Amazon camp was nearby. Thanks to nymph senses, they could sniff females out anywhere, anytime. Her hands were on his waist, holding tight. He had never felt stronger, more alive.

Valerian rode beside him, the nymph army lined in their wake.

"Brenna will not be happy if we slaughter the female warriors," Joachim said in his deep, gruff voice. He was a strong soldier, one of the best, and he was mated to the human Shivawn had once owned.

They were friends now only because Shivawn had relinquished all claim to the girl. That was a good thing, too. As he was learning, all things happened for a reason. If he'd kept Brenna, he would not have been free to mate with Alyssa, and he would rather die than be without his Alyssa.

"Clearly, they are hiding in wait. But they have not attacked us yet," Valerian pointed out, "so our charms must be working."

The lure of the nymphs, he thought, something he'd always been proud of but cursed today. He didn't want Alyssa upset for any reason.

There was a whoop, a war cry, and then the Amazons were flooding the edge of the cliff above their camp. "Halt," a female voice shouted angrily. "State your business, nymphs."

"Perhaps we aren't as charming as we assumed," Valerian muttered. He raised his arm, and the army obeyed. "We came to speak with the prisoners."

One woman stepped forward. She was fair-haired, tall and muscled, yet as pretty as an angel. "No," she said, and Shivawn recognized the voice that had commanded them to stop. She must be the tribe's queen, Kreja. "You may now turn around, Valerian, and return to your palace. We won't kill you. This time."

Shivawn had heard of her bloodthirsty nature, her unbending determination and the iron fist with which she ruled her people. What he had not heard was whether she'd ever spent time with Valerian. That familiarity...had they once been lovers? If so, Valerian would have cast her aside—females never left the nymphs. Correction: females rarely left the nymphs—and would not wish to help the nymphs in any way if they had.

"Tell us what you know of them," Valerian demanded. "Please."

Kreja smiled, smug. "A *please* from your lips... irresistible. They were given to us by the gods," she said. "Therefore, they belong to us."

A young girl pushed her way through the masses. Kreja grabbed for her, saying, "Lily, no!" but the child squirmed for freedom and rather than hurt her, the queen let her go.

She approached, spear in hand, eyes wide. "Pretty," she breathed, gaze locked on Dorian, an irreverent dark-haired warrior who preferred variety over quality.

"As are you." He winked at her indulgently. "Perhaps we'll meet again in a few years."

The queen watched the exchange, looking both proud that the girl was brave enough to approach the warriors and worried for her safety. As if the nymphs would ever harm a child.

"I'm old enough to have a slave," the girl called Lily said, chin lifting. "His name is Brand the dragon. I made him wash my clothes and fetch my breakfast this morning. I could talk to my mother about keeping you instead."

His lips twitched. Even Shivawn smiled at that. "No, thanks," Dorian said. "Perhaps another time."

"Lily!" Kreja shouted, and the little girl jumped.

"Until then," she said, turning and running back to the females. Instantly they absorbed her into their midst, leaving no sign of her presence.

A muscle ticked below Valerian's eyes. "Where are you harboring the men? They have information we need," he said, returning everyone to the business at hand.

"Information *I* now have. Information I will share only because I have every intention of demanding payment for it one day. You worry for your missing soldiers, I presume. They were taken to an island, far from us," she said. "They told me of sun, moon and sand, where mers swam and the gods could freely exercise their power. Something they did often, testing the warriors mercilessly. Both nymphs were alive when the vampire, Zane, and the dragon, Brand, were brought to me."

Valerian glanced at Shivawn with dread before refocusing on the queen. "What island?"

"They did not know."

"You realize the dragon and vampire armies will come after you if you keep those men, yes?"

"Yes." She grinned with relish. "Let them come. Amazons enjoy combat, if you hadn't heard."

"I am ally to both. Should they ask me, I will fight at their side and do all in my power to bring you down."

Rather than frighten her, the boast merely intensified her giddiness. She sent an eager gaze over the army. "Out of fond remembrance of our week together all those years ago, I will warn you not to try."

So they *had* been lovers. Curious, Shivawn thought. Before settling into their current residence, the nymphs had wandered Atlantis from palace to palace, race to race, taking their pleasure wherever they found it but never remaining in one place for long. The Amazons, however, they had always avoided. They didn't desire companions; they desired slaves. For a time. It wasn't in a nymph's nature to submit. Well, not outside the bedroom.

"One youthful mistake," Valerian said on a sigh. "I will do what I must, Kreja, memories or no."

She smiled. "You always do. Do it, then. Fight us. Mating season soon approaches." A horn sounded in the distance, and all of the Amazons stiffened. Frowning, the queen glanced behind her as the horn echoed once more. "Until we meet again…" What that, she and her followers stepped backward in unison and simply disappeared.

"Alyssa," Shivawn said.

Realizing what he wanted, she gripped him all the tighter and flew him to the top of the cliff. Down, down he looked. The women had stepped off the cliff and into a churning lake. They made a splash when they hit, then surfaced and swam to shore, waving coyly up at him.

"First they challenge you, and then they run," she muttered. "What odd creatures."

They floated back down, and Valerian sighed. "Where could this island of sun and moon and mers—" He pressed his lips together, head tilting to the side. "Wait. I know where it might be. Come with me."

As quickly as their centaurs would allow, they traveled to the nymph palace. Valerian's queen was waiting for him when they arrived. The nymph king dismounted and ran to his pale moonbeam, swinging her around while she kissed his face.

Alyssa bit Shivawn's shoulder, an action of possession, for Brenna waited atop the front steps, wringing her hands together, black curls billowing around her lovely face as she searched the sea of soldiers for Joachim. The warrior was pushing through the masses. When he reached the little female, he jerked her into his arms and she sighed with relief.

Shivawn turned until he was facing Alyssa. "I love you," he told her. "Only, always, you."

Her features softened, fangs retracting.

"The human means nothing to me, I swear it."

Alyssa looked away from him. "But you almost bedded her that day. Wanted to bed her."

What a fool I was. "Let us discard the past, love. We have started fresh."

"I guess I'll have to kill someone else," she muttered.

He chuckled. "That you will."

"This way," Valerian called.

Shivawn dismounted and helped Alyssa do the same. Side by side, they followed Valerian through the palace, past jewel-encrusted walls and men making love to nymph females in every corner. Decadent moans echoed as they descended the steps and strode into a cave.

Valerian pressed against a jagged rock in the upper corner of the wall and two boulders parted, revealing a breathtaking view of the ocean. Fish. Mermaids waiting to catch a glimpse of a nymph.

The king twisted another of the rocks and withdrew a small, round glass, extending it from the wall like an arm. He bent down and placed his eye in the center. Several minutes passed, warriors shifting from one boot to another as they waited.

What was he doing?

He moved his body left and right, angling for…what? Finally he stepped back and nodded stiffly. "I was right. Look."

Shivawn bent and peered through that glass, realizing he was looking up, up and out of the sea. Breath hitched in his throat. There was a patch of land, a large expanse of pin-pricked black, and a round golden sphere. Water lapped at the edges of a beach, white sand stretching into thick, emerald foliage. "What is that place?"

"I have never been sure if it is on the surface or if it's another hidden city like Atlantis."

"How do we get there?"

"The portals, perhaps."

Shivawn's attention slid to the portal in question. It was upright, surrounded by the mist that constantly seeped from it. Touching it pulled a person out of Atlantis and into the ocean. The one and only time he had done so, he had swum to the surface to steal human females. That's when he'd met Brenna and hurt Alyssa so terribly.

"Then we swim," he said. He turned to Alyssa to explain the need for such an action and apologize if necessary. Assure her again of his love, most definitely.

"My king is out there," she said before he could utter a word. "I, too, will go through the portal."

He glanced to Valerian, who nodded. Attention returning to Alyssa, he tenderly kissed her temple. "You are a true warrior, after all, love. Together, we will bring our people home."

WHEN THE SUN ROSE, Layel was tense. Afraid. So afraid. His night with Delilah had been the stuff of fantasies and dreams. He needed more. But would he get it? Or would she lose her emotions as Hestia had warned?

He'd been watching her sleep for hours, the gentle rise and fall of her chest a mating call. He hated to wake her and lose this peace, but it was necessary. "Delilah," he said, gently shaking her.

Slowly her eyelids cracked open.

And that's when he knew. His chest constricted with painful intensity. Once more her gaze was cold, blank. She rolled to her back, eyelids already closing. "What's wrong with me?" she asked groggily.

"Your emotions were taken again." Layel wanted to kill something. The goddess would be a nice choice.

"Oh." She didn't sound as if she cared.

"I love you," he croaked out.

She yawned. "I know. I love you, too."

At least she knew, even if she couldn't feel. Hestia had

been right in urging him to use logic. "Do you remember everything you promised me?"

"Of course. It's my emotions that disappeared, not my brain."

He sighed. "It's time to find and destroy the monster, love."

"All right." Unhurried, she rose and dressed.

He'd half expected her to insist he allow her to continue sleeping. Hopeful, he pushed to unsteady feet. After he'd donned his pants, he plucked several berries from a nearby bush and held them out. "Eat."

"I'm not hungry." She studied the length of several blades before sheathing them at her sides. She didn't look as if she cared to use them or even knew what to do with them.

"Eat. Please. You need to stay strong."

Reluctantly, she took and ate the fruit.

"You said you remembered what you promised me, but do you remember last night? What happened between us?"

"Yes," she said, looking at him. Blinking without concern. "Are you ready? I promised to win this contest, which means I need to fight a monster."

He grabbed her shoulders, desperation flooding him. "Delilah."

For a moment, one sweet moment, warmth fluttered over her expression, chasing away the cold, but it was quickly gone. And then the beast was roaring in pain and fury, the high-pitched scream enough to bust his eardrums. Layel stiffened, realization settling deep. "The monster has been found. Come."

He clutched Delilah's hand and jerked her into motion, racing through the trees, his heart pounding against his ribs. She stumbled several times, and he began to worry for her ability to do what would be needed.

Whatever would be needed. Not knowing what else to do, he picked her up and leapt into the air, flying high... higher...

An eternity passed, the mountain seemingly never ending. Trees knifed toward him, slapping, but then the beach came into view and he knew he was farther away from the action, not closer, the monster's newest roar weaker. With a twist of his body, he turned them around and headed back into the trees. Where in Hades were the other warriors?

Finally, in the center of the mountain, he caught a glimpse of Tagart exiting a cave, sword raised. Broderick jumped out and attacked him with a sword of his own, the two men swinging and thrusting at each other, grunting and slashing.

Layel didn't want Delilah fighting in this condition, but he didn't want to risk defeating the monster himself, either. Damn the gods! What should he do? He set her down. She didn't protest. Just sat there, watching the fight through indifferent eyes.

"Stay here," he whispered.

"I promised to win," she said.

"Worry not, love. I'll only be a moment and will find a way to ensure your victory."

She nodded, the easy compliance so unlike her, his heart sank a little.

"What's in there?" Broderick demanded of Tagart.

"Nothing." Tagart swung his sword. Missed as the nymph jumped out of the way.

"Sure?"

"Wouldn't matter. This is *my* kill. I found it first."

"Yes, but I'll be the last thing it sees."

Layel dropped to his stomach and inched forward. With

the combatants distracted, he could sneak into the cave and injure whatever was inside. *If* something was even in there. How could this be a riddle?

He didn't get very far.

A huge, monstrous creature with black wings and red eyes lunged out, teeth snapping at Layel, then at the struggling warriors, who leapt apart with shocked gasps. Heart drumming in a wild frenzy, Layel backtracked, shoving Delilah behind him. She wasn't ready for such a battle. Might not care enough to dodge a death-blow.

"I don't think we should fight it," she said, voice devoid of either fear or eagerness.

He wanted to look at her, but was afraid to tear his attention from the monster. Afraid that a single moment of inattentiveness would cause the beast to attack him, and thereby Delilah. "Why?"

"I don't fear it." Stated so matter-of-factly.

"Well, I do. And you would, too, if you still had possession of your emotions, brave Amazon warrior or not."

"No, you're not understanding. The gods said we would find something the likes of which even the bravest of men would run from, something that we fear more than anything else. We are to face it, defeat it. But the thing I feared above all else was being without you. Last night I faced that fear. I defeated it. I gave myself to you, without reservation, hopeful for the future. Don't you see, Layel? I don't need to slay this beast. I've already won the gods' challenge."

A riddle. Just as Hestia had said. He stilled, his eyes widening. Delilah had done it. Had truly done it. And she'd done it without him. The foolishness he felt at not having figured it out himself was no match for his pride in the woman who had. *His* woman. Grinning, he turned and hugged her close. Her arms wrapped tentatively around him, and the small gesture warmed his heart.

"Very good, my child. Very, very good. And so a winner has been declared," a laughing voice whispered through the trees. "Ah, but do not fear, vampire, nymph and dragon. No one need die this day. The losers shall be spared, as each of you proved useful in some way. And I know what you are thinking, vampire. I told you otherwise before. But how could you have faced your worst fear if there were no consequences for your actions?"

With the words, the monster disappeared, though its roar continued to echo throughout the mountain. Tagart and Broderick whipped around, confused, searching. "Where did it go?" they panted in unison.

Each of the five gods appeared in a blazing cascade of lights. As Layel blinked against their brilliance, he saw that only Hestia was smiling.

The goddess faced Delilah. "Amazon, you have surpassed my expectations. Of all the warriors, you have displayed the most strength, courage, endurance and wit. At any point, you could have given up, yet you persevered, determination your beloved companion."

"Not true! My dragon displayed the most strength. You cheated," Poseidon growled at the goddess.

"As did you," she replied smugly. "Do you honestly believe none of us heard your meeting with the dragon last eve? You told him exactly what his greatest fear was, and still he failed to understand. The Amazon is unquestionably the winner of this game. And that means I have won our game, as well."

Ares clenched his fists so tightly blood ran from his palms.

Artemis regarded them coldly, as if the outcome didn't affect her one way or another.

Apollo was popping his jaw, the glow around him more diminished than before.

Then they each nodded in reluctant acknowledgment.

War cries abounding, an army of nymphs suddenly burst past the trees, and stopped. The roars became gasps and snarls. Layel raced forward, his goal to protect the nymphs, his friends, from the gods. But before he reached them, the gods repositioned themselves, beside him one moment, blocking his path in the next. Layel ground to a halt.

"Valerian," he called.

"Layel," the nymph king responded. "What's been going on? How can we—"

Hestia waved her hand at them and they disappeared as quickly as they'd arrived. "Good riddance."

"You," Apollo said to Broderick, as though there had never been a disruption. "I have a task for you, nymph. As I am no longer welcome inside Atlantis, I feel the need to return to the surface world. And there is something you can do for me there. The least you can do, really, since you did not win me this contest." The two vanished. At least Broderick had appeared amenable.

"And, you," Poseidon added, pointing to Tagart, eyes narrowed. "You cost me sole claim to Atlantis. For that, you will be punished. And then you will exist simply to amuse me." They, too, disappeared.

"And then there's you," Ares said to Layel. "Victory could have been ours, but you chose to put love first." Despite his words, there was no anger in his voice. "I would punish you, but you seem to have saddled yourself with a permanent mate. That is punishment enough, I'm thinking."

A mate was not punishment, Layel thought. A mate was a reward. But he gave no protest as Ares, too, vanished.

For several heartbeats, there was silence. Then a female sigh echoed. "Enough distractions. I will now award Delilah's prize." Hestia merely blinked at them and they were suddenly standing in front of the Amazon camp, a cliff rising in front of them. The women obviously couldn't see them, for they were readying for war, unconcerned by the vampire in their midst.

There was the young girl, the one who had been locked in the dragon cage what seemed an eternity ago. To Layel's delight, she was leading a scowling Brand by a chain, as though he were nothing more than a pet.

"Lily," Delilah said. She reached out stiffly, as though the action were automatic rather than heartfelt.

"Delilah," the goddess said, stopping her in her tracks. "As you know, my precious, you have earned a boon. What would you like? Name it, and it's yours. Remember, your sister Nola is out there, perhaps in pain."

Layel's jaw clenched. Low blow, he thought. *Remember your promises,* he projected to Delilah. *Remember my promises. Please remember.* During their night of passion, he had vowed to help her search for Nola, and he would. However long it took. He would not rest until her sister was safe. The boon wasn't needed for that. Would she remember? Would she care?

"Or I could give Layel back his mate," the goddess continued. "That would please him, I think."

Layel locked gazes with Delilah, letting all of his love pour from him.

"May I ask a few questions first?"

"Of course," the goddess replied magnanimously.

"What happened to the nymph army?"

"The army was returned to Atlantis, healthy and whole. If your fellow competitors Broderick and Tagart are lucky, they will someday follow suit."

Delilah nodded, satisfied. "Since you have already agreed to spare Layel's life, I ask for my emotions," she said, and Layel sank to his knees in relief. "I want my emotions returned. My love for him."

"I planned to return them anyway," the goddess surprised Layel by saying. "After you chose your prize. Logic aids us so much more than sentiment, after all. Besides, mere emotions don't seem a large enough reward for your efforts. Is there nothing else you would like?"

"Loving Layel, being with him, is what I desire most. But as you are giving me that, as well, I ask for Nola's safe return."

Hestia studied her a moment, then nodded. "Very well. All that you have named, you shall have. But not all at the same time. Nola has much to learn first."

A moment later, Delilah's body jerked and she screamed in pain, just as she'd done the night before. All Layel could do was gather her close and hold on to her until the throbbing subsided. Finally she collapsed, panting, sweating.

"Thank you, thank you," he said, raining kisses all over her face. "Thank you for remembering. Thank you for loving me."

Her violet gaze lifted, piercing him. "Does some part of you wish I'd asked for your mate's return?"

"Ah, but you did ask for exactly that. *You* are my mate. My greatest prize."

Slowly she grinned. "A prize," she said with wonder. "Me. It's what I've always wanted to be, what I secretly dreamed of each night in camp and every time I saw other creatures holding hands and basking in each other."

"It's what you've always been, what you will always be." He kissed her forehead, her nose and then her precious lips. "We will never be parted again, I vow it. We can live in my palace or I will be your eternal slave at the Amazon camp."

Her eyes widened. "You would be my slave?"

"I *am* your slave, love."

Now those widened eyes filled with happy tears, her smile brighter than the sun. "I would love to live in your palace. To have you all to myself, no war or battle-training to distract us. Maybe, though, we can visit my tribe upon occasion." She looked down, as if it was too much to hope for.

"Anytime you wish. The girl, Lily, can even stay with us when we return, if your queen will allow it. Perhaps she can help us practice our parenting skills."

"Oh, Layel." She kissed and nipped at his face. "I would like that. And I think Lily would, too." Her head fell back and she laughed, a sound of true joy. "We'll have to deal with her new slave, though. Are you sure—"

"My quest to kill the dragons is over." He shrugged sheepishly. "But perhaps I will torture Brand a wee bit. Or perhaps he will prove useful as we rescue Zane and Nola. Because if I know my Amazon, you will not be content to wait for Hestia to send the girl to us, just as I am not content to leave my soldier in torment."

"You, Layel, are a wonderful man. My dark and passionate king." She cupped his face, her thumbs tenderly brushing his lips. "So…now that you have me, what are you going to do with me?"

"That's easy, love," he said, holding her tight. "Cherish you, all the days of my life."

* * * * *

*More enthralling paranormal romance is coming your
way from*
GENA SHOWALTER
*and HQN Books
in 2009!*

*In September 2009, the dark and sensual journey of the
LORDS OF THE UNDERWORLD continues with
Sabin's story in* THE DARKEST WHISPER.

Turn the page for your sneak peek....

THE DARKEST WHISPER

THE WOMAN was going to kill him, and not because she was stronger and more vicious than he was. Which, if Sabin thought about it, she was. He'd never ripped a man's throat out with his teeth, and he was damned impressed that Gwen had. But two full days had passed since he and his crew had rescued her from the pyramid and she had not relaxed. Or eaten. She hadn't even showered in the portable stall he'd had Lucien fetch her.

She didn't trust them, didn't want to risk poisoning, unconscious vulnerability or nakedness, and that was understandable. But damn it, he was seething with the need to *force* her to do those things. For her own good. She had to be exhausted and couldn't possibly be comfortable, dirty as she was. Forcing her, however, was not an option. He liked his trachea where it was.

The only thing she'd taken from him was clothing. A camouflage tee and military fatigues. They bagged on her, even though she'd rolled the arms, waist and legs, but there wasn't a female who'd ever looked better. With that wild fall of strawberry curls…those take-me-to-bed lips… and knowing the material she wore had once touched his body…she was utter perfection.

I need to get laid. Soon.

The moment he returned to Buda, that's what he'd do. Find a willing woman who only wanted a good time and, well, show her a good time. Maybe then his head would clear and he'd figure out how to deal with Gwen.

Something else that bothered him was the way Gwen had planted herself in the corner and watched him no matter who entered his tent. Him. As if *he* were the biggest threat to her now. He'd snapped at her that day in the cavern, yeah, telling her not to touch him. But he'd also ensured that she remained on her feet on the trek through the desert to set up camp. He'd stayed with her, guarded her while the other warriors went back to the pyramid to search for anything they might have missed the first go-round. Did he really deserve the death glares?

Maybe...

Shut up, Doubt! he chastised his demon. *I don't need your opinions.*

Don't know why you care what she thinks. You've never been good for women, now have you? Remember what happened to Darla?

Crouched on the sandy floor, Sabin closed the lid of his weapon case with a forceful snap, locked it and turned to the bag of food he'd had Paris bring him. "Shut the hell up. I've had all of you I can take."

Gwen, once again in the far corner, jerked as though he'd screamed, those strawberry blond locks tumbling around her like a curtain. "But I didn't say anything."

He'd lived among mortals for a long time and had trained himself to converse with his demon inside his head. That he'd forgotten his training now, with this skittish yet deadly woman with the smile to die for...mortifying. "I wasn't speaking to you," he muttered.

Paler than usual, she drew her arms around her middle. Since the tent framed her, it rattled as she moved. "Then to whom were you speaking? We're alone."

He didn't answer. Couldn't. Not without lying. While lying wasn't something Doubt could do, instead spreading its poison like butter over bread with questions and suppositions, Sabin certainly could. However, he preferred not to unless the outcome of a battle was at stake.

Thankfully, Gwen didn't press the issue. "I want to go home," she said softly.

"I know. But I'm afraid I can't let you do that…"

ATLANTIS

Glossary of Characters and Terms

Alyssa—half-vampire, half-demon, second-in-command of the vampire army

Amazon—Atlantean race of female warrioresses known for their thirst for war

Apollo—god of the sun

Ares—god of war

Artemis—goddess of the hunt

Atlantis—a hidden city under the sea, populated by creatures mistakenly created as the gods attempted to form man

Brand—second-in-command of the dragon army

Brenna—human; mate of Joachim

Broderick—elite nymph warrior

Cassandra—siren formerly enslaved by the demons

Centaur—Atlantean race defined by half-man, half-horse features

Darius—king of the dragons

Delilah—Amazon warrioress

Demon—Atlantean race of horned, scaled flesh-eaters; most reviled of the creatures

Dorian—nymph warrior

Dragon—Atlantean race of men able to shift into fire-breathers

Forest of Dragons—land surrounding the Inner City; property of the dragon king

Formorian—Atlantean race with one arm and one leg; wings are their great strength

Gorgon—Atlantean race with snakes for hair, able to turn men to stone with a glance

Grace—human; queen of the dragons

Hestia—goddess of hearth and home

Inner City—center of Atlantean commerce

Irren—formorian warrior

Jada—female nymph warrior

Joachim—elite nymph warrior

Kreja—queen of the Amazons

Layel—king of the vampires

Lily—Amazon child; daughter of Kreja

Marina—slain queen of the demons

Minotaur—Atlantean race with the head of a bull and the body of a human

Mists—portals from the surface world to Atlantis

Nola—Amazon warrioress

Nymph—Atlantean race so sensual, no one can resist them; they need sex to survive

Outer City—home to Atlantis's criminals and assorted unwanted races

Poseidon—god of the sea

Renard—dragon warrior

Shaye—human; queen of the nymphs

Shivawn—elite nymph warrior

Susan—slain human mate to Layel

Tagart—dragon warrior

Valerian—king of the nymphs

Vampire—Atlantean race of blood-drinkers; most can fly and teleport

Vorik—dragon warrior

Zane—vampire warrior